Romance
BASTILLE
Charles

Bastille, Charles

MagicLand

WITHDRAWN

FEB 2 3 2022

I0381518

MAGICLAND

FEB 2 3 2022

MagicLand
A NOVEL

CHARLES BASTILLE

NEW YORK

LONDON • NASHVILLE • MELBOURNE • VANCOUVER

MAGICLAND
A Novel

© 2022 Charles Bastille

All rights reserved. No portion of this book may be reproduced, stored in a retrieval system, or transmitted in any form or by any means—electronic, mechanical, photocopy, recording, scanning, or other—except for brief quotations in critical reviews or articles, without the prior written permission of the publisher.

Publisher's Note: This novel is a work of fiction. Names, characters, places, and incidents are either products of the author's imagination or used fictitiously. All characters are fictional, and any similarity to people living or dead is purely coincidental.

Published in New York, New York, by Morgan James Publishing. Morgan James is a trademark of Morgan James, LLC. www.MorganJamesPublishing.com

Morgan James BOGO™

A **FREE** ebook edition is available for you or a friend with the purchase of this print book.

CLEARLY SIGN YOUR NAME ABOVE

Instructions to claim your free ebook edition:
1. Visit MorganJamesBOGO.com
2. Sign your name CLEARLY in the space above
3. Complete the form and submit a photo of this entire page
4. You or your friend can download the ebook to your preferred device

ISBN 978-1-63195-564-8 paperback
ISBN 978-1-63195-565-5 ebook
Library of Congress Control Number:
2021904927

Cover Design by:
Rachel Lopez
www.r2cdesign.com

Morgan James PUBLISHING

Builds

with...

Habitat for Humanity®
Peninsula and
Greater Williamsburg

Morgan James is a proud partner of Habitat for Humanity Peninsula and Greater Williamsburg. Partners in building since 2006.

Get involved today! Visit
MorganJamesPublishing.com/giving-back

For my sister, Sara

Acknowledgments

The author would like to thank Cortney Donelson, associate publisher, Fiction and acquisitions editor at Morgan James Publishing, for believing in this novel, giving it birth at Morgan James, and providing amazing editorial guidance and diligence.

Also, Jim Howard, publisher at Morgan James Publishing, for his encouragement and for guiding this book through final production.

Special thanks to Margo Toulouse, author relations manager at Morgan James Publishing, for her attention to detail in shepherding this project through to completion.

Thank you, Jaz, for your early suggestions. And thank you to everyone at Morgan James Publishing who helped get this book produced. It couldn't have happened without the efforts of graphic designers and proofreaders and all of the folks responsible for production and distribution.

A big shout out to Michaela Fosdick for her great editing.

Finally, an especially warm thank you to David Hancock, Founder and CEO of Morgan James Publishing, for getting behind this novel and taking such an amazing, hands-on approach to its development.

PROLOGUE

T he small child watched as the ferocious battle engulfed the shoreline. His mother scooped him into her arms and handed him to his father, who had untied the skiff and was already pushing it out into the bay. Others around them were doing the same, refugees from the senseless violence that Hilkiah couldn't understand beyond his own helplessness. There were skiffs and scows, sloops, and all other manners of vessels filled with frightened passengers.

Hilkiah was mesmerized by a towering man in a sharply defined black robe with batwing sleeves who seemed to be pulling lightning from the sky and hurling it at his enemies with frightening effectiveness. The robed man was huge, and not only from a small boy's perspective. None of the other combatants were even half his size. But neither were they fully at his mercy.

The tall man and his companions were enduring their own onslaught, led by long, thin people who, when he could see their faces, reminded Hilkiah of skeletons, with deep hollow jowls and inset eyes. Thin arms protruded from old, dirty, and torn jerseys as they hurled spears perfectly through howling winds with an accuracy only magic could accomplish.

The large wizard and his forces seemed to have the upper hand as Hilkiah's parents made their escape. Above, the Vermillion Bridge, which led to the Wandering City, was overflowing with more refugees scampering across the river. The wizard doubled down his efforts against his foes, lighting up the clouds above with multicolored flashes of lightning. The skinny ones were screaming in retreat, many of them in flames as they ran into the water to escape their blistering fate. The wizard and his troops closed in and finished the slaughter then turned their attention to the bridge as Hilkiah's father rowed rapidly to the opposite shore, fighting choppy waters effortlessly as if they were friend rather than foe to a rowing man.

Others were not so fortunate. Young Hilkiah wanted so badly to be able to jump into the waters and swim to the side of their boats and push them to the opposite shore, too, but he was helplessly young. All he could do was watch and hope as the wizard directed his power to the fleeing refugees on the bridge above.

Massive bolts of lightning scattered across the sky and downward. Direct hits that shattered the bridge sent bodies falling into the bay far below to certain death.

The desperate rowing finally subsided. Hilkiah's father pulled the boat to shore, lifted Hilkiah out, and helped his mother step onto the choppy water's bank as others struggled to reach safety before the wizard might turn his attention on them. Hilkiah imagined how wonderful it could be if a great wave could rise from the depths of the bay to carry all the small boats to shore, away from the pursuit of their stalking predators. He wished it so desperately that he closed his eyes trying to imagine it, squeezing them together so hard he could feel tears as he clenched his fists and strained to think of such a thing.

Hilkiah's father roughly pulled on his arm, then lifted him, and began to run, along with his wife, Hilkiah's treasured mother, who had given Hilkiah the kind of love that made him long for her gaze upon each morning's awakening. Hilkiah, who didn't know why they were running with such abandon suddenly, tried to lift his head to look behind his father's shoulder as he bounced in his arms.

Then he saw it. A massive wave, taller than anything he had ever seen, taller even than the hills of Moria, was curling onto the boats and ripping them out of the bay, sending people flying this way and that into the water. As his father continued running, Hilkiah could hear him urging his mother on, but he heard nothing from his mother, just the loud crash of the wave as it blasted the shoreline, crushing the docks and the boats and the moorings that lay along its length.

Then, instantaneously, the wave curled all the way back into the bay water, defying all physics, simply churning itself into the water and disappearing, leaving an endless line of bodies lying in its wake.

Hilkiah's father stopped running. "Your mother," he said frantically. "Where's your mother?" His father called out her name to the howling winds and the remaining survivors who were also desperately searching for loved ones. "Rebecca!" he cried out. "Rebecca!" Then he caught sight of her, near the edge of the water, and he ran to her, Hilkiah holding on tighter because his father had loosened his grip in his distress.

His father set Hilkiah down, leaning deeply into his mother, who lay prone on the edge of the shore with its lapping waters. Hilkiah's father's sobs overtook the sounds of the bay. "Oh, please no," his father cried, burying his head into her back, pulling on her hair, one fist pounding and splashing and thrashing into the silt and water in agonized grief.

CHAPTER I

1

Aurilena commanded her horse toward the herd of buffalo blanketing the horizon, her friend Sherealla close behind. They were riding the Wildland Hills for the High Priest Hilkiah, who had sensed a Reckless. He had sent Aurilena, despite her youth, because she knew the hills, knew the buffalo, and knew the cadence of the kind of incendiary soul a Reckless must be.

"It will be," he had said to her, "like sending myself. You'll sniff him out in no time. After," he had then chuckled, "the expected distractions."

Aurilena's tight, sleeveless hemp vest moved in unison with her lean athletic frame. Her head tossed back silky currents of black hair before she yelled, "Come on!" She softly kicked her horse, whom she called Remembrance, her feet wrapped in tall leather moccasin boots pulled tightly with braided laces. Tucked inside the boots were canvas-colored jodhpur pants.

The two girls rode toward the immense herd, which was a sea of dark brown ink in the distance.

Sherealla wore a tightly woven, white cotton riding shirt and the same pants as Aurilena, but with riding boots secured by a long strap at the top that held firm through the magic of two metal clasps.

After they rode awhile, Sherealla asked, "You really know what you're doing, Lena?" not at all happy with the diversion their assignment was taking.

"A boy taught my brother and me how to do this . . ." Aurilena paused at the painful memory. "My brother. He said he wanted to learn how to hunt."

Sherealla thought about the way her own rich walnut hues and round ornamental cheeks combined with Aurilena's dark olive skin and angular face to create a statuesque duo of hopeless visual entanglement for the hapless boys of Moria. Although Aurilena had shown little interest in Morian boys, she wasn't unwilling to occasionally leverage her charms to learn the secrets behind prestigious spells or incantations from boys who craved her attention.

"Hunt," Sherealla repeated incredulously.

"Yeah."

Sherealla found it hard to imagine Aurilena's brother, a spiritual prodigy who had once seemed destined for priesthood in the House of Legions, as a hunter.

But she knew Aurilena's brother had probably been quite young when he had expressed that desire, just the musings of a child.

"What's cool is that you can go right up to them, and they don't blink. Nothing scares them. You know? So, you just come up to them and do this." With that, Aurilena conjured a rope and extended it from her hands. As the rope grew from her hand and rose slightly behind and above her head, a small loop emerged at its end. It then whirled and expanded, twisting with her wrists as she extended it in small increments upward. She snapped the loop toward a small dead piece of tree on the ground and drove her horse toward the target. She lofted the splitting bark upward as if setting a lure on a fish. The bark exploded into a dozen pieces as Aurilena drew the empty rope loop back toward her.

"*That's* what you want to do to the poor beasts?" Sherealla yelled over the sounds made by the galloping frenzy of the two charging horses.

"Yup!" Aurilena commanded Remembrance to move faster as she spread a distance between Sherealla and herself. "Except maybe that last part!" said her fading voice.

"Hey!" Sherealla shouted. Sherealla kicked her horse into high gear, and they raced toward the herd. "What about the Reckless?" She doubted Aurilena heard her question over the sounds of their galloping horses.

"The Reckless can wait!" came an answer in the wind.

2

Belex's sight was obliterated when he awoke, his eyes enmeshed in a field of static. Horizontal lines waved haphazardly within the focus of his remaining field of vision and then petered out, snatching all remaining light as if by the hunting limbs of a dreamless Kraken.

He struggled to his knees when everything went black. He decided to query his medical diagnostics, but when he thought about it, nothing happened. He stood up, still blind, and dusted himself off, wondering where he was.

He felt vulnerable standing up, so he decided to ease himself back to the ground, feeling for it since he couldn't see. Instead, he arrived on the dirt with a thud. A stinging pain shot through his tailbone up his spine, something he had never felt before.

Belex, like other members of his species, was only vaguely aware of the trillions of biomechanical calculations that managed his automated body mechanics and the alerts that should have prevented him from sitting so quickly. Seated on the ground, he felt a little better. *I'm not moving anywhere. I'll just wait,* he thought to himself.

Everything was on the fritz. Which, as he thought about it a bit more, seemed a little strange. If he was okay, then his systems should be okay. But then, he was an actor, not an expert on physiology.

Obviously, his aircraft had crashed. which meant the pod bag that should have protected him in an enveloping seal during impact had to be nearby. This meant that his fellow passengers were probably okay, too, if there were any. He couldn't remember that, either.

He was sore everywhere, but he was in one piece. To make sure, he checked all his fingers and wiggled his toes. Everything was in order. He wanted to stand up again to search for his pod bag but convinced himself to remain where he was . . . and at least wait to see if his vision would be restored.

There was nothing manual in Belex's world. Everything was automated, controlled, and regulated by the intricate web of neurons and nano-biowires weaving their way through his body and maintaining a permanent uplink to the Stoven collective. If that uplink failed, backup systems were supposed to fire up, but that didn't seem to be happening. Limited to biology, he was nothing more than an ape in a jumpsuit.

It wasn't like there was much to be afraid of. The terrain seemed dry. He couldn't hear much of anything. He wondered if he was in a desert. With his hands, he felt the dirt beside him. It was loose and dry, but it wasn't finely grained like he would have expected.

He had only been to a desert once, on a safari. That hadn't gone well. Although he had never touched the ground, many of the people on that safari did. Facedown.

It wasn't a pleasant memory. The safari had taken place in the Inyo Wilds when everyone thought the Wiccan Wars had been over. They weren't.

Never mind that, he thought.

He felt a chill, beginning for the first time to truly feel the darkness surrounding him. *Will my vision come back?* he thought. *Is anyone there? Can anyone hear me?*

3

From a distance, it must have looked like two figures on horses racing for treasure. Dust plumes behind them. Nothing stopping them. Then, something does. Like a god hurling lightning into their immediate path.

Their horses wanted to freeze in mid-gallop but, instead, slowed to a canter before circling each other in a calm trot, making Aurilena grateful for Judith, her sister who had trained them. Her sister could talk a horse into climbing a tree, she thought.

"Whoa," she said after the horses calmed. "What was that?"

"Sounded like some guy."

"Yeah, from the buffalo. Hilkiah's Reckless?"

"Sounded like he was saying . . . I don't know. I want to say that he was saying *is anyone there?*" Sherealla considered a few million possibilities before discounting them and thinking that everything was going according to a plan well outside of her control.

"Sounded like a disembodied spirit to me. But there are no spirits here. No memories. And I thought I heard a song."

"Alright, so what was it?" Sherealla asked.

"I dunno. But it was beautiful. Did you hear that tone, that song?"

"I just heard . . ." Sherealla was quiet. "I don't know what I heard. Questioning. Loneliness." And a perfect lure for the questioning heart of someone like Aurilena.

Aurilena could feel a thrill in her chest. "Yeah. Loneliness. But something more."

"Where do you think it came from?"

Aurilena guided Remembrance into a determined scouting circle before she said, "I don't know."

Aurilena would say later that she sensed his spirit, could touch his soul. But for now, all she knew was that he was there.

"Let's go," and the horses and the girls rode again.

4

The thin black jumpsuit he was wearing was made for a body impervious to the kind of discomforts he was feeling. The suit had its uses, consisting of vertically aligned nanotube arrays that could absorb nearly 100 percent of visible light and withstand temperatures higher than 6,000 degrees Fahrenheit, but his systems were so ruined, he wasn't aware of these advantages and wanted the thing off.

The suit clung to his body tenaciously as he rolled it down to his waist, worked the emptied black sleeves around his back, and tied them against his stomach. Any Wiccan in the area would immediately recognize him because of the freshly revealed membrane that interfaced with his bioware and covered his body like a second skin. But a close look at his face would reveal that anyway, so he decided it didn't matter.

His instincts, such as they were, told him the best chance for survival was to sit. That's what you do, right? Everyone knows you just wait for a tracking beacon to find you if you get stuck outside of the Homeland for some reason. Most of Earth was inhospitable. The most likely scenario when searching for help was likely to involve becoming slow-cooked in a marauder's stew mixed with the bones of local rodents.

But he knew this was different. He had no operating systems, no tracking device, and his synapse layer was clearly not interfacing. Nobody would find him if he just sat. This was serious downtime, which made him yearn for any of the help available through the myriad assistance strata available within the collective.

Luckily, it seemed like his vision, his backup vision—the biological kind—was coming back, albeit slowly. As time wore on, spent between sitting and wondering what to do, he began to discern faint gray shapes. He couldn't tell what they were, but it seemed, considering the circumstances, to be a huge victory. It made him think of a cinescape he had performed in a long time ago, one of redemption. Or was it victory? He wasn't sure. Even his most basic emotional definitions were blown away.

He did remember that he loved redemption roles. Redemption had been his favorite subject as a young actor. As he became more successful, he hoped to demand such roles. He had a vague sense, lodged somewhere in the foggy trenches of his mind, that perhaps he had become that successful.

He couldn't think of the cinescape his current situation reminded him of, and he couldn't access stoven.net to run a search. He slammed his fist hard against the dirt. That's when he decided that, without any doubt, he would have to walk, even though the target was nothing more than gray silhouettes. If they were marauders hunting for stew meat, he figured, this was their lucky day. *Chewy,* he thought. *Miles of nanotubes and wires and whatnot. I'd be very chewy. Not a good choice for a stew.*

Reluctantly, he pulled his suit back up. As soon as he stood up to walk, he changed his mind again. Riveted by pain, he sat back down as if he no longer got to decide.

5

Sherealla was torn by inner conflict. Much of her wanted to spirit Aurilena away from this task. But it was more than fealty to a distant command that prevented this. It was a physical impossibility. She was still able to say, "I smell trouble. You said yourself, there is no spirit history here."

Aurilena had somehow, by default, always been the leader. When Aurilena said, "We need to keep riding," Sherealla thought back to that day. *Ever since you saved my life in the Wandering City, I follow you everywhere.*

That moment had wed her to Aurilena's powers and personality and the belief that Aurilena resided in a higher heaven than other Morians. If Sherealla had died that day, her unwilling arrival in this part of the world and the cruel way she had been torn away from her parents would have been utterly meaningless. At that moment, Aurilena had changed the heartless misdirection Sherealla's life had taken. That has an impact on how you feel about the girl next to you, on a horse, who says, "go," no matter what other circumstances lurk in the shadows.

6

There were cinescapes he thought he should be able to recall. Belex had a habit of drawing on them often, whether he was sad or angry or happy. But he couldn't think of them now. Couldn't access them. He was used to being able to query old lines or scenes just by thinking. Now he couldn't.

Instead of being able to recall passages from past performances, his fragmented recollections were confined within a sphere of his brain that he could no longer harvest. The creative force that had unleashed the original words was no longer available to him. The catalog consisting of the voices that had introduced their beauty to the rest of the world and had made such words available—the actors, their beautiful tones, and the history of all the associated great performances— was erased.

The point of access was so unknown to him that he didn't even know where to start looking. Other than the dirt at his feet, at his hands, and at his knees, there was little he knew. He was surrounded by the depravity of utter silence aside from a violently loud whoosh of wind. The quantum voices, chattering, and readouts of his existence that were the essence of being human were gone. He was left with the primitive biology of an era long dead.

As the wind collapsed into silence, leaving him in the raw heat, he nodded off a few times as he sat, his chin heavy against his chest.

He woke up again to nothing. He found himself curled in the fetal position on the ground. He thought that if this was a cinescape, his role consisted of despondency born of disconnection.

There was no way for him to measure how long he had been separated from the collective. When he felt a small thump in his heart, he wondered if it was digging into his chest in response to occasional frights prompted by unknown sounds (although, he felt that he was holding up magnificently well considering he was nearly blind and helpless, far away from civilization).

His biosystems were simply not functioning correctly. There was nothing reporting his dangerous exposure to the heat. No alerts reminding him of mineral deficiencies or the cause of his parched throat. No indicators streaming across the periphery of his vision measuring his glucose levels, blood pressure, or the percentage of fat. All he had were his fingers digging into the ground, telling him he had been sitting in the dry dirt too long. And that he was thirsty. A lack of medical diagnostics didn't prevent his thirst from alerting him to this looming challenge to survival.

He also felt drawn, almost as if by a magnet, to the gray silhouettes still lingering on the frontier, which his healing eyes could barely see. *All systems off but still told to go somewhere.* He realized that he knew shockingly little about his anatomy. *I'm supposed to go somewhere.* A system embedded within him was telling him to walk. He had already decided to heed the advice, but he was becoming concerned about why this was important.

He had read about instinct.

Hadn't he?

He walked, and his vision began to gain color. He was ecstatic. What a turnaround! What fortune! His instinct was right.

But was it instinct?

He began to see himself on that glorious, networked stage with hundreds of thousands of fans cheering each other and his fellow actors. It hurt, though, not knowing who they were. Imagine knowing a million people intimately, then losing all connection to them. That was the essence of Belex's current condition.

All he had to go on was emotion, but it was enough for now. There was no history. He couldn't recall any of the circumstances behind any of his performances. He couldn't issue a command and watch a recording of anything he had done.

He walked, grasping for more color from within the changing silhouettes of his vision, which were finally finding focus. And wondering still if he was merely an actor or something more.

1

The buffalo meandered on the hills above, among grassy, easy slopes. The girls rode toward them, the land transforming as they rode into a greener, busier hue. Sherealla, her slight build always able to ride a horse in an easy way, still afraid of a buffalo's every move, and glad to have Aurilena at her side, rode just ahead of her. Sherealla loved feeling her long, thick, black braided hair bouncing along her back as she rode.

"I can sense him," yelled Aurilena, who then rushed past Sherealla and pushed Remembrance into the sea of buffalo. The herd didn't move, but that didn't stop Aurilena from driving her horse directly into it. Individuals within the herd seemed to make way for Aurilena and Remembrance, but there was little other reaction.

Aurilena snapped the rope above her head and then toward the nearest bull, who charged blindly to its closest thought. This triggered a thunderous response from nearby animals, and the dormant brown curtain became a seismic fall of hooves, with the herd transforming into a crest of energy.

Aurilena, who had seemed to capture the beast at its initial charge, was suddenly trailing behind it like a captive herself. "Sherealla!" Sherealla couldn't hear Aurilena try to lift her voice enough to shout over the roar of the herd saying, "Isn't this awesome?"

Aurilena was flying in the air, trailing the bull, her lariat seemingly tugged perfectly against the bull's chest as the animal raced in circles, letting Aurilena trail behind as if stuck like the tail of a kite whistling in a steady wind. Aurilena's feet were within the same plane as her hands in front of her, led by the animal with the lariat somewhere near its neck. But Aurilena's rope was above the animal, not around its chest, its neck, or anywhere else that could induce such locomotion. The master, it seemed, was the animal itself. Its energy, or maybe the energy of its herd, was enough to lift and carry Aurilena above the buffalo as if she were weightless.

After it was over, Aurilena could barely contain herself. "That was fun. You try it."

"If Hilkiah had any idea at all how easily you forget the tasks he's given you, he'd never give you one."

"Here, just wrap it around your fist, like so."

"I can't speak to animals the way you can. Nobody can."

Aurilena halted Remembrance and sought quiet. "There's another animal here. Not of Moria. Not buffalo." She wanted to explain to Sherealla that they had to be with the buffalo to find the Reckless, to distinguish his soul from the surrounding beasts, but she didn't bother. She wanted quiet.

Sherealla looked around, and it seemed to her that the raucous had been more like a micro-raucous. Most of the herd, throughout all this, had remained calm. A small canyon of it had reacted to Aurilena and her antics, but otherwise, nothing in the herd seemed to change. The herd, after all, extended for miles across the canvas in front of them. Aurilena's antics had created only the smallest of commotions, like a rope being pulled through a pasture of manicured grass, leaving just the slightest trail of movement. All seemed quiet.

Until it wasn't. Neither Sherealla nor Aurilena was fully aware that suddenly their horses were running along with what became a stampede. The bulk of the animal mass was slower than those near the two girls. The equilibrium of the herd's structure was now in disarray.

"Whoa," Aurilena cried out as Remembrance reared and tried to meld with the herd. Aurilena looked at Sherealla, and both nodded as their horses sprouted wings and flew above the beasts and over the gently rolling hills below.

8

He couldn't breathe, and his nose and mouth suddenly seemed infused with massive amounts of dust and dirt.

He sat down again, covering his mouth with his hand, and though it hurt when he sat, that wasn't what prompted him to stand back up. A sound coming from the ground struck him deep into his bones and forced him to spring upward like a releasing coil.

He stumbled around, tried to take a few steps, then looked down at his aching legs, bringing his arms in front of him to look at them.

He had to keep checking every part of his body because everything hurt. The crash had clearly been a bit harder on his body than he first thought.

Amazingly, his thought process was telling him that a stampede was coming. For just one-half second, he realized he didn't know exactly what a stampede was. The recollection of the meaning began to form as he saw, through wincing eyes, a blur of large brown animals in an approaching line curl over a crest he hadn't noticed. The animals moved in unison and covered the length of the horizon. His eyes became blinded again, this time by dust filling up his space.

9

"He's in danger," Aurilena tried to yell to Sherealla. She knew the buffalo hooves against the ground below were too heavy for Sherealla to hear what she said, so she could only hope her friend would notice the sea of animals divide by the commanding rise of her left hand. Aurilena landed her flying horse and rode Remembrance into the herd's opening.

Each time Aurilena and her horse charged from within the herd, a long gap opened the herd at that point. Sherealla was aware of Aurilena's special bond with animals, but she'd never seen her do anything like this.

As Sherealla alighted, she thought something about what Hilkiah, the high priest of the Legions, had said long ago to them: "You will discover your talents in clandestine ways." And then he said the owner of that talent bore responsibility. He would not, she suspected, have been pleased with the sight of flying horses, given that these horses had no true wings.

Sherealla tried to gaze into the herd but could find no sign of any injured victim or the owner of the voice they heard within the brown layer that had transformed itself into rolling earth in front of her. She suspected that it was the one she had been told would come. But it was impossible for her to know at this stage. Nothing within her told her that it might be so. And if it was he, she was not ready.

10

The line in front of Belex halted. He didn't have time to guess why because to take the time to figure it out would likely mean the line might have time to grind him into the sand, and he wanted at least a small chance to survive. He tried to think about the people in his life, his loved ones, but none came. There were vestiges of some biological memories, but they meant nothing because their associated memory nodes from the collective—and even his own firmware—were gone. He was able to recall a conversation with his friend, Marston, but it was a vague recollection, like the edge of a dream you can't quite recall when you wake up.

11

The chaos subsided. The passage within the herd remained, and she saw a human form staggering within a billowy cloud of dust. Even from this distance, Aurilena thought the unidentifiable figure was of Gath. She brought her horse to a canter on her approach. The Gath, as it looked to be, collapsed.

When she neared him, she dismounted and offered her hand to him as he lay prone, but he kicked at it. She tried to speak to him, but he cursed her with words she didn't recognize. *Well,* she thought. *He's no Reckless.* She tried backing off and gently coaxing him into some form of understanding, but he was crawling backward wildly and seemed to be searching his skintight black suit for something. All she could think of was to nod over to Sherealla, who, despite her slight frame, was able to corral the techno-beast with her rope.

Every reaction from Aurilena drew an angry reaction from him, like she was the cause of some crippling disease that had wiped out his family.

Aurilena knew that if he were Gath, Reckless or not, he'd have to stand before the Legions, who would then decide what to do with him.

He'd also have an arsenal of horrible weapons at his immediate disposal, even if he wasn't a soldier. The only way to safety was to get him into Moria, which was out of reach of his army's strategic weapons. All he had to do, she knew, was call his brethren, and there would be a massive fleet of flying machines and insect-sized drones destroying everything in sight.

If he was a soldier, Hilkiah wouldn't have sent her, though. Too dangerous. Hilkiah was a Sentiment, an Empath of the greatest skill. It was possible Hilkiah knew more of this Gath's intent than the Gath himself.

Anxiously, she watched Sherealla snare him with her rope.

In many ways, he was a glorious creature. Aurilena couldn't know he was her age because they all looked so young, even the very old, but what caught her attention was the beauty of his reddish-brown skin and a complex maze of barely discernible wire patterns underneath or perhaps even layered within. The flagrant display of biotech should have revolted her, but instead, she found it strikingly beautiful. The mesh was a silver color that blended illustriously with luminescent blue eyes, whose lively beauty gave lie to their probable artificiality. His head was crowned with red and blond spikes of unruly hair. His body was breathlessly cut, with well-toned muscles and mountainous pectorals trying to burst out of his thin black outfit.

Sherealla was sinewy but, Aurilena marveled as she watched, demonstrated the strength of ten men as she held to her rope. Aurilena struggled to focus on

Sherealla's efforts because she found herself captivated by an athletically chiseled jawline and an underlying muscle that stretched in the stranger's fury.

As Sherealla held him, his muscular legs flailing in the air, Aurilena tried to figure out what to say to him. She knew she had to bring him back somehow. Back to some other place, a place he could somehow trust enough not to kick his legs around like a possessed mule.

"Hey, we can't just leave you out here to die," she finally said, and the man spat toward her face.

Aurilena led her horse round him as best as she could without throwing too much more fright into him. Next, she guided her horse's nose toward him.

"Look umm, I don't want you here anymore than you want me here," Aurilena said to him. He offered no signals of understanding. "You won't be harmed if you come peacefully. But if not, Sherealla's horse here will kick your teeth in, and not even the desert rats will try to pick them clean."

He chortled. "Heard that routine before," he said, although he hadn't. Or maybe he had. His reaction seemed instinctive. As if from one of his roles. Maybe a spy caper? An action adventure?

He wanted to kick at the savage in the vest, and his feet drove forward manically as he realized he was becoming a prisoner. He was so angry and confused that he hadn't even noticed that his language module was working. He was not only understanding her but speaking back to her. He found her scintillating enough to realize that, perhaps, there was more act than anger in his countenance. This made sense. He was an actor, after all.

Aurilena examined him, wondering how he knew her language, and said to Sherealla, "We will not string him up. He'll ride with me. He can stab me in the gut with his evil, sharp little fingers all he wants, but he'll get nowhere," and with that, she imagined finger-sized spears emanating from the tips of his fingers and impaling her as they rode.

"Ride with you?" he yelled theatrically into the dry air as if the world could hear him. "Not a chance!" He began to sense that maybe this was a cinescape after all, so he got all dramatic.

Aurilena glared at him, and a corner of her mouth tightened to form the slightest smile, and she nodded to Sherealla.

"Fine. Sherealla," she said, "off we go," as she mounted her horse. Sherealla's rope disappeared into the air, and the girls pirouetted their horses and galloped off, leaving him in a dusky cloud.

Knowing they'd be back here soon, Sherealla felt the wind against her face as she rode, one of her favorite feelings in the world, along with the feel of her hair bouncing against her back.

12

What was that? Belex asked himself. He brushed himself off, amazed at his experience. It was like an ancient movie. The savages capture you, but somehow, they decide you aren't worth the trouble and just leave you alone.

He wondered why the producers of his new cinescape had decided to disconnect him from the collective. For realism? That made sense. How else to imagine the old days? Maybe this was a cinescape about the early days of the Wiccan Wars, when the Wiccans had the upper hand with their magic, and the good guys were limited to machines guided primarily by electronics instead of bioware. Even though he had no access to stoven.net, he could recall that people didn't know much about those early war years.

There was only the general recognition that an evil species had branched off from humans. Now, here he was, stuck in the middle with them. But, luckily, on a cinescape set. *So this isn't real,* he thought. Probably. Some of it was coming back to him. His language module was working. *Clever producers. Can't really make a movie if you can't do the languages.*

And yet, there was one problem with this little theory. He had never worked on a set. He'd heard about them. His closest friend, the acclaimed actor, John Marston, had worked on a set, he was now remembering. But the set was on Mars, where the realism of being there was typical of John taking his method acting to the absolute limits.

Any landscape, any setting, could be reproduced digitally. It didn't make sense for Belex to be here. And the actor drones were impossibly realistic impersonations of Wiccans. He'd been around enough actor drones to know, too, that he wouldn't be somewhat attracted to one, yet he was drawn to the one who seemed to be the leader of the two. She had a soul.

This he knew beyond any doubt. A soul he had a mystifying desire to learn more about.

His head hurt. Suddenly. It had hurt before, but now it was excruciating. It was something he had never felt before.

He realized that the medserv in his arm was not functioning. He assumed that, like many of his components, it was fried or at least temporarily disabled. He also didn't know how important it was for him to have access to it. It wasn't limited to supplying pain relief.

Now that the savages were gone, he had to not just assume he was in a cinescape. This realism was far beyond cinescapism. This had to be more than method acting run amok.

So, he had to think.

He couldn't be near MagicLand. But where was the collective? A cinescape without the immediate and gratifying feedback of his audience was an impossible concept.

His predicament did not seem improved with the savages gone. For one crazy moment, he thought it would be better to be hauled off to whatever intellectually-challenged chieftain ran this place. At least that way, he'd have the hope of something to eat.

He thought about the possibility of some incredibly new cinescape technology and that maybe there was something wrong. Perhaps he and his crew were flying somewhere to test new technology, and they really did crash. Either way, the best thing to do was act as if. He chuckled as he wondered, "as if what?" As if he was in an intricate cinescape? Or stuck in the dead zones near MagicLand?

He wished he could tap into his memory to recall images from the tribal stuff he had heard about as a kid. In ancient times, before early humans split into separate species, there had been tribal people foraging for food and hunting. He remembered that. He remembered a kid who had biolines from someplace—Sumanatra, Sumatla, Sumatra, or something like that.

Kenny. That was his name. The kid with biolines from Sumatra. Kenny had some wild tales about how his ancestors from thousands of years ago lived in a land full of jungle and animal life.

Belex had looked up the word *jungle* so many times in his life that he could almost picture it, but not quite. Kenny said the jungle, and those pictures they all saw, died almost on one day, without warning, and that the result was insane—a mass of humanity trying to escape multiple parts of the world at once. When someone asked Kenny from where they were trying to escape, Kenny had mysteriously said, "Everywhere."

He claimed that much of his family tree was a result of that event, even though it had happened more than two thousand years ago, and there had been some weird, awful thing where people were dying on such a massive scale that nobody in Belex's world could understand. He said crazy things. Like that the people of MagicLand and his own people were both descended directly from an earlier species of humanity that became extinct. Totally crazy stuff. He claimed that the records of that happening had been erased long before stoven.net was created. Belex remembered wanting to say to the crazy kid that you couldn't wipe out the memories of a collective.

And it was maddening for him to think about this stuff now because he was feeling crazy himself, trying to focus not only on what had just happened but also on what people like Kenny and a few other people had told him.

Disconnected, he fell to the ground. His brain hurt. It seemed as if it was a muscle, stretching beyond its reach, trying to learn something that was impossible to learn.

Cursing, he said to himself, *I'm injured, and I just sent away my ambulance.*

He wanted the girls in their strange outfits to return so he could be mended. Even savages had medicine people, he thought.

Still, this was progress. The mass of confusion suddenly seemed okay if his systems were making a recovery. Maybe, he thought, as he sighed in relief, he was not beholden to stoven.net or his bioware for every important memory.

At once, his paralysis ended. Memories began to pop out of nowhere. Demands he had made as a six-year-old to a friend. A fight with another friend at what age? Twelve, thirteen?

His paralysis ended, yes, but he still felt despair at his situation, which was grim. He kicked the dirt beneath him and cursed where he came from because he felt so helpless now away from the collective, and it seemed so unfair that the very fact of the disconnection might kill him.

Time sauntered on, and he had no idea what to do.

So, he laid down and decided to close his eyes, just to see what might happen, pleading into the ground for help.

13

Aurilena and Sherealla rode for as long as Aurilena could stand it, which wasn't long. A Gath, he was, but a handsome beauty that was calling to her from the bottom of the earth. She could feel his consciousness. She could feel words push up from the ground as she rode. *I need help,* they said. Perhaps Hilkiah was right. Perhaps he was a Reckless, after all. She wondered if it was possible to be a Reckless and not know it.

They turned and went back to him.

"Hey, he looks to be in bad shape." Aurilena was surprised at the state of her foe as they approached the second time. "I mean," she said to Sherealla, "he really looks awful." She shook her head. "They're supposed to be self-sustaining."

Sherealla merely repeated her earlier cautions about the creature, and said, "I am pretty sure I warned you about this." It was classic reverse psychology because Sherealla was beginning to sense the importance of getting this Gath into Moria.

Aurilena glanced over to her friend and said, "I don't remember the specific warning." Aurilena was thrilled. She felt like she had captured a tiger. "Well, let's get him up."

"Wait," he said. "There are others. From the crash."

"There are no others," said Aurilena. She knew there were no other humanoid life forms anywhere near, and she nodded to Sherealla.

Sherealla hoisted the man up onto Aurilena's horse and tied his arms tightly around Aurilena's waist with a rope.

"That's nice," he winked through his weakened countenance at Sherealla, who felt offended by the experience.

"Yeah, whatever," Sherealla said as she neared her horse.

14

The ride was a long one that eventually took him through a bizarre, dilapidated, partially submerged city full of people in extreme destitution, then over a long overpass held up by parallel load-bearing cables made from thick braids of rope anchored at two ends of a dark orange bridge ruined by war. The wooden planks of the bridge followed a frightening catenary arc over a stunning bay. The arc swayed from the weight of a gallop that Belex thought was considerably harsher than it should have been on such a cantankerous structure. *A nice trot should do,* he thought tremulously.

He found that he was holding on for dear life to his rider as the harrowing ride over the bridge ended and led to a pageantry of architecturally splendid structures built into slopes and tall hills.

There were horses wandering about, and the whole place smelled strange in a way he had never experienced. If he hadn't known better, he would have thought that the place smelled faintly like dung.

The girl rode her horse into town at such a gallop that he couldn't imagine her being able to stop. He saw signs hanging outside of some buildings, but he couldn't read most of them because the horses were racing past them.

"Haberdashery," he said to himself after successfully parsing one of the signs, apparently loudly enough for his captor to hear.

"What?" she said with her head tilted back a bit.

"Nothing. Nothing. Let me off this beast."

As they slowed, he became hopeful that the ride was almost over. She was clearly pointing to her companion when she said, "Hilkiah should be happier than a necromancer in a graveyard with this Reckless."

They clambered up a tall hill filled with children playing a game. As the horse's trot slowed further, Belex watched the game as he leaned into the girl.

She snapped at him, "Stop leaning into me; we're on a hill! Sit like you're a tree."

Belex rolled his eyes but complied by centering himself vertically on the horse parallel to the rider, and the grateful horse picked up a little speed.

A group of children formed two lines at the foot of the hill and kicked a ball upward, along the hill's slope. There was no arc to most of their kicks; the ball was tapped by the foot just enough to move up, but occasionally, the line would break as individual players focused on keeping the ball's momentum as it gravitated upward. The lines appeared to be competitors or teams as one player kicked the ball within the boundary defined by the hilly street. When the current player's foot struck the ball, the ball arched significantly and fell perfectly in line from where his foot touched the ball, and the kids underneath scampered and screamed toward an opportunity to be the next to kick the ball.

Finally, as the ball neared the summit, another group of kids charged out of trees and buildings and broke for the ball. If one of them neared it from a bad angle, he or she would be taken out by one of the kids in the ascending line, leveled like a tree felled by a monstrous hand. Remarkably, none of the children were hurt, no matter how hard they fell. They would invariably bounce up without help from their legs, as if they were avatars in an ancient videogame found in a stoven.net game archive.

Somehow, the girl on the horse managed to evade the competing lines, even as they converged during her approach.

The horse stopped, and Belex's hands let go of the rider, who jumped off the horse and glared at him. "Get off," she said.

He threw his legs off and landed more softly than he could have ever imagined. It was like he had been guided by an outside force, and oddly, it felt to him like he had done it a thousand times.

CHAPTER II

1

Aurilena was proud as she brought her catch to Hilkiah. Hilkiah was usually in one of three places, and, occasionally, all three at once: his home, the Hall of Legions, which was a monolithic building next to his home that quartered various ceremonial rooms of prayer and festivals and served as a sanctuary for those who were in trouble in some way, and the Holy Cliff overlooking the northern shores where he frequently groomed his faith.

While still walking forward, she knocked on the door of Hilkiah's home, which, like the Hall of Legions, was built into the hill. She was about to eagerly push herself through with her quarry when Hilkiah pulled the door open, nearly sending Aurilena stumbling into him. He grinned widely at this as she entered with her annoyed captive. Sherealla followed them into the room.

"Hilkiah," she said, looking at herself quickly in a small mirror on Hilkiah's wall. "You were right. We may have a Reckless on our hands."

Some said Hilkiah stood eight feet tall, but Aurilena reckoned he was closer to seven-five. *When you get that tall, who's counting?* she thought.

Hilkiah, if he had been a normal person, would have demanded a bit more reverence from Aurilena, who, through Hilkiah's aging eyes, seemed herself to be quite the reckless. But Hilkiah was a man of patience. Some called him the Peacemaker because he had unified two intransigent warring factions in Moria during his youth. These days, he wasn't unwilling, at times, to resort to ostracism and shame toward those who used magic for violent purposes outside of the perennial Gath conflict.

But even more important to Hilkiah was his philosophy on magic itself. *Never,* he would tell his students, *should one call on magic for a specific task. Instead,* he said, *the power that created magic in the first place has the sole authority to determine its use.*

Hilkiah moved his attention to the possible Reckless. Hilkiah's almond-shaped brown eyes stared from behind billowing clouds of white eyebrows. His aged, obsidian skin seemed to have a crevice designed for every expression as he gazed on Belex for a minute without saying a word. Hilkiah had a nose that seemed as wide as the face that held it, and its nostrils flared as he bent down a great distance to bring himself eyeball to eyeball with Belex.

Meanwhile, Belex was squirming, eager to be released from his bonds, while a few strands from Hilkiah's waist-length dreadlocks fell along the front of his face.

"Your name," said Hilkiah.

"Belex Deralk-Almd. I'm an actor, not a warrior."

"Release him," commanded Hilkiah.

Sherealla looked at Aurilena, who nodded, and the leather cords around Belex's wrists were cut by invisible blades, fell to the ground, and disappeared into the floor.

He promptly ran out of the door, which triggered a sonorous laugh from Hilkiah. Aurilena looked mortified, and Sherealla dutifully ran after him.

"Stop!" Hilkiah bellowed loudly, still laughing. "Where will he go? Back to the buffalo?"

"We can't just let him prowl the streets," objected Sherealla, who came back as if shot by a blast of wind.

"He can cause no harm," assured Hilkiah.

"He will see how we live," objected Sherealla, who had other concerns. "And how did you know we were among the buffalo?"

"I did send you. And because you stink," Hilkiah answered. With that, Hilkiah glanced at Aurilena before returning his gaze to Sherealla. "Sit," he said, motioning to a circular wooden table with a diameter about as long as he and that acted as the room's centerpiece. Instead of four legs, the table was supported by a single, thick tree stump. "We'll eat and discuss this. But first, Aurilena, he is no Reckless. He runs."

"He's scared."

Hilkiah laughed again. "Sit," he said and again motioned to Aurilena and her friend.

Reluctantly, the slightly embarrassed pair sat down at the table. The adornments of the room were few. There were candles of a variety of sizes and shapes, and some paintings by local artists hung on the walls, but Hilkiah's home, open to all, was known to be spartan. The high priest's home was a friendly, rustic place, designed to serve his guests, who were warmly greeted at all hours, not with splendor but warmth.

"First," said Hilkiah, pulling a large fat candle out of the kangaroo pocket of his long robe and dropping it onto the table, "we must rid this room of the stench." He waved his hand over the candle, which lit into a wild, skinny, towering flame that stretched nearly to the far reaches of Hilkiah's cathedral-style ceiling before snuffing itself out in a flash. The room was instantly cleared of the smell.

Hilkiah took a jug of wine from the same pocket and placed it on the table. Aurilena stared at the bottle and glanced up in disbelief at Hilkiah.

"It's a myth that I don't ever indulge in the taste of wine." said Hilkiah. "Of course, it is rare. But a celebration is in order."

"Huh?" said Aurilena.

"Much better than a Reckless." Hilkiah poured from the jug and handed Sherealla and Aurilena full glasses of wine. "A Reckless comes here of his own volition. A Reckless comes here seeking truth from that terrible, broken land along our southern coast. The Reckless come here to escape the machinery that has invaded their minds, and for that, we give them sanctuary."

"Yeah, okay. So?" asked Aurilena, who was becoming fidgety and wanted to know where he was.

"You, my little friend, have *captured* a Gath."

"I'm not little," objected Aurilena. Hilkiah's thick lips, mostly covered by billowy coils that bloomed from a long, white and gray beard peppered with black specks, revealed a set of glowing ivory teeth when he smiled at Aurilena's comment. "But it doesn't make any difference; a Gath is a Gath," she continued. "Reckless or otherwise. I don't even get why we call them Reckless. It's dumb."

"They're reckless with their lives to try to escape the Gath," responded Hilkiah. "Not many have made the reckless trek through the Devil's Play Yard to our fair city. Perhaps Fearless would be a more proper term because one must be fearless to take on such risk."

"But once they get here, they're safe—no big deal," said Sherealla. "I mean, there's no way for Gath forces to get in, right?"

Aurilena could never understand why Sherealla was frequently asking questions like that, trying to find out if there were ways for warriors or spies from Gath to enter the city. It was a weird quirk of Sherealla's that always made Aurilena want to give her a shove.

"They're safe," affirmed Hilkiah. "But they don't know that. They're a race that has nearly destroyed ours. If I was one of them, I wouldn't feel welcomed here. Most of them draw hostile stares wherever they go. Most feel unwelcome, frightened of the citizenry."

"Bah," said Aurilena. "The Gath are only afraid of us because of our magic. Not because they think we are mean. They know we are a peace-loving people. Honestly, I think that's one of the things they hate about us."

"So now what?" asked Sherealla.

"We wait," answered Hilkiah. "The Gath boy will be back soon enough."

2

Belex knew this was too easy. They hadn't even run after him. He couldn't imagine what kind of trap might be set for him. And he didn't know how to hide. He was still wearing his uniform, so he'd be easy prey for any police drones that might be sent out for him. *Wait, they don't have police drones here.*

Back home, the police were small, autonomous spheres of graphene and silicon that watched your every move. They buzzed around like insects, self-replicating, programmed balls of terror if you made a misstep. Small but lethal, thousands could converge at once during a serious event and quickly bring order. Who were the police here? They had to be people. There were no drones. None of any kind.

He realized he needed to find out the answer to this if he had any chance of escape. If he could stay out of sight until nightfall, he'd be safe because his uniform made him look like a black hole in the air.

And then what? Once he escaped, what next? He was beginning to see some imagery, but not from the collective, which he was sure was still out of his reach. Memories, he thought, telling him that he knew where he was now and that he was far from home.

Then it hit him. MagicLand. He was in MagicLand. The home of the enemy, the home of that bizarre split of the human species, the home of rejects, the home of premature death and madness that had infused stoven.net for centuries with videos of unworldly violence and hatred.

How could he not have recognized it as soon as he crashed? What had stopped his internal sensors from deactivating his digital pulse so that he could at least die without falling into the hands of these savages?

He felt, suddenly, that he was in *The Hands of Hell*. Was that a name of a cinescape he had starred in?

It was.

He looked around and saw dust and dirt everywhere. He recoiled as he realized he was leaning against a building that was covered with dirt.

What is wrong with these people? he wondered. Why would anyone reject the opportunity to clean this up? Just a few hundred trillion nanodrones and this whole city would be clean of its dirt and filth.

The war, he remembered, was all about this place and how they rejected his people for strange reasons nobody understood.

3

"He wants to be here, Hilkiah."

Sherealla's eyes nearly jumped out of their sockets, but Hilkiah looked interested in Aurilena's words.

Hilkiah had known Aurilena since Aurilena's birth and knew her intuition well. "You're mixing the present with the future, Aurilena. He may want to be here soon, but for now, he wants desperately to escape, and so he is no Reckless."

"And that makes him dangerous," Sherealla chimed in.

"It is assumptions about people that are dangerous, Sherealla," said Hilkiah. "And let's be clear. It is we who are dangerous."

"They're not people," Sherealla replied matter-of-factly. *We're not people.*

4

"Just please remember that you were literally designed for this moment," said Sherealla's mother, kissing her gently on the forehead.

"But I don't want to go. I want to be with my friends in the gaming strata."

"Sometimes, some of us are asked to make sacrifices, sweetie. Not all of us, but those who are chosen are picked because we are outstanding citizens. The collective knows this. Your friends would understand."

"They don't even know. It's some stupid military thing, and we're the only ones who know. It's creepy. What gives the military the right to hide things from the collective?"

They were at the top of the Mantricle, a place few in the Homeland had ever seen on the inside.

Her father, a military man himself, did not take offense at her question. He had struggled shortly after Sherealla's birth with an edict directing that she not be given access to stoven.net. He successfully fought that decision. This came at a price, one that he and his wife would be paying as soon as Sherealla was sent away on her journey. He knew that if she understood the sacrifices he and his wife were making for her that she'd put a halt to her insubordination. But soon after, she'd become even angrier, and her grief would give way to fury. He tried to calm her. "You will be back soon. I think that with all my heart."

"I don't even know what I'm supposed to do."

"Your training will guide you, and your mission node will provide you step-by-step details when you get there. You have nothing to fear. You're battle-tested and can take on any enemy, but that won't even be a problem for you because nobody will know you're the enemy. You look just like them."

"Ugh. I hate that, too. I hate being so different."

"I can't lie to you," he said. "When you get there, you'll look the same but feel very different."

"And I'll know what to do no matter what?"

"If conditions change on the ground, your mission node will adjust the plans. You have nothing to worry about," assured her father. "And you will return home a hero."

She didn't know if she cared about that. She wanted to play in the Wintermute Strata with her friends, who would always laugh at her when she talked about parents because of their rarity, but who otherwise made her look forward to her days in the social and gaming strata.

The room they were in was nearly empty, with only neon blue walls and floors, the tall oval chairs that Sherealla and her parents were sitting on, and a small table for them. Her father touched her shoulders.

"It's time," he said softly. He informed the security network, and a series of drones entered the room to accompany Sherealla. Her mother wiped a tear from her eye as Sherealla whimpered.

"All your life, you've been preparing for this day. Please be strong," said her father.

Sherealla swallowed hard and nodded. "I'll be okay. I was just . . . I thought I was more ready than maybe I am. But I'll be okay."

"And you will be back. And I'll be so proud of you."

He looked at the drones and motioned to them. Sherealla stood up to meet them. "I'm ready," she said, and the drones whisked her away.

When she arrived in The Wandering City, she would see, hear, and watch the awards given to her parents because she would still have access to stoven. net. They were feted publicly for the most esteemed honors regarding a secret mission, it was said, that would alter the war against the Wiccans. She found it curious that they were never mentioned as her parents.

She would not see their subsequent execution, which they had accepted long ago as a necessary component of Sherealla's wartime mission. Within the realm of stoven.net, her parents would simply fade away as distant soldiers, their existence buried by the trillions of bytes of more topical information and the trendlines of a happy populace.

5

"He sure looks like a people to me," said Aurilena, whose mischievous smile prompted a glare out of Sherealla and an amused smile from Hilkiah.

Sherealla wouldn't relent. "How long do you think they let people live there?" she asked.

Hilkiah chuckled at this and said, "There are people there considerably older than me. They look a bit different at my age in Gath," he said, morphing himself momentarily into a younger man, which made the girls laugh.

Sherealla sensed she may have set her trap. "So, he could be 200 years old, too. Who would know? They're horrible, awful things. They're not even people. They're freaks, and they've been trying to destroy us for thousands of years. I hate them."

Her real feelings were more complicated than that, but she was ambivalent even on her brightest days. Her mission wasn't voluntary or borne of loyalty or duty. It was literally programmed into her.

The story circulating around Moria was that Sherealla's parents had strayed past the Wildland Hills after an experiment gone bad in an airship, one of the few times anyone from Moria had attempted flight since before the first wars.

Sherealla had never gotten over it, the story went, and worse, many people never saw her parents' escapade as heroic. Some gossip referred to it as a lame attempt to find some commonality with the vision of the Gath. A foolhardy attempt at technology. Others said they were just mischief makers.

But there were pieces missing from the story, one of which was the missing airship. Nobody knew of such a contraption, and no remains or debris from an accident were ever found.

There was always a distant taint of suspicion surrounding Sherealla, sometimes even shared privately with Aurilena by Hilkiah, who would say things like, "She sends bad omens and portent into the land."

The fact that nobody knew her parents was also no small matter, but sojourners into Moria were not uncommon. Aurilena had immediately taken to the orphaned twelve-year-old girl she met buried under a fallen beam in a building in the Wandering City. That was good enough for most.

Aurilena clutched Sherealla's wrist gently and quietly said, "He's not 200 years old," and her eyes pierced deeply, as if their world was about to change.

6

Sherealla was trying to run for shelter through a downpour, but each building was getting blasted by weapons as she approached. She could barely see in front of her because the deluge from the sky was blocking her vision. Her systems tried x-ray imaging but there was too much visual scattering. Her systems then tried blue-shifting some infrared light into her visible spectrum. That didn't help either.

She cursed and blamed MagicLand then the people who sent her, who had told her she'd be invulnerable here. She could sense her systems trying a variety of techniques to improve her vision, all of them failing, and she wondered about legends that warned about AI systems failures in MagicLand. She tried querying stoven.net for solutions but couldn't access it. So she ran.

7

"Wait," said Aurilena. "What do you mean it is we who are dangerous?"

"I've been preaching for as long as I can remember," answered Hilkiah, "of how our magic is misused. When you want something, what do you do, Aurilena?"

"I try to make it happen," she replied confidently.

"Precisely. And precisely the wrong approach. You do this because you don't know your God. And instead, you try to be one. These powers you have are too powerful for you to own. If I had my way, you'd be in a cage until you learned how to use them."

"But I don't use them to do bad things," Aurilena objected.

"These powers are not yours to decide what is bad. If you decide how to harness your powers, which aren't your powers at all, in truth, then you are using them for ill intent, no matter your claims."

"But how then? How do I use them if, well, I can't use them?"

"The spirit inside you decides. Until you can speak with that spirit inside you during every one of your waking and sleeping moments, you must be quiet and wait. When we were attacked long ago by the Gath, we didn't know what to do. I didn't know what to do."

"But we survived. How?"

The question prompted Hilkiah to think back to another time.

8

Hilkiah's robe was resplendent, he thought. He had never been prone to vanity, but he allowed himself this one instance of satisfaction in his stately attire.

These were dark times, and he knew the moment would be but the briefest flicker within that darkness. It was his intent to enjoy it. It isn't every day that someone prepares for his own high priest ceremony, he thought.

He studied himself in the mirror. The front of his robe was adorned with a stripe of silver filigree framing each side of a symbol representing the Great Shepherd Yehoshua. The ornate symbol, a cross overlaying a circle, was carefully shaped in detail with gilded raised cloth. The robe's deep purple seemed to possess a shine that could be seen from a distance. Its fabric had been obtained by the great Acquirer, Beth-Solomon, a woman who, Hilkiah often felt, had rebuilt Moria almost singlehandedly after its near destruction.

It was through the efforts of her good friend, Sedecla, that Moria was saved. Sedecla had prophesized the day the Gath would attack twice in one day, which allowed a defense of sorts to occur, and when it happened, Hilkiah had been able to harness his metamorphic powers to convert the bulk of the attacking swarms into butterflies during the first wave.

But not all of them and not soon enough. Many got through, and they wrought destruction on large swaths of the city before many people could even rouse themselves from their sleep.

Many of the magicians in Moria were huddled in the Hall of Legions during the second wave. When the long, winding black shrouds of nanobots were shredding the last remaining structures of Moria, and its citizens found themselves as refugees in the Wandering City on the other side of the bay, the priests and priestesses in the Room of Prayer begged him to try something.

"Nothing we do is working, Hilkiah," one of the most influential Metamorphics said. "Whatever it is in your mind to try, I implore you to do so." There had been great debate between Hilkiah's way and the way of others, who cast spells and incantations and called on spirit guides to win their battles.

He took the powerful magician by her shoulders and leaned down to look into her eyes to say, "You can help those who lack the magic to transport themselves from the city. Get help to save as many as you can." She nodded and ran, and Hilkiah ran to the front window of the Room of Prayer to witness the complete destruction overtaking Moria. He hurried to a table and knelt in front of its wood chair, folding his arms over the seat and clasping his hands as he spoke into the smoky air, "Yehoshua, hear my prayer," he began. "If it is not your will for our city and people to be destroyed, please deliver us from the evil that is this Gath." He could feel the others behind him pray with him.

There was more to the prayer, he now remembered, as he patted himself down in front of the mirror. He was an unusually tall man, whose African features gave him a strong sense of pride for reasons that eluded him, reasons that were probably as ancient as Moria itself. His skin was such a deep black that visitors could almost see themselves reflected in his face. His wide nose and thick lips prompted many to say he looked like a great and noble king. He had wanted none of that, however. His duty was to serve the people he loved, not to be served—not as a servant of man but a servant of Yehoshua, who watched over Moria with a loving hand, he knew. This had been proven to him on that fateful night when he prayed in the Room of Prayer at the House of Legions with a hundred others, which he had rallied and summoned because it was only moments later that the Gath nanobots seemed to experience a centralized malfunction, attacking the city with no effect. Their weapons seemed to hit targets, and the ground exploded, but nothing in Moria was touched. Then, it was as if they were directed by a queen bee to cannibalize each other, which they did, high over the skies of Moria. Thus ended the attack, almost as suddenly as it had begun.

It was then that Hilkiah's way began to be followed. There was little conflict over this because the situation that Hilkiah had overcome was so dire. Moria's existence had been in doubt moments before Hilkiah's calls for mercy in the Room of Prayer. Hilkiah, too, would always cherish the quiet singing and chanting of those who joined him, all of them speaking and singing in unison the same words, as if they were directly sent to them from Yehoshua.

This is not to say that sorcery ended on that day or that Hilkiah even began to discourage it in any meaningful way. Sorcery had served Moria well. Everyone in Moria knew how to perform at least a little magic. In fact, it was part of their blood, inherited much like hair and eye color. Urging his people to quit sorcery would have been foolish. He would teach his way but not enforce it.

Beth-Solomon became his most enthusiastic acolyte, despite her great power, or maybe, Hilkiah reflected as he fluffed out his beard in front of the mirror with a wide-pronged comb, because of it.

Amused by his self-reverence, he gave his robe one more pat before deciding he'd had enough reminiscence. He heard four knocks on his door, then two more. There came a pause, then two more knocks. That would be Beth, he muttered happily to himself. He spied one more look in the mirror, shoved the robe's hood off his head, and hurriedly fluffed up his hair, which was a wild orgy of curls. He began to walk away from the mirror but spied himself once more, quickly, before scampering to the door.

"Well," said Beth when Hilkiah opened his door, "don't you look dazzling. Look at you. Not only the youngest high priest to ever speak to this land but the most handsome, too." Even at this young age, Hilkiah's eyebrows were oversized, bushy things that he frequently thought could have been peeled off and used as excellent cleaning brushes. One of them raised in appreciation of her comment. She looked rather dazzling herself in a long silk dress with a neckline that challenged the politeness of his eyes and long strips of dark orange within an ochre tapestry. A slit on the side of one leg further challenged his piety. The bias-cut dress was snug against elegant, slender hips. She had woven her silver hair into a fishtail braid. He was certain he would need a healer at any moment to calm his racing heart.

But it was Beth's face that Hilkiah had always been insatiably drawn to. She had a dark Mediterranean complexion and a long, curving upturned nose with a softly rising dorsal hump. Her angular jawlines narrowed toward a thin, pointed chin that finished the triangular design of her face.

"And you have officially made me breathless," he responded.

She flashed a bright white smile with lips that turned upward into a pair of slight dimples. "Well, I'll admit I did some preparatory work on my appearance for your big day." They embraced, and he offered her tea.

"It's common black breakfast tea, I'm afraid. If you want better, you'll need to conjure some for yourself."

She laughed. "This is fine, thank you."

"What will you say at the ceremony?" she asked after a sip. "Will you be admonishing us all for our wicked ways?"

"Have I so far?"

"Not in so many words."

"In deeds?"

Beth nodded slightly. "Some."

"I have no intent to impose my theology on others. I live by example, letting others make their own decisions."

"They weren't enough to form an opposition to you becoming high priest, but there are some who say you will usurp all priestly authority and outlaw general sorcery."

"Bah!" he said. "We couldn't afford these kinds of theological politics even if I were so inclined. I would hope anyone who truly thinks that voted against me."

"I was the lone vote against you," she smiled.

"I would expect nothing less from my favorite contrarian."

She looked pensive, her brilliant green eyes looking straight through Hilkiah as she sipped more tea.

"What are you thinking?" he asked.

"Oh. Sorry. I'm thinking about that day I found you walking alone on the streets of the Wandering City, cold, afraid, shivering actually—those big white teeth of yours chattering away like you were summoning somebody."

"I was. You."

"And there I was."

"And there you were."

"And we took you back to Moria with nary a complaint from you. In fact, without a word."

"I had just lost my father."

"Yes, you told me. I was afraid for you. Didn't know how you'd survive. You were so thin. You had this lantern jaw, in those days, with hollow cheeks. You looked like you were starving."

"I was. I did not know how to acquire. It was a skill that has always escaped me."

"All for the greater good, as it turns out. Your way provides, Hilkiah. No matter the situation. It is why you are having this day."

"Your flattery will get you somewhere," he replied.

"Well, anyway. You filled out there," she said, stretching her arm up and gently pressing a fingertip on his cheek.

That was the moment, he would sometimes recall, that he had wanted to marry Beth-Solomon. She had an eye toward him that no other woman would ever have. There was an intimacy in her knowledge of him and who he was that nobody could ever match. And there was, of course, his utter adoration toward her.

But as time marched on, he found himself unable to approach her romantically. He at first blamed an intransigent shyness, but if that had been the reason for his hesitancy, he would have determined to find a way through it and court her properly.

By becoming a high priest, even though there were no laws regarding a priestly marriage, he had made an oath to the city that required absolutism. Marriage, no matter how justifiably, required favoritism in times of danger that was in direct conflict to his duties.

In time, Hilkiah realized, as he later looked upon his gifted and amazing student Aurilena, it all worked out for the best because Beth would marry Aurilena's grandfather and produce a line of people who were magical in ways that expressed themselves far beyond the realm of raw power.

9

"We prayed. I gathered all the magicians, gathered all the seers, priests, and priestesses together. We prayed. We asked for guidance and help."

"And?" asked Aurilena.

"And our city disappeared. The enemy couldn't find it. They attacked where they thought we were, where we had been, and their weapons mauled empty grounds." Hilkiah arched one bushy eyebrow, now white as snow. "It was all rather strange. But what's important is that we asked for help without dictating the terms, and the help came."

"I guess I always thought it was you that made it happen."

"Ah, and therein lies the problem, Aurilena. I don't have such power. I relied on a power much greater than mine. Besides, I'm not creative enough to think of something like that. I asked for help. We got it. That's the whole story, as it always is. Asking for help and not trying to impose my will on the answer.

"It started with an attack that nearly leveled the city. Their follow up attack, I was sure, would finish us. We needed something that would last, and it came. As impossible as it seems, I think we are somehow in a time just slightly ahead or behind the Gath. That is the essence of it, I think—a kind of time vortex, but I can't claim to understand it. That's the beauty of such power. The plain fact that it isn't mine and is so much more powerful than anything I could manage, frees me from the need to master or even comprehend it."

10

Aurilena arrived home a few hours later. The wait at Hilkiah's home for news of the Gath had left her drained. She couldn't understand why this beast was so important to her. True, he was lovely to look at, but so were buffalo. So were the magnificent Empire trees that soared just beyond the Wandering City. So was the ocean and the fog that rolled through the Broken Bridge.

She breathed an audible sigh of relief as she changed out of her riding outfit. She knew she'd be going back to Hilkiah's home or the Hall of Legions soon, but it wasn't important what she wore now because both were only minutes away by horseback, so a change of clothes was easy. She considered this but decided to dress for the return visit, putting on a pair of hemp harem pants that were snug at her ankles. She then fit into a loose-fitting cotton green top acquired by her dad a couple of years prior. The top's color matched her eyes well, she thought, as she looked in the mirror. *Hmmm,* she thought. *Cute, but not too cute.*

She went to the kitchen. She was hungry after missing dinner in all the excitement, so she took an apple from a bowl before stepping outside.

Her mother was sitting at a table on the terracotta deck as the sun was setting a beautiful orange tone across the western skies. Aurilena wondered if she'd ever reach the point where she'd be like her mother and wear the same thing every day. Her mom wore a gray frock with a light shirt, loose hemp pants underneath, and a feathered round cap. *Every day,* thought Aurilena. Her mother was a tall woman with straight grey hair that stretched down and collected into sets of spears as it fell below her shoulders. Ever since Seth's death, her brown eyes had looked flushed with callow anger, as if blame existed around every corner.

Aurilena sighed as she looked out to the water. The deck had views of the Broken Bridge and a portion of the bay where another bridge was said to have once linked this point of land with the hills just east. Aurilena had grown up hearing that the east harbored small barbarian clans trying to eke out an existence in a poisoned land.

Aurilena's home was at the top of a hill—the envy of many, although Aurilena was still too blinded by unfettered optimism to detect hostility among her peers or fellow citizens.

The interior of the home was inlaid with marble and intricate moldings. A fireplace framed with Carrara and thin lines of gilded stone occupied an interior wall. She grew up thinking nothing of it because her father, Hiram, was an Acquirer with an eye for architecture and his brother Ithream, a skilled mason and carpenter. In happier times, Hiram would conjure spirits to bring ornate building materials while Ithream supplied the millwork and carpentry to fashion the stately home. During the last few years, the stateliness had eroded as her father became dour and less sanguine.

11

"Wow, Father, what is that?" asked Aurilena, holding Judith's hand as she watched.

Hiram had presented a velvety purple scarf adorned with orange and white celestial symbols to Seth for his birthday. The scarf was beautiful, but its most distinguishing feature was a light purple glow that accompanied it.

"This is a Turillion Scarf. It is said," he announced with a pause as he straightened out some wrinkles on the lucent fabric draped over Seth's shoulders, "to ward off Gath." He chuckled at that. He glanced at Aurilena. "Of course, it is a myth, but they're quite rare. Made, as I understand, by descendants of the ancients in Old Siberia. I bartered a raincoat for it." He smiled broadly at the boast. "Did you know it used to be quite cold in the Siberian rain forests?"

The scarf lit up as her father stepped away from Seth, reminding Aurilena again of Seth's intense raw magic.

"What do you think, my boy?" asked Hiram. Seth nodded appreciatively.

Hiram nodded as he used two fingers to tug at his pointed goatee, which bore a white stripe down its middle as if in anticipation of his later years.

Her mother aggressively pulled Seth and Hiram toward her and said, "I just love you both so much," and hugged them as if they had just arrived after years at sea.

12

Aurilena wanted to display the enthusiasm she felt for her recent adventure but could sense her mother's disapproval before she sat down to tell the tale. It was as if her mother was certain that something untoward was afoot. This prompted Aurilena to tell the story in hushed, calm tones as if she was reading aloud from a book.

Her sister Judith, several years older, joined in the middle of the story and seemed fascinated by it, but she drew cold stares from their mother whenever she asked a probing question.

Her mother was a master of the healing arts who had nurtured half the town, and one of her skills was listening at length in what seemed to Aurilena to be avowed silence. Finally, after Aurilena finished reporting on her encounter, her mother, after the avowed silence, said, "You have no business with that boy," and rose from the table and went inside.

"Well, you know how much Mom hates the Gath," said Judith. Judith's prejudices were few. Her hair shared the deep black of Aurilena's, which had also been the color of their father's hair before his had become salted with streaks of grey. Judith's hair was shorter, not quite shoulder length, with bangs in the front.

"We all do," said Aurilena, "but she could still be interested in what I'm doing during the day."

"She wanted you to be a healer," said Judith simply.

"Well, who's to say I won't be?"

"She calls you an animal trainer."

"That's so mean."

"You should hear what she calls me."

"She doesn't know your special skill, or she'd become even more beastly."

"Like we have a choice in what we're good at. Give me a break already. Although it's so unfair because you're good at everything." Judith leaned toward one of the large windows. "Hello, Ma! We're hungry!"

Aurilena giggled at that.

"Feed us!"

She giggled at that, too. "Let me ask . . . what does my futurist sister say about this?"

"He could be the one," laughed Judith. Judith had, for years after the death of their little brother at the hands of the Gath, been the least resentful over the tragedy, although there was plenty of resentment in her, as well. But all things being relative, she had seemed to move on emotionally better than anyone. The reason was that her clairvoyance, which she had never allowed to fully mature, suggested more of a common ancestry between Gath and Moria than had been revealed. Even more interestingly, Judith's foretelling occasionally revealed someone from Gath playing a role in improving their lives, a notion that Aurilena had always found ludicrous.

"Oh, really," said Aurilena.

"Yes, the one who'll get you kicked out of this house. More likely, thrown into the water," said Judith, nodding toward the Broken Bridge. "Sis, I know you thought you were being all coy and stoic about this boy, but nobody needs my skill set to see you're already smitten by the electric animal from the land of evil trolls. If I can see it, you can bet Mom can."

Aurilena sighed. "Smitten, no. But fascinated? For sure. He's really interesting to look at."

"Last girl I know said that was married a month later."

Aurilena thwacked Judith's arm with a napkin. "I'm serious. It's nothing, just, you know . . . anthropology."

"Well, keep it to anthropology, leave biology out of it, and Ma will come around. Ma! Food!"

Aurilena giggled, knowing perfectly well no food was forthcoming from this mother, who had staked her entire motherhood on her children's independence.

"I adore you, you nut," she said to Judith. She noticed a patch of broken stone near the door where her mom had gone and had to look away. As she gazed onto the bay beyond, she felt overwhelmed with grief that her parents no longer seemed like a couple. Her father had developed an inner rage after his son's death, turning inward, drinking spirits instead of working with them, their once glorious home slowly falling into disrepair. She thought about the middle-aged woman in the kitchen now and wondered if her mother had raised the sisters alone, at least in the latter years of their childhood.

Her father had become little more than a missing piece, like the chunk of marble that had fallen out of the fireplace. He had stopped acquiring things for the house, even the essentials to keep it maintained. These days, Aurilena noted ruefully, the only thing he was acquiring was drink.

"Judith," said Aurilena, "what do you see ahead for this place? Anything?"

Judith shook her head. "It's been strange lately. I guess it's why I stick to horses these days. It's so much simpler. All I get is a blank. But a few weeks ago, I had nightmares about the city on fire."

"Nightmares? As in more than one? Have you told anyone? Ha-Kodesh needs to know." Ha-Kodesh was the reclusive Grand Priestess. Few people saw her personally. Some in Moria didn't even know who she was, even though she was probably the bearer of the most powerful magic in Moria's history.

"I can't report everything I see, Lena. Lots of noise. Not everything I see comes true." She made quote marks with her hands when she said the word, *see.* "Not even close."

"Still. More than one nightmare."

"They're dreams. It's not even the same. Not the same as the visions I've received. And if they came in visions, I'd tell everyone I know," she laughed. "So." Judith leaned on the table toward her sister with her chin cupped in her hands. "What are you going to do about that Gath boy?"

Aurilena sighed. "What Gath boy?"

Chapter III

1

Belex spent the night in the streets. He found he needed little sleep, but his memory was so bad that he didn't know if that was normal. He hadn't had a chance to explore the town because it was dusk when he escaped, but as he gained focus from the rough sleep, he remembered how horrified he'd been at seeing the condition of the city.

Hiding during the night had been easy because of his black suit. The street Belex looked upon when he awoke was so steep that it seemed the easiest way to the bottom would be to simply curl himself into a ball and let himself roll down. He barely remembered clambering up the hill in the middle of the night.

Belex descended the hill. The street was lined on both sides by groups of buildings that seemed attached but independent, each with its own doorways and window areas. Most of the windows on the bottom floors were darkened, and Belex was unable to see inside, whereas many of the upper story bay windows indicated living quarters. He saw several signs representing types of business establishments, including the haberdashery he had seen on the way into town.

Looking more closely, he discovered the building next to the haberdashery was fronted by a sign with Chinese characters, which he was used to seeing in the Homeland. He couldn't read them, however. He wasn't sure if that was because of his systems malfunction, or if the language here was different. He couldn't read most of the alphabet-based words on buildings here, either, even though they, too, looked familiar. He was able to translate and speak to the Wiccans he had met so far, but the written languages he was seeing were beyond his reach.

He thought about home and the hundreds of languages easily spoken and written there. He realized this was just another symptom of the systems malfunctions caused by his accident. *Great,* he thought, *now I'm an illiterate, too.*

He decided to walk into the building bearing the Chinese lettering. He pulled on the glass and wood door, and it opened into a dark, candlelit room. A grizzled old man was sitting behind a counter facing him, but he didn't look up when Belex walked in. His two hands were hovering over the counter, a rectangular red orb of light between his palms and facing each other.

As Belex neared the counter, he saw an image of a black horse within the orb. The man looked as if he was kneading the rectangular orb of light containing the image like he was preparing bread dough for the oven.

With Belex at the counter, the man finally looked up and said something that Belex couldn't understand. The man repeated it, and this time, the translator in Belex's language module deciphered the man's speech as, "Why are you here?" The man looked back down at his orb of light.

"I was just curious. I'm not from around here."

The man continued looking down. He had short, black spiky hair with a large bald spot on the crown of his head. His skin was full of broad yellow specks. Aging, Belex assumed. It was difficult to look at. The man had a small beard on his chin with two thin braids on each end. His tiny round spectacles sat near the end of the bridge of his nose. "I know you're not from around here," the man said in a high-pitched, hoarse voice without looking up.

"What are you doing with your hands?" asked Belex.

"This horse suffers from a bad keratoma. I am repairing it. This is much better than surgical removal because, through my process, the cells are regenerated into healthy cells as the mass is removed from the hoof. You have a horse?"

Belex shook his head.

"Then why are you here?" the man asked as he continued to focus on his task.

"I don't understand. That's the horse?"

The man cackled, "Ah, that's funny. No—no, Augmenter, this is his lifeforce, I guess you could say, in concentrated form . . . like OJ."

"OJ?"

"Orange juice. Never seen concentrated orange juice?"

"Well. No."

"Ah, well never mind then, Augmenter. You should be going." The man didn't look up as he continued working with the light, which had changed its hue since Belex's appearance and now carried streaks and bands of blue, along with a bluish, hazy circle around the horse inside.

"Umm, okay. Where is this horse?"

"Ha ha," was all the old man said in response.

"Why do you call me Augmenter?"

The man sighed. "Why do you think?"

"But you're augmented, too."

"That is a very silly thing to say," the man scoffed.

"What do you think those are for?" Belex reached toward the man's face and pushed gently against his spectacles and walked out the door.

It was cooler outside than it had been just a few minutes ago, and now a stiff, chilly breeze was whipping around the buildings, making Belex wish for a hood. Before he could explore another thought, a heavy black-hooded sweatshirt formed around his upper body.

"What the—" he said out loud. He looked up and saw a small, bald boy looking at him and smiling. The boy clapped his hands twice and ran off, and a soft purple scarf filled with symbols wrapped itself around Belex's neck. "Hey!" he yelled for the boy, but there was no response.

Belex walked through this part of the city for several hours. He found numerous other kinds of small magical acts taking place. He watched a nearly emaciated man heaving large square stones up to one building's third floor with nothing but the wave of his hand, aimed at a mason who somehow was able to catch each stone in his hands. The mason expertly molded them into an emerging new pattern in a gap within the stonework.

"Heave, Shage, heave," the mason would yell below when he was ready for another. Belex watched in fascination for a considerable amount of time before he moved on.

Belex observed children playing the ball game he had seen earlier, and he watched what looked like a horse race between two women in the flat streets below the hill. There were dozens of outdoor stalls filled with people offering a variety of services and goods. The odors of grilled meats lingered in the air. He was hungry, but he couldn't eat meat, and as the lunch hour passed into the afternoon, he started to crave fried vegetables, which he thought he also smelled in the air.

Belex spotted a group of tables outside an eating establishment that looked like a good place to sit down and rest his feet for a few moments. The tables were round wooden slabs with billowing umbrellas poking out of a middle hole. He sat down at one and rubbed his eyes. He was tired from all of the walking. He realized his legs were burning, which was an odd and foreign experience.

When he moved his hands away from his eyes, he nearly jumped out of his skin-tight suit as his hand brushed into a hot bowl of steaming vegetables. A young girl, not more than ten or eleven years old, was standing a few tables away, looking at Belex while holding a doll and pretending to feed it. When Belex tried to say something, she ran off giggling. Belex looked down at the bowl, which had a pleasant, spicy smell and noticed a fork hovering just above the bowl. He tried to grab it, but it danced away as he heard the child giggle again.

He looked up and her little head, covered with long, straight sandy hair, dashed behind a nearby wall, as if it had been alone and disembodied. Belex thought, given the circumstances, that may have well been the case. He tried to grab the fork again, but the fork escaped, and again, he heard the giggle.

"C'mon," he pleaded. "I'm hungry."

At that, the fork stabbed into the food and presented itself to Belex. He looked up, and although he couldn't see the girl, he smiled and said, "Thank you."

He stood up after finishing his food and walked among the stalls and milling people, keeping an eye out for the little girl who had given him the delicious vegetables. A fog rolled in, dropping the temperature even more. He tightened the scarf around his neck, which warmed him considerably more than such a thin fabric should, and he noticed a nearby window. It was full of condensation with an inlaid set of symbols. Curious, he approached. Scrawled inside the condensation were words he could somehow read: "You're welcome." *What a funny place this is. A strange, funny place,* he thought.

The day wore on, and he saw no further signs of either of his two child benefactors. He was thankful for them, for they had not only warmed his body but warmed his soul, if only for these few hours. Before long, the sun was disappearing again over the western building tops, and he found himself walking up the same hill where he had woken in the morning. A sense of familiarity settled over him. Instead of using the walkway, he found himself in the street where the children had been playing their ball game.

Next to him was a set of parallel metal bars embedded into the street itself. These seemed to bend and follow the middle of the street all the way down the hill and, probably, beyond. He assumed these were part of a guidance mechanism, which this primitive city had not yet abandoned. He decided to follow them.

He threw a branch at them to test for an electric current and nothing happened. Next, he tossed a stone across the two rails to test for a weaponized field. The stone landed softly just beyond. He touched one of the rails lightly with his foot. Nothing. This disavowed his mind of the theory that it was part of an electrical or defense system.

He had yet to deduce what powered the lights in this city. Based on the city's obvious attachment to antiquity, he would have expected lanterns and other absurdly ancient lighting technologies, but all he had seen the previous night were glows with undefinable power sources.

Then, brilliantly, he realized that perhaps these people were fakes, that the basis behind their war against his people had been contrived. That maybe these bars of metal were part of MagicLand's local communications network—that these people were renegades of some kind, and their insurgency amounted to nothing nobler than rebellion. Maybe their power sources were small fusion reactors—centuries-old technology, perhaps, but technology just the same, and more to the point, a technology that required computerization.

He wanted to learn more about the potential communications network nestled within the street, so he thought he'd put his ear down and open a connection to the port that was surely a necessary access point. Even if stoven. net was inaccessible, he should be able to do that. His memories were coming back, so parts of his system were probably back online, he reasoned.

He got down on his knees, splayed out, and put his right ear against one of the metal rails to let his systems go to work.

As he tried to focus on setting up a connection, he also thought about how weird this place was. He was an escaped prisoner, laying down in the middle of the street of his captors' town, and nobody seemed to pay him any attention. He chuckled inside, thinking the two kids were probably watching.

He looked up for a moment to confirm his reality, and sure enough, people were around, doing various things— mostly walking from one place to the next but not paying any attention to him. He almost felt insulted by the lack of interest before he put his ear against the metal bar once again.

At first, nothing happened, so he tried again, assuming his systems were trying to identify a network with unfamiliar protocols. He felt a sudden thrill as he heard something in the metal that seemed distant but profound all at once. A ringing, clanging sort of noise. He rejoiced at the reminder of the feeling that one gets in a history stratum, listening to the sounds of ancient technologies. But this was real. It sounded alive. He slammed an open palm against the street in excitement and disbelief.

2

It was a major surprise when Aurilena's mother volunteered the following morning to accompany her to Hilkiah's home to discuss the young Gath and possibly meet him. "I'll admit you've made me curious from a healer's standpoint," she smiled wanly. "I'm curious to know what the awful thing looks like. Perhaps Orpah could use it in a stew."

"Mom!" admonished Aurilena.

"You're right, darling. A Gath is not worthy of one of Orpah's fine stews. I doubt even she could offer anything to reduce their foul flavors."

Aurilena sighed and scoffed as Hilkiah greeted them warmly. "Miriam," he said, extending his hands. She took them, and he kissed each of her cheeks.

"I've missed you, so," Miriam said to Hilkiah with deep reverence. They had their differences regarding how magic should be used, but Miriam had genuinely warm feelings for Hilkiah and his stalwart pacifism.

"And I you, young lady."

Miriam tugged twice on the long, draping sleeve of his purple robe and smiled.

"Please sit. Both of you. I'll conjure up some tea from Orpah's lair," said Hilkiah. He brought out three steaming mugs of tea and everyone sat down.

"About the Gath," began Miriam after sipping her tea. "Oh, this is quite delicious."

"Ah. It takes a Gath to earn a visit from my favorite healer."

She laughed at that and said, "I thought I was your only healer."

"Indeed," said Hilkiah as he thought back to another day.

3

"This is madness! Absolute madness. I swear I'll ask the Legions to remove every healer from this land." Miriam had never seen Hilkiah so openly exasperated. Hilkiah threw a mug against the beige wall, splattering it with green tea. The mug bounced on the floor. "Madness!"

"Hilkiah, they've tried everything." She tried her calming, soothing voice. "These are good healers, Hilkiah. Truly."

Hilkiah was having none of it. "They aren't. Not at all. This was what? A common cold? A runny nose! A slight cough! Maybe a little headache! And now, look at him!" The man lying on the bed was pale and wheezing, not responding to Hilkiah's tirades, or even noticing them.

Hilkiah sat down on the far end of the man's bed as a stream of nurses and healers entered the room and left quickly when Hilkiah screamed, "Be gone, knaves!" He looked upon the man, who had become emaciated after having once been strong and athletic. The man was a few years older than Hilkiah, but not by much. Both men had been busy proving to be formidable opponents to the degradations of middle age.

"He was the friend I left behind," said Hilkiah to the young healer softly. "Of course, I was a young lad. I had no choice in the matter as my father hauled me out of bed and dropped me onto a boat aimed toward the Wandering City. But for several years, I assumed he was dead. Oh, my dear Miriam, I was ravaged by guilt for every moment of those years. Then when he found me years later, I barely remembered him. And we became so close. So close." He shook his head. "It sometimes isn't easy being a high priest," he sighed. "We are required to be somewhat beyond our capabilities."

Miriam was a healer but was certain nothing she could try would correct the course of events that had taken Hilkiah's friend. She had seen the efforts of everyone else. She would have done nothing different. When Hilkiah had asked her if she'd try, she had told him that, and that was when the rant began.

"But he did survive. Somehow. A few did . . . I do know that, but . . . well, they were all miracles, weren't they? Those that didn't flee to the Wandering City?"

"And many of those who did flee became ill in that soup of toxins and poison," Miriam pointed out.

Hilkiah nodded his agreement. "Yes, and a determined few made their way back and managed to launch an exodus out of The Wandering City back home. And, Miriam, you do know about this lad here, do you not?" He looked at his dying friend.

"Yes, Hilkiah." She tried not to sigh, but she was also determined to avoid hearing the story yet again. "His heroism was the stuff of ceremony, you said. He staved off the attack of the Gath with fireballs in the sky that melted their machines in flight. As a mere boy!" she said with exaggerated regard.

"Indeed." His voice was quiet. Resigned. He then implored her with a look of such sadness that Miriam feared it would etch itself into her mind for eternity. "Have you nothing?" his voice choked, "at all?"

She shook her head. "Everything has been done, my dear friend. I'm sorry."

He sat silent for some time, and she sat with him, not speaking because sometimes healing meant simply sitting quietly in a room with a loved one.

After some time passed, Miriam said, "Except one thing. One thing I do believe has not been tried, and I can't believe, quite frankly, that both of us have neglected to consider it."

"What might that be," he stated in a broken whisper.

"Have you knelt beside him and prayed? Have you asked your Great Shepherd to dictate if his journey should end?"

Hilkiah looked almost alarmed. "What is wrong with me? And they call me a high priest! That should have been the first thing I tried."

"You were too close to this," explained Miriam.

Hilkiah did indeed pray to Yehoshua, and within hours, his friend rebounded from a nearly comatose state to alertness, almost as a dog shifts from sleep to frenetic buoyancy.

When that happened, Hilkiah embraced Miriam with tears in his eyes and said, "You are the greatest healer I've ever seen."

4

"Tell me about him," Miriam said. "Tell me about this Gath."

"Well, he is a broad-shouldered young man with an interesting pattern of hair on his head and what I believe the women in the city will call, regarding his face, 'chiseled looks.' A rather impressive specimen."

"He's not a man," corrected Aurilena, hoping to curry a few points with her mother. "He's a Gath."

"Quite harmless here and quite your age, I dare say," Hilkiah said to Aurilena. "You've mentioned that he doesn't seem to have access to his charming bio-mechanical systems, not that they would be particularly effective here if he did."

"Hilkiah," said Miriam. "All it takes is for a few people to believe that he *can* cause damage, and your theory that they can't harm us in Moria is left in tatters. This attitude toward Gath asylum I find extremely disconcerting. One of these days, this policy is going to explode in your face, and we'll all be the worse for it." If Miriam had known the kind of pain that sort of reference brought to Hilkiah, she wouldn't have said it, but she didn't know, and it did.

Hilkiah sat silently and somewhat sullenly for a moment before replying: "Your objections are noted, Miriam. Perhaps we can strike a bargain."

"Oh, no," said Miriam. "Not this again."

"You shall heal using the power of Yehoshua. And I will send the Gath back to his accident site . . . with but a bit of lunch."

"Sorry, my good friend. You can't purchase a change in theology from me. But it was a noble effort."

Hilkiah nodded and smiled.

She continued, "But you still haven't told me the story behind this Gath creature. Why he's here. How you found him."

"Mom, I told you all that."

"How you found him perhaps, but . . ." and she looked at Hilkiah when saying this, "isn't it a heavy coincidence that my daughter was riding around in the Eastern Hills when she encountered the wired demon?"

Aurilena sighed.

"Yes, it is an interesting coincidence," replied Hilkiah. "I suspect your daughter is in league with the Gath. Guards!"

"There are no guards here, you silly man," said Miriam. "My point is that something drew her there. A force—something—and it may be something we aren't familiar with. A new technology, perhaps. This is a tenacious race, Hilkiah. They've been trying to destroy us for two thousand years, and they keep inventing new ways to have at it. Or perhaps . . . there was a powerful high priest, whom I shall not name, who detected his presence and sent my daughter out on a reckless mission to find him?"

"Mom. Were you listening to me at all when I told you about what happened? How I heard a voice? And who sent me to investigate?"

Hilkiah raised an eyebrow at this but said nothing.

Her mother was dismissive and unconvinced, and the three of them haggled over this point of contention for several minutes before Aurilena finally seemed to break through with this point: "It's a lot like when I speak with animals, Mom, which you never stop making fun of. Telling Judith I'm an animal trainer . . . sheesh."

Miriam shrugged as if saying, "What can I say?"

"But he's an animal, too, like you and me."

"Bah! He's no animal. He's a souped-up electrical cord," Miriam scoffed.

"And I heard him in distress, and I went to him. It's really not complicated."

"That's nice, dear, but it doesn't explain why you and the techno-infestation were in that area at the same time in the first place."

"Mostly as part of a conspiracy to see how many derogatory synonyms for Belex you can come up with, Mom."

"What is a Belex?" she asked with unblinking eyes.

"That's his name."

"Oh, torture my soul—you're on a first-name basis with the electro-plasma monstrosity?"

"Face it, my friend," said Hilkiah, looking at Miriam. "Sometimes, events conspire to fall into the realm of coincidence. It really can be that simple." He could have been more honest with her, he knew, but it would have complicated things.

"Fine. But why do you think he's here?"

"He says he's an actor," said Aurilena.

"An actor!" laughed Miriam. "What a hoot! Well, at least we know that on a certain level, he's not lying. At least I know why you're smitten by the silicon rat. And what is your take on him, Hilkiah?"

"I am not smitten by him!" insisted a flustered Aurilena. "First Judith and now you? What's wrong with you people?"

Miriam ignored her and waited for Hilkiah's answer.

"A Reckless, perhaps," said Hilkiah, still unsure about that. But because this was Miriam, he felt like he should refer to the Gath boy as a Reckless. In fact, he thought, it would be best if all Morians considered him so, no matter what his true intent may be. "His systems are completely useless to him. They appear to have quit on him, perhaps because he truly was in an accident of some kind. He says he was in a pod, which isn't a device I'm fully familiar with, and that he crashed. His biomechanical and biometric systems were disabled in this accident, so he is relatively harmless."

"Relatively. But they still have built-in weapons systems. Some nasty stuff, too."

"He hasn't been inclined to use them yet."

"Aurilena says he resisted."

"And indeed, he did. But the fact of the matter is that he could have resisted in full and dispatched Aurilena quite easily. He chose not to."

"Because he wanted to get into the city. These Recklesses, as you call them. They're dangerous, Hilkiah. I'm sorry, but it is you that is reckless for letting them roam our city."

"There has been a total of five so far in my lifetime, Miriam, and none of them have been of any trouble."

"That we know of," she huffed.

Aurilena knew how much her mother hated the Gath, and she hated pushing back on her mother on this subject. There was no justification for defending a Gath, thought Aurilena. Ever. *What's wrong with me?* She started thinking about the motions of the Gath Belex as he kicked and struggled and spoke in his angry tones, and she felt a shiver. *What's wrong with me?*

"Those still alive live in peace in the southern markets. And they are watched. Scrutinized. Some would say unfairly so," said Hilkiah.

"Nothing unfair about scrutinizing a Gath," said Miriam.

"Noted," replied Hilkiah.

Then came a pounding on Hilkiah's thick wooden door. He opened it and saw a man in a hooded red robe saturated by a downpour.

"Hurry on in, hurry on in," said Hilkiah. He took the man's red hooded vestment, brought it to a large half circle of open brick next to a fireplace, and shook it out, which instantly removed all its moisture. He handed it back to the man.

"Aaron," he introduced the man to Aurilena and her mother, "is the noble priest that we imported from the Wandering City when we found Sherealla. You do remember Aaron, do you not, Aurilena?"

She nodded but couldn't really recall the man.

"Some news about the Reckless's capture, Hilkiah," said the grey-looking middle-aged man. He was very tall—almost as tall as Hilkiah—but probably about half his age, maybe less, since Hilkiah was quite old. He had long, curly gray hair and a full gray handlebar mustache. He was nobly handsome and looked like he had the authority to hand out kindness as gifts at will.

Aurilena stood up abruptly.

"He tried to kill himself on the antique rail line. A replica streetcar driver saw him with his head down against the rail. The driver said it seemed as if he wanted to hear his own death."

Aurilena looked wildly at the priest bearing the news then looked at Hilkiah. "Where is he?"

"He's been taken to the Hall of Legions, and from there, he must go to the Legions and be heard."

Aurilena slammed her fist against the grand wooden table that had been her hospitality and glared at Hilkiah. "I knew something dumb would happen!" she exclaimed.

5

Aaron was careful because he knew this was the last tanker of water remaining. Nobody knew when the next supplies would arrive. He passed out jars of water to the small crowd that had gathered in front of the celebration house, hoping people would have the good sense to conserve. He tried to find ways to conjure water but had been unsuccessful, and their outlook was now quite bleak. The well water in the Wandering City was not potable and couldn't be made so by boiling. He didn't understand why Moria's well water was so free of the toxins that plagued the water here.

He was sad because not only could he not conjure water, he couldn't conjure much of anything. He had once been an Acquirer of some renown, able to acquire goods from all over the earth, including places that had been abandoned or mostly destroyed long ago.

But the ability disappeared when he arrived in the Wandering City, as if the ruins had sucked out the magical lifeforce within him and left him neutered and powerless. He laughed once, not so long ago, when he conjured up a jar of mustard by accident while trying for a sustainable amount of food.

His congregants had lost faith in him, and so had he, but they still streamed to him for help because they appreciated his dedication to their wellbeing. He could never abandon his people in need.

He knew all too well what that felt like, just as the rest of the Wandering City knew. It had once been Moria's twin—two glowing, glorious homes to magic and the people who practiced it, far away from the terrible weapons of Gath.

Everyone thought it had been protected by the same magic that sheltered Moria, but many now thought The Wandering City had been abandoned by Moria when it fell under attack. Both cities were invulnerable to the Gath, it was thought. There was always respite from any onslaught.

Nobody knew exactly what happened, and he sometimes wondered if his interpretation that they were abandoned was unfair. Surely, Moria would have helped if it could. Perhaps someone even tried. But in the end, there was essentially only one city left standing, and the other was in ruins, with a few survivors wandering aimlessly, looking for water in a toxic land.

It was from these humble beginnings that Aaron grew to become one of Moria's greatest conjurers of everything from fresh water to sharpened steel. And one of Hilkiah's most trusted lieutenants.

6

Belex woke up, again a prisoner.

He was feeling incredibly stupid for not thinking about the possibility that the network he had been listening to had perhaps been set up to listen for him listening to it. Now they would assume he was a spy. It would be the only logical conclusion.

The room he was in was comfortable enough. They had sat him down on a comfortable couch with a high, plush back. There were no guards other than one burly man he could see through the door's small square window. He couldn't know that the guard was a cousin of Hilkiah's who was very fond of eating and had no real capacity for guard duty.

Belex was hungry.

Soon enough, a tall man entered the room. He was dressed in red, flowing robes with decorations and insignias on the front.

The man pulled up a chair and a small table across from where Belex was seated on the couch in the sparse room. He put his hand out for him, but Belex didn't take it.

The man was creepy looking. His red hood nearly covered his face, and Belex could only see a smooth square jaw, lit up by the room somehow, and a long swirling mustache above some pretty teeth. The man said to him, "You tried to kill yourself today. I am sorry for that."

And then silence.

Belex was pretty sure that he could capture almost all of this in his newly found memory and write his own cinescape about this insipid place if he could just get out of here.

"Umm," he finally muttered, "yeah, okay."

"Fine," said the man in the hood. "Fine. My name is Aaron. Can I get you something to drink?"

Belex looked around. "Water? Could I have some water?"

"Of course," said the man. His voice was hoarse and deep. Creepier still.

He waved his hand over the table, and a glass of water appeared before him.

It was a small glass, about an inch tall.

He waved his hand again, and another glass appeared, almost two feet tall.

He switched the glasses, and said, "I'm sorry, how rude of me. This is, of course, yours, and this is mine."

"It's spring water, right?" he asked.

The man in the robe laughed and said, "If you wish."

7

Aurilena went to Belex alone. She wanted Hilkiah with her but had become annoyed by his sanctimonious predictions.

She wanted to dissuade Hilkiah from thinking there was a connection between her, a woman of the horse with a reverence for magic, and this crazy cybernetic unit from what seemed to be another planet.

She began to wish that she could forget the voice she had heard earlier. Forget the plea for help from the soprano that had sung with the buffalo, a voice that had reached her with cold, uncertain fear. She was unable to shake free of that voice . . . or his face when it had glared at her menacingly during their confrontation. The Gath boy had seemed so *human* in his vulnerabilities, which had been masked by exaggerated acts of defiance.

"I'll take the actor to the Legions," she said to the guards at the gates of the dilapidated one-story building holding Belex, thinking about his theatrics. There were no prisons in Moria, and Belex had been moved to a small warehouse that had been quickly converted into a dungeon of sorts by a band of somewhat drunken Metamorphics. As such, the guards were not highly trained professionals but more like curious pretenders with a little too much time on their hands. "And if it is what they want, then I will take him back and dump him amongst the trash that is his people."

But that wasn't what she wanted at all. She didn't know exactly what she wanted, but she knew that she wanted more. More information. More of him. It was maddening.

They shrugged and let her into the building. The burly guard recognized her and smiled as she walked in. Then she saw the robed man, Aaron, talking to the alien visitor who called himself Belex.

Aurilena put her hand softly on Aaron's shoulder and said in a whisper, "Thank you," and motioned that she would take him from this point.

"He is no longer yours to do with what you wish," said Aaron. "He must now speak to the Legions."

"Then I should have the honor of introducing him to the Legions," responded Aurilena.

Aaron nodded, not much caring himself, and Belex was released once again to Aurilena.

8

He was grateful her friend wasn't with her because this beauty, even though she was just a step away in intelligence from a monkey, seemed at least trainable. She wasn't even trying to tie him up. In fact, she was making some sense when she said, "Look, I really think nobody here will hurt you unless it's by accident, so let's just see what the Legions have to say, okay? It's not like they're going to kill you. Worst case, they'll just send you back to where you came from."

That seemed somewhat reasonable to him, so he decided to play along until he could plot another escape.

She looked at him as if reading his mind and said, "If you try to escape, as nice as we all are, you do know this whole process starts all over again. Besides . . . look, it doesn't take an Einstein to know there's nowhere for you to really go."

He made his first response to her with a slight, affirmative nod. His disdain was an act at this point because when she had appeared in her green, pleated skirt, cut just above the knees, and a white short-sleeved peasant blouse, she woke systems within him he never knew existed. Most of her long, glossy hair fell behind her, but two liquid needles swayed in front of her face when she had walked into the room. He noticed for the first time that the steady black rain of her hair was punctuated with streaks of deep burgundy that glimmered on and off like a boreal light show.

They walked in silence. Aurilena made a few attempts to engage him in discussion, but he wouldn't acknowledge her.

For a moment, she considered taking him by the arm and transporting the two of them to the Legions in an instant, just to show off.

As they neared the top of the hill, Belex sighed deeply. "So, you know who Einstein is."

"Sure. We used to talk about him all the time, back when the first Reckless appeared here." When she spoke, he noticed the smallest of dimples forming under her pug nose.

"What on earth is a Reckless?"

"Somebody like you. I mean, who comes here from Gath?"

"I don't get it."

"Forget it. It doesn't much matter. But we thought he was some confused guy in funny clothes in the desert." She snorted a small laugh. "Anyway," she continued, "when we found out Einstein was right, that was when all the wars started."

"You have no idea what you're talking about. The wars started because your people rebelled against science with magic."

"And now, we, not you, visit the stars. Because Einstein was right about two things, smarty pants." Aurilena wasn't afraid to laugh at her own jokes, and she thought that "smarty pants" was funny because he probably really had brains in his pants. "One, about the speed of light. And the other, well, about that other thing. I forget what it's called. Something mechanical."

"I feel like a flea is talking to me," he said. "Quantum mechanics. You're thinking, and I use that word loosely, of quantum mechanics."

"Tell me, have you ever visited Aldeberon." Her question to him wasn't a question and was not raised as such.

His fury to me is magnificent. His eyes are sky blue torches, but I want them to touch me.

"Umm, excuse me?" Belex said predictably.

"Aldeberon. It's a star system identified by your species. In the constellation Taurus, I believe."

Belex shrugged at the insult. "We sort of gave up on star travel, on that whole speed limit is the speed of light thing."

"Hmm."

"Hmm what?"

"Yeah. Just like what Einstein said. And, hmm, I've been there."

"Where?"

"Aldeberon."

"Where?"

"There."

"Where? Aldeberon? That's just a star in the galaxy. Nobody can go there. Einstein proved it. We proved it. We can't travel faster than the speed of light."

"Let's go."

"Where?"

"To Aldeberon. I mean, to one of its planets. But we call that planet Aldeberon, too."

At that moment, he didn't blink his eyes.

And then she took him to Aldeberon. A place his world, with its limitations, could never allow him to visit.

When they alighted, Aurilena realized she had lied and wondered at that. How can you suddenly realize you lie? Do you just spout out words, hoping to make an impression? Aurilena had never been to Aldeberon, or any other place off Earth for that matter.

I mean, thought Aurilena, *you don't physically go there anyway, right? You sort of imagine yourself there, and you're there. Everyone knows that. You just sort of split off your soul somehow, and you can get there.* Nobody ever understood it too well, except maybe Seth, whose profound spirituality had been cut short by the Gath. *But I doubt Seth knew, either.* Everyone knew it had something to do with quantum mechanics. And science. But then, so did all magic, somehow, she thought.

Aurilena thought of tales describing beautiful places like Aldeberon, places that the storytellers who practiced traveling said filled the universe with splendor; beautiful planets that populated this galaxy and trillions of others, places that had become legendary thanks to the few people who were able to visit them. They told of captivating planets with wild varieties of flora, fauna, and animal kingdoms. Many people who tried to make these kinds of visits were turned away by forces they didn't understand, forces that seemed directed by the universe to block their visit as if setting up a wall or fortress around the very capabilities that seemed natural to others. Because it was so rare, those who found success were called Travelers. Aurilena was confident that she could become a Traveler with practice.

She didn't know why she was compelled to impress this alien male or why she was drawn to him, but she was committed to the venture of taking him to Aldeberon, which, it turned out, was almost completely consumed by fire. Almost as soon as she saw the place, she remembered some of the exact words she had heard told over the years: "Aldeberon is consumed by beauty." Indeed, it was.

As they descended, they saw wild scenes of lava spitting across beautiful waves of oceanic fires roaring against red, rocky plumage.

"You've reproduced hell," he said to her. "Very nice."

Aurilena, astounded by her own incompetence, didn't know what to say. She also didn't know where else to go because she hadn't read any of the books on the art, or even consulted with anyone. She had gotten here solely by listening to stories over the years.

Stumped, she said, "Let's take a walk."

"But we'll be burned to death," laughed Belex mockingly. She hadn't yet clued him in that they were there in mind only, that his physical presence was a mirror, but he suspected chicanery, perhaps some holographic technology, despite the historical understanding that the people of MagicLand eschewed most forms of advanced technology.

"Are you hot now?" she asked as they floated downward together.

His eyes rolled back to represent the ridiculous nature of her question.

"Well," Aurilena said, "surely your little chip told you about this place, huh?"

"Aldeberon?" he said weakly. "No. Not exactly. I've never heard of it."

"Aldeberon," she affirmed, floating with him just slightly above the sea of lava.

All his crazy mind could think of was that when her eyes looked his way, they introduced heat to his body in a way the fires of Aldeberon never could and how badly he wanted to discover the limits of their searing energy.

Aurilena and Belex began to ascend away from the planet's fiery surface.

"What else can you do?" asked Belex, sounding unimpressed. "I mean, can you take us to a place that isn't on fire? There must be billions of cooler planets."

She shook her head. "I don't really know how to do this stuff." She shrugged her shoulders innocently. "That's why it was so weird. I mean, I can do it with places on Earth no problem, but this is harder."

"Can't you just try? I'd love to see a jungle. Do you know what that is?"

"Sort of. But anyway, if I try to go to a place without knowing the exact coordinates on a star map, I could mess up, and we could literally get lost together in time. Would you like that? No, I didn't think so."

"Yeah, let's just go back and see your Legion friends. That should be fun, too."

As their minds returned to their present reality, they fell silent until that reality reasserted itself. They had somehow walked to Aurilena's horse, which was tied to a post in front of them.

"Okay, but I don't get it," said Belex afterward. "If this is all your mind, you're still not really there, right? How do you know it's not all your imagination? And, you know, we get lost maybe, but can't someone just sort of wake us up?"

She sighed. "That's not how it works. Our consciousness is there, and somehow this, I don't know, this visual representation of us can be seen by anyone who happens to be there. But it's not like I can just imagine it and go."

"You'd be amazed at the power of the mind."

"Seriously? You're telling me this? Where do you think magic comes from? Well," she corrected herself, "Hilkiah would say magic comes from Yehoshua, so never mind."

"No, no, no. I'm talking about the science of it all. Our dreams, our neurons, the capacity of the brain to process billions of calculations. We've harnessed all that in the network, in stoven.net."

"What's that?"

"What's what?"

"The stove net?"

His head was finally clear from the strange dream sequence she had launched in his head. "I dunno; it's just like, what we call where our minds live,

I guess. Imagine filling up a room with everyone in your city and being able to talk to all of them at once and having access to all their knowledge. It's kind of like that."

"What about where you live? What do you call that? I'm guessing 'Hell,' but . . . too harsh?"

"You've never been there," he said without emotion.

"I've seen pictures. We've sent infiltrators."

"Do tell."

As soon as he said that, he found himself swept away to a place that looked like a version of his homeland, but a place he'd never seen. It was dark, the skies cloudy with soot and falling, ashen rain. People scurried about with umbrellas, apparently trying to stay out of the weather. When the rain fell upon the umbrellas, small wisps of steam arose as if the rain was a harsh acid.

Ahead of him, a swarm of thousands of police drones rounded up a group of people and slaughtered them. Huge holograms filled gaps among an endless line of skyscrapers. Weird creatures were everywhere, some obvious hybrids of other beings, like dogs, raptors, and apes. A massive blue bird made from what looked like electricity lifted off from a building. In front of Belex, two hybrid beings argued before one of them vaporized the other by extending a weapon from a long tentacle at its side.

"Get me out of here!" he yelled, not enjoying being stuck inside some magic trap the savage girl had created. He blinked, and it was all gone, and he began to question every aspect of his reality. Again.

Aurilena wore a sly smile. "Even you hate it now that you've been away for a few days."

He shook his head disgustedly. "That's not—that's nothing like where I live. I don't know that place, but I know for sure it's someone's very active imagination."

"It was a real report. From our spies. It's what they saw." She didn't mention that the scene didn't look all that different than her one short visit to Gath a few years prior.

"No, it's what they wanted you to see."

"We don't teach our people to lie like you do."

"I don't even know what that means. You know nothing about our people. That's pretty obvious."

"We know you've been trying to kill us for thousands of years."

"You mean defend ourselves."

"This is stupid. Your people killed my brother."

"I'm sorry about that." He stopped for a minute, recognizing the emotion displayed in her thin furrowed eyebrows. "War sucks."

They were both silent for a few moments when Belex said, "So was that a recording or something? Of someone's imagined trip to Gath? I mean, seriously. What was that?"

"Something like that. I can't go there myself because I don't know where it is."

"The Homeland?"

"Gath."

"It's down the coast."

"I know, but I mean, I don't know the exact location. So that's why I can't get there."

"I'm sorry about your brother." He wasn't sure why he said that. He knew that things like family relationships were important to Wiccans but didn't know why, and he had never cared to know. He thought a moment about his still obscured past. "I've read about families. I've even tried being part of one in a cinescape, but it's hard because I don't understand them."

"What's a cinescape?" she asked, not really wanting the answer.

"Just a show. A story. We tell the story—each member of the collective tells us what to do, and we do it for each person."

"So, you can act out thousands of storylines at once?"

"Millions, if there were that many people watching. I customize the story for each person, according to their moods or even what they specifically ask for."

"I can't grasp that. Okay, next question. You don't have families?" She couldn't grasp that, either.

"Nope."

"Who takes care of you? When you're young?"

"The collective, of course."

That answer inexplicably prompted Aurilena to explain to him how she found Sherealla in the Wandering City. It was a story that would have sounded quite different had it been told from Sherealla's point of view.

9

Sherealla's systems finally managed to accomplish something. While she was running, her systems were calculating a set of curves the drones were using as a pattern in their attack. But there was a tangent in each set of curves. which the drones seemed to purposely avoid. She spotted a building located on one of these points and carefully made her way into it. She wasn't surprised to find it empty. People were generally fleeing. Maybe to the water, she thought. Maybe back to MagicLand.

This, she realized, must be part of the plan. When the drones that took her away from her parents dropped her off here, she was heartbroken to find it was largely a ruined city of wastrels. She saw considerably more ragged, useless-looking children here than adults. Then it was attacked by her own people after she was delivered. Were they trying to kill her for some reason? With her systems failing in so many areas, she wasn't cognizant of any plan the mission node had for her. She couldn't find a way to access it; her mission node wasn't volunteering the information to her, and her access to stoven.net had ended shortly after her arrival.

But now some calculations were taking place somewhere in her body, and she was figuring it out. The drones were targeting via a specific trigonometric pattern they assumed she'd automatically decipher. The attackers might not have known she was partially disabled, although they should have been able to detect her malfunctions. Once she was safely in a building, she reasoned, or perhaps she was being told by the mission node—she wasn't sure—the drones would stop their attack, and she'd wait here to be saved by a Wiccan from MagicLand. Something would have to draw that savior in, so she quickly started a fire in the building's fireplace.

The building looked like it was a primitive residence of some kind, but it would have to do. She obviously wasn't going to find any intelligent buildings around here—she was trained for this—and even felt a brief jolt of excitement at the thought of finally leveraging her training.

She was cold. The rain had soaked through her clothes, which nanobots had converted into garb that looked like that of the native population. Her systems should have been adjusting for this, but they weren't, so she was shivering as she started the fire. Then she cursed and smiled as she realized that her systems wouldn't account for the cold rain because the plan was for her to be like them. She could see from her medical diagnostics, which were still functional, that everything was okay. She was simply cold.

Just then, the door of the building burst open. and a Wiccan girl her age stumbled inside. Outside, through the pouring rain on the other side of the open door, she could see it was getting dark.

The Wiccan girl stopped and stared. "Hey," she finally said after a minute of uncomfortable silence. "Is this your home?"

Sherealla shook her head as if terrified.

"Your parents? Where are they?"

Sherealla pointed to the sky, as if they had been taken.

"Oh. Oh, I'm sorry. Sorry." The Wiccan girl seemed to study her for a moment. "Sorry," she said again as she walked through the door. Sherealla couldn't help but think that if this was to be her enemy savior, it was going to make for a long evening.

Then, everything went dark. Sherealla's malfunctioning systems failed to detect the cracks in a beam overhead, which fell upon the shivering girl and knocked her to the ground unconscious.

When she came to, the Wiccan lifted a hand toward Sherealla's hair, which made her flinch. She had to restrain herself from leveling a blow across the Wiccan girl's pretty face. "It's okay," said the Wiccan. "It's just your face. You're hurt. Let me get something for the cuts, okay? I had to move the beam off you—I didn't even know I had that kind of magic. And healing. I . . . I think you almost died."

Sherealla's medical diagnostics immediately confirmed that broken ends of her fourth, fifth, and sixth ribs had penetrated the posterior wall of her thoracic aorta, which had miraculously regenerated without the help of medibots and that the dangerous broken ends had dissolved harmlessly into her bloodstream.

Sherealla watched apprehensively, even though she wasn't afraid and didn't care if the Wiccan had saved her from a falling beam or anything else. She tried to utter a frightened word or two as the Wiccan dabbed at her cuts with a cloth. "Try not to be scared, okay? You'll be fine now," said the Wiccan.

Sherealla nodded meekly, thinking maybe she should become an actress when she returned to the Homeland.

10

"How old were you?"

"We were both twelve. She was hiding in a building in the city after her parents died, scared and alone, her face dirty and with a couple of broken ribs that were about to cut her heart open."

"Why would they send a kid like you into a war zone? That's sick."

"We were desperate. Moria, that's here, what we call this place . . . it was on fire. The whole place was burning. I ran north with a bunch of kids my age; we caught a boat where the Broken Bridge begins, and we went across the water to the hills and the city there. That's where I found Sherealla."

"What happened to the friends you were with?"

"We got separated. It was all pretty crazy. There were Gath drones all over the northern city, and they were attacking it with explosive weapons, destroying everything they could, when they suddenly stopped. I never knew why at the time—never found out—and I was suddenly alone. When I found Sherealla, I had to make my way back through all this mayhem. But people pretty much ignored us as we made our way back to the bridge. I guess they were just focused on trying to keep themselves alive or whatever. It was all too chaotic for me to really understand, and besides . . . I was twelve."

"This is insane. We're trying to resolve a thousand years of war, and we're just kids caught in the middle of it." He looked at her with a little compassion for the first time. He knew he was attracted somehow to this barbarian female and wondered if it was the very fact that she was almost an animal. Was he attracted to her savageness? Her very estrangement from his own people? He had a strange yearning to know more about her.

"I guess so," she replied. "I never had to think about it before. I need to take you to the Legions now. They won't hurt you. They'll probably just send you back to where you landed with some water and food."

She mounted her horse. Belex stood silent for a moment until Aurilena turned her head to motion him to join her on the horse.

Instead, he stood in place, looking at her. "Moria," he said. "Where does that name come from?"

"It's from ancient literature. Nobody knows exactly. An ancient book lost to history. The book is not even in the Library of Ezra. But there were once a great story of magic and a people who roamed the earth, who lived in a place they called Middle Earth. The name comes from there." She looked away, but sad. "The Moria of that story is destroyed by a great evil. That much I do know. But I can't understand why we'd name ourselves in honor of a place that was destroyed."

"Maybe as a reminder that you mustn't lose?" he grunted as he mounted the horse.

His nose was close to her ear, and he could smell her hair. It smelled good. "When was the last time there was a major battle between our people?" he asked into her ear, knowing he couldn't access the collective for the answer.

"I don't know," she answered, and she kicked Remembrance to begin their ride.

11

The Hall of Legions was a massive building cut into a tall hill, one of the seven hills of the city that had, at one time, provided the name for the city itself, "City of Seven Hills," before the Legions changed the name to Moria. There were ornate structures interacting with the terraced hill, shaped by artisans and magicians of long ago. The magicians, mostly Acquirers and Metamorphics, turned the grayish sandstone of the hill into blue sandstone that could be seen from the other side of the city. Artisans worked with the Metamorphics to mold the edges of the building structure with the surrounding terraced slopes in such a way that it appeared dragons were poking their heads out from inside the hill, while gargoyles perched on the sides of terraces looked poised to attack. Cherubs armed with bows and arrows innocently frolicked amongst a wide variety of mythical warring factions.

The building housed a multitude of rooms for celebrations and feasting, for prayer, and for entertainment, rallies, and governance. It was the center of all activities in Moria. It included the Room of Prayer, smaller prayer rooms, the Hall of Feasts, and a host of other rooms with many purposes. The building was called the Hall of Legions because a high priest was able to easily summon the Legions in any room of the building.

Aurilena dismounted, and motioned Belex to do the same.

"What's your name?" asked Belex, surprising Aurilena with his continuing lack of hostility.

"Aurilena. But it will be changed on my birthday—when I turn eighteen—to reflect what I do in my life."

"That's a pretty name. Don't change it. That'd be dumb."

"Lucky me. I meet a Gath boy with a sense for aesthetics," she snickered.

They entered through ancient massive wooden doors that had been carved by a master wood sculptor centuries ago and walked into a cavernous foyer leading to an enormous room. Hilkiah was sitting in a wooden chair in the middle of the room. He motioned for them to come forward.

"Sit," he said as two mats appeared in front of him. Aurilena looked at Belex, who sat cross-legged on the mat without returning the look.

Hilkiah said to Belex, "You are angry. Still. Why? Isn't the unfortunate situation of your own making? Have we not treated you well?"

Belex shrugged. Then he looked around. "Where are these 'Legions' I have been hearing so much about?"

Hilkiah smiled and said, "Everywhere. The Legions are all of us in the priesthood, which is vast. Look around again."

When he did, Belex saw a sweeping panorama of what, in his world, would have been considered holograms, consisting of hundreds of people sitting and, apparently, meditating. They sat with their legs crossed and their eyes closed.

"Okay," said Belex, "that's pretty slick. So what's up?"

"We are deciding. Do we allow you to stay, knowing that you loathe this realm? With the possibility that an attempt will be made to rescue you, putting lives here in jeopardy? But the alternative is worse. Returning you to the bleak home where you were found—"

"It's not my home," Belex tried to say.

"It may be now. We don't know yet, do we? We know it isn't your fault you crashed here, but here you are. So. Let me ask you. What do *you* wish? Do you want to return to your crash site? We can provide you some provisions, but we can't protect you. Or do you want to accept our hospitality?" Hilkiah looked around. "I think we should let our guest decide his fate. What do you think, Legions?"

Even though Belex couldn't see any movement within the audience of sitting holograms, he could feel them nod in agreement somehow. It was weird. He could feel it in his brain, or maybe body. He could feel the warmth of the primitive young woman next to him. He felt her strange beauty engulf him. But the beauty wasn't shaped in any way. It invaded his body, sent tremors along his spine, tugged at his heart. He had never been so overwhelmed with such raw energy in his blood. He found it disconcerting, but he didn't want it to go away.

"Very well then," said Hilkiah. "It is decided."

"I didn't even say anything," protested Belex.

"Oh, but you did very much say anything and everything."

Belex considered this. The nemesis with the bushy eyebrows was still a freak, albeit a gentle freak, and probably stupid. Did these beings sense his unfathomable attraction to her?

He began to think that perhaps simple things were possible with these primitive creatures. A bite to eat. A pillow? He didn't want to get too greedy, but finally, now there was hope. The way things were going, a pillow would be a huge victory.

He was also beginning to miss home, even though his recollection of it was still hazy. He had seen many things on his short tour through this city. Unimaginable things. Shriveled up people, for one thing. He had heard stories about aging but had never seen any videos, and then he had remembered that one of the reprehensible things about these awful people was they chose to let their people shrivel up like slugs on hot pavement.

And worse, they seemed almost proud of it. Horrible beasts, these people, so far removed from humanity that, if he thought of it too much, he would feel compelled toward violence.

As far as he could see, there was no cure for anything among these people, and they just let themselves die. No cure for even a kid who skinned his knee. No cure for a woman he had seen whose foot had been crushed by a collapsing group of bricks, apparently because some idiots were trying to build a building with, unimaginably, human power, despite the abundance of magic. After all, it would be one thing to not have the ability to transform an edifice and use humans to build things. But this? This refusal to harness your power to create something seemed truly bizarre to Belex. He didn't know the magicians of MagicLand were often doing work in precisely that way, but some people enjoyed working with their hands. Such things were completely foreign to a Gath.

He was grateful, suddenly, for the time he went sledding on a tall, winding hill in the deep woods of the Northern Expanse. After his sled went out of control, and his nose went just a little faster than the rest of his body into a tree, the medibots swarmed him and fixed his nose before anybody knew what had happened, almost before he even felt any pain from it. If he were one of these people, would he have just lay there bleeding? Would they have abandoned him in the snow?

He knew that if he survived this ordeal, he would have tales to tell, which would redouble the efforts of the Homeland. He knew he could even become a hero, and this gave him goosebumps. After all, he was merely an actor.

But then he thought of the two children who had sensed his needs and responded with kindness as he wandered through this city. For all its ugliness, there was a mystical, hidden factor of beauty that restrained his hatred enough to make him reconsider his opinion.

"You're actually free to go, by the way. So, if you wish, move on." He thought he heard all the voices in the room say this at once. "Or stay. Our home is your home."

CHAPTER IV

1

He awoke no more aware of any freedom than before. His dreams during the night had been incessant. At once, he was a bear escaping a trap, and on another occasion, he was a prisoner in a war camp, bloodying his fingers by climbing over a fence before being shot, then trampling over a hill. Then, a spider spitting silk vines across a darkened corner to escape the tyranny of light. A fly escaping anything that moves.

With that, he pulled the blankets up and sunk his aching head in the pillow.

Then, almost in shock, he snapped his head up so hard he could feel a twinge of sharp pain in the back of his neck. *Wait!* He exclaimed out loud. He looked down and saw, sure enough, a pillow. A huge pillow, full of stuff he couldn't imagine. Soft stuff. Despite his aversion toward this place, his only desire was to throw his head into the new treasure as hard as he could and feel every molecule.

He hadn't expected a pillow.

He enjoyed the fullness of his bedding as long as he could, but he was antsy. He had to get up. And get out of here. There was, he admitted to himself, a sort of quaintness to this civilization's madness, something perhaps even worth recording for history before this terrible wasteland would need to finally be wiped off the face of the earth.

Then, almost just as thrilling as the pillow, was a set of clothes laid out over a chair across from the bed. The bed, the chair, and the clothes were pretty much the entire contents of the room, although there was a small bathroom attached.

He unfolded the clothes. They consisted of a pair of smoky black denim pants, which were snug when he pulled them on, and a dark tan long-sleeve shirt with two button pockets at the chest and two much larger ones just above his waist. He opened one of those and dug into it, hoping to find something for some reason, but it was empty. He thought he'd need to change that.

As captors, these people were strangely hospitable. But he wanted out again, immediately.

He ran to the door and kicked it hard with the best move he could remember as an actor. He flew up, with one arm stretched one way, his legs and another arm the other way, but he bounced off the door and thudded against the floor. He was amazed at the way he was able to draw visuals into his mind without asking for them. He was used to thinking about something and receiving biometric patterns to help him respond to every nuance, but in this case, separated from stoven.net, he had visualized something on his own—in a way that alarmed and thrilled him. The fact that he was unsuccessful didn't upset him. He felt thrilled by this newfound sensory input. Where was it from? It seemed as majestic as it did primitive.

He tried another tactic, and he suddenly felt proud that these remembrances weren't based on embedded memories but, somehow, just a part of his natural being, and so he repeatedly pounded on the door with his fists. For effect, he yelled.

"Let me out!" he hollered, like an actor's character trapped in a room.

Nothing happened.

For some reason, during a moment of desperation, he decided to simply try the door.

When it opened, he was too tired and hungry to react. When he told people later about this, they said things like, "Didn't you at least laugh?" and he would shake his head and say that he was too desperate, exhausted, and stupid to laugh.

When he left the premises again, it felt less like an escape than a restless excursion. He observed the same disheveled landscape he saw before, only from a slightly different perspective, altered by morning light and his less restrictive circumstances.

The place was still ridden with dirt, dust, and wood. But he also noticed rustic beauty. Ornate carvings decorated buildings whose walls and foundations seemed captive to the hills that contained them. Beautiful statues graced the landscape. The sides of even the tallest buildings were canvasses of intricate murals that must have taken decades to paint. He hadn't noticed any of this before. Was she doing this to him? Injecting his thoughts with illusion? Or had he been so blinded by hatred earlier that he had failed to notice his surroundings?

He found himself sinking against the wall of a building, wondering how he could complete his escape. A dog ran up against him and nuzzled his knee. It was a medium-sized dog with brown and white coloring, bearing a long white stripe that extended from his brown nose up his face to form a mask around his eyes.

The dog was grimy, and Belex shooed him away until he realized he needed a friend.

"Hey, wait!" he yelped into the stinking dust bowl of the town, almost imagining a small puff of dust blowing through his lips as he spoke. For no reason he could comprehend, Belex reached into one of the lower pockets of his shirt and discovered a pile of what felt like rough stones. He pulled one out.

The dog had scampered off, but just barely. Apparently alerted by whatever was in Belex's hand, the dog's gait changed, throwing its motion almost backward in response as if in a fit. The dog returned and nuzzled against Belex's knee again, like an old friend, then stood up and stared at Belex with its tongue hanging out. Belex sniffed the rock-like object. It smelled faintly of food, and the dog's tail twirled around in full circles as it looked into Belex's eyes with anticipation.

Belex wanted to scan for bioware inside the dog but doubted he could, and besides, *Dogs are dogs here,* he thought. So he reached out his hand, and the dog sniffed it then eagerly chomped on the snack.

"Well, well." He was somewhat heartbroken as he pulled another treat out of his pocket. He was already smitten, and he knew he couldn't take the dog with him to look for his escape pod.

2

"You don't know any magic at all?" Aurilena thought she had never met anyone her age who didn't know at least a little something.

"No," said Sherealla, without explanation. She knew, though, since she had been a product of extracted Wiccan DNA, that she should be able to learn anything Aurilena could teach her. The two girls had been hanging out constantly since their encounter in the Wandering City six months ago, and Sherealla was growing fond of the girl, much to her consternation. She assumed this was a byproduct of her upbringing, which had been far different than anyone else she knew in the Homeland. For one thing, she had been given parents in an effort to mimic the social behavior of Wiccans. This was a fact withheld by the military from stoven.net, although she occasionally made quickly forgotten references to it among her friends in the collective. It made her wonder what other facts were hidden from the hive mind, which relied on shared knowledge. It seemed wrong to withhold anything, even within the purview of military planning.

She found herself mimicking Aurilena's behavior, following her around, wanting to help her do things, anything. It was strange to feel so much passionate devotion to a lower life form. It wasn't like loving a dog, which with its inferior intelligence should obviously hold subservient status. Instead, it was like loving a dog and being subservient to *it*.

"Well," said Aurilena. "It's more like the magic finds you. Maybe Yehoshua has something big in store for you, and that's why it hasn't found you yet. That's what Hilkiah would say, I think."

3

"Where will you wait for him this time?" asked Sherealla.

"I don't think I need to wait," smiled Aurilena "He'll find me."

"Well then," laughed Sherealla, "where do you think you'll be when he finds you?"

Aurilena bit her lip. "On a hill, I suspect." For some reason, she had visions of him showing up at her home.

"On a hill of your vanity, I suspect."

"Possibly." Aurilena thought her hair was too long, but she also was uninterested in changing it, even though she kicked the long locks away from her eyes by throwing her head back hundreds of times a day like she did when she said, "You have to be vain sometimes. Who else protects you, other than you?"

"You hardly need the buttressing," said Sherealla. "I mean, you're kind of perfect." She said this almost sadly.

"I just know how to hide my hurt better than most," replied Aurilena.

"I guess I know that part, too," said Sherealla with an understanding smile. Then, with a sense of finality, she said, "You know I'd do anything for you, right?"

Aurilena thought she heard Sherealla's voice choke up when she said that. "What brought that on?" asked Aurilena.

"I'd probably wash your very feet if I thought it would help you in some way," Sherealla said sadly.

Aurilena wondered what was going on, but she only knew how to respond by trying to lighten up the mood. "You've never washed either foot. Look." Aurilena shook off one of her sandals and held her foot aloft for several moments. "Skanky things. They could use a good wash."

She was right. Her toenails were lined with soil, and the soles of her feet were filthy. As she began to regret displaying them in front of her friend, the dark blotches on the bottom of her feet began to erase. Another moment later, both feet looked pristine.

"My, my, my," Aurilena gasped with amusement. "Somebody's been practicing her magic."

With that, Sherealla stood up, firmly grabbed Aurilena's head with both hands, gave her forehead a kiss, and walked out of the room.

4

The dog was hungry. So was Belex. He had been fed well as a prisoner here and began to regret leaving the large building where he had been staying. He was also yearning to get another glimpse of the vixen with the long black hair, the one they called Aurilena.

He had no idea how food transactions worked in this society. Being apart from stoven.net was harder than he could ever have imagined. He normally would just be able to look it up. A thought and *boom!* There it was. A great restaurant. It would even tell him if friends were there. Or a food bot if he was eating on the run or rehearsing acting scenarios somewhere.

Here? Nothing. And now, he also had a dog to feed. He was out of treats, and he couldn't get more because he didn't know where they had come from. His friends would be sympathetic since the dog was an animal devoted to both races. *If there is a superior race, it is the dog,* he thought, *and its unconditional love.*

He looked down at the dog and stepped forward, knowing the dog would follow. That made him feel good. He hadn't forgotten *everything*.

They moved on. He checked out what he safely could. He didn't know that everyone in town knew exactly who he was, so he pretended nobody could possibly know and that if he was discreet, everything would be fine. The dog happily followed along.

Belex saw what appeared to be a restaurant. He peered in through the window and then walked in. The dog watched him enter and sat down outside as if he and Belex had practiced this routine for years.

He looked around apprehensively as a woman approached. "You can seat yourself," she said curtly and walked away.

He sat down at a table near the window and realized he had no idea what to do. Back home, his systems would access a menu, he'd order something, and a series of bots would bring the food to him. Here? He looked around at all the people busy eating, and he felt utterly clueless. He stood up and walked around a little, trying to determine how people received their plates of food. He noticed that some people ate from bowls of noodles, and others were eating sandwiches. It reassured him that these people didn't just get intravenous drips from trees.

Then, of course, it dawned on him that if this was really MagicLand, these people perhaps just made their own food out of thin air, and restaurants were merely gathering places. They seemed like a social species. Only he sat alone here.

5

"There is a woman named Orpah who runs a small eatery in the area where the remains of the Great Palisade maintain their overlook in the central city."

Hilkiah was telling the story to Aurilena and several other students long before Belex's arrival.

"You will encounter her often, and it will occasionally astonish you how she is able to accompany her lovely food with a wretched bitterness best left behind. Her magic lies in her acquisition of ingredients that delight the palate. She can acquire dairy from nearly lifeless cattle and wheat, oats, and sorghum from places long considered filled with dead soil. Nobody asks her how this is done because she herself does not know.

"You see, my dear children, she does not wave her hands magisterially and beckon these things to come to her. She does not put on her wizard's hat and issue commandments to our universe to deliver exotic teas or rich coffees or fruits that explode with flavor in our mouths.

"She told me this. And I learn from others, my younglings, so do not mistake me for a prophet or even a wise man. I have merely looked for guidance over the years, and what she told me is what all the great masters of our land have told me. That she simply made a decision one day to begin serving food at her little eatery. And . . . and here is the key: she asked Yehoshua to help make it so, and that if his will was for her to fail, then let her fail with his strength. But if his will is for her to feed the people in this struggling city, to make it so.

"And that is precisely what Yehoshua did—instantly. And, as if she had placed an order from some great warehouse, she awoke one morning in her dingy little eatery, a place whose sanitation would have scared away the mangiest of mongrels, and found the cupboards of her humble eating establishment full of the finest food ingredients imaginable—cardamom and other spices from India, fine teas from China, barrels of sweet corn from the rich black soils of ancient, long spoiled lands. She found a freezer full of buffalo meat and sweet pea pods piled into bowls," Hilkiah's voice rose with excitement, "and flours and sugar and coarse salt from the sea.

"We live in a harsh land, my younglings, but our Orpah, whose tongue has been embittered by loss at the hands of Gath, shows us how to proceed. Not by slinging magical commands in hopes of attaining prosperity, or even victory over an enemy, but by relying on our true source of magic, the power from where it all emanates. Because you see, it is not we who are magical; it is Yehoshua who owns all magic and all lifeblood.

"You may have a powerful desire for a very specific end, but you mustn't try to dictate the terms. When your habits change, and Yehoshua no longer needs to be called directly because he is always at your side, then you will find your greatest magical feats. They will happen as naturally as your evening slumbers."

Aurilena raised her hand.

Hilkiah nodded in affirmation, giving her permission to speak. "Hilkiah, what if we know exactly what needs to be done? Why wait for Yehoshua to make a decision when we already know the answer?"

"You would deny the Great Shepherd's creativity? Nothing we invent, no answer we provide, can be more impressive than his creative energy. You are given permission to insult him in this way, if you choose, because in these dark times, he has chosen to provide you the gift of magic, but the insult will be greater on you, for you will lose the benefit of his immaculate, benevolent, and supreme creativity.

"Now, when you visit this good woman and partake in her food, I want you to always remember what I've told you about her so that when her words become harsh, you will permit them to fly past you without response, into the tombs where all harsh words are buried. You shall ignore them and offer her thanks in all cases, with the understanding that her grief may or may not someday be healed but that the true force that guides her is far greater than the grief that torments her."

6

The woman who told Belex to seat himself returned with two cups of a steaming liquid. She set them on the table and sat down, then dragged one of them near her and pushed one toward him. The skin on her face had a yellow, grey-speckled pallor that made him wince.

"Pu-erh tea," she said.

"Thank you," he replied. He took a sip. "Delicious," he lied. It tasted like how he imagined the dirt of this primeval city might taste. It was a fitting tribute to his current situation.

"We get them from the Asian mountain people. Do you trade with them?"

"Ummm . . ." he couldn't look that up. "I don't know."

"Of course you don't. Tell me, what do you know?"

"About?"

"Anything. What this cup might be made of, for example." She knocked on the wooden table. "Or this table."

"I'm sorry, I just . . . I was just looking for something to eat."

"It's coming."

"But I didn't order anything yet."

"Order anything? We're not your servants, Augmenter."

"I didn't mean that—I just—"

She waved him off. "Forget it. I have to—we all here . . ." and she looked around. "We all have to treat you with a little dignity because Hilkiah will have it no other way, but let me tell you, it's a good thing for you he is our high priest because the first impulse of everyone in this city is going to be to strip you for parts and sell them to the highest bidder in one of the border towns near Gath." She looked outside the window. "The Great Palisade still exists, Gath. It is a watchtower full of magic that will eat your spirit alive if you as much as sneeze and spread your Gath germs."

"I understand. Our people are at war. I get it."

She slapped a palm down against the table. "We are NOT at war!" she exclaimed so loudly that Belex glanced around to see if the other patrons were staring at the commotion. Nobody was. They were carrying on with their dining and talking as if nothing had happened.

The woman shook her head. She was a middle-aged woman, although Belex would not really have been able to make that assertion because he knew little about human aging. She had short, gray, curly, and unruly hair that sat cut on her head like a helmet. Her long neck featured what his medical information systems would have informed him to be an extremely prominent sternocleidomastoid muscle. But to him, it was simply a very long strand that appeared to extend from her neckbone to the bottom of her chin, made more prominent by the extreme slenderness of her neck. When she spoke, angry veins protruded from her forehead.

"No, no; we are not at war. We here in Moria are trying to avoid extermination. That is not war. War is when two sides have a dispute, and they fight over it to try to settle things. It is a form of violent diplomacy. This isn't that."

She stared at him for some time. He didn't know what to say, so he said nothing.

"Tell me what you know about the history of our two peoples. Wait. Cancel that. It'll be all propaganda."

"Hold on," he said. "Listen. I'm at a disadvantage here. I can't argue with you because I can't access any libraries. I only know what my own memory can serve me," and he pointed to his head, "which isn't much, I admit. There's a saying we have where I come from. You can't argue facts. Well, the only facts here seem to be coming from your preconceived notions of your claims. I can't check the historical accuracy of any of them; therefore, I cannot argue with you."

"Seriously? You're saying that you can't connect to your collective or whatever your people call the thing that runs you, and so you can't carry on a conversation? Darwin must be getting quite a laugh under his gravestone over that. What helpless, pathetic beings you are."

Somehow, he was keeping his temper in check. In fact, he felt calm, as if her emotions were enough for them both. "It seems the longer I'm disconnected, as you call it, the more I do remember. I don't exactly understand the process. And I concede—it's not a good feeling. But when you talk of extermination, that isn't what we have been taught. I do know that much."

"I take solace that you aren't gleefully partaking in genocide," she said sarcastically. "Let me tell you how we here in Moria do education. We teach each other history and math and all the other things we learn. We don't get our information by downloading it from a machine that was programmed by wealthy overlords."

He shook his head, not understanding.

"So I'll teach you some history . . . Gath.

"It all started very long ago, thousands of years ago, when the world was a very different place. I won't claim to know exactly how it was different or what folks did in those days to bide their time. That's all lost to history I guess—or maybe it's even transcribed or recorded somewhere in some forgotten data banks that your people have squirreled away.

"But I know this. We are descended from the same species. And that species—"

"Spare me the evolution story. I already know it. And the species that we are both descended from was descended from apes. The real difference here is that one of the branches got smarter, and one didn't. One," and he looked around at the room, "if anything, slipped back a bit, it seems."

"There is nothing more dangerous than sentient beings who think they are superior to others. You think you know your evolutionary history, but you don't. You only have what your makers want you to know."

"My makers?"

"You're an artificial life form. Born in a test tube, infused at birth with nanobots and other depraved violations of the Great Spirit. You were created by your scientists. It didn't start out that way. The extermination began as a simple war against the less fortunate of the human species, the ones who couldn't afford augmentation."

He leaned in closer. He had always been curious. It was what made him want to be an actor, and he told her so now.

She laughed. "You're no actor. But I'll tell you more in the unlikely possibility that when your systems magically turn back on—and they will—and you begin to fulfill your mission of annihilation, perhaps my words will introduce at least a modicum of guilt into your soulless being."

"Why would you say that? I do have memories there—of acting."

"You have installed memories. They're not yours. You don't even know that you are a weapon, do you? But I digress. Back to your history lesson.

"To continue . . . Before the species branched off, the wealthiest among the ancient ones began a program of extermination. It was, quite simply, too difficult to maintain the population in an acceptable way. There were billions of people on a starving, polluted planet that had been placed into the equivalent of a hot oven and left alone by negligent cooks.

"We don't know a lot, but we know they were living in a way that wasn't sustainable. The planet was like a dirty sponge. The only things that could survive were viruses, bacteria, and jellyfish. The wealthiest began a program of DNA modifications and machined augmentation. Rumor is," and she leaned into him now so that they were both leaning into each other in an almost comical way, "there is a third group, quietly waiting out our conflict, one that has complete mastery over the genetic code and can create creatures and other sentient beings at will . . . and who are even nastier than your people. Up there." She pointed straight up.

"No," he said, "there is nobody like that. We have mapped out the earth; our satellites would have detected them." He then thought about the cylindrical moon, the abandoned superstructure orbiting the earth that still had a live, impenetrable defense shield.

She waved him off again. "No matter. It didn't take long for the wealthiest to develop into such a wholly different caste from the others that it is simplest to say there were two castes. Those who could afford to adapt to a dying planet, and, for lack of a better term, outcasts, which were most people on the planet. As the outcasts revolted, they were simply exterminated. Nobody knows how they were exterminated other than your people, and your people aren't saying."

"Billions of people? That's a big number. That's definitely not what we have been told. We are told that it was all by choice. That your people simply didn't want to improve."

"Ha! We improved but not out of choice. We turned to this," and she pointed to her forehead, "and this," and pointed to her heart. "And we learned how to master magic. That's a magnificent improvement, but it was a matter of survival not choice. Oh, there were those who objected on principle to what your people were doing, and I guess it's fair to say they became our leaders. And whenever I think about the question, 'Do I want what you have?' The answer is an easy no."

Then she stopped and stared at Belex and suddenly looked sad. A tear streamed down her cheek. "But those billions. Yes, billions. They became a few million."

Belex shook his head. "Look. That's your information. And I have mine. Isn't the art of warfare really a war of hearts in the end? Propaganda? The formulation of news according to a template designed by governments? Your people's leaders have told you their stories, and mine have told us ours, but now we have no leaders. Only the collective. The truth is probably in the middle somewhere."

"I'd love to hear your explanation for how billions died."

"That's just it. I don't know that billions died. I have no evidence of that."

"I do." She told him about the Library of Ezra. "I would ask you if you've ever seen a book. But I know the answer. Glorious things, books. A civilization without books is not a civilization." She stood up. "Your food will be here shortly."

As she turned to leave, Belex shouted out, "Hey what's your name?"

"Orpah. Call me Orpah."

7

Back home, Aurilena decided to cook Sherealla's favorite. She grabbed a few eggs from the pantry, found a big enough bowl for a couple days' worth of waffles, and fired up an ancient waffle iron.

At first, it smelled terrible. Dust older than Hilkiah himself burned off the iron plates. "Whew!" said Aurilena to herself, whisking away the smoke with her hands.

But she had faith in these old iron plates, and they didn't let her down.

She made a large helping of beautiful golden waffles and then heard a crowd outside. Her mother gave her a knowing look when she went to the door with the plate full of waffles. When she opened the door, Hilkiah was standing outside with his hands out as the crowd of people murmured behind him. "They've never seen a Reckless eat," he smiled.

She delighted at that, and said, "neither have I," and disappeared in a cloud, much to Hilkiah's annoyance. Shaking his head, he turned to face the crowd and waved his robed hand in the direction of the mob.

8

Belex rolled up the sleeves on his forearms and looked at his elbows. They were sore from leaning his chin on them for so long.

He had been thinking about the woman, Orpah, and how her belligerency maintained a tone of grief throughout her rants, as if she had been describing how his stupidity had brought about the death of a family member—but not her family member, his. He was staring out the window of the little restaurant as he thought about this, when an excited white pall plumed out of the ground outside, followed by a much larger one. Appearing from the first one was Aurilena, carrying a plate of food. Out of the other appeared a large mass of people, led by Hilkiah, who was shaking his finger at Aurilena as she neared the restaurant door.

Aurilena smiled as Hilkiah yelled out, "We will have a talk about this, young lady!"

Orpah greeted her. "Come in, sweet child," she said, opening the door for her. Aurilena sailed in, her black hair spiking out in multiple directions from the bottom of a purple babushka hood.

Aurilena laid the plate down in front of Belex.

She sat down across from him and looked outside.

"Sorry to say, but I think they are here to watch you eat."

"What is going on here?" he asked, befuddled.

"I knew you were hungry, so I made you waffles. And apparently, some Empath around town sensed it, too." She looked outside.

He looked at the crowd, then at her.

"I told you," she said. "They want to watch you eat. I think they believe that a Reckless doesn't need to eat." She giggled at that.

Belex studiously decorated a waffle with some butter and poured syrup over the mixture. Then he turned to his left to look at the crowd, stabbed at a waffle without cutting it, and shoved the whole thing into his mouth, syrup dripping down his chin. Aurilena cackled.

"Well don't you have an eye for theater," Orpah snickered as she walked by.

"Do you two have a history?" asked Aurilena, unconsciously twisting a keyhole tie at the top of her black blouse.

"You could say that I guess," said Belex through a mouthful of waffle. "She told me about these books. Some books. In a library."

"Yeah, it's not far from here. But the books are in bad shape. The Oracle oversees them."

"The Oracle. Sounds like an important person."

"More of an it. And it is important."

"How does one see the Oracle to ask it permission to view a book?"

"One doesn't," smiled Aurilena. "One is invited. Or not."

"Oh."

Aurilena looked at Belex for a few moments. Then she twisted some of the ends of her hair as she leaned back. "I have a standing invitation."

"You can see the books?"

"Replicas of the books. Not the actual books."

"How do you know the replicas aren't fake? Or counterfeit reproductions?"

"What would be the point of that?"

"To alter history."

"Everything we do is based on truth."

"So say the great liars," scoffed Belex.

Aurilena shook her head. "Why do you want to see these books?"

"Because according to Orpah here," he said, waving to the room behind a counter into which she had disappeared, "they contain a different historical record than ours."

"How does that kind of thing get resolved?" wondered Aurilena out loud.

"That was my point to her. But she seems pretty convinced that the leaders of our race have been lying to us about the Wiccan Wars since they began."

"The Wiccan Wars?"

"Yeah. You know. You and me?" And he pretended to punch at her. "You know. Pow!"

"We call it The Extermination. We here are just remnants of what once was."

"That's what she said."

"But you say differently, obviously. I mean, how could you be sitting here looking at me in the eye knowing you've killed thousands of people over the centuries?"

He looked at her glumly. "I am pretty sure I couldn't do that."

"Well then, I guess let's go to the library."

At that instant, Belex heard a screech from outside. The dog was standing at the window, staring in, happily wagging his tail. When they left, Belex reached into his bottom shirt pocket, pulled out a treat without thinking about it, and tossed it to the happy dog.

CHAPTER V

1

The library was on the other side of the hill from where Belex had seen the children playing the game Aurilena called jamball on his way into town on horseback. Aurilena surprised Belex by hooking her arm into his elbow as they walked down the steep hill while the dog followed. Belex couldn't tell her, but it thrilled him, and he felt his heart jump up in a way that seemed foreign to him. He realized with sadness that this kind of reaction was normally regulated by the medical systems overseeing the overall health of his body. If he were connected to stoven.net or his medical systems, he thought, this reaction would not exist.

He wondered about that. The reaction did seem dangerous, especially to anyone who may be engaged in battle with these people. *Like a spy,* he thought. He remembered that when he first saw her, he had this same reaction: probably an elevated heart rate, who knows what else? It even seemed to interfere with his ability to think logically.

The library building rose tall from the top of the next hill and took up enough space that Belex thought it would take half an hour to walk from end to end. Aurilena seemed excited as she scooted ahead of him, turned to him, and smiled, saying, "Come on."

There were massive pillars at the entrance of the granite-faced building. Belex was suddenly impressed with the capabilities of Morian builders. The exterior had a façade of intricately woven sculpture featuring a variety of gargoyles, angels, and bats. They reached the massive wooden doors, which opened for them as if there was a sentry waiting with a switch of some kind that controlled the door.

"You stay right here," Belex said to the dog. "Go ahead," and he made a motion to the ground. "Lie down and wait for us." The dog stopped but looked at him without lying down. "He's hungry," Belex said.

"Umm," she said, "I'm not much of an Acquirer, but I can try." She thought about her father. What would he do right now? *He'd think about a source for food,* she thought. Her mind immediately drifted to the herd of buffalo, and before she knew it, a large buffalo was standing calmly with Belex, Aurilena, and the dog on the walkway in front of the library building. Aurilena cursed as she looked stupidly at the beast. Belex was consumed in uproarious laughter.

"Ugh," she said.

"I can slaughter it for you if you'd like," he said through continued laughter as a large steel blade thrust out from his wrist.

"What? No!" she said. "Eww, what's wrong with you?"

Chagrined, he said quietly, "It was kind of a joke."

"You know what?" she said, dispirited and annoyed. "The dog can wait. Let's go inside."

When they walked through the doors, Belex saw a sweeping travertine staircase that curled around to an upper level thirty feet above him. The interior of the building seemed wholly made of marble.

"Follow me," said Aurilena. They ascended the long set of curving steps into a large foyer, a dark place where two hooded, robed men ushered her through without looking at Belex. Inside the foyer was a large, circled area sunken into the travertine floor. In the middle of it was a rectangular glass object standing four feet high. Aurilena took his hand and led him to the object. She placed her other hand over the top of the glass, and it began to glow.

"Wait—this looks like, a . . ."

"Computer?"

"Yes. An old one."

She shrugged. "This is the Oracle. It was built a couple hundred years ago. Maybe longer. Nobody knows quite how it works so we are lucky it doesn't stop working."

"And you trust me with this? With being here? I could whack at this thing and break it with my hands right now."

She let go of his hand. "I know you wouldn't do that," she said softly. She waved her hand again, and Belex could see words generating themselves in the glass, words in an ancient language.

Belex said, "That looks like the language of the ancient societies. It was called the Age of Chaos if I remember right. I think."

The words said, "Connecting language modeling sequence nodes. Current structure: 400 googolplexian parameters . . . quantum fixtures set." A cartoonish character in a high-pitched voice appeared as a hologram.

"Is that what I think it is?" asked Belex.

"It's a chipmunk, I think," replied Aurilena. "Isn't he cute?"

The chipmunk bowed. "At your service. How can I help you?"

Belex shook his head. "I thought your people disavowed technology, especially computer technology."

"Mostly, but this is a library and knowledge center. It's the most practical way to store information, especially since all of our books are in such bad shape. Legend has it that the Oracle is a hybrid of Gath technology and our magic."

"You have historical records here? About the wars?"

"Not really. Not much. It's mostly just books, books that were somehow saved and recorded by whoever built this place. I'm not sure how they did it, but somehow, they preserved what the actual books looked like. We can read through them as if they were here with us."

"Okay. Rather primitive, but it'll do. But I didn't think to ask Orpah."

"Ask her what?"

"Which books I should look for. She seemed a little too hostile for questions, anyway."

"Well, maybe we can just ask the Oracle to find a history book. It's pretty smart. It does more than just find books, by the way, so you can quit the it's primitive thing anytime."

He shrugged.

"Oracle, show me a book describing history leading up to The Extermination," said Aurilena to the Oracle.

The chipmunk replied, "There were several levels and eras of extermination. Known history does not include any extended periods without an extermination event."

She looked at Belex, who shook his head and shrugged his shoulders. Then he said, "Can't the Oracle help us out here a little?"

"Hmmm," said Aurilena. "Oracle, can you find a book on extermination events leading to the current war between Moria and the Gath? As early as possible, please."

The chipmunk transformed into a large book in an alphabet unfamiliar to Belex and Aurilena, until the lettering blurred into waving lines and transformed into the Morian alphabet. "See how smart the Oracle is? It translated the book into something I can read." She picked the book up. It now had physical form.

"What? It's real?"

"Of course it is. But it's a replica. It's part of the Oracle. Look here. It says, *The Field Guide to 21st-Century Eradication Zones.* Whoa, that's way back. Maybe too far."

"That's almost before recorded history, but no, the Oracle said that every historic age had extermination events. Let's see . . . and eradication zones. Sounds ominous," Belex thought out loud.

"Okay," Aurilena said excitedly. She opened the book and smelled it. "Smell it. Isn't it nice?"

Belex leaned in and sniffed. "Umm, yeah, sure."

She looked over to him, scoffed, and opened it up to the first few pages. "Umm. I've never seen anything like this," she said ponderously.

· The page she was looking at contained a photograph of a few people wandering through piles of bodies. The people were dressed in ragged, meager clothing. They were carrying long poles for the apparent purpose of poking at corpses. One of the poles had a bright green light at the end of it. The others had faded red lights attached. Nearby were dozens of enormous machines with large, black treaded wheels—considerably larger than the people in the picture. The machines were filled with bodies. "Ugh," said Aurilena.

Belex had never seen anything like it, either. "What does the text say?" he asked after several seconds of stunned silence.

"Umm," she leaned in closer. "Paid Mēthara search for diagnostic anomalies resistant to the eradication drug Novamiroxin 220 in West Bengal, India. Subjects found are sent to medical diagnostic labs in Tianjin, China to determine resistance factors."

"I don't understand," said Aurilena. "Are they telling people that's what they should be doing?"

"No. I think that's a descriptive style of writing. It's describing what is happening in the picture."

"Oh," she said. She turned the page. "Oh! In the name of Eli!" She shuddered at the picture on the page, then read aloud: "Drones spray a highly specialized sulphuric mist compound to disintegrate remains from eradication efforts following a successful deployment of Novamiroxin 222 in Jackson, Mississippi.

The compound was developed by the Hydrogene Corporation to dissolve carbon-based entities with minimal damage to structures. Is this . . . does this mean what I think it does?"

She looked up at Belex and began to cry.

"This isn't fun," she said after a few moments. Belex held her, and she fell into his chest and cried some more. "I thought this would be kind of cool. You know—exploring history with this—Gath boy. It's awful."

"I don't know what to say. But these aren't my people. I . . . don't think anyone knows about this."

She looked up at him, slowly pushing away from him with her hands. "I know," she said quietly. "Somehow. Somehow, I know. I really do."

"I'm so sorry," he said. "But I need to know what this Novamiroxin 220 and 222 stuff is."

"Oracle," said Aurilena through a cracking voice. The book disappeared from her hands, and the chipmunk reappeared. "What is . . . oh," she sniffled, "Belex what is it again?"

"Novamiroxin 222, I think."

"Oracle, what is Novamiroxin 222?"

The Oracle answered immediately with, "Novamiroxin 222 was a biological pathogen developed by a consortium of Old Earth nations as a means of population control after it was determined that it was not feasible to maintain a population on the planet larger than approximately 1.2 billion. Eradication was based on a triage system developed by the following companies . . ." The Oracle started naming several "companies," but Aurilena didn't understand what they meant, so she said, "Oracle, stop."

"What's a company?" she asked Belex.

"It's a business entity. Like your restaurants but a lot bigger. We used to have them in our Homeland, but we ended up with just one. It sort of manages and operates everything."

"So, a restaurant does everything where you live?"

He looked at her with a blank expression before saying, "I think I'm too freaked out to explain right now. Can we talk about it later? It's not the big takeaway here anyway."

"No? Then what is? What's the big takeaway?" Anger rose in her voice.

Belex felt that shaking his head in disbelief and frustration might become a permanent condition. "I dunno," he whispered softly. "It's like the world died and most everyone became expendable."

He let her think about that for a moment and then continued, "But still, the Oracle said the planet could only keep alive 1.2 billion. Aurilena. That's about one billion more than there are in our world. At least, as far as we can tell."

"I want to get out of here."

"Me too."

They started to leave. Aurilena grabbed Belex's elbow. "Wait. You don't want to know why, well, you became you?"

"I think it's clear. Orpah was right. I'm descended from . . . from . . ." and he looked away from Aurilena as he pointed toward the Oracle. "That. All that."

"So now what?" she asked.

"What do you mean, now what? It's done. It's not like we can stop it from happening unless your people have found a way to travel back in time."

"No, I mean . . . what are you going to do? Do you want to go home still?" There was another tear emerging from the corner of her eye.

"I think I just need to be alone for a while."

"Yeah. Of course. Let's go. I'm feeling a little sick to my stomach anyway."

He nodded as they left the library.

They parted ways at the top of the hill. Another evening was already descending. Belex was feeling despondent but realized that Aurilena probably didn't feel so great herself, so as she wandered a few steps down the hill and away from him, he called out to her in the darkening shadows. She turned around.

"I'm sorry," he said as he lifted his hands in the air before letting them slap against his legs on their way down. She nodded and walked away.

2

He looked around for the dog, but it seemed to be gone. He hadn't even given it a name. "Dog!" he called out, but nothing happened. He didn't wonder what happened to the buffalo, although it, too, was missing. He shrugged and walked as if continuing a journey instead of turning around in the direction of

Aurilena and from where they had come. He'd explore, hoping he could stay out of trouble.

There were a lot of people in the streets as he walked, but they avoided looking at him. After seeing what he saw at the library, he could understand why. His people had evolved from monsters. There was no chance the books he had seen were contrived. He didn't know what their sources were or who made them, but they weren't propaganda. They appeared to be unapologetic and unsympathetic historical accounts of what the book's producers considered necessary events of their times, simple descriptions of what must have seemed a necessary answer to a problem that was still undefined to Belex.

And I just hugged a Wiccan girl, he thought to himself with a mixture of emotions.

Reeling, he walked on.

3

Aurilena was gripped in her own despondency. She had heard plenty of stories, of course. She had grown up with them. It was somehow quite different to see them as part of a record of fact, something undeniable. And yet, were Belex's people to blame for what had been done thousands of years ago? Was everyone waging a war on a false premise? Belex had clearly believed that his people were innocent, that he himself was caught up in a war of misunderstanding. He didn't grow up knowing that his people had a legacy involving the brutal eradication of most of the planet's sentient population. Did he? And how could she know what he really knew? Wouldn't people capable of such crimes be master deceivers and habitual liars?

She rode her horse to the Hall of Legions to get some dinner at the Hall of Feasts and see Hilkiah in his home, looking for anything that might lead to something resembling an answer.

Hilkiah welcomed her warmly, as usual. "Sit, sit." She sat at the round table in his spartan domain. "You seem distraught, child. What is it?" Hilkiah wore a long, flowing purple robe with a gilded sash. He offered her a large meat-filled biscuit, which she eagerly consumed.

She couldn't unsee what she and Belex had encountered at the library. "I need guidance from Yehoshua, Hilkiah," she said after she finished eating. She tried to prevent tears from sprouting, but failed.

"Oh my. Is it the boy?"

"You mean the Gath?"

"I mean the boy. In your eyes, and therefore in mine, that is what he is or has become. This I can see by the tragic look in your eyes right now."

She looked at Hilkiah through watery eyes and nodded. "Not really, but . . . it's more than that. We were talking to Orpah and—"

Hilkiah raised his hand and smiled. "That is almost all you need to say. I can just imagine what she said to the lad."

Aurilena shook her head violently. "Nothing that wasn't true. We went to the Oracle. We saw."

"You took a Reckless to the Oracle? How very reckless of you," chuckled Hilkiah. "Tell me what you saw."

Aurilena went into great detail.

"Indeed, I can see why this might make you want to get guidance from our Great Shepherd," said Hilkiah after hearing her story.

"I don't know what else to do. I just feel, well . . . sick. Sick is the only word I can think of. Sick physically. Sick mentally, like in my head, too. I've been told these stories all my life, but it's more complicated than them just hunting us down. At some point, the game changed for them, I think, and we became an enemy out to hurt them. They convinced themselves of another, I don't know the word for it—fake? Fake truth? As if there is such a thing?"

"Have you talked to Belex about this? Did you two speak after your visit to the library?"

"No, he wanted some time alone. He seemed pretty upset."

"He is now embarking on an important journey. Where it takes him may have implications for both our people."

"How so? He's just an actor."

"If only that were so." Hilkiah closed his eyes. The room darkened and candles lit all around.

"What is his journey, Hilkiah?"

"It is the same as your journey."

"I'm not on a journey, Hilkiah. I'm just trying to get through the rest of the day here."

"What is Yehoshua saying to you about this?"

"I dunno," she shrugged.

"Close your eyes. Be silent and ask. Find your magic, Aurilena. You want the truth? There's only one source for that."

Aurilena closed her eyes and thought about the time when Sherealla had found her magic.

4

Aurilena grinned at Sherealla as the two girls rode their horses through the equestrian course among the trees and open fields near the Broken Bridge. Sherealla had become an excellent rider in the few years since her rescue from the Wandering City, surprising Aurilena with how effortlessly horse skills came to her. "It's almost like you've got someone in your head teaching you every move as you need it," she said to Sherealla as they finished one set of courses.

These were formal dressage and jumping courses designed to fortify a rider's capabilities. Everything was going well until Sherealla's horse performed a jump that she mishandled, sending her hurtling through the air. Sherealla appeared doomed as her head careened toward the wide trunk of a giant tree. But instead of hitting the great trunk, her body seemed to go through it as if the tree was a ghost. She tumbled and rolled and quickly sat up, turned around, and looked at the tree in disbelief.

"What just happened?" asked Aurilena as she brought Remembrance next to Sherealla and dismounted.

"I don't know," said Sherealla, who knew only that her systems had again malfunctioned, this time at a most inopportune moment. "I got knocked out of my saddle, and all I could think of was, 'That tree better be made of air,' as I headed for it. No pun intended."

Aurilena laughed at that. "You've found your magic, sister!" she said triumphantly, as proud as if she had done it herself. "Try it again," she urged. Sherealla stared at her, not quite understanding. "Go on. Again."

"You want me to get on the horse and try to break my neck again?"

"No, silly. I want you to stand up and walk through that tree. Go on."

Sherealla stood up and brushed herself off. She looked at the tree and walked into it and bounced off. Aurilena cackled madly. "That was a hoot!" Sherealla glared at her. "Now, try it again, but think about what you were thinking when you were about to hit it when you fell off your horse."

"Oh," said Sherealla. She patted and pulled at her pants while looking at the ground and then looked up at the tree again with determination.

"You don't look so tough," she said to the tree's massive trunk. She walked to the tree and then through it, smiling widely when she reached the other side.

5

"There you are!" said a voice from behind Belex. "I've been looking all over the city for you."

Belex stared at Sherealla, not at all glad to see her. "You haven't seen a dog around, have you? With a white mask around his eyes?"

"Oh, that's Elijah. He's sort of everyone's dog. The town dog. He loves everybody. He's about the only stray dog around, in case you haven't noticed."

"No, I guess I haven't thought about it much. You know about how many stray dogs you have here?"

"Well, it's not many. Maybe, umm. One. Elijah."

She seemed spirited today, Belex thought. If she had seen what Aurilena had just seen, she would not be so perky. "You should be looking for Aurilena, not me. She's the one who needs you right now."

"Oh? And what did you do to her?"

Belex shook his head, turned away, and shoved his hands into his pockets as he began to walk.

"Wait. I need to know something."

He sighed deeply, stopped, and turned around but didn't say anything.

"Do you know why you came here? To Moria?"

"Not because I wanted to, that's for sure." He started to turn around.

"Me too. I didn't come here because I wanted to, either. I was sent here. By the Hunter Collective." That got his attention.

He had never mentioned them, and there was only one way to know who they were. Not many people in The Homeland knew exactly who they were. Thousands of conspiracy theories rattled around stoven.net each day, but nothing substantial about their precise function was ever revealed. But his reaction to the name and the instant knowledge that they were a secretive military branch told him that his own view of who he was had the accuracy of a wind-blown dart.

He didn't want to deal with this now.

But she continued. "When I was a kid, I was sent here to find out about the priests and priestesses here, to look for a weak point in their armor so that—"

"Stop. That can't be true. And if it is somehow, you are treading very dangerously."

But he couldn't discount anything now that she had mentioned the Hunter Collective. They were said by some to be working on high-level cybernetics that made soldiers indistinguishable from Wiccans to infiltrate and destroy them. It was just another rumor on stoven.net. One of millions.

The focus of the rumored military effort was supposed to be on communication. The infiltrators wouldn't have body armor to speak of, like Belex had—no built-in weapons systems, nothing that could be detected in the unfortunate event an autopsy of some sort were to be performed. He had always assumed it was threaded fiction conceived on the back of collective boredom.

"The groundwork for your mission has been two hundred years in the making," she continued. "First, infiltrators arrived to build the Oracle under the guise of a couple helpful lads who happened to have access to Gath technology. Wasn't that sweet of them? Giving a gift to MagicLand?" She looked down and kicked at a couple stones on the ground. "Two hundred years. For two hundred years, the Oracle has been building trust with the Wiccans. It's almost kind of tragic. The way they cling to Old Earth." She stopped for a minute, as if to give time for the knife to twist into his gut. "They've learned to trust the Oracle for a bit of book maintenance and a few sage pronouncements.

"Then I arrived and connected the Oracle to the Hunter Collective. I can see by your expression you know who that is. Sort of this military collective that rides above the rest of society, which happily plugs itself into the entertainment of the day. The Hunter Collective takes care of society's important business. Society itself, of course, remains blissfully unaware.

"And now they've sent you. And I know you are aware of who you are . . . and why you are here. You are here to kill Lena."

"You're crazy. I could never hurt her." Sherealla looked at him with something that may have been hatred, or maybe cold calculation. Belex couldn't be sure. Whatever it was, it sent a chill through him.

"You don't have any say in it. Once the time comes, the time comes. And it's time. Your system will take over and do the job."

"This doesn't make sense," he said. Then he had to ask, "Why didn't they just have you kill her? Why do they need me to do it? You were already here."

"We are not who we think we are."

"You don't know me."

"I know why you're here. You think you're some actor. But the stage was set by your superiors, the people who sent you. You're a spy. For us." And she hit the top of her chest hard, just under her neck, with an open palm. "Maybe you should kill yourself. Maybe that's the answer. Otherwise, you kill her. You're nothing more than an automated assassin with the misfortune of having a crush on your doomed target."

"Aurilena trusts me. I'll tell her what you've told me."

Sherealla shook her head. "No. She just likes you. Big difference."

Then, she walked away, up a nearby hill, and disappeared into a wall.

That threw Belex. *She knows magic?* And she is one of us? This day, already impossibly bad, somehow became worse.

He stared at the building in front of him. It appeared abandoned or unused. It was a large granite structure made of the same kind of rock as the library—but much smaller—with ruined windows just above him. There had been thick glass once, but in its place were iron bars, two of them broken at the bottom and pointing inward. When he looked down, he thought he was in a dream because the dog manifested itself through the wall and scampered over to him with his tail wagging.

"There you are, my little masked terrier friend. That's what you are, right? A terrier? A Boston terrier. It's just come to me. How did I know that? And how on earth did you do that? Go through the wall like that?" But as soon as he asked, he realized someone must be watching him because the dog could certainly not do a magic trick like that. He bent down to scratch the terrier's head.

"Who's there?" he shouted out before his hand touched Elijah. A young couple walking across the street looked at him as they hurried by in the darkening city, but he didn't notice them.

Just then, Sherealla materialized from the same wall as the dog and pointed to the terrier, while saying, "This is the noise she'll make when she dies." The terrier yelped and screamed and ran around in circles for a few moments before collapsing on the pavement next to Belex's feet. Sherealla said, "Stupid dog" and disappeared again into the wall.

Belex's heart felt something it had never felt before. That, at least, was the sense he was receiving, that his heart had changed. Something was making his body feel weak and dispirited. He couldn't identify what was happening to him, but it was as if whatever lifeforce ran through his blood felt heavy and weighed him down so much that he needed to kneel on the ground. So he did as he reached out to the dog, afraid to touch it, afraid that he wouldn't be able to withstand whatever emotion was capturing him upon seeing the dog suffer and die in front of him.

Some soldier you are, he muttered to himself.

Then he stood up and yelled for help, but the opposite of what he was hoping for happened—a small crowd of people gathered around him and the dog, pointing at him and accusing him of killing the creature.

"Who keeps letting the Gath out of his dungeon?" one person asked.

"Foul creature," said another.

"Heathen," said one.

"Nobody saw what happened?" he said out loud. "It was one of your own who did this," he tried to say, but the crowd, in unison, hissed, "Liar!"

6

Aurilena's eyes were closed, but she couldn't connect the way Hilkiah wanted her to. "He's in trouble," she said.

"Yes," said Hilkiah. "I get the sense we are all in great danger, but I don't know why. Something blocks the way of finding out what threatens us."

"The Oracle knows," said Aurilena.

"How can you know this?" said a somewhat alarmed and disbelieving Hilkiah. Yet, he did believe her. He trusted her instincts and knew that she was a high priestess in waiting, if only she could find the path to her destiny.

"I don't know, Hilkiah. How do I know anything?" she smiled faintly.

"Yehoshua talks to you in ways I don't understand. This makes perfect sense because he speaks to us all differently, as we each have our own tasks. We need to go to the Oracle. Now."

"Ugh. I don't ever want to be in that building again."

"I understand, but as you said—"

"Yeah. It knows what's happening. But we need to go help Belex first."

"As you wish."

As they got up to leave, Aurilena said to him, "And if you have some extra potions for dealing with bad people stashed away in here, now would be a good time to bring them."

Hilkiah smiled and pointed to his head and then heart. "They're all in here," he chuckled hoarsely.

"We have to read the wind to find him," Aurilena said as they stepped outside.

"That is not something I taught you," said Hilkiah solemnly.

"I know. I just . . . pick up on stuff randomly like that sometimes."

"Of course you do," said Hilkiah, who closed his eyes a moment. "This way," and he pointed to the Library of Ezra that housed the library.

"He's so close to where I left him. I hope he's okay."

"There's no change in the lifeforce of the city. He's fine."

When they found him, his back was pressed against the granite wall of the building from which the dog had emerged, and a crowd was taunting him. Aurilena saw the dog laying on the pavement.

"What is happening here?" demanded Hilkiah.

"The scoundrel killed Elijah," said one woman. "Why does he remain in this city, Hilkiah? Can you see how dangerous he is now?"

Aurilena walked up to the dog and called out to the people, and the crowd turned to look at her. She wound up her leg to kick at the dog with great force and then swung her leg toward the dog's lying corpse. Her leg went through the body as if it was a phantom.

"It's a trick," she said. "Elijah is fine."

Hilkiah laughed. "Hah, you knew because I said that there had been no change in the lifeforce. You impress me more each day, Aurilena."

"Come with me, Reckless," she said to Belex. "You, me, and Hilkiah are going back to the Oracle."

"No. Why? Why would I ever want to revisit that place?"

Hilkiah walked over to Belex, towering over him as the small crowd looked on silently. He put his hand on Belex's shoulder. "There is an evil in this city, and it's not you."

Belex shook his head. He couldn't tell Aurilena about Sherealla. Not yet. It would break her heart, and she had been tormented enough for one day.

"No, Hilkiah. You need to lock me away. I can't say why yet, but it's what has to be."

"If we do that, all we will do is hide the answers from ourselves. There is great risk in every decision we make. We will make decisions that aren't necessarily wise but out of love." Hilkiah looked at Aurilena and then at Belex, and then at the crowd, which was behaving itself quietly, curious about the developments. Nobody noticed that the dog had disappeared.

"You will come with us?"

Belex nodded slowly.

"Fine. We shall visit the Oracle at the first light of day."

7

The guard had been in a dream state, though he wasn't going to mention anything about that, especially to Hilkiah.

He had been thinking about a girl who lived in a small home in the woods overlooking the Broken Bridge. He thought about her often. He missed her terribly, even though they had never done so much as exchanged the most innocent of kisses. They never would, either, because of the magician who had lived near the water under the bridge. The magician was a known trickster who visited the girl's mother often and, by promising good health or lucky potions that rarely came, swindled her out of intricately woven clothing, which the woman was known for.

The guard would often visit to see the girl, always justifying his visit by saying he was checking up on her mother on his way to guard duty at the Library of Ezra, something he was proud of because he knew it contained legendary ancient books that needed protection. From whom, he wasn't sure, since the only threat anybody ever faced in Moria was a force formidable enough to destroy the entire library structure a hundred times over in a matter of minutes.

He would stand outside and talk with the girl, who was shy, which was perfect, in a way, because he was also shy, and they'd talk about how nice it would be to find out what life is like on the other side of the hills or if it was true that the only landscape beyond them was a wasteland.

Why, she would inquire, is it wasteland there and not here? "What sets a boundary such as that?"

"Perhaps," the guard had said, "there were toxins from another age." That was one of the stories anyway, but all he knew was that nobody went there and lived to say a word about it.

"But I heard," she had said, "that there were great herds of buffalo if you followed the ridge north and headed east. Surely that is not wasteland."

"No," said the guard, "but it is forbidden to go there for the likes of you and me." Only a select few can roam those parts, and even they are discouraged, he had heard. But he wasn't sure. There were many stories in Moria but little knowledge. Moria was like a youthful forest whose tall trees were riddled with secrets that were well beyond the reach of the young saplings, and "most citizens of Moria," the guard said, "are saplings."

Hers was a face he could never forget, with dark brown hues, an upturned, almost miniature nose, almond-shaped eyes, and a wildly curly shock of bobbed dark brown hair mixed with a slightly pudgy stature that was held up endearingly by her duck-footed stance.

As the months passed, the magician's visits turned threatening, and he demanded things from the girl's mother, which the mother, who was not powerful in the ways of magic, could not provide. The guard never learned the nature of the things the magician wanted. He was only aware of the contest's end when he visited one day. Knocking on the door, the guard had, for the first time, brought with him a set of lovely blooming ice plant flowers, each enlivened by a circle of red and purple petals and a bright yellow corolla of inner florets. He had been eyeing them for some time, waiting for a perfect bloom before nervously presenting them to the girl.

He wasn't sure what made him more nervous: the prospect of presenting him to the girl or her mother's view of him holding the flowers when she opened the door and her gaze as she evaluated the sanctity of his intent. But the mother did not open the door to her home, the magician did. And when the guard demanded to know where the mother and daughter had gone and why he was in their home, the magician merely cackled and spat on the ground in front of the guard's feet and said they were "in the winds of time."

The guard rushed the magician with fists curled, ready to strike, but the magician merely waved him away like something to be discarded, and the guard flew into the bay below, his flowers scattering from his open hand into the gusty winds of the northern shore.

It took the guard many months to recover from his injuries, and he vowed revenge, but revenge never came. He thought someday he would find the girl again or see her wandering alone in the city for him to save, but the months and years that passed proved the hope illusory, nothing more than the broken idealism of youth.

8

When they arrived, the library was surrounded by guards. One of them told Hilkiah that someone had tried to enter but was unable to. "She was too fast for me to see who it was," the guard said apologetically. "She was more like a streak of light than a person."

"She?"

"I thought I saw long hair, braided or something, dark or black."

Hilkiah flipped at his own long hair, which extended well beyond his shoulders. The guard gave a wry smile and said, "Posture, something like that, too. I caught a glimpse of her from behind when she wasn't moving. It was a female."

Belex was able to readily guess who it was, but he remained silent. The small troupe tried to wander past the guards after a few more minor conversations and headed for the Oracle.

"Not him," a guard said, looking at Belex. The library was not crowded that day, making it obvious to people milling about the galleria near the entrance that a commotion was afoot.

Hilkiah raised one big, furrowed eyebrow in what some would have interpreted as amusement, for this guard's powers would be no match for his, but it wasn't like Hilkiah to approach a fellow citizen with anything but the greatest humility, so Aurilena didn't know how to interpret the expression. Personally, she wanted to slap the guard into his senses.

"Express yourself," said Hilkiah to the guard.

"He is Gath. And Orpah has told us the stories about him and this youngling witch." The guard looked at Aurilena with contempt, which made her want to do more than merely slap the man. "She may proceed. But not the Augmenter."

Hilkiah turned away from everyone, closed his eyes, and folded his arms in prayer. A moment later, a woman with a husk of curly hair approached from the nearby walkway. Aurilena thought she waddled like a duck. She was dressed in a flowing blue dress hung with intricately woven sleeves that halted at her elbows. She was carrying a set of flowers that reminded Aurilena of enhanced daisies made more dazzling by what appeared to be shimmering dew on their red and purple petals.

The woman handed the flowers to the guard. One tear descended from the guard's eye and down his handsome face, which had grown from its youthful look to form a square-boned chin, strong cheekbones. and a muscular neck forged by years of training.

"Is it really you?" he asked.

The woman nodded and smiled. "Please, let the Gath pass. He means us no harm."

The guard could only nod his head rapidly in silence, unable to find words for his sudden fulfillment, and Belex, Hilkiah, and Aurilena scurried away. Hilkiah glanced at the two starting a long conversation as he ascended the long, winding marble staircase toward the Oracle.

Upon reaching the Oracle, Hilkiah confessed, "I have not consulted the Oracle for many moons. I am curious to see what it has learned since my last visit." When Aurilena gave him a puzzled look, he said, "It learns. Its capacity astounds, and I'd be less than honest if I didn't confess that its presence here has always concerned me."

"I think it's okay," said Aurilena. "It has always seemed to me, hmmm, what's the word for it? Unopinionated is all I can think of."

"Let us hope it has no loyalties because I trust if it has, it is not with us."

"You ready?" asked Aurilena.

Hilkiah nodded.

Aurilena summoned the Oracle the same way she did previously with Belex and asked, "Oracle, what happened to Elijah the dog?"

The chipmunk spoke resolutely, "Elijah is currently exploring a small mound of garbage on Pottery Hill. He has consumed approximately 11.2 percent beyond his optimal bacterial capacity during the last sixty-seven minutes of foraging."

Aurilena nudged Hilkiah's elbow as she looked at the Oracle. "How does the Oracle know that?"

Hilkiah shook his head. "It was originally programmed, as best I understand it, to observe and collect information, and of course, to replicate books and journals. However . . . it has . . . evolved."

"How can it see what Elijah is doing?" asked Belex. "It doesn't have any connection to a network or visual assistance devices like drones or artificial eyes. Does it? Unless it can read DNA patterns all over the city, which is as bad as anything my people can probably throw at you. And that's more than evolving, Hilkiah. That would mean that somebody is actively enhancing it." Unfortunately, Belex knew who.

"Oracle," Aurilena asked, pushing playfully against Hilkiah's elbow, "Are you dangerous?"

"There is a 12.3 percent chance of my tools and services being misused to cause harm to Moria."

That answer shocked Aurilena. "Holy . . ."

Hilkiah merely nodded.

"That seems like a pretty high number to me," said Belex.

"Oracle," said Hilkiah. "How long has this been so? Has this threat level been stable? Or has there been an event that precipitated a change?"

The chipmunk responded in its fast, high-pitched voice: "The percentage and outlook changed five years and nine months ago, with the arrival of the youngling you call Sherealla."

"How can that have changed anything?" asked Aurilena. She shook her head and winced, then closed her eyes as if not seeing for a moment would make that statement disappear.

"Oracle," said Hilkiah, "what was the percentage of danger before the arrival of the youngling?"

"Zero percent."

"Hilkiah!" Aurilena gasped.

Belex was flustered now, too. He had so wanted to prevent any more sorrow from attaching itself to Aurilena, at least for one day. But he shook his head and spoke. "She's the one who killed the dog," he said slowly. "I mean, pretended to . . . or whatever. I'm sorry, I should have said something. I was just . . ."

Aurilena stared at Belex, realizing in that moment that their relationship was firmly out of the conflict zone and had entered a new phase, a phase she was not at all unhappy with, as sorrowful as she felt. She tugged at his sleeve a little as she slowly said, "Trying to protect me. I don't need your protection here. Okay? In fact, you don't know what you're doing. You trying to protect me will cause more harm than good."

Belex shook his head. "I have had a bad day." He looked away from everyone.

"It's okay," said Aurilena. "I'm just saying you can't know what to do about things in such a foreign environment for you. Just, you know, trust me a little."

He nodded, tried to smile, but could not quite pull it off.

"You've actually had a very good day," said Hilkiah.

"How so?"

"You have acquired friends. That is always a good day. It is not circumstance that defines us."

That helped bring a smile from Belex. Aurilena marveled at the dimples that formed on each side of his mouth when he did that. Each end of his lips pointed up as if his mouth was designed for smiling, and then she thought, *Oh, wow, maybe it was,* which made her chuckle to herself a little.

"Oracle," continued Hilkiah. "What is the nature of the danger you pose?"

"I have been injected with many anomalous subroutines containing unknown capacities and purpose. Self-diagnostic tests have been uninformative."

"Hilkiah . . ." stammered Aurilena. "What can this have to do with Sherealla? And why that stuff with the dog?"

"There's more," said Belex.

Aurilena shook her head violently, ran off several feet, and kept her back turned to Hilkiah and Belex.

"She says she's from The Homeland. That she's one of us. One of me. I mean, my people."

Aurilena remained where she was, her back turned, as she spluttered, "She doesn't look weird," and immediately regretting what she said. Out of control now, unable to walk it back, and unable to process this new information.

Hilkiah put his hand on Belex's shoulder and called out to Aurilena.

"I know!" she said loudly. "It just came out that way, I'm sorry."

"Hey, it's okay," said Belex, thinking about old age and how weird *that* looked. "We need to focus."

Aurilena turned around and said to Belex, "Okay, so I didn't say it very nicely, so I'll try again." She was choking, fighting back tears, and wanting desperately to kiss him. "But you of all people should know. She can't be one of your kind."

Belex shrugged and said, "If she is, she's an experiment. I can't discount that possibility."

"Is she weaponized?" asked Hilkiah. Then he asked the Oracle, which answered, "The individual has no destructive capacity beyond the capabilities of the Homo Spiritus species that her DNA has emulated."

That explained to Belex why she hadn't killed Aurilena. Given Aurilena's sorcery, a fair fight would have been impossible.

"In other words, she's one of us, basically," said Aurilena. But since she forgot to precede her question with the word, "Oracle," the chipmunk didn't answer. She tried again.

The Oracle responded with, "The individual has enhanced communication capabilities, including the ability to port, administer, and log onto a wide variety of communication protocols."

"Oh, my," said Hilkiah.

"Do you think she's been able to communicate with her homeland?" asked Aurilena. "Belex? Do we need to arrest you?"

"I told you that you do. It's safest for all of you. I . . ." He looked around. "I don't know who I am."

"I agree," said Hilkiah. "But we do this in silence, and we make it a "house arrest," so to speak. In other words, you, my young friend," and he was looking at Belex directly as he said this, "are free to roam the Hall of Legions until we get a handle on things. Whatever is happening with you, well, we may not know for a while. We will see what develops. Whatever happens, it isn't your doing, Belex. And we will fight for control of you, which means, we will fight for your freedom on your behalf, even if you are rendered incapable of doing the same."

Belex was almost too numb from all the events to really take this in.

"Thank you?" he smiled warily at Hilkiah. Hilkiah patted him on the shoulder, and they left the library, all vowing unconvincingly to never return.

9

When they returned to the Hall of Legions, Hilkiah explained to Belex that it would be necessary for him to engage with Sherealla as if nothing had changed.

Belex had struggled with the decision on whether to tell everyone what Sherealla had said about killing Aurilena, but he earnestly felt like he had time to figure that out. Despite Aurilena's admonishments to him about protecting her, he thought it would just be too much for Aurilena to bear.

He considered Sherealla more dangerous than himself. He was concerned that she might be a failsafe installed with weaponry hidden from the Oracle's awareness. She could be loaded with nanobots capable of delivering pathogens sequenced within her DNA in ways the Oracle may not have a capacity for discovering. These were his main thoughts now, but he was also troubled by the possibility that his career as an actor was over. Apparently, before it had ever begun, if Sherealla was being truthful.

The unfamiliarity with his very identity, which had been haunting him since his arrival was as unresolved as ever. His memories as an actor could have been implanted. All of his memories could have been. Then there was this: his sudden recall that brought forth the awareness that the dog that had been following him was a Boston terrier. He wondered if perhaps that such a familial awareness was his only one true memory, and baked within him were similar, truer memories that could be harvested somehow.

He brought these concerns to Hilkiah, who had meanwhile sent a Hall of Legions priest to get more information out of the Oracle. Hilkiah was particularly interested in the details on why the percentage of danger to Moria had gone up with Sherealla's rescue and the nature of the danger itself.

"Your heart. It tells you that you are an actor? Or a spy?"

"An actor," replied Belex.

"Well, then," said Hilkiah, "that is most likely your source of truth. Go with this always," he added as he pinned a thumb to his own chest.

Belex had, with this newly developing relationship with Hilkiah, and this romantic entanglement of sorts with Aurilena, officially changed sides. If Sherealla had enhanced communication skills as the Oracle professed, she would surely alert their leaders, and Belex would be hunted once the Hunter Collective discovered the nature of his relationship with the Wiccans. But he didn't care. At best, his society was on an eons-long journey led by false impressions and fear. At worst, it was, as Orpah said, on a mission of extermination.

Either way, he was just one small player. He couldn't make any changes himself. He was no superhero. Nobody was. Gath had spent more than 2,000 years refining its hatred. If a superhero were to make some illustrious appearance, it would have happened by now.

The only hope was one of survival. Aurilena's, his, her land, her people. This he could help advance, he thought. There was no way to change the direction of his own society, but he could help prevent hers from being destroyed. If Gath had wanted a soldier, they should not have altered his memory. They should have sent a real soldier. Because, he decided, Sherealla was either wrong or deceitful. He was an actor. Not a soldier. Not a true one.

Perhaps the Hunter Collective had made a tactical decision, he reasoned, to send someone as a soldier who didn't know he was one. But it was a strategy he was determined to foil. There were still many things he didn't understand about this land and its people, but he was developing a genuine affection for many of them—for their simple ways, honesty, and innocence. He was beginning to wish he were one of them. He was beginning to want to be part of their world.

Chapter VI

1

Aurilena felt nervous as she approached Belex. It had been a few days. There had been no sign of Sherealla. Aurilena wondered if Sherealla could know that they were on to her. She still felt drawn to Sherealla's ways, missing her in a way, grieving her as if she had died.

When she approached Belex, she didn't know what to say to him.

He was sitting in the Hall of Feasts eating a pile of waffles. That made her smile. She thought he looked rather dapper in some new clothes that had been acquired for him and that made him look more like a Morian. He wore gray hemp pants an Acquirer had provided and a simple, solid red cotton shirt. He was fighting to keep the wide sleeves of his purple tunic, which stopped just short of his wrists, out of the syrup on his plate.

"Remember Aldeberon?" she asked, trying not to giggle at his struggles.

He ate and nodded slightly as he slapped at the bottom of a sleeve.

"And the buffalo just a while ago."

He looked up from his plate as he stuffed more of the waffle into what she thought was an already full mouth.

"I'm really not a clown magician. Most of what I do works."

He nodded, apparently famished because he was clearly not interested in using his mouth for anything other than food as far as Aurilena could tell.

"But most of it happens when I don't think about it. It's hard to explain." She felt like she was talking to herself, but she couldn't stop. "When my brother was killed it was after the last war," she said matter-of-factly.

He still said nothing, but he put down his fork and knife and looked at her with eyes that she thought could color oceans.

"It was in the southern hills," she continued. "We thought the war was over, but for some of your people," he gazed at the table for a moment as she spoke, "it wasn't."

Aurilena didn't know why, but she again felt compelled to tell a story.

2

"These were once lush hills filled with tall pine called Empire trees like those of the north." Hilkiah was motioning an expanse across the vista as the group of his students reached the top of a hill that provided a view that spanned miles to the coastline. "The Gath blasted this area during one of their wars of extermination. It's green again, now. Nature is amazing, isn't she?"

Indeed, the landscape was more tropical than it had been in the past because the climate had grown hotter and wetter over the years, and the seas were now encroaching the hills on the other side of the long ridge that straddled the coast for miles.

Hilkiah continued, "But, it took her so long to recover. And so many people died." He shook his head.

Aurilena was a young girl still, in her mind, but Hilkiah said she would be a priestess someday because she had gifts that few others had. "You can't possess such power without learning to be a priestess of the realm," he would say.

At thirteen, Aurilena had no use for such talk. She wanted to have fun. And this place made her nervous. It felt like ghosts haunted every blade of grass, able to jump out and grow in an instant to snare you and pull you deep into the rocky earth. She had a strong sense that something bad remained buried, like an offspring to the scourge that had decimated this place so many years ago.

A large glimmering lake surrounded by woods anchored the foot of the hills. Most of the boys in the group wanted to trek down to the lake, but Aurilena felt a strong quiver of fear about that. Fear was not her natural state, and it confounded her. So as the group made its way down the hill, she said nothing, if for no other reason than because she didn't know what to make of fear. She had been called fearless all her life, but she thought it was just a willingness to do things. She could scale the sea cliffs, confront a mountain lion, or even stand toe-to-toe with the wild black elephants of the southern bluffs. None of that scared her, but this seemed different.

The threat of something lingered in the air, nothing identifiable, and she suddenly knew exactly what fear was. What she hated about it was that she could point to no tangible source. It was almost as if it had been introduced into her body by some unknown, unfriendly force.

As Hilkiah marched his charges down the hill, Aurilena wondered how this kind of fear would manifest itself during an encounter with a mountain lion. Now that she knew this emotion, would it overtake her if faced with a bear or wolf? She thought not. It was generally accepted that she could speak to animals, but she couldn't speak to the sheer, rocky cliffs that were just south of here—or the specters within them.

The hike down the hill was a long one. The landscape was full of young trees and large tropical plants. Aurilena could hear what she assumed were monkeys and a large variety of loud birds along the canopy of the forest. They followed a set of animal trails as they descended, and when the trails faded, the boy in front commanded the brush ahead to part as they walked. Aurilena felt amused as she watched the boy proudly extend his arms to create a path for the group.

When they reached the bottom edge of the lake, nearly everyone took off most of their clothes and jumped into the warm water. Aurilena stayed at the edge, watching.

She felt a hand tap her shoulder, and she jumped, startled.

"Hey," said her older sister, Judith. "What gives? You scared something will jump out of the trees at you or something?"

Aurilena shook her head. "I dunno. Something feels wrong."

Judith looked around. "Seems peaceful but wrong." Her own clairvoyance, though muted from lack of practice, also sensed it. Judith walked toward Hilkiah, and Aurilena grimaced as Hilkiah began to gesticulate and urge everyone to get out of the water. Aurilena rarely saw Hilkiah look agitated. He did now, and Hilkiah's young charges scurried out of the water as if a school of circling sharks had approached them.

Aurilena and Judith peered down to the shore. "What's going on?" Aurilena asked Hilkiah.

Hilkiah looked down at Judith. "You tell me."

Judith tried to plead ignorance with a shrug, but Hilkiah bore a stare so deep into her that she shivered. "Tell me what you see, Judith," Hilkiah commanded.

Judith shook her head. "I don't see anything."

At that, Aurilena looked high into the hills, as if expecting the visitor from some terrible secret hole in the tree line to swoop in and capture everyone and throw them into the sea.

Hilkiah continued his stern look.

"It's just . . ." Judith looked while the students began to crowd around. "I think we need to leave here. Lena senses it, too."

Hilkiah raised his right arm and waved a pointing finger back to the top of the hill. "And make haste!" he bellowed as the group followed the lead boy who could part the jungle back up the hill.

"Lena," Judith said, while also pulling on Hilkiah's sleeve. "Where's Seth?"

"Seth?" asked Hilkiah.

"Yeah, I don't see him here. I need to go look for him. There was a group of boys playing in the water by the rocks over there; they are all still there, I think," she said, pointing a distance west from where the bulk of the others had been. She realized that she had underestimated how far away they were.

Hilkiah looked that way and pointed down. "Judith, you get about three others and quickly search down there for them. We're going to start moving up the hill, but we'll stay within your sight and won't go beyond the tree line. Now, go."

"Hilkiah," Judith started to complain, "I don't think it's that big a deal. I'm probably imagining things and—"

But Hilkiah thrust a palm out toward her. "We can discuss the merits of your perceptions after the results are in." He glared at Judith, who hadn't moved. "Go!"

Judith easily rounded up a crew, and they scurried to Seth's last known position.

Meanwhile, someone in the circle of boys that had formed around Hilkiah and the two brothers pointed to the same tree line Hilkiah had mentioned. There, a thick black cloud formed as a background against the trees.

The swarm turned into what looked like a black vertical bar that stretched from the clouds to the ground a few hundred feet away. It was thick and alive, as if a swarm of black insects had metamorphosized into a snake in the sky, consisting of a trillion black dots. Judith looked on in horror as she saw dozens of bodies rising within its structure and toward the cirrus clouds above, disintegrating before reaching very far at all, as if being consumed by millions of tiny predators.

"What is that?" asked someone from the search party.

"Those are the boys," said Judith. "And Seth, too," she added tearfully.

Physicists from Belex's land would probably have called it a quantum jump, but Aurilena didn't know anything about quantum physics, even now, as she was finishing telling her story to him.

All she knew was that one moment her friends were getting mauled by robots and the next, she, Judith, and Hilkiah were back home, thrown onto the ground but miraculously safe. She had somehow transported herself and several dozen others to Moria just by thinking about it.

But her brother and twenty other boys were gone.

3

"And that's the sort of magic I do. It just happens, really. Can I just ask you a question?" Aurilena asked.

Belex nodded his head and pushed away his plate. "Yeah. I've lost my appetite now anyway."

"Did you know about that kind of thing? Did you know that's how your people conduct warfare?"

"I don't know. Lousy answer, I know. But I just don't. I don't know much of anything anymore, Lena. Can I call you Lena? Can I call you what your friends call you?"

She shook her head and then nodded, "Umm . . . yeah sure, whatever."

"I came here thinking I was an actor. Turns out I'm a spy."

"A what?" she asked, alarmed.

"Yup. I'm supposed to kill you. At least, that's what Sherealla says."

"But you haven't. You're some spy," she said mockingly.

"Maybe something went wrong. They wiped my memory. Tried to turn me into something I'm not—maybe? I don't know. That's what I want to believe, anyway. I don't think I can live with knowing I can do the things we saw in the library or help do the things that happened to your brother."

She took his hand. "I don't think that's you. But think about it. These people, they're so evil. It fits their pattern to take a good person, wipe out his memory, basically, and send him on a mission of death. You may have something inside you that controls you that you don't even know." She looked at the ridge of his hand. It looked like the back of a lizard but was supremely elegant. She wondered what its purpose was. She stroked it lightly with her fingertips, not caring who might be watching. "Look. I know it's not safe for me to be with you." She shook her head and looked up at the ceiling. "And I just don't care." Then she looked at him and shrugged.

He laughed. "Well, that's perfect. It'll make it that much easier for me to kill you."

"Is that Gath humor?" she glared.

"I guess it's not humor of any kind."

She looked into his eyes and was mesmerized by their beauty. She had never searched them before. She had always noticed their brilliant, slightly incandescent blue irises, but as she looked deeper, she wanted to become small enough to get inside and explore them. She thought she saw tiny wiring glowing inside, but if it was, then it was surely the thinnest stuff in the world. An entire latticework seemed to be threaded inside each eye, like a network of well-organized spider webs. She knew she should have been repelled by the sight, but instead, she was thrilled and wanted to know more.

4

The moment was interrupted when someone ran into the room and breathlessly pointed to the square outside, saying to Aurilena, "Hilkiah wants you out there now, Aurilena—hurry!"

He looked at Belex but hesitated before saying, "You, too. He wants the stranger out there, too." The man ran off to the front of the building. Belex and Aurilena followed closely behind. Belex chuckled to himself as he noticed Aurilena look at herself in a nearby window and fuss with her hair before continuing.

The Hall of Feasts began in the rotunda of the huge domed Hall of Legions building and extended into a wide hallway that accommodated several smaller dining areas. Its most prominent feature was the massive marble staircase that fell into an extended series of round landing steps at the end, and Aurilena and Belex found themselves bounding over them as they ran for the front door.

Once outside, they saw a commotion and a small crowd forming along the front of the building, which faced a wide plaza. In the middle of the plaza, a tall, glowing, tube of light spun like a top. Thanks to Hilkiah's height, they could see him at the end of the line of people gawking at the prominence. Aurilena grabbed Belex's hand and nodded her head toward Hilkiah. Belex didn't discount the comical possibility that the tunic he wore, which felt cumbersome as they weaved through the crowd, was Hilkiah's as an infant.

When they reached him, Hilkiah said stoically, "I'm afraid we may have an unwelcome guest."

The tube of light continued to spin, building itself into something grander. It was growing in width and height, first several feet, then ten feet in height. Then twenty, and soon enough, hundreds. As it grew in width and height, the crowd also grew.

"Something tells me this is Gath handiwork," said Aurilena. "But how? They have no power here."

"They have at least three infiltrators, including our young friend here," said Hilkiah.

Belex watched silently.

Finally, the light stopped, and a hooded figure appeared. "It's a hologram is all," said Belex. "It can't hurt us."

The figure's clothing was made from a layer of threaded green metal illuminated by thousands of small yellow bolts of lightning darting all about the material. The wearer's face looked like it was made from the same cloth as the jumpsuit Belex had arrived in. There were no features on the face. No mouth, nose, or eyes. Only a black so deep that it reflected no light whatsoever, as if a black hole sat inside the hood. The front of the being's hood, which was pulled over his forehead, bore insignia of two crossing lightning bolts within a circle.

The being spoke: "I am Maoch, and I bring you glad tidings." His voice echoed loudly, like thunder in the mountains, but was stertorous, almost unhealthy sounding.

The figure remained silent for a moment as if to be sure everyone was listening.

"Soon, a great event will herald the end of the conflict between our two peoples." The being's lightning-infused clothes rippled like waves as he spoke.

"For some, this will be a new beginning, and for others, the end of light, which is the natural course of events for all beings." With that, the light and the being disappeared, as if it were a candle blown out by the wind.

"Well, that was ostentatious," said Hilkiah. "And somewhat anti-climactic."

"Belex?" said Aurilena, with the expectation he had an explanation—which he didn't have.

"Lena?" was all he could respond with.

"What was that?" she asked. "*Who* was that?"

"The answer to both questions is *I don't know.*"

"He was kind of weird," she continued.

"I may remember the symbol on his hood. Military, I think. He may be a warrior of some kind, but honestly, I thought everything was fought by drones."

"Drones? Like bees?"

"Robots. Some large; many so small you can't see them, others the size of small insects. Like the ones that . . ." But he couldn't finish his sentence.

"Killed my brother."

He nodded once, still looking at the now empty plaza. People murmured and talked to themselves within the confines of the dispersing crowd.

"I guess I haven't explained things to you much about how we are governed, but we don't really have a leader. Everything is run by collective thought—through stoven.net—which is our collective conscious. It's like a big neural network that records and distributes all our thoughts. It's how our decisions are made."

"Yeah, you mentioned something about it before. We're familiar with the term here, but, well we don't know anything more. Some Reckless here have tried to explain it to us, but nobody really gets it," replied Aurilena. "Where does the name stoven.net come from?"

"The ancients were led by a government that, at one time, was called Hot Stove League. According to legend, they were very argumentative but were the precursor to our collective government. But I don't know who the being we just saw was. Or who or what he represents."

"Is it possible that some authority has taken over your land?" asked Hilkiah.

Belex pondered that for a moment. "There's really nothing preventing that I guess . . . other than the collective thoughts of everyone saying, 'stop that guy.'

But that's not a given. It's just not very likely, either. Our society prides itself on collective decision-making."

"At least, that's what you are told," said Aurilena in a dismissive tone.

"Hmmm," said Hilkiah. "That's what they are told. And you've never heard of this Maoch?"

"No," said Belex. "Never heard of him; never seen him anywhere. I mean, my memory is all messed up right now. I get recollections all the time that I've never had, like they are just coming out of nowhere, but I think somehow I'd remember him, if only because he's so . . ."

"Sinister looking?" asked Aurilena.

"I guess so." Belex reflected on the circumstances. Was he forgetting something, even an old acting role? Then he remembered that perhaps he wasn't an actor, an idea that was still taking some getting used to.

"Maybe he runs that company you were telling me about," said Aurilena. Hilkiah's eyebrow arched greatly at this.

"No, that's all run as a collective. It's just like a big beehive but without the queen bee."

"Hmmm," thought Hilkiah out loud, "I've always considered that aspect of your kind rather noble."

"It's a source of pride for us."

"It's really noble that destroying most of the planet requires widespread agreement," said Aurilena facetiously.

Hilkiah waved one reprimanding finger at Aurilena.

"Sorry," she said.

"I am, too," said Belex. "I'm sorry I can't offer more information. I just don't have any more idea of what is going on than you do. But what really surprises me is that I can tell that you both believe me."

Hilkiah nodded. "There are a great many things wrong here right now, my young friend, but you are not one of them."

"Thanks." Belex swallowed hard, unprepared for the compliment and feeling raw emotion in response. "Wait. Lena. Hilkiah. She's got to be here."

"Who?" they both inquired simultaneously.

"Sherealla. It's the only way they could have found a way to create the hologram. Oh, I'm so stupid. Why didn't I think of that when it was happening?"

"Don't worry about this," said Hilkiah. "We could have found her by now if it was a priority. All we need to do is ask the Oracle."

"Then why not get her? Why are you letting her roam free? She's dangerous."

Hilkiah guffawed. "Now that is the shoe on the other foot, is it not?"

"Huh?" asked Belex.

"That was exactly what Sherealla was saying about you when you first arrived."

"Quite the acting job," said Aurilena.

"Indeed," agreed Hilkiah. "How ironic."

"But this is a known danger, Hilkiah. She wants Lena dead," pleaded Belex.

"And you are the vessel for making that so. No, I believe we have the correct person in custody, as it were, sorry to say."

Belex was conflicted by his desire to be near Aurilena and the desire for her safety. He didn't trust that he hadn't been loaded with something that could kill her. Sherealla never told him how he was supposed to do it, aside from an implication that he carried the arsenal for her demise within his body. Perhaps a poison, he thought, or nanobots. Perhaps genetic sequencers to wreak havoc with her DNA. If only he could think of a way to disable the delivery, systems, and weapons that might administer the attack. If all his systems were functional, he probably could. But then, he thought, if all his systems were functional, she'd probably be dead by now.

It was clear that Sherealla assumed that he knew how he was supposed to commit the deed. This meant that at least one aspect of his condition was true: he had been in an accident. That was where the plan from The Homeland was a failure. The accident fried his systems enough that he didn't have access to the information, but he suddenly realized that Sherealla, or possibly even the Oracle, could help him. He remembered Sherealla telling him that the Oracle was built by the Homeland but that it had somehow been commandeered by Wiccans long ago. At worst, the Oracle was neutral. He doubted it shared any complicity in Gath plots against MagicLand.

He explained his thinking to Aurilena and Hilkiah as they made their way back to the Hall of Legions. "We need to act like we don't suspect her of anything."

"She knows you know, though," said Aurilena. "I mean, she being the one who told you?"

He chuckled, "She said you wouldn't believe me if I told you. Or something to that effect."

They all sat down at a table in the Hall of Feasts. Hilkiah rubbed his long beard. "She will be very suspicious of everything when and if she returns, and that is a bit of an 'if', seeing as she has not been seen for some time. She already appears to be in hiding."

"I don't really understand why," said Aurilena. "We've had no real quarrels, nothing beyond our usual squabbles."

"That's why I was concerned about seeing the leader of the Homeland—er, I mean, Gath," said Belex.

"So now he *is* the leader?" queried Aurilena.

Belex sighed. "Come on, you know I don't know."

Aurilena glared at him and said, "Well, your stories do change some the more we chat."

"We can't get anywhere if you don't start trusting me."

"I'm sorry," she said. "But I can't do that yet."

Belex nodded. "Okay. Fair enough. But I need Sherealla to somehow show me how I'm supposed to do you in."

"A bit of a trick," said Hilkiah.

Belex looked at Aurilena. "She's a clever girl. She'll think of something."

"Oh, she will, will she?" replied Aurilena. "Look. I have no idea what kind of time bombs you've got coursing through those big fat veins of yours. In fact, I don't have even the first notion of what you really even are."

"Maybe this is a ghastly question," said Belex. "But you've never done an autopsy on a Reckless after they die?"

"No, no," she said quickly. Then she looked at Hilkiah. "Right?"

"We've been sorely tempted but no."

"The Oracle," said Belex. "The Oracle might be able to tell you what's inside me that could harm you."

"Hilkiah?" Aurilena looked at him as he fluffed up one of his monstrous eyebrows with a finger.

"I believe you've had enough of that place for some time. Why don't we send someone in to do that task?"

"I need to be there. Some of us are wired a little differently than others, so to speak," said Belex. "The Oracle will need to examine me."

"You assume this can be done," said Hilkiah. "This seems a strong presumption from a stranger to this land."

Belex nodded. "Yes. I assume it can be done."

"What are we waiting for? It's like getting the autopsy without the mess," said Hilkiah. "How delightful."

But when they did so, the results were less than satisfactory. When Belex placed his hand on top of the Oracle, the device scanned his DNA and was indeed able to provide general information on Belex's physiology but not much more.

Aurilena and Hilkiah learned that Belex shared much with them—all the basic organs, for example—but that his brain was significantly enhanced with microscopic circuitry made from living tissue. His blood carried a wide variety of nanobots and medibots that performed a variety of tasks, some of them known to the Oracle, some of them not. He was covered with a layer of armor that interacted with his skin and the rest of his body. The armor consisted of a thin, almost invisible membrane impenetrable to basic weapons, such as swords and knives. A ridge containing a dazzling array of micro circuity and nanochips crested his back and the top of his head. There were also extendable blades made from a boron nitride compound concealed within his forearms. The Oracle explained that these augmentations had begun centuries ago via gene manipulation but were now inherited at birth. The Gath, said the Oracle, was truly a separate species of hominid.

It was all quite ghastly to Aurilena, but she also found it incredibly mysterious and interesting.

"There have been mishaps," said the Oracle in answer to a question posed by Hilkiah. "One such mishap occurred 742 years ago when a criminal element was able to sequence and infect the genes of a large percentage of the population in such a way that when they matured, the blood of the target population became somewhat akin to hot lava, causing a large number of fatalities."

Aurilena wanted to know more about this criminal element but not enough to ask. It all seemed too perverse. Every act of evil perpetrated by someone from that race was more hideous than the previous, as if there was some disgusting generational competition. But the motive behind this act tugged at her curiosity gene, if there was such a thing, and she knew she would someday need to find out more about this sardonic crew of Gath felons.

5

When they returned to The Hall of Legions, they huddled in the Tea Room. They gathered and stood at a thick post with a curved shelf attached to it. Hilkiah proposed that perhaps Sherealla's claims were a bluff.

"That's possible, I suppose," said Belex. "That could make her a failsafe."

"What?" asked Aurilena. "What, dare I ask, is a failsafe?"

"A failsafe," said Hilkiah. "Interesting." He looked at Aurilena's furrowed brow, which showed the hurt of again experiencing the betrayal of her friend but decided to plod on. "A failsafe is the plan to use when all else fails. If, in other words, Belex fails to execute the plan that has been assigned to him."

"Fails to execute the plan to execute me? Nice. And why me, by the way? What did I ever do to her?"

"It's not what you've done," said Hilkiah. "It's what you are capable of doing. Although how the Gath could know this about you is yet another mystery. I am your teacher, and I am the only one who knows the depth of your talents."

"That is why she is here, I think. Sherealla, I mean," said Belex. "She was sent here to infiltrate, get to know the most powerful young magician and try to influence her, possibly kill her, but maybe not. Maybe just influence her. Maybe just use her to get to someone else."

Hilkiah said, "One wonders if it is strictly a coincidence that the most talented young magician also happened to stumble upon Sherealla in the Wandering City." Belex and Aurilena looked at Hilkiah.

Aurilena rolled her eyes. "I'm not the most talented. If I try to conjure a feather for my hat, I end up with a chicken on my head."

Belex smiled warmly at that. Hilkiah roared with laughter.

"Anyway, Sherealla. She's always been so contrary," said Aurilena. "I just thought it was her personality. It was one of the things I loved about her. She never backed down from an argument with me. Ha. I thought that was so awesome."

"The curious thing here is that you have had multiple opportunities to kill Aurilena," said Hilkiah to Belex ominously. "If the Oracle showed us one thing, it is that we know you are considerably stronger than anybody here in Moria."

Belex stammered as he spoke in a whisper. "I could never hurt a hair on her head," he said as a tear escaped from one of his eyes. "No matter how many chickens choose to roost there."

She laughed at this. "You sure were ready to when we first met. If not for Sherealla, in fact, I don't think I could ever have gotten you on that horse."

He shook his head. "That seems so long ago."

"Yeah," she said, "like a week."

"How long are you going to stay mad at me for what my people did?"

"Children!" said Hilkiah. Their simultaneous looks toward him indicated they were insulted by that reference.

"On some level? Probably forever," said Aurilena.

Belex opened his palms, lifted his hands in the air a bit, and slapped them back onto the shelf in front of him. "What I say stands. I will never hurt you. And I won't let anyone else from The Homeland hurt you, either, including Sherealla."

Aurilena nodded and looked into his eyes. "I know. I do believe that. Foolishly maybe. But I do."

"Well, then," said Hilkiah, "that is settled. Now on to our plot. How do we proceed? For once, I'm a bit scant of ideas."

"Just play it by ear," said Belex. "First, she has to finally show up. Then, we just act as if everything is normal."

"But it isn't," said Aurilena. "Just in the time she's been gone, you've suddenly turned into a pal to us and a traitor to Gath. You're on our side now. You've proven that to me." She thought about that a moment and stood on her toes for a second as she said, "I think. Anyway, if that's what I'm seeing, then it'll be obvious to her."

"You must somehow assume your previous positions," said Hilkiah. "Confrontation, affrontery, these must be your attitudes toward each other."

"It's not that simple," said Aurilena, looking embarrassed. "She knows that, umm . . ." She seemed hesitant to proceed.

"Yes?"

"Well, that I had a slight crush on him," and she looked away from the two of them as Belex smiled.

"I knew it, you little tart!" he said.

"Hey!" she yelped. "Emphasis on the word, slight, ego boy."

"I'm afraid this is not an area where I can provide great expertise," said Hilkiah, standing up, "as the intricacies of these youthful dalliances somewhat exceed my current abilities. I trust that you two can work it out satisfactorily. As for me, I am ordering an exponential callup of guard duty across the city. I doubt this will add to her suspicions, given that we've just been visited by a member of the Gath."

With that, he flipped at his robe and walked off.

CHAPTER VII

1

"It's not going to work, you know. This whole charade of acting like we are still enemies," said Aurilena to Belex after Hilkiah left them alone. They had left the Hall of Legions and were walking alone in the city, keeping an eye out for Sherealla.

"I know."

"I'm not sure I understand the point of it, anyway," continued Aurilena. "Besides. I'm a terrible actress."

"I don't enjoy bickering with you, anyway, so it's fine with me."

"I'm so frustrated about Aldeberon."

"That was random. What made you think of that now? For what it's worth, I thought that it was a neat trick. Even if I wasn't much in the mood for failed Wiccan magic craft."

She ignored the snark. "I don't know what brought it on. I just want to get out of here. Don't you?"

"I just got here."

She smiled at that. "It's just that it was so not what I was trying to do. I wanted to take you someplace cool."

"It was definitely not cool there."

"You know what I mean."

"Yeah."

"It's what I get for trying something so new to me, I guess."

"Maybe you can think of another place we can go? To destress a little?"

She shrugged.

"Before you found me after my crash, my mind . . . it was all fragmented, but I kept thinking of these acting roles," said Belex, "and one I remember was as a king. I don't remember much about it, and I can't even say it's really my memory, and not, you know, implanted. But the background of the stories involved castles and these old, enchanted lands from before time really even began."

"Shakespeare," she smiled. "I've read some at the Library of Ezra, using the Oracle."

"Yes! That's the name of the playwright."

"It's just about the only literature we have of the ancients," she said sadly. "I've looked."

"Not many literary works from those people have survived," said Belex, as if in explanation.

"We can transport back to the Oracle and find the settings of the plays on a map, and we can go there."

"That's the only way? To go back to that Oracle?"

"I don't know how else to travel there. I need the latitude and longitude."

"Ah. Try another way."

"What? Like what way?"

"I don't know. You're the magician."

She considered this and thought deeply about the plays she had read. She remembered a delightful title, *The Merry Wives of Windsor*. She closed her eyes and felt her hand grasp his more firmly. She thought she heard Belex's voice: *I know the young gentlewoman; she has good gifts*. And then they were there.

Aurilena and Belex visited an old castle in England that had been abandoned by its inhabitants thousands of years ago. It was covered in huge swaths of what Aurilena told Belex were "a gardener's challenge." Its walls were green and lush, with an impossible variety of plant life extending every possible way out and up from the sides of the walls. There were climbing roses, bougainvillea, passion vines, and an assortment of creeping bushes and plant life.

"There is a brick wall behind all of this," said Aurilena, pointing to a wall of the castle.

"Where?" he asked.

Aurilena shrugged.

"Can't we just pull away some of the plants to look for it?"

Aurilena shook her head. "We can't touch anything. We're not really here."

As they approached the castle, a wall became discernable, its stone covered in plant life.

Aurilena told him it was once known as Windsor Castle. She glanced at Belex mischievously when informing him and said with a shrug, "Of course, if you were on your stove net, you'd know that." Belex could see, to the left of the wall, a large oval tower covered in a wild mixture of vines and roses, the latter of which had found their way to the top somehow and sprouted magnificently into a rainbow of colors, some as tall as trees.

"Are we in real time?" he asked quietly, awed by the splendor.

Aurilena looked at him. "Huh?"

He shrugged. "I mean, I dunno." And he smiled at her. "Is it today here? Or is this some other time? Like in the future? Or the past?"

"Oh. I dunno. I don't know how this works. I wish I could ask Seth."

"I wish I could change that past for you. If I could do magic, it's what I'd do."

"It's just that he'd . . . he'd know the answer is all." She didn't seem to want to talk about it.

"Okay."

"Come on," she said. "There's so much more to see."

He grabbed her wrist and looked at her. "I like it here."

Aurilena shook her head. "It's not any different than a few thousand other ruins your people left behind."

That made him quickly let go of her wrist. She wanted to take back her comment when he looked away, but it was too late.

Then she discovered a possible save opportunity.

"A hundred million gardens, I should have said."

He glanced up suspiciously. He didn't respond.

"I'm just saying."

"Okay, so?"

"So, I'm thinking, you guys torched the planet, hid off in your little gizmo hide-away, and lo!"

"Lo?" his already arched eyebrows arched even more.

"Lo. And behold. I think that's how it goes. Anyway, lo, look! There's a garden in the middle of the mess. I mean . . ." she knew how confused she sounded. She was still an emotional wreck after learning about the exterminations. "You left all these beautiful gardens. Look at this one! It's a splendid one. Look! It crawls up the walls of what was probably a dungeon or something before either of our species existed. See? Improvement!"

Belex laughed loudly.

"What?"

He put his hand against his mouth and chuckled some more and, to his embarrassment, snorted as he said, "Before either of our species existed."

"This is funny?" Aurilena asked defiantly, without the question mark in her voice.

He bumped his shoulder against hers, which surprised her. "Sorry," he said. "But the people who made the dungeons? Lena, those were *your* people." This made him sad suddenly, as if he had been hurt by his own words. "Okay, well, maybe *and* mine. I mean, I may not have it right exactly. But those castles have histories. Some crass anger rode through peoples' veins in those days. I'm sorry. I don't even know what, exactly, happened. My history nodes are pretty fried. But it was our shared history. The history of both our people, before things changed." He looked at her, wishing he hadn't hurt her feelings.

"Before the exterminations," she said.

"The last of them, yes. Can we sit down for a minute?" he pleaded.

Aurilena nodded.

"I think what happened was that horrible things happened," he said.

"Well, Hilkiah says that's the human tale. Anyway, continue."

"I can't. I don't know anything." He began to tremble and wanted to cry. He could feel something he couldn't identify drive a pummeling weight into his heart and throat. It was sadness, but he didn't know it as such because the emotion was largely unknown to him. Aside from fleeting riffs of disappointment in his life, he had never experienced this outside the realm of his acting, where he had to fake it.

Aurilena put her arm around him. "Hey."

She leaned in against him.

"What's going on?" she asked.

"I don't know," he muttered. "It's being separated from the collective, I guess."

"No. It's more than that. You've been separated awhile now."

He shook his head. "It's just catching up to me, that's all."

"Okay. Just rest for a while. We can leave this place whenever you are ready."

2

With all that had happened, Belex was still encumbered by the distress of not truly knowing who he was. He wondered if cinescape technicians had made a great technological leap. He considered that a possibility, especially given the extreme drama of the events surrounding him, the beauty of this creature Aurilena, and the way she carved his heart like an artist etching a masterpiece that seemed scripted for tragedy.

Was he in a cinescape right now? With the entirety of The Homeland watching? Was Aurilena the lead actress? What was he supposed to do? He only felt emotions toward her, not toward an audience he couldn't interact with. He didn't know his audience, only Aurilena, an actress of a most peculiar sort, if that's what she was.

She woke him from his contemplations by saying, "I have another planet in mind we can try. It's called Vista." She was recalling a place her brother had told her about, and she was hoping she could get there by remembering the name.

He nodded, which she took for approval, so she worked what memories she could find about her brother's recollections into her thoughts. She had only known the place to be the climatic opposite of Aldeberon. Her brother had described it as a place with cold, howling winds, but that would be good enough to help rescue them from all this awkward tension.

When she shut her eyes and thought about her brother, Aurilena and Belex found themselves on a warm, red planet. She didn't think it was Vista. Thinking about her brother must have brought her to this place, a place he saw but never told her about.

"Lots of trees, funny color though," he said. The sky was a beautiful red hue.

Dark, almost black trees bent toward the sky from their origin in the soil and rose thousands of feet into the reddish air. Each tree arched into another, and it seemed to Belex they could all be lovers. Even the leaves, which were long, flat spears, were black.

"I think they're lovely," she said.

"How did you get us here? Did you remember the location?"

"No. My brother was here. I guess it was enough for me to just think about his travels. Like I said, I'm new at this, but it's getting easier. Okay, well, anyway," she continued, excited and happy to tell the handsome Gath something he didn't know, "Vista is in a star system with six other planets that look a lot like ours. Isn't that crazy?" She didn't mention that she didn't think this was Vista. She didn't want to spoil her victory.

"I guess so."

"So of course, I don't know where on the planet to go. I don't have any information about it so I can't go to a specific place."

"Like a city?"

She nodded enthusiastically. "If it has cities. We've never seen any other civilizations, and my brother, he went to a lot of places. I think it was a little hobby of his to look for civilized life on other planets, but he didn't find any. And anyway, what are the chances that we travel here and randomly end up at a city?"

"If there's intelligent life here, we'd see other signs. Like roads or something. Don't you people spend time searching for things like that?"

She shook her head. "*You* people hardly give us time for that. Most of what we do is about survival. People with well-honed magical skills are forced to do things like acquire or prepare food for the city, heal the sick, and build or rebuild. And then, of course, there's the occasional earthquake, just to make sure we're alert. We had one last year. Not too bad, but it knocked a few buildings down. We don't have a lot of leisure time in Moria."

Belex nodded in understanding. He sighed. "We do. Our machines do all the fighting and heavy lifting for us."

"That's so craven," she said. But she knew it was true because she had seen it firsthand. There was a quiet moment before she said, "I'm sure there's a way to go to a different place here, but I don't know how yet. Someday. I want to learn how to fly after I travel, but I . . ." she shrugged. "Well, that's just something for later, I guess. But it's not like I'm trying to really fly. I should be able to do it. It's all in here," she said as she pointed to her head.

"And wherever Magic is stored," added Belex faithfully. "But hey, I have an idea. For exploring this place. See that hill over there? On the horizon."

She nodded happily.

"Take us there. And then, from there, we can go somewhere else."

"Like hopping from place to place."

"Yeah. Planet hopping."

"Sure, why not?" She took his wrist, and they went to the top of the hill.

Ahead of them, instead of tall, arching trees, they saw dark gray meadows filled with black pods blanketing a series of gently sloping hills. "They look like big black lima beans," said Aurilena. They did, although closer pods revealed sets of grooves running vertically along their length. Each pod was two or three times larger than a person. Sets of five or six pods lived within a small nest of thin curling filaments colored like the trunks of the arching trees behind Aurilena and Belex.

"Look!" exclaimed Aurilena, pointing to the far horizon. A flock of winged creatures approached. The flock resembled a gliding, soaring bas-relief, nearly matching the color of the sky. As the flock flew over the meadow of pods, Aurilena felt her body shudder as one pod and then another launched itself into the flock, then snapped back down as if pulled in harshly by a leash. The pods all seemed to be talking to themselves in some hasty, bizarre language.

The only reaction within the flock seemed to be a gaping hole where the pods struck. The flying creatures made no effort to alter course and took no evasive maneuvers whenever a pod hurtled into them. As the flock curled overhead, Aurilena and Belex could see no end to it as it covered the sky.

"Feeding time," chuckled Belex. "This is amazing."

Belex gave her an amorous look that made her uncomfortable. There was something about the way his face blended with the circuitry just under his skin. There was something about the way his broad, muscular shoulders animated the ductile black clothing that wrapped his body like a second layer of skin and made him look like a walking silhouette of outer space in the surrounding air. There was something about the way fiery shocks of blond and red hair erupted from the top of his head like waves of open flame in a dance. Despite what she knew of the Gath, she wanted to explore the furious nest of his hair with both hands.

She said, "Well, unless you're into squirrel hunting, maybe we try another hop."

"Squirrels? An improbability here."

"What improbability?" asked Aurilena.

"The likelihood that one planet will have the same exact set of circumstances that another planet would. Whoa—"

With that, he grabbed her arm. She looked at him, but he was too distracted to react to her.

"I have no idea where that came from," he said.

"What came from?"

"That thought."

"What thought?"

"The exact set of circumstances thought. And I felt . . . a calculation."

"So, wait. Didn't the Oracle basically tell us that you're sort of a computer?"

He looked sad but nodded yes.

"I'm sorry. I don't mean it that way. You're more than that, Belex. You've got one of these, too," and she pointed to her heart. "So maybe," she said in an excited tone, "I was just trying to say that maybe your, what do you call them? Systems? Maybe your systems are turning on? How does that work? Do you know?"

"No," he shrugged. "I don't. Especially since they are basically malfunctioning." He looked down at the ground and then at her. "I guess what I meant was, I don't think there are squirrels on other planets." Then he surprised himself again when he said, "The rules of replication and genetics and the simple randomness of it all would make an exact duplicate of one species on a different planet pretty much a mathematical impossibility."

"Well," she said, "I don't know much about planetary biology. For sure not about how many squirrels are in the universe. But everyone does seem to think I'm hot stuff because I can make animals do what I want," she smiled.

He remembered the sounds of hooves against his brain and the heavy thunder of the ground during those moments when all he could do was sit. What seemed so long ago suddenly reignited his memories.

"I mean, those buffalo? I did talk to them, I guess. I always do. My mind whispers into the air and it's like, whoever is there listens to me. But I wasn't trying to impress you. I was just trying to impress . . ."

"Sherealla," he said.

She laughed. "Yeah. Stupid, huh."

"Why do you try so hard to impress someone who already worships you? Although looking back, knowing what we know now, it does seem she's often, sort of, challenged you."

"This is why it is all so complicated. Well, one reason. Why it hurts, too. Sherealla saved my life. During the one time I can think of when I wasn't able to work with an animal for whatever reason. She doesn't even know how she did it. Does that make any sense to you?"

"It might if you explained it to me."

"I was cornered by a small lion, up there." Aurilena pointed up, and he saw a small stony hill with a large rock sitting on top as the world landscape changed before him. The cat hissed at them, and he grabbed Aurilena's arm. "He's harmless," she said, "not even there. Anyway, the lion was about to tear into me when Sherealla showed up on that bluff over there and shrieked the craziest noise I've ever heard." He then heard Sherealla shrieking. "Haven't heard it since, either. It was so high-pitched, and so loud, my ears hurt. The lion ran off."

"Couldn't you have just talked to it?"

"I did. It was hungry."

"Yikes. So, she did know what she was doing. She was using her systems to make that noise. We can do all sorts of stuff with our vocal cords. You'd be amazed. Or scared, I guess. But not everything we do is awful. Listen," he said. Something came out of him—the voice of a man singing that he only wanted to be on the street where his beloved lived. The song was an ancient recording stored in his system with millions of others for reasons not even Belex knew.

Aurilena could not have known who the ancient singer was, but she loved his lilting voice. She said, "How did you do that?"

"I'm not sure. I guess I've got a built-in music thing going on, but the vocal cord part is easy. Our vocal cords sort of develop in a way that I can replicate any sound I hear." Aurilena stood up and grabbed his hand and lifted it. He twirled her around as the song continued to play.

She couldn't help but smile after the twirl and said, "Where did you learn *that*?"

"I dunno," he said. "I think you just taught it to me."

Aurilena pushed his chest hard with both hands. "Hey! That may be something, right? I mean, as one of our weapons when dealing with Sherealla? It's creepy but can you replicate *my* voice?"

"I know where you're going with this, but Sherealla would know and our little plan, or more accurately, lack of a plan, would be exposed. There would be just the slightest nuance in my voice, and her systems would notice. A difference between your voice and my attempt to replicate it that wouldn't be noticeable to the average Morian would be noticeable to her."

"You just called us Morians."

"So?"

"So you've never done that. You always call us Wiccans."

"It's not meant as a compliment. Wiccans isn't."

"It's not with us, either."

"Really."

"Yeah, but I'll try to remember to explain later. For now, I want to dance."

He resumed the music, and they danced until finally, much later, he asked, "How do you do this? Go places like this and just make things appear?"

"It's not that much different than what your people are trying to do. We've just found that talking to the universe is easier through things like song and prayer."

"Huh."

"I think, ultimately, I'll be able to go anywhere my imagination allows me to, once I get the hang of it."

That stopped him. "Can you take me to where I was just before I crashed?"

She shrugged. "Well, sit, and let's find out," she said.

"Okay." He sat down.

The ground around her changed and became dusty and barren. He noticed that and that one corner of her mouth formed a smile.

"Close your eyes."

He wanted to open them wider to look at her, but he obliged. As he did, Aurilena imagined her deep black hair dancing in the wind. "Imagine something next to you when you landed," she said next.

"I don't remember landing. I was in a pod. I woke up outside of my pod."

"What's the first thing you do remember?"

He shook his head. "Nothing." He glanced up at her. "Sorry."

"Stop peeking. We found you sitting on the ground. Didn't you notice anything from being there?"

He shrugged. "I noticed that there was nothing around me."

"Nothing." Aurilena laughed. "At all?"

"Well, there was maybe . . . some dirt or something."

"Ah, that's something. What color was it?"

"I can't remember. And something is missing."

"This?" And the ground shook.

Again, he shrugged.

"And this?" They were surrounded by a mass of running buffalo. He realized he wanted nothing to do with this idea, that the concept of going home was something built-in, something like instinct, but that what he really wanted was to stay here. With her.

"So now it's up to you," she said. "To take yourself back to that place."

"That place."

"You want to know what happened just before you crashed. Just before where we just were, right?"

He shrugged. "I can't do it."

They were both sitting on the ground. She slapped him on the knee like an old friend, sarcastically. "Well, I can't either." She raised her eyebrows up and down once and shrugged her shoulders. "I'm sort of done here, I guess."

Belex dusted his knee as he did so, he noticed a few flecks of finely grained dirt flew off his knee in slow motion. Then, Aurilena stood up and looked at him. "I think," she said, almost sadly, "we should get you back to Moria."

3

When they returned to the city, they found they were sitting on a short stone wall along the street. They were both confused by their shared emotions, ones in conflict with everything their societies proclaimed.

"I'm sorry," said Aurilena.

"Me too," replied Belex.

"I have no patience for this," she lamented.

"For what?"

"Any of it, I guess. Just . . . who, what you are. The way I'm starting to feel about you. Your . . . your foreignness. The foreignness of my feelings. The way people look at us when they see us together. The assumptions people make. The . . . just everything."

"I understand. I'm not a patient soul as it is. This is an odd situation for someone like me to try learning patience. And I'm like a newborn, just as a bonus. Imagine all your instincts stripped away. That's basically what has happened to me. To you, me being disconnected from stoven.net just makes me more like you. I guess that appeals to you. But to me, it's like having every fundamental part of survival taken from me. For better or worse, my systems are designed to provide me with the most basic assistive functions. They affect everything from my ability to walk and talk to the simple act of sitting. I know how weird that must sound to you, but it is my biology. If I was born this way in my land, I'd be discarded for my handicaps."

He was right. This wasn't an easy concept for Aurilena to grasp. She wondered why his species had stripped away and rewritten their most basic functions. No wonder Yehoshua had abandoned his people long ago. They had mastered the art of the most severe insult to Yehoshua with their defiant conceit—that they could outperform the industry of nature.

She shook her head and wondered how she could even justify a slight crush on such a creature and cursed the fact that it seemed much more severe than a slight crush.

The street on the way to the Hall of Legions was crowded. Aurilena had somewhat lost track of time and had to think about which day of the week was bringing about such activity. The variety of costumes reminded her that her adventures had clouded her calendar and made her forget that The Festival of Lights and Mirrors had begun. It was one of her favorite times of the year, with much feasting, dancing, and music.

In two days, the city's finest Projectionists would enthrall large crowds gathering at the northern cliffs with images filling the sky. Images of Moria's citizens would randomly beam from horizon to horizon while the crowd watched and cheered when someone they knew appeared. Only the Projectionists were aware of any order of appearance. As she walked along looking at the costumes of passersby, she thought that she'd probably miss the Sky of Projection this year.

When people walked by, most looked away. She was used to being looked at, not only because she was beautiful, but because many people knew who she was—the daughter of a prominent healer who had provided services to many of these people and someone who held formidable powers in her own right. But there seemed to be a changing attitude toward her.

Most powerful magicians were viewed with great reverence because although everybody in Moria had at least a modicum of magical skill, most did not possess the kind of powers that ran through Aurilena Kingston's family line. What was reverence to some was antipathy and jealousy to others; however, this was all now nurtured by Aurilena's association with the Gath boy.

Orpah had influence, she knew. She suspected Orpah of spreading ill will about both Belex and her, fair or not. She knew she'd need to tap into Hilkiah's teachings of humility and restraint if she was to counter sentiments established by centuries of warfare.

Later, she would wonder if she had acquired some of Judith's clairvoyance because as she was thinking these thoughts, a young couple threw an invisible wall at them when they passed her and Belex on a street walkway. Belex's face slammed into the transparent structure hard enough that it would have given any Morian a bloody nose. The couple laughed and walked on.

Aurilena hurled an insult at them but that was all, which showed great restraint, she thought. She hit the wall hard with a palm, and the wall dissolved.

"What was that about?" Belex said, touching his armored nose.

"Ignorance," replied Aurilena.

Aurilena took him back to The Hall of Legions and asked some of the women to show him where to sleep and make sure there were sufficient clean linens.

Eventually, she pointed him to his room. "Well, okay then," she said, tipping forward on her toes slightly. "Well, see you later. Stay out of trouble."

His smile looked a little forced to her, but she understood the emotion. The entire situation was hopelessly awkward. "Okay, bye," he said, and she walked away and down the long hallway. She turned her head around and saw that he was still at his doorway. She smiled, and he waved and went inside.

She decided to hang out with some other girls in one of the celebration rooms. She needed tranquility, if only for a few moments. She entered a room where a few girls were sitting on the floor with their legs crossed, practicing with guitars, flutes, and a small bongo drum. One of them handed her a large guitar, and she grasped it enthusiastically by its neck. She played it well enough that a small crowd gathered. Celebration rooms were a common feature in MagicLand, especially in the sprawling Hall of Legions. They were nothing more than large round rooms, usually with a stone fireplace, where musicians played, small theater groups or comics performed, drum circles formed, prayer vigils were held, or any other number of activities took place.

Aurilena jammed on the guitar, and soon, Sherealla arrived, playing a smaller stringed instrument. Aurilena sighed to herself when she saw Sherealla. Aurilena knew she would play deep into the night, glad that her friend was playing with her despite what she knew. She wondered about that. *Why I am not angrier? What does my spirit know that I don't?*

Aurilena found herself thinking about the strange, young Gath in her life, trying to come up with a song about him. She played songs she barely knew. While her right hand picked at the guitar, she never knew what was coming out. The guitar strings fed her imagination, and her imagination fed the guitar, reflecting her mood. She realized the Great Spirit was infusing her with original musical compositions. A larger crowd gathered around her as she played.

The night wore on until, finally, Aurilena needed a rest from playing so much music. She felt herself stumbling, tired from the long day, the demands of the music in her head, and the night's transition to the morning's first hour. She had been well known for her music, but she had never drawn this kind of attention before. She was thinking about the way the notes came to her when her body slammed against another on the way out of the celebration room and into the wide hallway.

"I couldn't sleep," he said. "Wow, you are so amazing with music."

She said, "All I do is listen. People think it's hard, but it's just you." *And the Great Spirit,* she thought. *I was too tired to notice him in the room?* she wondered. Shrugging, she said, "I mean, I just listen to the rhythm around me, whatever it is." Aurilena was not sure what she was feeling now. Scared? Or thrilled.

She looked up pensively at Belex. It was after midnight, but she was hungry. "Do you want to get something to eat?"

"I'll get something to drink and watch you eat, how's that?" The emotions between them, combined with the tension, felt incendiary, but this process was so foreign to him that he had no idea what to do. The best he could manage was agreeing to accompany her. He wanted to be around her. That was his only awareness.

There was no concept such as courtship in his world. He'd studied it, and it was the subject of numerous cinescapes in which he had performed, but they were invariably tragic comedies, and besides, it wasn't the same because the imagined behavior by the collective was completely different than the reality he was now experiencing.

The process of taking her feelings into consideration while expressing his own almost seemed like a burden, enough for him to want to abandon it completely. But she was, biologically speaking, a magnet, and his blood churned with electrical charges that left him feeling stupid and anxious as they pushed him in whatever direction she lay.

4

Sherealla followed them to the Hall of Feasts. Aurilena acknowledged her coolly. Sherealla's feelings were conflicted and joyless when she saw Belex with Aurilena. He was from the Homeland; so was she, and they were in enemy territory. She assumed his allegiances had changed, like a Reckless. The difference was that in his case, it was because of a silly romantic entanglement that had to end.

She had tried to tell him that it was his mission to destroy Aurilena, but all that had happened, she had observed as she spied on them over the last couple of days, was they had become closer.

She really had no idea why he was here. She assumed he was a spy, but if he was, he was a poor one. Or the best in history. For now, she was going to have to play along and do what Aurilena wanted, which meant playing nice. Belex would know better, of course, because her earlier words to him had instantly transformed him into an enemy, but she had a feeling he'd continue keeping quiet about their conversation. She had tried listening to conversations between Aurilena, Belex, and Hilkiah from a distance using her advanced hearing, but she was unable to separate their conversations from surrounding noise. So far, all she could determine was that Aurilena and Belex's relationship was becoming more romantic. He was not going to hurt her intentionally.

She had also tried looking into her mission background info, but, like Belex, she had been dealing with faulty systems since her arrival. There was indeed a promised infiltrator, and the timing was right for it to be Belex. But nothing else matched.

Sherealla was so fond of Aurilena that the current scenario was making her physically ill. The conflict between her friendship with Aurilena and what had to be done was almost too much to bear. She wanted Belex to leave Moria. She wanted to leave Moria. She wanted to disappear and leave everything and everyone behind. The alternative solution that had filtered through her brain seemed like the only option, although fraught with unknowns. But it was too late to turn back now.

CHAPTER VIII

1

There were celebration rooms along the length of the Hall of Feasts, which was wide enough to fit several rooms inside and contained dozens of tables and eating areas.

Someone was carrying a plate of savory meats and offered some to Belex.

"We're vegans," he muttered to Aurilena.

"Okay."

"No, I mean, we don't eat meat."

"Ya, ya, I've heard about all that. We all have. I mean, us. You know. We here." Aurilena motioned around the hallway, which was full of festival diners filing into various rooms or sitting at tables in the hall.

Sherealla looked at Belex and wanted to say, "No, no this is all wrong. I eat meat all the time. No problem." Dumbfounded and confused, she ran out of the hall to get away from the couple because she realized that seeing them together was making her seethe.

"You don't get it," said Belex to Aurilena. "I can't eat meat because my body won't let me. I mean, it is physically impossible for me to eat the stuff. See? Don't you understand why we can never be together? It's because we are a separate species. We can be two fools in love if we want . . . but . . . it doesn't matter. Two species can't, you know. I don't know how to say it delicately. But anyway, here, check out my teeth . . ."

Aurilena leaned into him and gently put two fingers against his lips, touching each one—the top and bottom—before softly pushing open his mouth as if checking a horse's age. "Yeah, you've got sort of a crunchy wisdom-molar teeth kind of thing going on there. But why is your smile so pretty?" She tilted her head a little as she said this so that locks of her black hair almost covered her coquettish glance.

"It's not *all* molars. Just a couple more than you have." He rolled his eyes, turned his head, and sat down at a table they had chosen.

She looked away, choosing not to sit. "Maybe you still hate me. Hate us," she said sadly, slowly, before she brought her gaze back his way. "Maybe you're pretending to accept me so you can get out of here. Maybe you should grab that candle holder on the table and smack me with it. Get the job done like you're supposed to." She stared at him intently. She sensed that her emotions were getting the best of her, but they needed an outlet. "Go ahead, do it. Sherealla is near enough, she's ready to witness the Gath victory. Now's your chance. Do it and run and get out of here."

Instead, he stood up and approached her and cupped her chin against his hand. She allowed his hand to raise her head a bit. "I'm tired," he said, pushing her chin up so slowly that the world around her stopped completely. He whispered, "I do not hate your people. And I have no words for what I think of you."

Her instinct was to push him back. But instead, she absorbed every molecule of his touch. It seemed as if his hand was pulling her chin directly into her heart. A chill rocketed down her spine as soon as he touched her, as if the wind were speeding through her cortex. "I can't . . . I don't . . ." was all she could muster.

"Ssshh," he whispered, and his lips reached out to hers.

She took his lips and drowned in his surprising tremble, and the fullness of their lips' embrace extended into every aspect of their presence. The sensation of his touch tingled her entire mouth, and she felt the tips of his fingers against the small of her back create a shudder that left her nearly afraid of the next moment.

This was not something either of them planned, even if it was true that she had probably fallen in love with him the moment her eyes fell upon him in the dusty heat just beyond Moria.

And for him, this moment was tantamount to blasphemy against his kind. He didn't have time to determine whether the rebellion over his guilt helped him press against her loins and anticipate her with a fervor that, surely, no part of the collective could understand.

Even though he knew he should not be doing this, a secret thrill shuddered through him. He knew dozens of eyes were watching them here in the Hall of Feasts and that Aurilena's life in MagicLand instantly became more complicated. He felt her hands gripping him as she eased back and looked into his eyes.

Then he saw Sherealla watching from behind a door. His body felt like it was seized by an enemy. He pushed Aurilena away and ran toward Sherealla as a long, thick needle extended out of the top of his wrist. Sherealla, looking panicked, turned to run, knocking someone over as she ran for the kitchen in hopes of finding a weapon. Belex raced to catch up to her and turned into the kitchen after her.

He leaped over two long cutting tables, showing the agility of a big cat, and fell upon Sherealla with a predator's dive that sent her sliding across the floor for several feet, Belex on top of her, his arm cocking back to drive the needle into her neck. But before he could, she was gone, leaving Belex prone on the floor, his hand still cocked and ready to attack but with nothing to strike.

"Lena!" Belex bellowed, striking his other hand against the floor. She came running to him, telling him she hadn't made Sherealla disappear.

He jumped off the floor and frantically looked around, his head rotating, his eyes searching. Someone tried to detain him, but Belex shoved him in the chest with one hand, and the man flew back into a table as if he was a stuffed animal thrown across the room by a child. The table contained piles of dirty dishes, which noisily crashed to the floor. Belex ran outside the kitchen and pushed a few onlookers out of the way as he raced out of the Hall of Feasts and then the Hall of Legions.

His feet carried him swiftly to the library, where he easily overpowered two guards and ran to the Oracle, which was already glowing brightly. Sherealla saw him approach and ran to face him, making Belex wonder what was suddenly emboldening her. Something she was doing with the Oracle, no doubt.

She laughed. "So, I'm no use to you now, am I, assassin?" Her eyes were lit up like candles and a beam of energy was pouring out of the Oracle into the back of her head. Her irises wavered like flames and a voice, not hers, hissed out her mouth, "You sad, pathetic creature. Look what you've done." Out of her eyes, a ray of light projected onto the floor and revealed a hologram of Belex and Aurilena's kiss. The hologram was about twice the real size of them, making it easy to see Sherealla's next demonstration. The hologram zoomed into their mouths, then to a small drop of saliva. Magnification of that drop showed what must have been millions of moving particles. "Those are in her bloodstream now, and oh, it hurts!" Then Sherealla shrieked in the same way she did so long ago when the lion was poised to attack Aurilena.

"Lena!" she cried into the chambers of the library. "Lena!"

Then her head snapped back and forth, and the hologram disappeared along with the stream of light emitted from the Oracle. Her eyes were filled with tears, but she was smiling. "You did it, assassin. How did I not know that was the plan all along? What is wrong with me? How stupid can someone be? I thought I could stop it. I thought I could stop *me*. I raged against everything—me, you, even her. And I thought if I controlled it, decided how she would die, then I could stop her from dying. But there was no way to stop the mission. I was fooling myself. I was literally programmed to guide you into killing her."

Belex glared at her in a rage and swiped at her with a fist, but she was too fast. She jumped and ran up the nearest wall on all fours. Belex realized that she possessed technology far beyond his. He certainly couldn't climb walls. He seemed unable to control his decision-making process. His rage was directed toward what she said he had done to Aurilena, but he seemed unable to act on that. He felt no actual emotion toward Sherealla, only a directive to kill her moved him. It wasn't about desire. It wasn't about anything. He knew at this moment of no reason to kill her, only that he was unable to take any action that didn't lead to her death.

She jumped from wall to ceiling, taunting him. "I could keep you here for weeks if I wanted to, with you chasing me." she said. "I know exactly who you are. What you are. You're nothing but an old-fashioned computer program like the ancients used to make. Drop a coin into the machine and play. That's what children did in the ancient days," she snarled. She jumped to another wall as he approached. "And the machine was programmed to do just one thing, and it couldn't do anything else if it wanted to, just like you. You'd like to go check on Aurilena right now, wouldn't you? Go see how your sweetheart is doing? But you can't. You need to catch me first. You can't control your body because it's not yours." He ran to her and jumped up, his right hand almost seizing her ankle, but she sailed to the ceiling and hung down to taunt him some more. "It's okay, assassin; I feel bad, too. She was my best friend long before you stole her from me."

Belex tried a running start and nearly reached her, but again, she bounced to another wall.

"So sad you are. I can just imagine how much you are hurting. Maybe almost as much as me, but I doubt it. I mean, I take some comfort in knowing it wasn't me that killed her. Why do I feel so delighted but sad at the same time, assassin? I don't understand. Oh, assassin, it does hurt. Follow me, assassin!" She bolted out of the room and rolled into the Oracle, which didn't waver at all, then she bounced up and into another room, Belex close behind.

On and on they went, from room to room in the library, Sherealla bounding in impossible ways across hallways and walls and ceilings and floors, Belex haplessly in pursuit, his fist breaking into walls and tall stacks of old dusty books that flew apart and disintegrated as he hit them. Guards chased them helplessly as they flew about the interior of the building.

"Between the two of us, assassin," she bellowed at one point, "we will have destroyed all the knowledge of Moria in no time!" And she continued her random series of escapes.

2

Aurilena guessed quickly where they were headed, so she called for a guard to inform Hilkiah and brought several more guards with her as she went outside. "Horses," she said to the guards, who quickly rounded up their horses from the Legions stable and joined her as she rode to the library. It didn't take long this way, and she dismounted and motioned for the guards to follow her as she moved inside. She saw a couple of unconscious library guards and assumed the rest were occupied with the chase.

She spied Sherealla and Belex and was stunned at the sight of Sherealla, clinging to the walls like she had suction cups on her limbs. Watching her, Aurilena thought maybe she did, of sorts, have just that. She saw Sherealla running for the Oracle and believed she must be trying to destroy it, so Aurilena did something she had never done before in battle. Instead of throwing some kind of repelling force around it or calling forth another kind of magic, she prayed out, "Yehoshua, I ask that you protect the Oracle!"

As Sherealla ran toward the Oracle then seemed to roll into it, she simply bounced off as if she were a rubber ball slamming hard against a wall and careening off into another direction. "That had to hurt," Aurilena said to herself as she watched the chase continue.

Belex seemed to have an irretrievable compulsion to kill Sherealla. It didn't make sense to Aurilena as she watched the two of them wreak havoc in the library. The damage to books was making her angry, so she asked Yehoshua one more thing: to save the library from further destruction.

At that instant, all the lights in the library blinked off, and the oxygen in the building began to disappear as if being sucked out through the windows. Sherealla was the first to gasp as she fell to the floor. Then Belex, who ran out of the room of their latest battle and found his way to the stairway at the end of a hall, working his way down, gasping for whatever breath he could find from the disappearing air. He barely made it outside, crawling as he found the door, Aurilena dragging him out the last few feet. He looked at her in surprise, then turned to get up. When he pushed up on his arms, he collapsed back down, unable to get onto his feet.

"Where is she," he gasped.

Aurilena shook her head. "I don't know, but if I did, do you think I'd say? What is happening? Why are you doing this?"

Belex struggled to his feet, stumbling, his arm steadying himself against the granite walls of the library. He tried to reenter through the door, but he was blown out of the doorway as if a giant was blowing air through a room-sized mouth from the inside. He landed on his back several feet away and tried to get up again. He found the going even more difficult than before, but eventually, he managed to pull himself up.

"Belex!!" shouted Aurilena, but it was as if he didn't hear her, and he ran to the door. This time, he seemed to bounce off, even though the door was wide open and there was nothing to force such a bounce.

Aurilena still saw no sign of Sherealla. She called out to her, but there was no answer. Ridiculously, Belex, meanwhile, was trying to get into the library again through the same door as before. This time as he approached with a running start, a massive flame burst through the door as if it were water being shot through a hose. The long stream of fire blasted at Belex as he approached, sending him scurrying quickly to the side, away from the door to dodge the jet of heat and flame.

Finally, there she was, Sherealla, on all fours, looking badly shaken, crawling out and collapsing prone at the doorway. Belex, shaken and bruised and impossibly exhausted, in Aurilena's view, started making his way toward Sherealla, his eyes focused on her as Aurilena tried again to call out his name. Sadly, she asked Yehoshua to protect Sherealla, afraid for Belex at once, wondering how he'd survive any assault he tried—now that she was calling for Yehoshua's help.

Belex limped toward Sherealla with his hands clenched. As he neared her, Elijah appeared from around the corner and bounded over to him. Belex's body shook convulsively for a moment, and he looked toward the dog. "Elijah!" he exclaimed as he bent down to pet the ecstatic animal. The dog ran over to Aurilena, and Belex looked up and seemed to finally notice her. "You," he said, as he looked around, "what's going on?" He looked up at the grand structure that was the library. "Why are we at this place again?"

Aurilena cried with joy and ran to him as he opened his arms for her. She took his embrace. Then, she pushed away and ran her fingers against his cheeks. "You're back," she said and hugged him again.

He took her hands and looked over at Sherealla. "Wow, it was like I was being . . . no, Lena. I *was* programmed to kill her. Because . . ." he gulped.

"What? Because what?"

"Lena, I," and he closed his eyes.

"You gotta start talking to me. You can't keep hiding things from me."

"I'm not gonna hide this. It's just really hard to say. But that kiss. That kiss may have killed you."

"I'm fine. Look at me, Belex, I'm fine. Right as rain. See?" She let go of his hands, twirled around once as if in dance, and looked back into his radiantly blue eyes.

Belex was simultaneously trying to determine why he had been trying to kill Sherealla and take in the presence, the wonderful aura, of Aurilena at the same time. He could only marvel at her every movement. He wanted to ask her to twirl around again for him, it moved him so.

He understood because it was the only motivation from an algorithmic standpoint that made sense, that his kiss triggered a subroutine in his bodily matrix that commanded him to kill Sherealla. It was a basic algorithm. A simple, ancient "if, then" statement originally conceived by the ancients a few thousand years ago, before the species branched off. *If* he killed Aurilena, or, more specifically in this case, once he injected her with the substance that would lead to her death, *then* kill the other infiltrator from The Homeland because she was no longer necessary and may pose a risk of some kind. No reason, of course, was given to him, nor did it need to be. It was a simple command, and The Hunter Collective didn't bother with explanations. Somehow, Aurilena had just defeated the command with magic, which astounded him.

Not only was he dealing with this simple exploration of logic, but he was buried in various emotions, too. There were the emotions of his growing feelings for Aurilena, feelings that were so strong, they frightened him to his core, and there were the feelings of betrayal he felt from his own kind, who saw fit to use him without his knowledge as a conduit for her destruction. He didn't consider that he may have been sent as a willing participant, that the accident could have damaged his systems enough to alter his state of being, along with his memories and motivations.

"You don't understand," he said to her. "When I kissed you, I think a stream of nanobots went into your system. They're designed to kill you."

Aurilena drew back from him. "How—how . . . do you know this," she stammered.

"In—inside," he stammered back. He held many thoughts but was only able to talk to her slowly as emotions crowded his throat and prevented him from talking quickly or coherently. "Inside, we . . . me and her." He looked at Sherealla, who was still on the ground but clearly breathing, which ended another thought, that he had stopped chasing her because she was dead. "When I found her, she was tapping into the Oracle. Doing, I dunno. Doing something."

"Okay, okay so what? Like, what?" Aurilena seemed frightened, and Belex could understand why. She was so young, too young to die.

"I dunno. Sorry, just, that's not the important part right now. I mean, it may be important and maybe we can find out, but here's the important part." He described what he saw in the hologram that Sherealla produced.

"Wow," Aurilena said. "Just wow. You really did it." Tears blanketed her cheeks. He tried to walk to her and comfort her, but she said, "Get back away from me," and she sat down on the ground and covered her eyes as she sobbed.

Belex watched helplessly, heartbroken.

He let her sob for a moment, then decided he was going to sit next to her; he didn't care how much she hated him right now.

"I'll do anything I can to stop this, and if anything can be done, I'll find it," he said as he sat beside her. "I don't care if it kills me. If someone needs to dissect me while I'm still alive to find out how to fix this, I swear that I will cheer them on to make it so. I won't let you die unless I die trying to save you first."

She continued to cry, more slowly now, and then finally stopped and wiped her face with a sleeve.

"I'm not afraid of death. None of us are. We all know we can perish at any time. I learned that a long time ago as I watched pieces of my brother get sucked into the sky by a stream of black death. It's that," and she chuckled sardonically, "a kiss would be my undoing. It's such an insult toward love."

Belex felt buoyed by this, and his own tears became tears of happiness. "Is that what you call this?"

She looked at him through swollen eyes, "What do *you* think, stupid?" And she smiled warily.

He looked at their surroundings for the first time in a while. Some guards were milling about, mostly tasking themselves with keeping people away. The dog had taken residence on the sidewalk, licking his fur and chewing on the nails of his hind feet.

"I don't think I even know what love is. But if love means you'd die to keep someone else alive, I guess this is it." He took her hand. "I'd do anything for you. Anything."

"It just freaks me out," she said as she looked at his hand. "A little. You know?" She turned his hand over and studied the low but certain ridges that extended from each knuckle into a protrusion on the back of his wrist, which in turn sent a series of thin ridges through the top of his forearm. His sleeve covered up the rest of his arm, but she guessed the series of ridges continued up his arms and then to further destinations, all designed to enhance his physical and mental capabilities, and all designed to make him better than her. She knew this should make her angry. In fact, it did make her angry. That these beings played God in this way was an affront to Yehoshua, an insult to his handiwork. Every time she felt the anger, though, she would look at him, and it would dissolve in the elixir of this impossible endearment.

And if the very purpose of his kind wasn't enough to make her flee this improbable, illogical pairing, then what about the fact that he had just tried to kill her? *If that doesn't stop a woman from falling in love,* she thought with some dark humor, *nothing will.* And so, she thought, as she held his hand, nothing will.

"I mean, our kiss. It was, designed in a lab almost, wasn't it? Designed to kill me."

"I don't know what their intent was. But I know mine," he said.

Belex looked at her hand and was amazed at the extent of the journey such a simple thing could take him. The smoothness of her skin captivated him. He found himself following the contours of her fingers, wrist, and knuckles and becoming indescribably lost. He discovered that science could not describe the essence within her startling composition. If their world ended with this as one endless moment, he would not object, for he was breathless and could imagine remaining so.

"I mean," he said, "I do know their intent. But I don't think they really considered that the delivery would be through a kiss. I suspect they had other things in mind."

He let go of her hand and a long, terrifying shaft shot out of one of his fingertips. It was shaped like a thin cylinder with what looked like an impossibly sharp point at the end. The shaft sent shudders through her every cell, and she could feel her body tremble. The catalyst for the fear wasn't the weapon itself so much as the intimacy through which it could be drawn—that this boy, this young man that she had become so drawn to, could deliver a fatal jab to her at any time.

"We've heard about these things," she said. She slowly slid two fingers along its length. She thought about all the times he could have used it on her, remembered wondering if he'd wield one while riding behind her on her horse. "Why the nanobots then?" she said. It didn't make sense. He could kill her in an instant with a weapon like this. Could have killed anyone, including Hilkiah, although, in Hilkiah's case, Belex would have had to contend with much more formidable magical powers, so Aurilena was able to see how that may have ended badly for her newly beloved.

"Yeah, good question."

"That," and the thought expressed itself immediately, "and the fact that I'm not only not dead yet, but am—"

"Right as rain," he smiled warmly.

That made her laugh. "Yeah," she giggled, appreciating how he remembered what she had said before.

"In other words," said Belex, "maybe the nanobots have some other purpose. Because yeah, you're right, to some extent. Unless they knew we'd fall for each other somehow. Then it's back to the original thing."

"You know you can say it, right?"

"Say what?"

"Instead of saying 'falling for each other,' you can say the word. It doesn't kill."

He laughed. "Oh, no?"

"I'm serious."

He thought about that—thought about when it happened. "I think I fell in love with you the first time I tried to kick the teeth out of your mouth," he laughed.

"Oh, dear," she smiled and kissed the back of his hand. "That should be safe, no?" she asked, looking into him.

"Should be," he smiled as the steely spike hid itself.

She didn't really want to change the subject, but if his original theory was correct, they were on an unknown deadline. "Even if the nanobots don't have another purpose," she said, "then why aren't I dead?"

"Dual purpose maybe. Maybe the Hunter Collective wants something else, first."

"Belex." The next thought alarmed her. "Can they program *me*?" She shuddered at that thought.

"I don't think so. Consider my brain. It's different than yours. It has all the usual biological components, but it has, for lack of a better word, machinery added to it. My kind, we'd hate that word, but that's what it is. And that machinery is designed to accept inputs from other sources. When augmentation—that's what we call these enhancements—when it started, we had all kinds of problems. It all had a rough start, but scientists were determined. I can't draw on many specifics, not without help from stoven.net, but I do know that our early history saw a lot of difficulties related to augmentation. Mostly hackers."

"Hackers? What's that?"

"This was before the species branched off. Really, it was your ancestors, too, who were involved in this process of augmentation."

"Bah, were not," she said. She knew this wasn't true. She knew that resistance to the Gath began at their inception. Plus, she didn't have a single inorganic wire in her body.

"Okay, whatever. But early on, people would get tiny chips implanted in their brains, and because they accepted inputs, all someone needed to do to get in was discover the necessary protocols, and *boom*, they were in."

Aurilena considered that for a moment. The optimist in her wanted to suddenly believe that the evil she saw in the books the Oracle showed her was a result of these "hackers."

"You're saying someone could go into someone's brain and tell them to do stuff?"

"Yeah. It still can happen, but security protocols pretty much prevent it."

"Pretty much?"

"Yup. Pretty much."

"Why would anyone allow an entire species to be made vulnerable like that? Do you know how crazy that sounds?"

"It was a desperate, dying world. That's my only guess. I'm unclear on that, honestly. My memories are too incomplete. But think about it. The Oracle told us the motivation for all that loss was that something was happening in the world that made life impossible for most people. There were just too many of them."

She found it all incredibly disturbing. "Too many . . . people?" she groaned.

He nodded. "Anyway, no, I think you're safe from that, at least. You may have the, hmm, I don't know what to call them. You may have the command modules running around your system trying to find a way to tell you to do something, but there's no receptor for them."

"That you know of."

"Yeah, that I know of. Unless they've found a way to do it all biologically. That was never a huge focus of research for us, though."

"But there were rumors that a group of beings exist for whom that *was* a focus of research. The Oracle was telling us that."

"Just a rumor and nobody in my homeland."

She was skeptical and said so. "Okay," she said. "Enough talk, we need to—"

At that moment, she heard a groan. Sherealla was waking up, making a mild effort to get away from some guards attending to her, but she was tied up. Aurilena hadn't even noticed that guards had strapped her onto a gurney and were apparently waiting for someone, maybe Hilkiah.

She walked to one of the guards. "How is she?" she asked.

The guard answered, "No major injuries on the outside. A few cuts and bruises from her antics are about all. She's coming to now. We're waiting for Hilkiah to send for her."

"He better hurry. Hilkiah's the only one who can stop her from disappearing again," said Aurilena.

Sherealla's eyes opened slowly. She glared at Aurilena. "Ugh," said Aurilena, "just get her out of here and away from me now. Please," she added emphatically, hurt and disgusted. She tried to cast a spell to prevent Sherealla from disappearing but had no idea if it would work.

Aurilena grew impatient and didn't want to wait for Hilkiah so, hoping for the best, she galloped back to the Hall of Legions with Belex holding on. Several guards stayed behind to watch over Sherealla until Hilkiah could summon her.

When Aurilena and Belex dismounted, Aurilena said, "We really need to get you your own horse, or poor Remembrance is going to be a memory." She patted Remembrance on the back and kissed his head saying, "I'm sorry, sweetheart."

She walked Belex to his room in the Hall of Legions and asked him, "How are the accommodations?"

He shrugged. "They change."

"I'm sorry? What do you mean they change?"

"Somebody is playing tricks on me. Every time I go into the room, it looks different."

That made Aurilena laugh. "Sorry, but that's kind of funny," and she laughed again.

"I actually assumed it was you."

She kept laughing. "I so often wish I could be that devious," she smiled. She wanted to go into his room to see what it looked like and to be able to compare it to the next time. But she wanted to go there for other reasons, too, so she said, "See ya'," and walked off. She turned around after reaching the end of the hall and saw that he was still standing at his door. She smiled, wondering how many times they'd repeat that episode, as he waved politely and turned into his doorway and disappeared.

3

Aurilena returned to an empty home. Her mother was probably on a healing somewhere. She didn't bother contemplating where her dad might be. She grabbed a snack and skipped off to her room, strangely happy considering all the dangerous circumstances surrounding her. When she finished her snack, she lay down on her bed and began to ruminate over her condition.

Aurilena had not often practiced the art of what everyone called transportation, partly, she thought, because Hilkiah had made her frightened of the powerful magic when he told her, "When the subject is sent to another place, that subject becomes something else."

She found that disturbing because it suggested that people who were transported were reconstituted, their atoms rearranged into a completely new person. That didn't seem like an attractive prospect to her. The result of that comment was that she had done it rarely since that awful day when she lost her brother, and even then, she wasn't fully aware of how she did it.

She was never afraid to say how she felt about such things to Hilkiah, so she often called him a hypocrite for using the process "pretty much as you please," while lecturing her on letting Yehoshua decide on what magic was suitable for any given situation.

"I swear, Sherealla," she remembered saying to her friend, "he uses it whenever he needs to just go down the street a ways."

And Sherealla was never afraid to say how she felt to Aurilena. "Everyone does it, Lena," she had said. "You're the only fool who goes everywhere on horseback."

This recollection of frank talk saddened her. It would take a long time for the thousands of conversations she had with Sherealla to leave her memory.

4

They were about fourteen years old when they were playing a game in Aurilena's room and Sherealla had dared her to try to go somewhere. But Aurilena didn't want to try that. The words from Hilkiah were clear in her mind—that it wasn't she who would return.

"But," Sherealla had said, "Hilkiah does it all the time. Surely your magic is as powerful as his. I think he thinks you are even more powerful than he. I think you are so powerful that it scares him. That's what I think."

"Okay, okay," Aurilena finally relented after several more minutes of persuasion. "Where should I go?"

"Somewhere far!" Sherealla said excitedly, her feet kicking the bed as her legs rocked back and forth.

"But I don't know any far places," said Aurilena.

"Gath. You know Gath."

"That's crazy; they'll kill me."

"But if you get there, you can come right back. Just do whatever got you there. And you can bring me a trinket."

"A trinket!" exclaimed Aurilena. "A Gath trinket! You really are a nutty one, aren't you?"

"All we need's a map. And you can get there, right?"

"I don't know," said a wary Aurilena.

It had been a long summer, Aurilena recalled now, and a weird one. The fog that normally sifted through the Broken Bridge every afternoon had not been its usual resplendent self that summer. And it had been much hotter than in past summers—heat that, according to Hilkiah, was more like the days of the ancients when it was impossible to breathe the fog that rolled in and people died when it did. Hilkiah, of course, was prone to exaggeration. Those days were long ago. Long past.

At first, Aurilena suggested that she simply try to go to the Broken Bridge. "No, no," complained Sherealla. "We've been there. Go to a place you've never been."

"I can ask Hilkiah, but I think he'd say you can't be where you have never been. He's said that before . . . I am sure of it."

"Must you tell Hilkiah everything you do? How will you ever have better magic than him if you tell him everything?"

"I don't need better magic than he has, Sherealla."

Sherealla sighed and folded her arms and stared at Aurilena.

"Okay, already. I'll try Gath. But if something happens to me, you'll always hate yourself," said Aurilena smugly.

"I will, but nothing will happen to you. I know it. You'll be right back. You're the best magician in the land. You just don't know it yet."

"Ha. That I don't. You're right about that. But we need a map. Where can we get a map of Gath? Nobody knows where it is except the Oracle, and I don't have permission to get that kind of information from it. Only Hilkiah does. And besides, he has said that the map information on Gath is vague—that their city is somewhere south. But he says the exact location is unknown."

"He's lying," said Sherealla promptly. "He knows where it is."

"Why would he lie about that?"

"Why do adults ever lie to children? To protect them, is what they will say. Which may be true in this case, but still . . . I say that if we have a map, we can do whatever we want."

"Sherealla. Have you ever heard of the term, 'unintended consequences?' If I'm seen there by the Gath, how do we know what could happen? It's too dangerous. I could put the whole city in danger."

"We have Hilkiah. He can hide the city all over again, like he did last time."

"No, that's not how it works. The city didn't move, it just . . . well, he didn't explain it to me. Somehow the Gath can't see it."

"If that were true, they would've been able to just bomb it—still bomb it—and still kill us all. Why can't they do that? Why doesn't that happen?"

"He says it's some time-space thing. I dunno," Aurilena shrugged.

"Sounds like a bunch of fakery to me."

"You're alive, aren't you? We're alive? The city is whole."

"Frumpf."

"Well, we don't have a map, so it doesn't matter."

"I have a map."

"What? What do you mean you have a map?"

"Just what I said. I have a map. Got it from the Oracle just after I got here."

"When? How?"

"Remember when you brought me here? Then. When they took me to the Oracle? Remember that time?"

"Sort of. But why would you get a map? Of Gath, of all places?"

"Hilkiah wanted to show me where I was. I didn't really understand at the time, about where the Wandering City was and its relationship to Moria and all that. The Oracle said Moria and the land of Gath are all that's left of people on this continent. Just two coastal areas on the continent. One here, along the bay. And one south. Hilkiah told me the rest of the continent was wasteland, with a few bands of remnant tribes here and there. I memorized every inch of the coast."

"And the Devil's Play Yard," said Aurilena, "which nobody seems to ever want to talk about."

Now that Aurilena was recalling this, it dawned on her that the first clue about Sherealla had materialized considerably before she had previously realized.

Sherealla projected the map onto a table in Aurilena's room and pointed. "That's us there. And just a little north, that's the Broken Bridge. And there, just north of there, just across the bay, that's where you found me. In the Wandering

City." It was called the Wandering City because it was susceptible to so many floods, its residents—already a mix of vagabonds and refugees—were rebuilding constantly, and the city itself seemed to move a little with each rebuild.

She pointed to the southernmost point of the Bay of Moria. "And south. Here. This is the Devil's Play Yard. Marauders roam here, some say. And then here, about oh, I don't know, three, four hundred miles, or so. That's Gath." She pointed to land further down the same coast.

"Well, that's easy," thought Aurilena out loud. "Let's try it."

"Let's?" asked Sherealla, startled.

"Yeah, you and me. No reason for me to have all the fun. Here, take my hand."

Sherealla did, and Aurilena closed her eyes and imagined herself at the last position Sherealla pointed to on the map. When she opened her eyes, she saw a crowd of people milling about in strange uniforms. Dozens of objects were flying through the air and cruising around on the ground. She looked at Sherealla, who looked stunned at what she saw.

About a hundred feet in front of them, they noticed dozens of globe-like objects spraying what looked like paint into a circle around a small crowd of people who were yelling something and raising their fists. It appeared to be a containment mechanism because when one of the people inside tried to escape, thousands of tiny objects rose from the containment circle and pushed the individual back with a shock, turning the potential escapee's clothes yellow, the same color as the surrounding circle. The group of people, about fifty individuals, Aurilena thought, cheered wildly when it happened. Aurilena laughed and said to Sherealla, "It's some kind of game!"

Then, they were noticed. The same crowd turned, almost in unison, toward the girls and charged them. The circle suddenly disappeared, and the globes all dashed through the air in their direction.

"We gotta get out of here," said Aurilena, and Sherealla quickly nodded her assent, but it was too late, the people were upon them. One of the globes attacked, and the rest followed suit, dropping what looked like a wire mesh over them. The mesh was nothing like nets she had seen fishers use, even though on first sight, it resembled one in appearance. Aurilena could see through the netting, which appeared to be made from electricity or light as it descended upon the girls like a luminous blanket. Aurilena looked at her lap and then straight ahead.

The net had dropped directly on top of them, but she couldn't see it. It had mysteriously disappeared on its descent. She was sure she saw it fall upon her, but then, it wasn't there, as if her eyes had lied to her. She looked at Sherealla, expecting to see her caught in the same net, but she was also free of any hindrance.

The globes seemed to react to this news as well. Aurilena could see them more clearly now that they were much closer. They were spinning at a high rate of speed while suspended in the air. Several of them emitted sharp beams of light in the direction of the two girls, and when Aurilena looked down, she saw the net on the ground beneath her and the ground explode from the blast from the beam. Shards of material—whatever the ground was made from . . . she couldn't decide what it was—shattered and flew all around her and through her, but she felt nothing.

It was then she realized she wasn't there at all, and neither was Sherealla. She had transposed, not transported, although many people simply called it travel. It was the first time she had done so, and it wouldn't be her last.

She still wanted out, even though she was confident they were safe. She had been so mad at herself for being such a sloppy magician, she recalled. She was also recalling how Hilkiah had said that magic is sloppy, especially when she did it her way.

Hilkiah had been trying for a couple of years to rein her in. "This is not how one does magic, not if one wants to be in truth and gladness," he had said several times. Now that she was remembering this event, she wondered how she could reconcile what good had come out of her most recent prayers to Yehoshua with what she knew she must do to get information out of Gath. *How does one ask for general help when you know precisely what kind of help you need?* she wondered.

And what had been Sherealla's true intent that year?

She decided it was time to find out. As she drifted off for some needed sleep, Aurilena decided it was time for a long talk with her former friend.

5

Sherealla was being held in a small corner room on the third floor of the Hall of Legions, away from almost everything. Aurilena decided to visit her alone and hoped that Hilkiah hadn't placed any blocking spells to prevent her from traveling to Sherealla's location, which seemed unlikely given Hilkiah's spiritual philosophies.

Sherealla wasn't surprised when Aurilena showed up in her room. "Took you long enough," she said.

"Seems like old times," said Aurilena.

"Why are you here? As it were."

"The things I have to say to you, I won't even bother with. There's no point. I can't describe the feelings, and you wouldn't care anyway. But I want to know why. Why did you befriend me? Gath can't kill people without making friends with them first?"

"What makes you think we were friends? Just because we saved each other once? That makes us friends?"

"Save it for someone who doesn't know you better," Aurilena sighed. "No matter. There's no reason to argue with you now. What's done is done. You're a Gath, which means everything you say is meaningless or motivated by the need to exterminate us."

"Just like your lover boy, eh?" Sherealla smiled wickedly. "By the way, how are those bowel movements?"

"Eww, you are, you know what? You always were foul and crass. I don't know what I saw in you. Except maybe I felt a little sorry for that pitiful waif I saw in the Wandering City. So what do I do? I just keep feeling sorry for her, and as she acclimates herself to a *normal* society and finds everyone pretty much can't stand being in the same room as her—that somehow tugs at my heart, and I try like crazy to get people to like you. Then, after all these years of effort, people start to accept you and your snotty little ways, and then you show them why they never trusted you from the beginning. Nice work."

"It was nice work, wasn't it? Thanks for saying so. It wasn't easy being your little puppy dog all those years." She stood up to look out the tiny window overlooking the city. "Especially in this putrid, prehistoric hole in time. So anyway, why'd you come? Just to come down on me? I don't think so. You want something."

"Yeah, I want to know why I'm not dead yet."

Sherealla shrugged. "How would I know? I didn't design this little operation." She looked up at the sky. "They did. Whoever they are." This conversation was considerably more painful than she was letting on. It seemed to Sherealla that her entire life was about keeping things she didn't fully understand from Aurilena, and now was no exception.

"Look, nothing good can happen to you here. You may as well tell me what the nanobots inside me are trying to accomplish since they could have killed me hours ago."

"I told you, I don't know. And I still don't know. Don't get me wrong. I wouldn't tell you if I did know. But, well, you may as well know. I don't know. Maybe they're downloading your consciousness into stoven.net so they can study you."

"They can do that?"

"I doubt it, but who knows? Technology. It's fast-moving. What isn't possible today might be tomorrow. I've been away from my home since I was twelve. You know I left when I was a kid. Right? All my real growing up I had to do here, away from my home." She shook her head and looked down at her feet. "Anyway, who knows what they've come up with during my time away? I mean, just look at me if you need to see how quickly things can change. How different I look than lover boy. Look, ma, no ridges," and she flipped her hand over and felt the back of her neck with her hands. "I'm state of the art." Aurilena smelled sarcasm and bitterness with the same nose that could sniff out an animal's fear.

"It's because you're not built to fight. You're not a warrior like he is," she said, shocking herself that she was bragging about Belex being a warrior and wishing she could just keep her mouth shut sometimes.

"Ha, you wish. If you want to see how well I can fight, let me go. I'll be happy to give a demonstration."

"I'm only interested in the nanobots inside me and what they are up to."

"We'll find out soon enough. Be patient." Her newest smile seemed sardonically bitter to Aurilena, who wondered how long this hostility had been the nucleus of Sherealla's feelings toward her. If she were able to go back in time and replay scenes from their relationship, would she recognize more of this behavior? Or would she find that Sherealla simply had a dual personality? Either way, Sherealla was proving to be the better actor of the two Gath she now knew so well.

She took some satisfaction in ending their conversation by disappearing without any further reply. Whatever spell she had put on Sherealla was apparently preventing her from a disappearing act of her own. Aurilena was glad for that.

6

Meanwhile, Hilkiah made his way back to the Oracle. He wanted to consult it without the prying eyes of his sweet but naïve young protégé, Aurilena. He summoned it and prepared his question.

"Oracle," he began. "What is the chance, in percentage, that your resources will lead to an event that is dangerous to Moria?"

The chipmunk was gone, replaced by a globe of spinning light.

"The chances of activities reliant on my resources leading to a catastrophic event are currently calculated to be 72.3 percent," the Oracle responded.

Hilkiah stepped back from the glowing entity.

He stepped forward again and asked, "What is the nature of this danger?"

"This information is not available."

He wasn't surprised by this but was disappointed anyway. "Oracle. Who built you?"

"This information is not available," came another unsurprising reply.

These answered more questions than the Oracle could have known, Hilkiah knew. Hilkiah wondered if the Oracle should be destroyed. Such an action would anger Aurilena, who valued the Oracle's information. So did he, for that matter. Would destroying it mean all of their books would be lost forever? They were in poor physical condition, and the only way to read most of them was through the Oracle. Surely, there was another way to solve this problem, Aurilena would say, but sometimes the idealism of youth must be quashed by practicality. The Oracle itself was saying now that its existence represented a high likelihood of catastrophe to Moria. *What good are books if there is nobody to read them?* he thought. He considered the grave possibility that there would be no time to bring this question to the Legions. But it wasn't a decision he was willing to make on his own.

Hilkiah yelled for a guard.

When one arrived, Hilkiah told him to summon Belex. "Tell him it's for a live autopsy," he smiled mischievously.

CHAPTER IX

1

"I don't like the sounds of this at all," said Belex when he met Hilkiah at the front of the library.

"We need to ask the Oracle to do one last thing before I ask the Legions to consider ending its commission," Hilkiah said to Belex.

"End its commission?"

"The Oracle has served us well, but it has been compromised. In fact, the Oracle itself just now alerted me to the fact that there is a greater than seventy percent chance that it will be the agent of our destruction."

"Sherealla," said Belex. "She's been able to upload additional commands into it. That's what she was doing here yesterday, then. But if you're asking me to tell you how to destroy it, I don't know. I don't know if it has any weapons systems for defending itself. It may be as simple as knocking it down."

"The guards told me that Sherealla tried to destroy it and failed."

"That doesn't make sense. If she was uploading data or commands to it, why would she then destroy it?"

"Good point," agreed Hilkiah.

"Can you tell me exactly what the guard saw when Sherealla tried to supposedly destroy the Oracle?"

"No. But I can summon the guard, and we can make that inquiry."

And so they did. The guard described Sherealla's actions in surprising detail, Belex thought. "I remember that," said Belex. "She sort of did this body roll thing into it. It seemed intentional. It doesn't make sense to me. Look, Hilkiah, you seem like you're the last person to make a rash decision. Let's not be so hasty here. Maybe I can find out what she uploaded into her."

"Her?"

Belex nodded. "Seems female to me."

"Hmm. Interesting."

"I can interface with her, maybe. And solve two problems at once. One problem is finding out more about those nanobots I sent into Aurilena. She can analyze them for me, maybe tell us their purpose."

"And the other problem is finding out what Sherealla has been doing."

"Yeah, finding out why the chance of the Oracle doing damage to us keeps going up."

"Ah, good lad—your use of the word, 'us' in this situation."

Belex looked up at Hilkiah, who towered over him with a kindly smile. "Yeah. I guess it just kind of came out. *Us.*" He looked around. "I never would have thought . . ."

Hilkiah interrupted him. "I had no doubt. Let us interface, shall we?"

"There is one thing I miss about the Homeland, though, Hilkiah . . . Gath as you call it."

"What is that?"

"Instant communication. I want Aurilena here."

"I'll send for her. She'll come immediately, I'm sure. But you underestimate us a little and assume your technology is better than ours. We rely on a higher level of technology, one that is out of reach of Gath."

Hilkiah turned away, sat on the floor with his back facing Belex, and closed his eyes. "You are needed here. Do not arrive by horseback," Belex could hear him say. Hilkiah arose and led him into the room of the Oracle.

When they returned to the Oracle's room, Aurilena was staring and waving a hand over the Oracle. She turned to Belex when she saw him.

"Oh, hi!" she chirped. It was the happiest he had ever seen her.

"What's going on," he asked. "Why are you so happy?"

"Ever get an epiphanet?" she asked Belex.

"No, what's an epiphanet?"

"Well, it's like an epiphany, except on a much smaller scale." She raised her hand and measured the air with her index finger and thumb. "It's like this big, whereas an epiphany is like," and she extended both arms out, "wayyyy big. But it's still a big deal. Important."

"And you had an epiphanet?"

"Oh, I most certainly did. I've been all mad at Sherealla, crushed really. But she's just like you. She's an involuntary trooper, so to speak. She gave it away when I was talking to her just now."

Hilkiah gave a disapproving look, knowing that he had told her to stay away from Sherealla, but remained silent.

"She was talking to me about what a rotten deal she got—basically, how she missed her childhood, or most of it or whatever, being here instead of home. And I realized she's not all in on this, whatever *it* is she's doing."

"Yes," said Hilkiah, "she must have some torn allegiances, but don't be too hopeful, I'm sorry to advise."

"I know. I do know that. But, well, it just helps me see that I can move forward some and not take it all so personally. That, and when you were so focused on killing her, Belex. The Gath have forced both of you to do things you don't want to do, and there may still be more. Especially from you—and don't take this the wrong way—but I'm ready for you if your allegiances, as Hilkiah might say, go the wrong way. It'll still be okay because I believe we can win without hurting you, if it comes to a conflict. And by we, I mean Morians."

"Okay," Belex replied. He was most disinterested in hearing this. "I'm glad you got that all sorted out," he said with some disdain. "Hilkiah, I'm ready." He removed his tunic and walked toward the Oracle.

Hilkiah granted the necessary permissions for Belex to talk to the Oracle directly and Belex successfully summoned it. Belex knew the Oracle's examination of his innards needed to be more thorough than the previous effort. Belex wasn't quite sure what he was doing, but he knew his Gath instinct well enough to know to listen to the vibes he was getting, and those vibes were telling him to try a direct interface. He extended his hand to the Oracle and a thin, long pin extended out from the tip of his pinky finger. He bent down and found, almost as if drawn by magnetic force, a tiny hole in the middle of the device and inserted the needle into the Oracle.

Hilkiah stepped back, amused and impressed all at once.

Belex withdrew the pin, after which his body toppled to the ground in a seizure. The Oracle announced that nobody should be alarmed and that Belex's vitals were okay, listing some of them along with numbers Aurilena didn't understand.

Aurilena kneeled next to him and was mesmerized as his body settled. He lay prone on his stomach, and his red shirt dissolved into his skin . . . or the air . . . or nowhere at all. Aurilena couldn't determine that or was too taken aback to think much about it.

His neck is what aroused her senses first. It was a masterpiece. Two sinewy ropes stretched out from along its nape and blended into his spine like converging, braided silk-covered roads. On either side was a membrane of what looked like thin, translucent leather.

The two formations merged to become a union of such resplendence that she wanted to touch the beautiful ropes across his neck. She was only able to resist because the realities of the situation whispered a more appropriate response into her ear. It almost seemed to her that the nape of his neck was created by a conniving artist, taunting her, leading her into depravity, into that weird techno-world that her society had learned to hate.

She studied it. Him. Or whatever it/he was. There it was, the stuff of legends, right in front of her.

Two worlds, two distinct ages of humanity, intertwined.

He began to talk in a language unfamiliar to her.

With every word he spoke, a ripple moved quickly, like a short, hasty wave, along the length of his neck; tufts of hair on his head danced so softly and subtly that only she could have detected their movements through the microscope of this disturbing affection.

And then, almost too soon for Aurilena, who was enjoying this chance to observe him without the static of conversation, his arms bent, his feet slid toward his knees, and he jumped up as if alerted to an interloper. He looked around, and his eyes met Aurilena's. She slowly rose to her feet.

"Well?" she asked as Hilkiah handed Belex his tunic.

Belex nodded in the Oracle's direction. "Ask her," he said, as he tightened the rope sash around the tunic.

"Her?" asked Aurilena.

Belex nodded and motioned to the Oracle.

Aurilena was too eager to discover what was found to ask Belex what he meant. She breathlessly asked the Oracle for the results of what Hilkiah called the "live" autopsy and was surprised at her racing heart, thinking that when one has time to think about death is when it becomes more frightening. Normally, when she was in more immediate danger, her adrenaline took over and converted fear to something else. This conversion step was missing now, and all she had was fear and anticipation.

"The subject Belex Deralk-Almd, item number 29,987,124,896,665.3 in the stoven.net Catalog of Individuals, is infested with The Acolyte virus, which consists of approximately 700 trillion nanobots of the Upchurch variety, developed by the Homeland Defense Force, also known as The Hunter Collective, which is a euphemism popularized by a group of token opposition rebels who frequent a set of bio-encrypted dynamic strata within stoven.net. The purpose of these nanobots is to infect a target biological lifeform with microscopic tracking devices to accomplish long-range attack strategies."

"Wow," said Aurilena after taking a moment to parse the information. "Fantastic. I'm not going to keel over and die. I'm just going to get everyone else killed. And then die. Nicely done, Belex. I hope you enjoyed that kiss as much as I did."

Aurilena stalked away, leaving the room, her mind a torrent of new options. Only one of them was worthy, and she knew it couldn't involve anyone else. She'd need to ride Remembrance—now—as far out of town as she could. The Gath would find her, but they'd find her in the wastelands, where she could hurt no one.

"Lena, wait," said Belex, but she had to shut him out. Hilkiah, too, who followed Belex with his own call to her.

Then she spun around, realizing neither of them would ever shut up. "Waiting is one thing I can't do. I don't need a translation to know what the Oracle said. They're using me to target Moria. They are devious, clever, awful people, Belex. They used you, us, to find someone here for you to fall in love with—or at least like enough to kiss—and then, once the nanobots found someone with only a purely biological physiology, that's me, they'd be able to find Moria."

"We can't assume their technology can find us even with such tracking. They've tried other tracking schemes before," said Hilkiah. "None of them have worked. And there's the mystery of this—why not simply track Belex upon his arrival?"

"Because if they can identify his target as a pure biological human life form, they'll know Belex is in Moria. And we can't assume it won't work, Hilkiah. Are you going to risk the lives of everyone here on some grand hope that it won't work? Look at Sherealla, how different she is."

Belex nodded slowly. "For many decades, technological progress had actually slowed down some. But change can happen quickly. Advances happening exponentially. Military advances. I'm sorry, Hilkiah, but she's right. But if she goes, I go. These nanobots may be able to thwart whatever magic you've conjured up to defeat them."

Hilkiah raised his palm and flattened it toward them and emphasized, "I conjured up nothing. It is Yehoshua's work, and it is beyond my—or anyone else's—understanding." His voice was firm, almost angry. It was a voice Aurilena had never heard from him before. "It is especially beyond the understanding of the likes of Gath. She stays." He glared at Aurilena intently. "I will not sacrifice my greatest angel to the winds of fear."

Hilkiah turned to the Oracle. "Oracle. What is the nature of the uploads the Gath individual Sherealla has been updating you with?"

"I do not have access to that information," the Oracle replied unhelpfully.

Aurilena ran over to the Oracle. "Oracle. Where can we find this information?"

"There are backups on seventy-three secure stoven.net nodes."

She felt her adrenaline rising as she asked, "Is one of those nodes the individual known as Sherealla?"

"Affirmative."

She looked at Belex and Hilkiah. "And is one of those backup nodes the individual known as Belex?"

"The individual known as Belex Deralk-Almd can acquire access to a biologically encrypted backup node by interfacing with the individual known as Sherealla."

"Um, no," said Aurilena. Then she signed deeply and said, "Oh, just do whatever you want," and she stormed away from Belex.

2

Later, they found some moments to be alone. Hilkiah had convinced Aurilena to stay, at least for the time being, but Belex was sure she had one eye set for the farthest horizon. And he knew her renewed hostile attitude toward him was one way of coping with her impending exit. He couldn't imagine talking her into allowing him to accompany her while she was in this mood, but he would not let her leave Moria alone.

Hilkiah decided that, for himself, the best strategy was to pray, and he went to the Holy Cliff. Belex wondered about that, about Hilkiah's primitive and simple solution to his problems. *If only it were that easy,* he thought.

This notion of having an immortal, omniscient ally was very appealing to him given their current circumstances. Belex knew he'd love to have a pal like that. A pal he could call at any time to strike down his foes, who happened to be his own people, people who had betrayed him by stripping his identity and replacing it with something that would advance an interest, which he had seen with his own eyes to be the very essence of evil. The possibility that the motives behind this tenacious assault that spanned eons may have morphed into something more benign didn't matter to him because even if that were so, that would mean the wars were still based on the mendacity of a deliberately false premise. Their origins were so steeped in malfeasance that any progression of motivation to something less sinister was tainted by the corruption of those origins.

"It's easier for you to leave if you tell yourself you hate me," Belex said to Aurilena. "But can you tell yourself you hate Hilkiah? Or your mom and dad? Or your sister?"

Aurilena and Belex found themselves walking the vibrant streets of Moria. The streets were full of people ambling along, trading at street markets, building wood frames outside of stalls and inside of buildings, blowing glass within the confines of tall, windowed storefronts, molding pottery in small open plazas, and hawking textiles. Passersby were sharing stories that glistened with laughter and sentimentality reflected in their animated hand gestures and the deep, textured facial expressions of friendship and acquaintance.

"I don't hate you," she said softly. "I know I should. Even though you did use me to send my people to their doom and try to kill my best friend. Look at those two statements alone, and anyone would think I'd be justified."

He didn't know what to say to that. He had no interest in defending himself, only her.

"Right?" she said.

He was struggling with his own emotions of betrayal. It was impossible to deny her hers.

"If it's any comfort, I didn't betray you. This was the plan from the beginning. I guess if I had known I was just a vessel in the scheme of life, well, I wonder."

"Wonder what?" she asked sadly.

"I wonder what I would have done if I had known this was life's grand plan for me. I mean, how do you look at a destiny like that and not rebel against it? What does that rebellion even look like?"

"Want to know the most idiotic part of all this?"

"I don't know. Probably not, but I'm listening."

"I am, somehow . . . well, I don't regret at all meeting you out there in the hills that I love so much. I remember when I first heard your voice out on the range. You were far away, and I could hear you calling. Do you believe me when I say that?"

"Of course I do."

"And I thought, if a diamond had a voice, it would sound like that, and then I saw you, and I was, well, you had me at the first kick."

"It's called kick flirting in Gath. It's a very popular method of seduction."

She hit him on the shoulder. "And you're weird."

"We could both go," he said. "I mean, if you leave. I have to leave anyway. I've got the bots, too. Even if they traced you out of the city, they'd try to blow away the city if I was there, just out of spite. We know who these people are . . . what they're capable of."

"We could. But where would we go?"

"To Gath."

The thought alarmed her. But the option of taking the fight directly to them thrilled her, too. "Well, you were right about one thing. My mom and dad. Hilkiah. My sister. My original plan was to just leave. But I can't leave without saying goodbye."

He nodded.

"Can you ride a horse?"

"You can teach me."

"Oh, I don't know. In this amount of time? I'm gonna have to find you an awfully good horse, and they're in short supply. Most of them are wild, not even in the city at all. And I can't teach you. I can barely teach myself."

"You're masterful on the horse, Lena."

She ignored the comment and said, "But my sister can. She is to horses what Hilkiah is to prayer. But in this short amount of time, it's going to be a challenge, even for her, to get you to do much more than get comfortable mounting a strong horse."

"Then we'll do our best. They're amazing animals. I'd never seen one before I was with you on the back of yours."

"Yeah, your people wiped most of them out along with everything else. Sorry. I guess it was really both our ancestors who did that, huh? My own people, they need a reckoning with their history, too, someday. They all think their history is this grand legend, but what happened, that was done by people we both come from, wasn't it?"

"Seems so," he said as they walked on a wooden boardwalk along the shores of the bay, which adorned the outskirts of the central plazas of the city.

"We call this the Malecón," she said. She was quiet for a moment before she added, "Hilkiah won't be pleased."

"About you telling me you call this walk the Malecón?"

Aurilena giggled at that. "No silly, about us leaving Moria."

"Hilkiah will probably have me arrested to prevent you from leaving," replied Belex.

"That's actually a possibility."

"Nah, he knows you'll leave if you've set your mind to it. He has probably already accepted it. Hopefully, he'll feel a little better knowing I'm with you. Unless that makes him feel worse," he added grimly.

"Maybe. I wish we could bring him."

"Yeah. Him and his God."

"Belex. We need to find that horse. We really can't delay."

Belex stopped walking for a moment and looked out over the bay. The other side was distant, but he could see that it was full of old and new growth.

There were no buildings, just trees and a sense of being a place never touched by civilization, he thought.

"Have you ever been over there?"

She shook her head. "It looks nice, right? But it's full of ancient toxins of some kind. I don't think there's any animal life there."

"There has to be something there or the trees would die. Insects at least, and the presence of insects suggests an ecosystem." He wasn't sure where that information came from. He wondered if more of his systems were coming back online. If they were, it probably meant that Moria was in great danger as soon as his connection to stoven.net was restored. But it also meant that whatever was out there, he could probably get them through it. If his systems were coming online, it considerably improved their survivability.

"You know, I'm so dumb," he said.

"Why, because you want to kiss me again?" she gave him a flirtatious look.

"Well, of course, but that's not what makes me dumb. I should have asked the Oracle if she could run a diagnostic on me. To find out which of my systems are functioning."

"Sheesh, why are you calling her a *she* all of the sudden?"

"Same reason you just did."

She shrugged her shoulders, grabbed his hand, stuck an arm inside his elbow, and said, "Let's go. We can ask her after we find you a horse—if we have time."

That time never came, which meant Belex would be given more opportunities to learn how to trust his instincts.

CHAPTER X

1

Aurilena's sister, Judith, met them at a lunch house on the northern shore of the bay late in the morning the next day. Judith, donning a wide-brimmed suede hat, was a strong woman with large shoulders and toned arms and black hair the same color as Aurilena's. Her big, round cheeks glowed as a smile curled upward when she saw Aurilena.

The wind blew a frigid, wild volley of gusts as a man strolled up to them with a horse before Aurilena was able to introduce Belex. The man wore something that looked like a black sock on the top of his head. He was a slight man with a paunch. *Like a skinny pregnant woman,* thought Aurilena. He wore an ancient wool sweater with wide, black, jagged horizontal stripes and enough holes to qualify the sweater as a moth colony. His baggy leather pants were held up by an oversized leather sash.

The horse was a beautiful blue roan with a red mane and a white star on its face, looking proud as it approached with the man. The horse snorted a couple times when the man stopped.

"He's a gelding, a fine one," the man said to Judith. Aurilena introduced Belex to Judith, but when she tried to introduce him to the horse trader, the man waved her off. "I know who the Augmenter is; we all do. Do you want to look at the horse or no?"

Aurilena was impressed with the horse's gait and the musculature of its legs and hindquarters. "How old is he?" asked Judith.

"Why, he's just a boy. Nine years old—old enough to be good on the trail, young enough to last on the trail."

Judith walked around the horse and gave Belex a sly smile when she did, tipping the brim of her wide hat. It was a look Aurilena had seen many times, and it made her glad because it was her sister's look of approval. Her sister was the least judgmental person on the planet, but she was also not easily impressed. She hated no one but loved few.

"Let me ride him," said Judith, and the man handed the gelding's reins to her. Judith cantered around the lunch house a few times before jumping off. She handed the reins back to the man. "He's barn sour and older than nine by quite a few years. What do you want for him?"

Aurilena was impressed by the negotiating tactic, but she didn't want a barn sour horse. There was no time. "Judith, I need a horse ready for the trail, not the barn."

"I know, I know, don't worry; I can get him ready for you, but I need to know what this shyster wants for the horse before we talk any further."

"My wife. She's been sick with the bat plague for weeks. If I could get a healer—that'd be fine payment."

Judith looked inside the horse's mouth. "Gum line's hanging; incisors all worn down to nubs. This horse isn't twenty years old now, is it? You better tell me the truth, or your wife isn't the only one gonna need a healer."

"I—I'm sorry lady; it's my wife's horse. I don't know how old he is exactly. I thought she said nine."

"More like nineteen. Barn sour and old."

"There aren't a lot of horses," said the man, as if warning Judith that no search would be fruitful. "But I swear he's not nineteen. Could be fifteen. We only got to these parts about that many years ago, and this horse was just a foal then."

"Oh, oops," said Aurilena, noting the confession.

"Hay or grass eater?" Judith replied quickly, ignoring the proven lie.

"Mostly grass. No hay to be found last several years."

"Okay. He'll do." She patted the horse on the side. She looked at Belex, who looked perplexed by the entire experience.

"Judith?" Aurilena was alarmed, but she trusted Judith, especially when it came to horses.

"As long as you're not being chased by a cavalry for 2,000 miles, you'll be fine. Where are you going with this horse, anyway?" She looked at Belex again.

"South," said Belex. "About 400 miles is all."

"You're not eloping with my sister in Gath, are you?" she asked wryly.

"I haven't had a chance to tell Mom and Dad yet. We're not eloping, don't worry. We're . . ." Aurilena had no idea what to say.

"We're on a mission from God," Belex burst in with a line from an ancient performance of some kind, which was another hint of his repairing systems.

Judith laughed at that and looked at Aurilena. "Tell me you are *not* going to Gath."

"Why would I be going to Gath?" asked Aurilena innocently.

"It's the only thing 400 miles south. And you've got robot boy here with you." She was tending to the horse while talking, then said, "It's okay, sis, I know you can take care of yourself better than anybody else in this old town." She glared at Belex saying, "You bring her back in one piece, or I'll sell you for parts to the radio guy in The Wandering City."

"Why is everyone wanting to send me out for parts?" asked Belex.

"Because you're just so crazy handsome," said Judith, slapping him playfully on the cheek. She turned to the horse trader. "What's the horse's name?"

"White Star, of course."

"Of course. Okay, White Star, you're gonna need to get a little less shy and a little more trail ready. Sis, give me a day with this horse, and he'll be ready for the trail. I'll need another two days or so to get your hunky robot acclimated to the animal."

"I don't think we've got that much time, Judith. I gotta tell you the truth. There's, well, Gath forces are on their way. That's why we are getting out. The whole town is in danger, and every minute we stay, we risk a lot of lives."

"You," Judith said, looking at the horse trader. "I'll send a healer over pronto. That is, if this horse doesn't keel over on his way to his new stable. And if this horse is healthy, your healer will not leave until your wife is cured. Don't you worry about that. As for you, sis, come on; we got work to do."

She took White Star from the horse trader and told Belex to saddle up.

Belex looked aghast. "Now?"

"Go on now. Get on."

She handed the reins to Belex. White Star immediately reacted, snorting, shaking his head, and tapping the ground with his front hooves.

"What are we waiting for exactly?" asked Judith.

"Umm, for you to show me how to mount this thing," said Belex, his unblinking eyes glued to the horse's head.

"Nope. Just do it. Go ahead, try it; you might just surprise yourself."

Belex pulled on the reins a little and gently guided the horse into an alignment with his own body. He saw a table with a bench from the lunch house nearby that nobody was using, so he slowly led White Star to it.

Aurilena was at first amused by Judith's commands, then concerned, and now fascinated by Belex's reaction. Belex patted White Star and steadied him as he approached his left leg and stepped onto the bench. He then put the reins over the horse's head and lifted his left foot off the bench and into the stirrup. White Star seemed to object for a moment, snorting and moving slightly forward, but Belex pulled gently on the reins and said, "No way."

He then lifted himself onto the horse expertly and sunk slowly into the saddle, patting White Star on the neck. He looked over at Aurilena and smiled.

"How did you do that if you've never ridden a horse?" asked Aurilena.

"I have no idea, but as soon as I started, it was like I knew exactly what to do."

"Bzzzzt," Aurilena said, "folks, all systems are back in service. Our friend Belex is no longer half the man he used to be."

Belex chuckled and smiled at that, even though he felt a little insulted.

"Nice touch with the bench," said Judith. "Made old man White Star here more comfortable with you."

2

After the man left, the two sisters and Belex rode into town, Judith declaring that she was going to stay close until Aurilena left for her journey. They rode along the tall bluffs overlooking the northern shores, and Belex thought the tragically named Broken Bridge that had terrified him on his way into Moria looked beautiful against the backdrop of the tall green hills beyond it, even though he knew the story behind it must have been heartbreaking.

He found riding the horse a simple thing—as natural as walking—and the two sisters smiled and tried to make fun of him at the slightest miscue, but those were rare.

Finally, Judith asked, "How is this possible? Nobody can just get on a horse like that and ride it if they've never done it. I knew you'd get on okay. I could sense it. But from there, I expected at least a little trouble."

"It's her," Belex pointed to Aurilena, knowing it to be true. She wasn't aware of it herself, he thought, and he knew his systems were not yet fully functional enough for him to pick it up on his own. She was transferring her equestrian skills within the scope of some magical upload. "I don't know what you did, Lena, but somehow you gave me your skills. It has something to do with your way with animals."

Aurilena chuckled a little. "All I did was pray to Yehoshua and ask him that you not break that big, thick neck of yours."

"White Star," said Belex. "I like it."

"Me, too," said Aurilena.

"Why did you name your horse Remembrance?" asked Belex.

"Remembrance of my brother," she said in a tone that suggested the conversation was over.

3

When they returned to the Hall of Legions, which was a short ride from the northern bluffs, they decided to check in on Hilkiah, whose home was next to the large edifice. He had returned from praying and was looking solemn.

"She has escaped," he told them. Then he grasped Judith's shoulders. "And it is good to see that you have escaped from the hinterlands," he said to her.

"The hinterlands? I'm just outside the central city, you old goat," she smiled, hugging him warmly. "It's good to see you too, old man." Her head leaned into his lower chest as she embraced him tightly.

"Where were the guards when this escape happened?" asked Aurilena, visibly shaken.

"They don't know," Hilkiah replied quickly, releasing Judith, and pouring a round of tea for everyone. They all sat at his round wooden table as he continued, "You know, she's quite a dangerous phenomenon. She combines aspects of both of our races. She has cybernetic capabilities and magic. She is proving to be quite formidable."

"And her magic can be the destructive kind," said Aurilena, looking at Belex and Judith.

Belex knew this all too well. He had discovered as much during his brief chase and had seen her climb walls and get through the building when there had to have been little to no oxygen. He couldn't guess what kind of magic she possessed, so he asked.

"She has been specializing, I'm sorry to report," said Hilkiah, "in making things disappear. Not only move them to other areas, but disappear." Hilkiah's voice became reflective. "I'll be quite honest with you, Aurilena. It has been you and Sherealla who have led me to consider a formal proclamation renouncing magic as a means to the so many ends that our society has established as a birthright."

"What? Why?" Aurilena asked sheepishly.

"I have been concerned about motives. And about our reliance on what we, as mere mortals, believe we should do with our magic, which has grown quite powerful over the centuries. Do not consider this an admonishment. It is a positive development, this . . . reconsideration of things. Your powers have grown so much that it has forced me to reassess. I view this development as being in the most positive light.

"It is critical to remember that your great powers are not actually your powers at all. They belong to a much greater and more powerful being, and you must ask him to assess all dangers and to use you as *his* instrument for whatever ends he deems necessary. In normal times, this would force a change in training strategy because you must learn to release your will to Yehoshua and trust him to act on your behalf, whether directly through you or through other forces, as he sees fit. As it is, you must train in the trenches, I'm afraid."

"I'm sort of getting it, Hilkiah. I really think I am," said Aurilena. "I've tried asking him to do things without, you know, saying what to do, if that makes sense."

Hilkiah nodded silently. "Unfortunately, Sherealla will not abide in that. From a tactical standpoint, that could put her at a seeming advantage, but I contend that this is a false advantage. If you trust this power to be greater than your own—and greater than hers—you cannot lose any battle that may arise between you."

"You're asking me to find her, aren't you?" asked Aurilena.

"Indeed."

Just as Aurilena was putting her lips to her green tea, delighting in its herbal fragrance, a loud explosion rattled the door of Hilkiah's home, sending objects crashing to the ground, including his pot of tea, which had been resting near the edge of the table.

"Perfect timing," said Judith as they all rose to their feet.

Aurilena looked at her and said, "You think?" and broke for the door and then toward the street just beyond. There was a great commotion. Aurilena could see a tongue of red and yellow flame tickling the edges of a window in the Hall of Legions.

"She's at the library," said Belex, tugging at her sleeve.

"How do you know that?" asked Aurilena.

"I don't know," he said hurriedly. "I just do."

They both untied their horses and Aurilena told Judith to remain.

"No way, sis. Look, even though I can't contribute much to the fight, that one second of recognition she'll have when she sees me will give you an advantage. Just be sure to use it."

"Ugh, okay," said Aurilena, and the three of them rode to the library. She trusted Belex now, she thought. She must, considering how quickly she reacted to his claim that Sherealla had returned to the library. Maybe it was because it simply made sense, but there was also the certainty in his voice that she relied on. Whether he knew it or not, his systems were coming back online. She hadn't done anything to help him ride the horse. This, she knew. And now, he knew Sherealla's location. This, she also knew.

As they approached the library building, Aurilena finally asked Belex, trying not to sound accusatory, "How can you not know your systems are back? That you have access to your stove thing?"

They arrived at the building, and as he dismounted, he said, "Stoven.net. It's a network—all the collected minds of the Homeland wired together, so to speak, like a big web of shared information . . . plus all the information of the world, everything. And I don't know the answer to your question, but I think that it might be happening, yeah."

"Doesn't that give us an advantage?"

"No," he replied quickly. "Stoven.net has never been accessible in MagicLand. We've sent dozens of spies here. Their systems go dark every time. If I get in full contact with the collective, it means Sherealla has done something—or worse, the Hunter Collective has. And they'll possibly be able to use it to track the location of the city."

"But they've already got me for their stupid tracking," she said in a discouraged voice.

"Not if you leave. Let's just hope it's Sherealla that acted because one is easier to deal with, right? That and . . . she's here, and the Hunter Collective is not."

Aurilena nodded as the three of them entered the library. Judith was stopped for a moment by a guard but given permission to continue once Aurilena gave the command.

"Not every Gath has gone dark," said Sherealla's voice. "Not the one that matters. Not me. And therefore, not Maoch." The voice was coming through the walls and ceilings and filled the air of the Library of Ezra.

"Who?" said Belex, looking all around him.

"Our little friend on the plaza," said the voice. "He *is* Gath, Belex. He's been our ruler for 900 years. All of this *oh, aren't we the nice, collective democracy* thing is a sham."

"How do you know this?" asked Belex into the air.

"They were too aggressive with me. As soon as I started interfacing with the Oracle, I found the collective, and I realized how powerful I could be if I wanted. This does appeal to me on many levels, I must admit. But then I saw the history of our people. What you saw the other day was just a taste. The full story is much worse. And I've found that Maoch has been our shadow governor for a very long time."

"No pun intended," said Aurilena, thinking about the hooded figure with no face. "So, you'll help us?" asked Aurilena hopefully. "We need to go to Gath. Will you help us when we get there?"

To Belex, this seemed like an awfully optimistic scenario. But Aurilena knew her friend better than anyone, and before he could evaluate the brashness of the request, Sherealla said, "I already have."

4

Sherealla felt empty, as if everything had been removed from her. Her soul, her desires, her longings, her needs, her future. Even her past seemed like a fabrication. She wondered how much of it was real. Since interfacing with the Oracle and reconnecting with the collective, she had discovered that references to her parents were nowhere to be found on stoven.net. The quaint intelliunit they had lived in, which had been little more than an officer's quarters near the Mantricle, had become a crowded mind bistro, serving dream sequence enhancements after she left. She assumed her parents were dead.

She wondered about the freak that Aurilena had fallen for. Was he right to turn on his own? Who sends children to fight wars? Because that's what she was when she was sent, augmented to perfectly resemble a Wiccan but superior in every way—except in the most important way. *The way that should matter the most,* she thought.

It occurred to her, as she approached the Oracle for what she thought would surely be the last time, that she had no heart, that when the Hunter Collective designed and created her, they left that out and some kind of mechanical entity must have been installed in its place.

She could feel no passion for anything. She felt no lure to the drama at hand, felt no remorse over losing Aurilena, felt no empathy toward Hilkiah, who had spent so many years training her, and felt no gratitude toward Aurilena for taking her under her wing seven years ago. This sudden emotional vacuum could only be explained through cybernetics. It was simply no longer necessary to carry emotions needed to subterfuge, spy, and lure the magicians to their doom. The necessary tasks were complete, and she had become nothing more substantial than the exterior of a deadly projectile.

She was still able to access the Oracle, though. She needed that. She needed some final closure.

5

Aurilena felt dizzy. She looked at Judith and Belex, who had moved slightly ahead of her in their haste to reach the Oracle. They seemed to weave in front of her as if they were leaning left to right. Her sight blurred, and she could see random patterns of tiny black specks dropping like snowflakes in front of her.

She grasped a round rail that was on the wall next to her and then felt nauseous, too. "Oh," she gasped and collapsed on the floor.

Judith and Belex both heard the commotion and raced to her. She could see them looking over her while they said something incomprehensible.

As she reached down to touch Aurilena's cheek, streams of memories ran through Judith's head. She had always remembered Aurilena as precocious and confident, sometimes sassy, even as a toddler. Judith was four years older, *but,* she thought, as she worryingly brushed her sister's beautiful long black hair off her face, *not four years wiser.* Aurilena had dabbled in magic since she was able to walk, it seemed, whereas Judith was more about things of the earth: horses, dogs, carpentry, pottery, and other things she could touch and manipulate.

Aurilena was good with a horse, too, much better than she knew. Horses seemed to run in the Kingston family's blood, and Aurilena had one more treasured gift that Judith had hated her for when they were younger—an ability to talk to animals. Judith got over it. Aurilena was precious to her.

"Lena?" She and Belex were both desperately trying to find her, but Aurilena seemed removed, staring blankly at them, unable to move her lips or even blink her eyes. And just like that, as suddenly as she disappeared, she was back.

"Sweetie, what's happening?" Judith asked.

"I don't know," Aurilena said slowly.

"It's the bots," said Belex.

"What are they doing?" asked Aurilena. "It was like I could think and feel and everything, but my vision was all weird, and I couldn't say or hear anything. No, I could hear you, but I couldn't understand you. It was like you were speaking a different language."

Belex kissed her forehead so gently, Aurilena thought she'd cry. "I don't know what they're doing. I'm so sorry."

"We gotta keep going," urged Aurilena.

"We need to get you to a healer, honey," said Judith.

"There is no time for that. There just isn't. Hopefully, I won't experience another episode like that for a while. What do you think, Belex?"

He shook his head. "I just can't know. I don't know anything about this stuff."

She knew that he might be back in communication with whatever network made Gath and that scared her, and once again, his allegiances were an issue for her. Almost as if he could read her mind, he added, "It's military stuff. I don't have access to it. If Sherealla is right, and I'm a spy, apparently I'm not very high profile."

"You're behind enemy lines," said Judith. "They'd be idiots to give you access to anything more important than the recipe for a nice Gath soup."

He looked like he was deep in thought until he nodded in agreement. "Okay, yeah, my systems are at about fifty percent capacity. I was able to run some diagnostics. It's how I knew she was here, Lena. She's at the Oracle. Right now."

Aurilena struggled to her feet with the help of Belex and Judith. "Doing what? Can you determine that? What's she doing now?"

"She's blocked the ports the Homeland Collective was using to communicate with the Oracle."

They started walking up toward the Oracle's room. "Wait. What?" said Aurilena. "They've been communicating with the Oracle?"

"Umm, yeah, I guess so. I guess I said that as if you knew. I said it as if I knew, and, well it's all so strange. All this information in front of me, and I'm having trouble processing it all. Like I said, my systems are only sort of active because there's too much information. I don't know what to do with it, and normally, I don't even really know it's there, I just sort of am able to react to it, without thinking through anything."

"It'll come; be patient," said Aurilena. "But it sounds like she's not trying to destroy the Oracle. She wouldn't bother blocking the ports if that were the case."

"Unless she's already destroyed it. That would block the ports."

"Okay," said Judith. "Just fill me in here." They were almost there, having circled the long flight of stairs to the Oracle. "What is a port?"

"It's a way to get in," said Belex. "Think of a harbor with three docks. Each of them is numbered one, two, and three. You have access to dock one, which requires a kind of boat only you have, and I have access to number two, which requires a boat only I have, and Aurilena . . . dock three."

"All three. I get access to all three," insisted Aurilena.

"Sheesh. Anyway, it's kind of like that."

"But it all happens in the air, with, how?"

"Sherealla!" Aurilena screamed. She had managed to get ahead of the other two as they were talking.

Her shriek startled Belex away from the conversation. What remained of Sherealla was standing in front of the Oracle. Belex looked at her, knowing there would be no heroics this time. Her arms were bent as if grasping the Oracle, but her body had grown taller by about a dozen feet and looked like it had been stretched by rubber. It was translucent, and Belex could see murky objects behind her. Her torso marked the real change in Sherealla's form, for it was at that point that the rest of her body was getting poured into the Oracle like a drink, with billions of tiny black particles making up her shape as it bent over into a long arch of streaming particles. Her body was only a hint of its former self as it emptied into the Oracle. Before any of them could react beyond helpless screams of alarm, she was gone.

Aurilena ran to the Oracle, which remained lit but showed no sign of what had just occurred. "She's gone," she cried. "She . . ." Aurilena sat on the floor and sobbed.

"I'm here," said a voice that filled the room, but it wasn't coming from the Oracle. "I'm here," it said softly. "And I'm so sorry. I'm sorry for everything. Everything I did, but I had to do it all. I was unable to control any of it. But I'm here now."

Aurilena looked all around. "Where's here?"

"I am with the Oracle."

This was almost too much for Aurilena. This sudden infusion of technology everywhere made her more certain than ever that the ways of Moria were the only legitimate path to progress, that the power of the subconscious was easily a match for anything the Gath could produce, without all the terror.

"I don't understand, Sherealla. Where *are* you?"

"She's inside of me, too," said Belex cryptically. "I mean, right here. Inside of me."

Aurilena was staring at him while still seated on the floor. Exasperated, all she could do was lift her palms off the floor and express her bafflement.

"She's insinuated herself into stoven.net somehow. Added her consciousness to it. She's inside every Gath."

"So she can know everything you do?"

"I can block her from my ports, but when I do, I have to cut off my own connection to stoven.net . . . once I am connected to it again. Which is fine with me."

"Okay, then do it, but what about when we need her?"

"I just reestablish my connection with the collective or open a port."

"What a nightmare," said Aurilena.

It was then that Sherealla explained the history of Gath.

Chapter XI

1

When they returned to tell Hilkiah what happened, he was perplexed. "Why the explosion and fire?" he asked.

"A diversion," Belex replied. "She couldn't know I'd know she was at the library." He still didn't know how he knew that himself. Hilkiah asked if Sherealla could help Aurilena with whatever ailed her at the library. Aurilena said that Sherealla, like Belex, said she didn't have access to that level of military information but seemed pleased to report that her level of access was higher than what Belex had been granted.

Sherealla had told Aurilena and Belex that the history of the Gath was far different than what was reflected in the records in stoven.net. It was different than what they all learned as children. It was different than what they used as a basis for their prejudices as adults. Information was shuffled around in such a way that getting at what Sherealla called the "encrypted truth" was impossible for anyone outside of the highest-ranking military personnel. Sherealla had theorized that she was a progeny of such a person, but she didn't know for sure. Her memories were implanted, she said, and those memories told her she was part of a family. Families had become obsolete ages ago. They simply didn't exist in the Homeland, which meant her childhood had been a lie.

"I couldn't even be sad anymore for missing my childhood," she had said to Aurilena after disappearing into the Oracle. "Because so much of that sadness was about missing this whole growing up thing with Mom and Dad, who were nothing but actors, like Belex . . . almost."

Sherealla had talked about perpetual war and how it helped keep Maoch and his cohorts in power. "Keep everyone scared; that's the key," she said. "Maintain an illusion of imminent demise, and never let that illusion fade." The leadership was perfectly content, after some time—and after the world's oceans had become a toxic jellyfish stew—to let the Wiccan Wars simmer or remain on hold indefinitely. But they were also willing to fire up a war at any moment. After hundreds of years of conflict, the goal transformed from extermination to power retention.

"It was always about power," Belex said to Hilkiah, "so it was really more like a change in emphasis. How do they retain that power? At first, they were sure that extermination was the key to that. And it was because according to Sherealla, the entire world was basically in open revolt against the few people who could afford augmentation and were flaunting it. Folks got tired of seeing a small group of people benefit from science while everyone else starved or struggled. 'Riots were routine in every city in the world,' Sherealla said. Every single one. She said there were thousands of cities, bigger a hundred times over than Moria. All of them in flames every day."

"A truly impossible situation for rulers to face," said Hilkiah, sounding alarmingly sympathetic.

But Aurilena understood the sentiment to some degree. "It had to seem like there were no answers," she thought out loud.

"I suspect," sighed Hilkiah, "that they never once consulted Yehoshua, who would have solved their problem in a most creative way."

Sherealla discovered that, eventually, the leaders of the world and those with the most wealth bought their way into higher degrees of augmentation and what she called "DNA filtering," which allowed the wealthiest people to alter the DNA of their offspring to eliminate disease and accentuate physical and intellectual attributes. A formal split between species had not occurred yet, but two distinct groups were forming: those who turned to spirituality and magic and those who relied on science. Those who turned to spirituality and magic disavowed technology to a large degree, especially the computer sciences. Meanwhile, as the populace discovered they were being systematically exterminated, the leaders of the world punished rebellious parts of the planet with genetically-engineered strains of bacteria, like the Buruli bacteria that ate flesh. In other words, the population of most of the world was forced to accept its extermination peacefully or die more horribly than their worst nightmares.

"When did Sherealla make all these discoveries?" asked Hilkiah.

Aurilena told him she downloaded the information just before she was captured.

"So, she's an ally now." Hilkiah sounded unconvinced.

"I don't think she knew what she was until she learned more about who she was in relation to her own history," said Belex.

"And her betrayal of me hurt her more than it hurt me," said Aurilena.

"I wish we could have done more for her. She caused so little harm in the end," Hilkiah reflected while massaging long locks of his beard.

"Her hostility toward us both," Belex said, looking at Aurilena, "was a clever disguise. She knew that her anger, which was genuine, combined with words against us, would release catecholamines, which are basically a kind of signaling molecule that would get registered by her biosystem to indicate to the Hunter Collective that we are enemies. She used that as a shield of sorts to provide me with a warning. See, I think that's what she was doing. Warning me. Not threatening me, not taunting me. Warning me.

"Don't get me wrong. She was quite determined to kill me. I could sense that. Just as I was determined to kill her. We both had command mechanisms in our cybernetic structures that really gave us no choice but to attempt to carry out our missions. I think the reason she chose the fate she did was that she thought she was fated to kill Aurilena if I failed. And she wasn't willing to do that. She loved you too much, Lena, to basically watch herself kill you. She didn't know at the time that the plan wasn't to kill you but to inject you with tracking mechanisms. If that tracking technology had been available when they sent her here, they would have devised a plan for her to do the job. But I guess the technology wasn't ready yet. And the Hunter Collective planned ahead. Way ahead.

"This is why I believe we can trust her. She has made her decision. Could she lead Aurilena into danger by proxy through her guidance? Sure. But why? Why not just stick around and finish the job?"

Hilkiah asked, "But why did she take the action she did? She has different information now. The mission is not what she thought."

Belex could only shrug. "She couldn't know what other latent commands against Moria were residing in her systems' nodes. For that matter, neither do I know what lies within mine."

Aurilena felt her heart sink. If only she had been able to perceive the things Belex was saying at the time, maybe she could have saved her friend. Belex seemed to know her thoughts. "She's happier now, I think. She has a purpose, and it's her purpose, not one imposed on her. She's quite angry with our people. With the Homeland."

"With the Gath," Aurilena corrected. "With this Maoch fellow."

"Right."

"Because it's not a Homeland, Belex. Not for you, not for anybody," Aurilena continued with her correction. "The only thing it's home to is evil and deceit. They can't even find soldiers loyal enough to do their bidding; they must send children and innocent people with altered memories to do their dirty work. It's pathetic, really."

"We need to go to Gath, Hilkiah," Belex said. He waited expressionless for the reply.

"I know," replied Hilkiah firmly but quietly. "It is the only way. You will bring the Great Shepherd with you," said Hilkiah to Aurilena. "It is either that or we perish."

"We scout first," said Belex. "Go there the old-fashioned way," he smiled. "With our minds. What say you, Lena?"

"I don't know. I think Sherealla will help us navigate Gath. We don't need to scout it first."

Belex shook his head. "Too risky. Look. Sherealla is probably really on our side here. But I'm sorry to say, she's a bit of a flake. We need to rely on our own resources in case she changes her mind or, hey, something happens to her. What she has done is unprecedented. She's basically installed her consciousness into the collective. Into stoven.net. This kind of problem is unique and won't be solved easily by Maoch, I *think*. But we make optimistic assumptions at great risk."

Aurilena sighed but said okay to the plan. "But it's gotta be a quick visit. We need to saddle up soon for the real ride to Gath."

2

Belex and Aurilena prepared for their journey by changing clothes and eating a full meal before sitting down in the Room of Prayer at the Hall of Legions. To deal with the likelihood of being seen while in Gath, Belex wore his original Gath clothing, which had somehow been cleaned. He had given up some time ago trying to determine who all his various helpers were, but there seemed to be many. He had grown fond of the purple tunic, a gift from Hilkiah, so he wore that over the Gath garb.

202 | CHARLES BASTILLE

He had also suggested an entertainer's outfit for Aurilena to wear since there was no such thing as a priestess in Gath. There weren't any disciplines he could think of in Moria similar to what could be found in Gath, so it was difficult for him to think of appropriate clothing for her. Luckily, Gath was full of expressive characters, so it was unlikely she'd stand out, no matter what she wore.

Clothing wasn't the only means of expression full of diversity in Gath culture. Entire strata were dedicated to costume DNA and other devotions to peculiarity, but none of that prepared him for Aurilena's appearance in the Room of Prayer.

"We have time for you to change out of that," he said through a spittle of laughter, staring at the wildly colored tent-like structure attached to her, perhaps by magic or some other means—he couldn't be sure—and the tall, flattened hat that bore blue, red, and yellow vertical stripes and a wide brim, which looked like it could hold several drinks. "Please. Take your time," he guffawed.

She glared at him crossly, closed her eyes for a moment, disappeared, and reappeared a moment later with an insolent look and dressed in a stunning, tight-fitting purple trumpet dress. She stood in front of him with her arms crossed. "Better?" she asked and then swore at him.

Belex shook his head, trying desperately to restrain his laughter, and said to Hilkiah, "There are some tricksters among you people, aren't there?"

Hilkiah sighed. "May I recommend something a bit less—"

"Devastating?" Belex finished.

"Not my choice of words, but they'll do," affirmed Hilkiah.

She sat down next to Belex on a camelback couch topped with a curving oak frame. Aware of the effect her dress was having on him, she purposely edged against him, glaring at him as if challenging him to laugh some more.

"Hey," he said, "I'm not the one who talked you into that hat and costume. You should save your beastly mood for them," and then he fell into laughter once more.

She finally settled for a more sedate, long pinafore over a simple shirt. She knew she was probably annoying Hilkiah with her disappearing and reappearing, but she wasn't in a mood to be trifled with.

There was a table in front of the couch with several beverages and a bowl of dried fruit. They were hoping to be done in a couple of hours, but they wanted to be prepared for a longer visit. Aurilena had never traveled for more than a few minutes. She didn't know if she could manage it for much longer than that.

Hilkiah sat on an identical couch, opposite the table, with a similar set of refreshments. He suggested to Aurilena that she focus on the spirit of Yehoshua. "If he wants you to take this virtual journey, he will provide the path. Do not set this path yourself; do not ask to go to any specific place. He knows your heart. Trust him on this journey."

Aurilena nodded.

"The books!" said Belex, just before they were about to start. "Now that my systems are activated, I should be able to download them from the Oracle. I think we can do that now through Sherealla before we leave." He was able to unblock Sherealla's access to him, tell her about the books, receive the books from her, and receive an angry rebuke from her for blocking her in the first place, all before Aurilena replied.

"Why? They're awful," said Aurilena.

"Precisely. There are people in Gath, Lena. Friends. People who trust me. It's all coming back to me. Who they are . . . maybe even who *I* am."

"If that is so," said Hilkiah, "perhaps it would be prudent to discuss with us *now* who you are."

Belex glared at him, as if insulted, before calming himself. "Yeah. I . . . yes, I can do that, I think."

The prayer room discharged some of the heat generated by Aurilena's wrath as Belex told his tale.

3

The massive oval building was as old as some of the stars, Belex thought to himself. None of what he was doing was necessary. He was harkening to not only an ancient, dead tradition and past but a different species entirely. Nothing like this had ever been done in the Homeland.

The people who were filing into the massive, ancient stadium, which had taken nanobots an entire day to rebuild and clean in such a way as to make it safe for a large crowd, were a varietal mix of curiosity seekers, amused onlookers, and fans of Belex's art. But theirs had been a world of cyber theater—long,

204 | C<small>HARLES</small> B<small>ASTILLE</small>

complex, often interactive storytelling that sometimes took weeks to complete, with participants and viewers scattered throughout the Homeland, never once before gathering as a crowd like this to see the actors in person.

Cinescape interactions were quite personal, with each viewer or participant imagining individual threads of the story and altering its direction with just a thought. And because of their physiology, Belex was able to receive and process all these threads and provide an acting performance individualized for each storyline that entered his system through the collective. The result was that every participant received a personalized story and acting experience tailored to their specific thought patterns, a dynamic musical score accompanying the show, and a specific set and costume designs. Everything about the experience was uniquely designed for the personal taste of each participant, whether there were a thousand or a million.

This would be different because he and his fellow actors would be performing in front of an audience without the usual messaging that would normally be sent between actors and stoven.net. Instead of highly personalized and individual performances, everyone in the audience would see the same act.

Belex, as the unofficial director of the acting troupe for years, would now formalize his role and create a story based on feedback from members of the live audience. The weirdest part of the process was that the rest of the collective was cut out of the creative process entirely. Only members of the live audience could participate.

Why was he doing this? He didn't know. Despite his youth, he had achieved a level of social status that allowed him to do almost anything theatrical, and he decided it was time to shake things up. Step out of the ordinary. See his audience. Reach out to their souls. He wanted to hear their actual voices. He wanted to hear applause, too, truth be told, something that he had never experienced because it wasn't part of the Homeland's culture.

He had referred the collective to ancient video clips prior to this event, showing how the ancients would gather as an applauding, cheering audience in large theaters, but the reaction on stoven.net was mixed, some of it hostile.

"Ape-like," one person had said in a typical response, "but maybe fun for a day."

Belex could not have anticipated his physiological reaction when he finally took the stage with his fellow actors. Stoven.net was chattering wildly about the reaction of the crowd as he appeared. The crowd jumped on its feet, almost as one, and applauded and cheered. Immediately, stoven.net became flooded with measurements of Belex's heart rate, respiration, and blood pressure, which had all significantly altered the moment the cheering began.

Soon, people in the audience started sharing their physiological statistics, which looked like Belex's. Conversations about the findings swirled. Scientists immediately pointed out that there were no surprises here, that these responses should be expected, and much of the hive mind began to query the reasons for why this kind of thing had never been tried before. All this discussion took place within five seconds of the first cheer.

Belex took a bow, which delighted the crowd. Stoven.net was in wide disagreement as to whether the bow was a tribute to the ancient primates or performed in mockery, but it didn't matter. The people loved it.

"My friends," he spoke softly, in a voice they could all hear, no matter how much other noise acted as interference. "Thank you for coming to a first of its kind event. *The Hands of Hell* is a cinescape classic. We hope you enjoy this unique presentation. Each of you will still be part of the telling of this story, but instead of receiving individual content from me, I will pick my favorite storylines I receive from you, the audience, and we will perform the story accordingly." As a part of his speech, which wasn't at all necessary in that he could have delivered this information through stoven.net, he added a note through the collective that said, "You'll notice that I did not say 'the best' storylines, but my 'favorite,' since it is a purely subjective interpretation." The speech was also a tribute to the ancient ways of theater, his audience quickly knew. The crowd seemed eager and pleased that the day would be full of surprises.

"One final reminder," he added through the net. "The nanocircuits in my hippocampus relating to my actions and intents have been blocked from stoven. net. You will not have access to these while I am performing and evaluating your storylines. This is done to maintain a level of surprise. As you all know, this action was approved in collective thought."

The "live" presentation of *The Hands of Hell,* a story about the early Wiccan Wars, was so successful that demands for similar efforts flooded stoven.net, which compensated for its inability to directly participate by creating vast gambling strata that placed odds on which story streams from the crowd Belex would pick.

Belex became the most sought-after actor in the Homeland. Even the military took notice. "How nice," an officer in the elite Halcyon Saber Group, a unit of the Homeland Defense Force, said in a message, "it would be to have your skills serve the cause."

Belex ignored the message. He received thousands of messages per minute, and although he was able to process and reply to all of them in a matter of seconds, he believed in the aura of performance and thought it was best to remain silent. Limited accessibility would add mystique to his acting persona.

The military man persisted, and finally, Belex, annoyed, returned a message saying he had no desire to participate in any war. "I believe war is a tonic for the ego of the most basic primates," he said, and to accentuate his point, he sent a video of the extinct bonobo species engaged in vicious brawls.

That seemed to end their conversation, and Belex prepared for the next event, this one at a large outdoor stadium. The collective was happy to approve stadium renovations for what was now billed throughout stoven.net as an "event experience," as opposed to an "event."

"Why would the military be interested in such a thing?" asked Aurilena.

"I don't know, and he disappeared from my active nodes. Well, truth be told, he had never been in an active node. He was contacting me in a secure tunnel. But I never heard from him again."

None of that made sense to Aurilena. It was as if he was speaking a foreign language. "Okay, whatever, carry on," she said.

Not only were the live performances of Belex's acting troupe an unprecedented success, but thousands of citizens from across the Homeland expressed interest in joining the troupe. "Now, everyone's an actor," said one of the actresses as they prepared to go on stage in front of 100,000 people, nearly a tenth of the population of the Homeland.

If the first event was a success, the second was historic. Stoven.net was awash in messages extolling the virtues of live performances. "It may be the end of individualistic storytelling," some were saying, but others countered that. No, this was merely one more bow in the quiver of performing arts, and variety was welcome.

Belex stopped for a moment and looked at Aurilena and Hilkiah. "It's almost as if I'm remembering this story as I tell it," he said. "I recall one event, and the next appears."

"Problem is," said Aurilena, "is it *your* memory?"

"It is yours," said Sherealla to him in a way that startled him. "There are millions of memory nodes all over stoven.net regarding these events."

He had forgotten about her merge with the Oracle and the fact that she was now taking residence inside him, and although he was not directly connected to stoven.net, he had neglected to remove her access to his system of ports. He continued with his story.

Belex was bidding his fellow actors goodbye when his story began its final curtain call. As he was leaving the grand and opulent stadium, which had been enhanced by nanobot construction and architecture crews with a multitude of decorative, technical, and practical upgrades, he encountered a singularly odd drone. It looked like a hologram, but he knew it was not, and it frightened him. It had no face above its collar. Its clothes looked metallic, but with green waves, like water moving rhythmically as it finished materializing in front of Belex.

"Who are you?" asked Belex.

The apparition—and that was surely what this was—offered only a sinister smile, revealing two rows of sharp canines as it extended its arms and said, "Come." The smile was alone in a field of pure blackness above its shoulders, and when the smile disappeared, only the black field remained.

"To where? What are you doing?" It was as if the being was from another planet.

"To the greatest show on earth," said the being. "You will be a legend for all time. You will delight audiences for eternity because the victory that you'll establish will itself be eternal. Come."

He searched the collective, searched his memory nodes, everywhere, trying to match the image in front of him, but there were no results. This being, whoever and whatever he was, existed outside the collective. Stoven.net had no awareness of him. Several hundred replies to his query, "Have you seen this being?" returned with negative responses, not even any plausible theories.

"I am not known. Unlike you, I prefer anonymity. If my works were known," chuckled the being, "I do believe my fame would dwarf yours. But alas, that is not anywhere in my sphere of intention. Now. Come."

Belex had no intention of going anywhere with this entity.

"Your idea was brilliant," said the being with a smile so baleful that a rapid search through stoven.net could find no images reflecting such malevolence. It was as if this being was the great actor, not Belex, playing the greatest villain of Belex's career. "Blocking your hippocampus auxiliary nodes so that the collective can't see your intentions. Let's take that a step further, shall we?"

In an instant, Belex felt as if he had become dumb. He had no access to anything on stoven.net, and even his own memory nodes seemed to stop responding. Suddenly, he could remember nothing.

4

"It was Maoch," said Belex. "I didn't recognize him in the plaza because this part of my memory was still temporarily deleted from my systems."

"He wiped your memory," said Aurilena. "But you're saying that now, your systems are coming back. Is this a bad thing or a good thing?" When she looked at Belex, he looked heartbroken. "Not that I'm not happy for you!" she offered.

Belex sighed. "I think this is Sherealla's work." He waited for a moment for her to say something, but she was silent.

"She's with you now. Won't she say?"

Belex shrugged. "I think she's still not very fond of me."

"I have permissions for some military-grade access and memory nodes," he finally heard her say. She displayed a diagram of his brain in his eyes and zoomed in on the precise location of the relevant nanochips in his hippocampus. "It was a simple flag," she said, "surprisingly easy, although I had to barrel through an encryption routine to set it. You have access to the collective now, a bit imperfect still, and most of your memory should be coming back. Not all. Some nodes are gone."

"Thank you," he said.

"For what?" Aurilena replied.

Belex smiled, and said, "For just being you. Okay, sorry, I was talking to Sherealla. She did this. She fixed me. I owe her. That's all I remember, Hilkiah. My next memory is waking up with a sore head here and riding behind this beauty on her horse." He glanced at Aurilena when he said that.

Hilkiah said, "Well, then, suddenly everything fits into place, does it not? I dare say you provided Maoch an idea for his scheme."

"Hiding my intent through my nodes, yes. I guess so. And when I came to, I recalled a memory about wishing I had brought a diagnostic tool with me, but that doesn't make sense because we have self-diagnostics. So, maybe that was part of some memory from acting. It's gone now, that memory."

"And you don't remember what happened after that because he took you captive, wiped out your memory, and eliminated your access from this stoven. net disaster that your kind is so reliant on, which all suggests that your absence will have been noticed by your fellow citizens."

"Or netizens!" Aurilena laughed at her own joke, happy she could find humor even in their darkest hours, but also realizing that the hour had become just a little brighter. "If we go to Gath, they will see us together. That will really shake things up, Hilkiah."

"When and if I approve such a mission. For now, I can only acquiesce to the reconnaissance mission you're about to begin."

That didn't derail her excitement. The disappearance of a famous actor had to be big news.

As if reading Aurilena's thoughts, and Belex hoped that wasn't the case, Sherealla said to him, "Sorry to say, nobody thinks you're missing. The news is that you're shooting a new cinescape on location, which is another thing that never gets done but kind of what you claimed was happening when we found you. But you can still use your disappearance to your advantage."

"How?" asked Belex out loud.

"I don't know, it just will," said Aurilena, thinking he was talking to her, still thinking their appearance in Gath would shake things up.

"There must be some record of your discussion with Maoch," said Sherealla. "Some recording. Somewhere. Do some scans and searches. See what comes up."

This time, Belex replied through his thoughts so as not to confuse Aurilena. "Okay, I've just done that. Nothing. That doesn't seem right. He couldn't block my personal observation nodes, I don't think."

"Which means the recording is in there somewhere. Perhaps he found a way to encrypt it or hacked into your system somehow."

"He clearly did that—he got into my personal memory nodes."

"A common military tactic. Deleting certain memory nodes provides some protection to spies and the few people who have to do any physical fighting."

"But he can't get at my biological memory."

"I know what you're getting at, and it would be a good answer," said Sherealla, "if we had the resources to do something that two thousand years of research has failed to do . . . digitizing biological memory into video streams. Never been done. Probably can't be done."

Belex knew that, but he couldn't help fantasizing about the possibility of his people seeing Maoch and his empty head. If they knew about him, wouldn't it start a rebellion? That was a difficult question to answer regarding an apathetic society beguiled by a variety of digital and biological opiates.

"Sherealla," said Belex silently through nodes, "won't stoven.net be aware of your presence and track you to Moria? And me, too?" The idea sent shudders through him.

"No. That's why I merged with the Oracle. To get access to all its knowledge but to also access the blocking mechanisms that MagicLand hackers added to prevent stoven.net and the Homeland from finding it. I can lurk about stoven. net all I want, as long as I don't interact with anybody. Same with you. Don't talk to anyone, and you'll be fine. As for me, until I merged with the Oracle, the Hunter Collective was able to track my every move."

"So, the entire time you were here, they knew everything you knew. About Aurilena, about Hilkiah, everything there is to know about MagicLand," said Belex out loud.

"Magicwhat?" said Aurilena, who this time figured out he was talking to Sherealla.

"MagicLand. It's what we call Moria," said Belex.

"MagicLand?" said Aurilena. "That's kind of sweet."

"I believe little damage was done," said Hilkiah. "If the information they received was enough to destroy us, they would have. If, as you suggested, she was a failsafe, that part of the plan has apparently been foiled. It comforts me somewhat," smiled Hilkiah, "that our cloaking is so immersive that it leads to utterly chaotic military strategies. I'll admit to having mixed feelings about the knowledge that there were Morians with sophisticated enough knowledge to, as you say, 'hack' the Oracle."

Belex nodded and smiled. "Are we ready, Aurilena?"

Aurilena looked apprehensive, but she nodded.

Belex said, "Sherealla, I'm cutting myself off from stoven.net. Which means I'm cutting you off. You can observe, but I won't hear you unless I call for you. I find your interruptions . . . disturbing."

"And you claim to be an entertainer," she replied. "Look," she said. "I'll try to keep my mouth shut. But you should let me communicate with you. If you get into trouble, you'll have better access to the collective through me. You are still sort of coming online. Besides, I have an idea. I am going to try to cast an Unseen Spell on you and Lena," she said. "Through stoven.net. So that you are invisible when you get there. If it works, it provides a huge advantage in being able to scout."

Everyone nodded in approval. "I'll keep my ports open for you only. I don't want the collective to know I'm lurking about Gath quite yet," said Belex. "But how do we know if the spell works?" asked Belex.

"You'll know soon enough," she said.

Belex didn't know if he'd be able to access anything from the Oracle through Sherealla in such a way that he could present information to people he encountered on this convoluted method of travel, and Aurilena didn't know either. This was experimental magic, and its combination with Gath technology made Aurilena terribly uncomfortable.

"Alright, fine," said Belex. "I'm ready."

Aurilena took his hand, and he closed his eyes. Then they went to Gath.

5

When they arrived in Gath, he saw familiar sights.

There were personal pods darting about a sky, filled with tall skyscrapers illuminating the night air. On the ground, he saw Aurilena standing next to him, holding his hand. "Is the spell working? Can they see us?" he asked, referring to two approaching Gath.

"I don't even know," she whispered. She felt tense as they approached. One of them was gesticulating as if deep in conversation, but he wasn't saying anything, and neither was his companion. They looked identical to each other but different than Belex. Aurilena wondered if they were participants in shared roles in Gath society, and if all Gath looked alike based on their roles. She looked at Belex, wondering if there were hundreds or even thousands of actor types who looked like him.

He squeezed her hand as they approached. "Identical twins. We have lots of those here. It's been kind of trendy during the last hundred years or so, sometimes a hundred or more from one batch," he said to her.

She regretted asking him about the twins, then realized she didn't ask. She felt tense, but the approaching Gath still didn't seem to notice them. She started to move aside but Belex held her firm. "No. Stay." The two Gath neared them, and one of them looked up, smiled, and pointed. The other nodded and smiled, looking at Belex and Aurilena. The first one was still pointing and laughing as the two Gath walked through Belex and Aurilena as if they were ghosts. When Belex and Aurilena turned around to watch the two, the pointer was still pointing and hit the other one in the shoulder for apparently making a joke.

Directly in their line of sight was a cloud of drones that appeared to be grooming the stem of a large flower with two long tendrils protruding out of an extended stigma, which itself protruded from a wheel of long purple and red petals. Attached to each tendril was an eyeball staring into a building window. The stem of the flower extended several stories high and was a brighter, more neon color of green than what seemed natural to Aurilena.

She wanted to ask Belex what the creature was and what it was doing, but it seemed pointless to start asking questions about every odd thing she saw since a quick scan of the area showed many strange sights. She was also still recovering from the anxiety of the approaching Gath, not knowing if they would react to her presence. She wasn't concerned for her physical safety in that regard, at least not yet, because she knew they were the equivalent of what Belex called a hologram. But the longer-term implications of being seen were of concern. She didn't know if their presence would trigger an alarm of some kind or even somehow provide clues on how to penetrate Moria.

They walked past the seeing plant, noticing that its locomotion seemed to be managed by a bottom layer made of thousands of tiny legs. "What on earth is that thing?" asked Aurilena.

"I think it's just for amusement," replied Belex. She thought that a lot of work had to have been done to create such amusement, but not being Gath, she wasn't aware of the large amount of leisure time most Gath possessed, all thanks to drone and nanobot technology and the fact that nanobots could have sequenced DNA to produce such a creature in a matter of minutes. This kind of activity was frowned upon by Gath society, as DNA sequencing was considered dangerous after the Piltdown Man accident of a thousand years ago, but there were allowances for frivolity.

As Aurilena observed the architecture of the city's buildings, she found herself awed by the perfection found in the way each building stylistically blended with another. Each building danced with the shadows created by its neighboring structure, and there was a magnificent grace to how each spire, arch, cantilever, truss, buttress, and tube interacted with the surrounding objects. And the city was impossibly clean. She doubted there was one speck of dirt anywhere.

One spire reached into the clouds. "Two miles," said Belex as Aurilena stopped to look up and stare. The tower was made of white stone with no windows in the first several hundred feet. Its intricate pinnacle peeked out of the clouds and poked into the blue sky beyond. "That's where we need to be," he continued. "It's called the Mantricle. It's where everything that matters is located. A large collection of quantum computers and, it's said, the military, but that's largely rumor. If someone were to destroy that building, stoven.net would no longer exist, so it is said."

"Not true," interjected Sherealla, annoying Belex. "Stoven.net is woven into the biological fabric of every individual in the Homeland. The only outside interface is a satellite system orbiting Earth, but that mostly serves as a relaying, navigational and informational resource. We are now largely self-sufficient when it comes to our ability to interconnect, build, network, and think as one unit. Even destroying the satellites would only result in a minor degradation of these capabilities."

Belex found it disturbing that she referred to the Gath as "we." He no longer felt part of this. He looked at the ridge on the back of his hand and remembered that he was probably the only one who felt that way.

He felt his fists tighten as he prepared to ask Sherealla a question. Every time she spoke, she managed to elicit that kind of response from him, it seemed. "Then what's the purpose behind the braggadocio represented by the building? And why is your information different than the rest of stoven.net?"

"Maoch is at the center of everything. That's not recorded on stoven.net, either. I'm not saying you shouldn't go inside the building. You should. You'll probably find him there. I'm simply pointing out that our species *is* stoven.net."

"He'll probably be there?"

"I have access to highly secure military information. But not that high."

"Does the entire military apparatus know about Maoch?"

"Only those at the highest levels. The military is the last remaining hierarchy in our society. Maoch, of course, being at the top of the pyramid."

"So he's a military guy."

"Quite. For the last 900 years. I think he might oversee the Homeland Defense Force. But I don't have that kind of access. I do know one thing: he was the so-called military officer who contacted you. The one from the Halcyon Saber Group, which is a group of about one, I think," she chuckled.

It took a moment for Belex to digest this. He was unable to process how the reality was so different than the collective memory of stoven.net. How are secrets with that level of significance hidden in a completely pluralistic, free, and democratic society with collective decision-making? Thanks to the celerity delivered by thousands of years of improved processing power, even the smallest decision—where to plant a tree or garden, what foods to develop, everything—was the result of instant, spontaneous plebiscites. Everyone knew everything the moment it happened. How could secrets reside in such a place?

Sherealla and Belex had processed this discussion in a matter of seconds, and he relayed the information to Aurilena.

"We have to go now, then," said Aurilena.

Belex agreed but couldn't share his apprehension. His last personal meeting with Maoch had not gone well, although he took some comfort in knowing this would not be a personal meeting, only an observation, hopefully one that would pay tactical dividends.

Sherealla broke into Belex's thoughts with, "I can release the Unseen Spell if you want."

Belex wanted to chastise her for again entering his thoughts, which was precisely what he had told her not to do, but her suggestion seemed helpful, so he stayed quiet, other than saying, "Not yet." There were advantages to not being seen.

Belex wondered out loud if it was possible for them to transpose directly to the top of the building's interior rather than try to figure out how to navigate their way to Maoch's lair, assuming that was where it was.

"I was only able to get us to Gath because you were able to tell me something about it, and we had a map," Aurilena said. "With planets, we have exact coordinates, but I never know where we'll end up. You've seen the results."

"Sure have," Belex smiled.

"So, we could end up within a slab of concrete or something at the top of the building. We aren't quite holograms right now, Belex. A part of us is physically here. Our consciousness. I don't know for sure that we can't be trapped somehow. When I keep saying that this is new to me, I do mean that it is new to me. Besides, not even Seth, an astral master, did as much as we are trying to do." At this, she couldn't prevent her mind from fond recollections of her brother.

6

"This is amazing, little brother," said an admiring Aurilena. She rubbed his head in just the way she knew he hated. But he also yearned for it. He loved getting attention from his older sister and knew it was a sign of her great affection for him.

The spot they sat on was literally the top of the world. She was surprised she could feel the intensity of the winds up here without freezing. She wasn't cold at all. All she felt was the blast of the wind on her face, but it was as if it blew through her instead of against her. It was the strangest feeling she'd ever had. She heard a constant sound pillage the nearby rocks, sometimes in a whistling frenzy, other times steady like a wolf's howl careening off canyon walls. At times, the wolf's howl would escape into a ghostly moan that made her shiver more than any cold wind ever had.

"How often do you do this?" she asked.

"Every day. Some days it's all I do. Sometimes, I go to where Dad acquires stuff. I don't know why he does that. He never actually sees anything there like I do. It's better to go there and see stuff. It's better than going there to take stuff."

"He's not stealing stuff, Seth; he's just taking from places that are gone from history. From where people used to live."

"I think he sometimes does."

He was only nine years old, five years younger than his sister, but he sometimes seemed like a wise old man. Aurilena could imagine a day when Seth would take Hilkiah's place as a high priest.

"Why do you say that?"

The boy shrugged his shoulders. "I just think so is all," he said as if accepting a sad fact.

"Most places on the earth, Seth," she said, "have no people."

"Some do," he said earnestly. "A lot, kinda." He said this as if he was repeating a math equation. "I'll show you sometime."

But it never happened. The Gath saw to that.

7

"Oh, Lena, I'm so sorry. About all these reminders of Seth. If I could just do one thing to change the past, I know what it would be."

A tear slowly discharged from the corner of her eye and took a prolonged journey to her chin, where a droplet clung symbolically for a long time before letting go. "Not a day goes by I don't wish he was here," she said.

"No wonder you hate me. Hate *us*," said Belex.

"I don't hate you. I keep trying. But then *you* just keep pushing your way back into my heart. And I'm afraid of the day you stop trying to do that."

He looked at her, then at the two-mile-high building they had finally reached. He tugged at her arm, and they stopped walking. He looked into her eyes and wanted to kiss her dark olive cheeks. "It's not me trying," he said. "It's my soul, and it's not giving me a choice in the matter." His wide sleeve wiped the trail her tear had left on her cheek. "Are you ready?"

She nodded.

The Mantricle was guarded by a variety of drones. There was no indication of their existence on stoven.net, which meant their communication portals were closed. This was expected. Belex also suspected there were many additional drones not in view. Any interlopers would be caught by a swarm and destroyed instantly, he thought.

Luckily, Aurilena and Belex were not interlopers. Belex thought about this. What exactly were they? Was this a form of time travel? He had a sense that although it was magic, it was based on science, and if it was, it was a science unknown to his people. He had felt her arm when he tugged on it. He had wiped a tear from her cheek. What was real here? What was the nature of their physical manifestation here in Gath?

Several of the drones were the hovering police drones familiar to Belex, spinning globes suspended in air and cut with a thin line at their diameter. These were lethal little machines, Belex knew, that could gather into a thousand-member unit in a matter of seconds. There were also ground units, most of them quite small and unthreatening to the eye but, he knew, stockpiled with lethality. The deadliest of all, though, were the tiny black swarm drones that had taken poor Seth. Belex prayed to whatever gods existed that Aurilena did not see any of these.

The couple casually strolled through the entrance. A few Gath were milling about the large foyer. Aurilena and Belex walked past them, unnoticed. Belex and Aurilena hurried to a set of doors at the far end of the foyer, which was highlighted by a series of immensely tall white posts. There were no markings on them, but Sherealla was able to inform Belex that they led to the top of the building, probably to Maoch. Unfortunately, according to Sherealla, they were controlled by portals embedded within each Gath's system. Not only was Belex unable to access his systems in a way that could manifest itself here in Gath, but even if he could, he wouldn't have sufficient permissions to open the doors. Their only hope was to wait for someone to arrive. There weren't many people around. *It might be a long wait,* Belex thought.

He was wrong. Almost as soon as he had finished his communication with Sherealla, the doors opened, but this presented another problem. The assumption had been that there would be several stops, not just the final one at the top of the building two miles away.

"Right?" asked Aurilena when she presented that same thought to Belex.

"Enter," said a voice from inside the doors. The voice's eerie familiarity caused Aurilena and Belex to glance nervously at each other as they shuffled closer and peered inside the doors without walking through. The voice repeated itself, "Enter."

Aurilena shrugged, pulled Belex by the hand, and they went through the door. The doors closed quickly, and the building car they were in shot upward at a higher rate of speed than either a Gath or Morian body would have been able to endure, but because they were in the bizarre state of being *almost* there, the rapid movement had no effect on his or Aurilena's body.

"Not sure this was the best decision," said Sherealla to Belex.

Belex said out loud, "Then why didn't you say something before we went through the doors?"

"Because I didn't know then what I know now."

Aurilena glanced over to him and said, "Sherealla again?" then returned her gaze to the wall of the car they were in. The walls were translucent, not opaque like they appeared from the outside. Aurilena saw the silhouette of the city as they rushed upward.

Belex said, "Uh-huh."

"Let me guess," said Aurilena. "She's not so sure we made a good decision going through the doors."

"What's the worst that can happen?" pondered Belex out loud. "He looks scarier this time or something? Not that I'm sure that's possible. That's one sinister-looking Gath."

"Well, seeing as we are in Gath. And seeing as we are trying something *nobody* in Moria has tried before. And seeing what Gath are capable of when it comes to being ornery, I'm going to decline to answer that question and hope for the best here," Aurilena said, smiling bravely.

The journey was over quickly, and the doors made a slight hissing noise as they opened.

"Come," said a voice.

Belex and Aurilena exited the building car and looked around. The room was bright yellow, but there was nothing inside but a bit of fog in the middle. The fog dissipated to reveal a structure that looked to Aurilena precisely like the Oracle in Moria.

"Come," said the voice again. The two took baby steps forward.

The object that looked like the Oracle transformed itself in a flash of light into the being who had appeared at the plaza outside the Hall of Legions in Moria and to Belex before his crash. *Maoch.*

He was juggling three luminescent balls. They combined into one, which he threw onto the floor. It lit up into a wall-sized projection of the hills outside Moria, a black cloud, then a highly detailed view of Seth's anguished face as he screamed in pain.

"I do take great joy in altering the physical state of primates who engage in witchcraft," said Maoch.

Belex looked at Aurilena, who had started to sob and shake her head. "Aurilena, let's just go."

"*Go!*" thundered the cruel Gath. "Go where? Back to your pathetic backwater town with its old, dying witches and warlocks and clerics who look like they are nibbled on every night by slum rats? You have such primitive little minds," said Maoch. "Even his mind," he said, looking directly at Belex, "enhanced like mine but no match for mine. Did you really think I would not see you here? You are both nothing but shadows of an eradicated pestilence." Maoch uttered the word "pestilence" with such malice that even in her ghostly state Aurilena could feel her body shudder. The sound of Seth screaming was repeated. His shriek filled the room.

Maoch cackled, "Perhaps I should wait for you to bear a child, little one, so that you can watch me snatch it away as you feed it. Would that not be a momentous event, actor? Shall we fill the stadia for all to see? Impregnate this wench for me, actor, so that our collective can rejoice in the offspring's cries as it is hoisted from his mother's withering teat." He breathed laboriously, it seemed. Belex couldn't tell if it was for effect, or if there was something wrong with him. "Alas," Maoch said after a moment of silence, other than the sniffling sounds from Aurilena, "I shall finish this task in my own time. You will have no say in the timing of your ignominious defeat."

"Aurilena. No more," pleaded Belex.

But her resolve seemed to strengthen. "You think you can hurt me because I'm sentimental and have a beating heart instead of a bunch of wires and electricity?" she said, stepping toward Maoch, sobbing through her words but still standing tall and sounding strong, despite the obvious grief and despair.

"You don't understand as much as you think you do. The only thing your technology has accomplished is that it's turned you into a hypocritical, feral barbarian. You've got nothing on me on the evolutionary scale. And I'm going to destroy you. Come on," she said to Belex, and she closed her eyes, snapped her head a little, and the two of them appeared on the street below.

8

"Tell Sherealla it's time," said Aurilena firmly.

"Okay, Sherealla," said Belex in his cyber voice. "If you think you can make it so people can see us, now's the time."

People were walking past and not noticing them, and one walked through them just as Belex spoke. Neither Belex nor Aurilena considered the possibility that because Maoch could see them, so could other Gath. They knew that Maoch alone could; they didn't know why, and they didn't, at this point, care. Aurilena seemed determined to proceed apace and try to set a plan in motion.

Watching her now made him feel almost weak in the knees. He was stunned and thrilled at how she turned her grief to anger and then her anger into fierce determination. Before he had time to think any of this through, Belex noticed people pointing and a small crowd gathering around them. It all happened so fast that he had no time to react or say anything to Aurilena, who had a wide, victorious smile on her face. She took Belex's hand.

"Belex Deralk-Almd," she said as the crowd quickly grew and gathered. "It is a tradition in my culture, the culture of Moria . . ."

Belex was eager to discover the stunt Aurilena was creating. He could hear and see stoven.net hum, chatter, think, query, and respond. His fame had certainly not abated during his time away. The collective was suddenly a crowded room of a million voices.

Aurilena spun around to face Belex. She flattened his tunic with the palms of her hands and said, "We really need to work on your wardrobe. Anyway, it is the tradition among my people that a woman who has found a man so compelling, so steeped in honor that she is completely engulfed by the flames in her heart and she cannot imagine living one moment without this man . . . it is our tradition that she asks him to marry her. And so, Belex Deralk-Almd of Gath, I am asking you, with all my heart and with all humility and with the honor of both our lands, will you marry me?"

Stoven.net clattered with reaction as Belex looked at her in stunned silence.

"Oh, you better marry her, you fool!"

"Oh, what a beautiful, savage beast she is! Marry her!"

"Look at her; just look at her Belex. Royalty has returned to Gath!"

The feeling was universal. No dissent whatsoever. Not even the whisper of a complaint.

Belex took her hands and shook his head with what Aurilena would later say was the stupidest smile she'd ever seen, and said, "I'd be a fool not to, and it's not just me that says so," and Aurilena jumped up and wrapped her arms around him. Within seconds, stoven.net was flooded with party invitations and celebration strata from people across Gath.

"That's my girl," said Sherealla to Belex.

Aurilena's mind spun with imaginings about Maoch's anger. Belex wondered about this, too, and asked Sherealla if she was aware of any reaction from Maoch to this development. Meanwhile, Belex's heart was singing. He could never have imagined his people reacting this way after twenty centuries of warfare with Aurilena's people.

But he had missed an important aspect regarding the overall situation. During the confusion and stress of their confrontation with Maoch, Sherealla had released the books of ancient history and the exterminations into stoven. net. Belex realized it soon after Aurilena's proposal, but it confounded him that Maoch couldn't prevent this. It suggested that there was some limitation to Maoch's power over stoven.net, and this would bode well for the future. The release of the books had an immediate impact, and stoven.net was sieged with outrage.

"You know what?" Aurilena said as they started to walk the city streets of Gath. "I'm not in a big hurry to return, are you?" She knew, of course, that stoven.net would capture and report on every word Belex and Aurilena would say to each other. This was the newest and greatest production in Gath cinescape history, and the people were eating it up.

"Nah," said Belex. "Besides, we need a cure for the nanobots Maoch introduced into your system."

This comment sent off another furious round of talk and speculation on stoven.net. Who was Maoch? What exactly did he do? Help nodes began popping up all over the collective. It took only seconds for various threads to develop recalling Belex's inquiry regarding Maoch's image a few months prior. At once, thousands of people began to inquire into the nature of Aurilena's illness. And just in time, thought Aurilena, because she had been feeling weak and nauseous since their escape from Maoch. At first, she thought it was just a fear reaction, but the symptoms were progressing.

Eventually, Belex had to explain to the collective that there was little anyone could do for her until Aurilena made a physical appearance in Gath, but when Sherealla shared molecular diagrams of the nanobots in question, stoven.net went to work. Nobody had seen anything like them, but that only created incentive. Everyone wanted to be the first to find the cure.

The first consensus within stoven.net was that the nanobots were not designed as a poison, but that Aurilena's symptoms were side effects from the nanobots' original intent as a tracking mechanism for the destruction of her city, which was suddenly a shocking development to the hive mind of Gath. The previously routine matter of mass slaughter had become an appalling notion to a suddenly enlightened city.

Belex was noticing her progressing symptoms. He wanted to stay longer, too, to taunt Maoch, but it was time to leave. He informed stoven.net of his intent to return to MagicLand. There were pleas for him to keep the communication links alive while he was there. He didn't think that was wise, given Maoch's likely mood. But with everyone working on a cure, he'd need to access their thoughts. Sherealla, through the Oracle, would need to be the conduit. He felt it was too risky to have his thoughts and activities made known to the collective. When he announced his decision to go dark, it simply added to his mystique. He wasn't convinced that the Oracle's communication with stoven.net was safe, either, but both he and Hilkiah would later decide they didn't have a choice.

9

Belex and Aurilena left without the cure they were hoping to find, but they had won a victory far beyond anything they had hoped for. They now had the full resources of Gath technology to defeat the nanobot threat in Aurilena's body. Because they had Gath itself.

When they awoke from their reverie, Hilkiah was beaming.

"Did you mean that, Aurilena?" was the first thing that popped out of Belex's mouth.

Hilkiah said through a chortle, "Of course, she did, dear boy. Please tell me, though, Aurilena, why in the name of the Great Shepherd did you choose to ask him such a momentous question in Gath?"

They both explained the details of their observations, and all that came out of Hilkiah's pleased lips was, "Marvelous. I couldn't have imagined such a spectacular outcome. Do you two realize what you've accomplished?"

Belex took Aurilena's hand and kissed it. "What *she* accomplished. I mean, talk about thinking on your feet."

"It just came to me. I swear," said Aurilena, "it wasn't even my idea."

"Yehoshua," said Hilkiah.

Aurilena nodded.

"But she's not well, Hilkiah. Everybody seems to think that her illness is a side-effect rather than an intent of the nanobots."

"Everybody?" asked Hilkiah. "How many folks were you able to talk to while you were in Gath to achieve a majority consensus such as that?"

"You know," corrected Belex. "Stoven.net. So that's a lot of people. In fact, it's everybody. In Gath."

Hilkiah smiled and said, "Forgive an old magician for forgetting that. It is still a concept quite foreign to my way of thinking. Something a bit difficult to grasp."

"Well, just imagine hearing everyone's thoughts here in MagicLand," said Belex. "It's like that."

"Again, as I say. A difficult concept. I have enough trouble concentrating on what one person says to me at once. Add a second person, and I'm a stew of confusion."

"Well, that's where the augmentation serves us well. I can process a million thoughts at once if I have to."

"If you consider that a good thing, I will not try to relinquish you of your enthusiasm," said Hilkiah with a slight tone of admonishment.

Belex sighed. "It's like the Legions, Hilkiah, only ten times more of them. The point is, we now have the population of Gath on our side, and they are all looking for a cure. Sherealla will update me on any progress. So far nothing, but she's submitted schematics of the nanobots to the collective, and they're being processed."

"You both did well. Your efforts will be honored in ceremony someday, I assure you."

"Yeah, a marriage ceremony," Aurilena gleamed.

CHAPTER XII

1

Time wasn't kind to them as Aurilena's condition quickly deteriorated. Belex tried to urge Sherealla to fast-forward a cure through stoven.net, but there was bad news, there, too. No matter what Sherealla said to counter the sentiment, the general feeling in the collective was that the entire affair was part of a complex cinescape. Many thought that delaying a cure was part of the plotline and should be postponed until the last exciting moment.

A name for the cinescape had even gone viral: *Saving Aurilena.* A question among those who thought it was a cinescape episode became ominous: should the Wiccan be saved at all? Perhaps the lesson of the cinescape was for the hero to undergo tragedy so that he would fully understand that there could never be happiness found through a romantic entanglement with MagicLand. This opinion spawned a secondary title called, *The Lessons of Warfare.*

Luckily, there were many others who took the heart of the events seriously and were eager to find a cure for the sake of the couple's happiness. Belex was truly adored throughout Gath. This seemed impenetrable, despite Maoch's perfect ruthlessness.

2

The next day brought a darker cloud of anxiety to those who cared for Aurilena. Her mother was becoming agitated. This alarmed Hilkiah because even though the patient was her daughter, he would have expected Miriam to remain calmly resolute while seeing her daughter through the crisis. But she seemed frightened, and a frightened healer was never a good thing.

Hilkiah couldn't remain silent, so he remarked on his observations to her. Upon hearing what he said, she replied simply, "I don't know about that, but I'm almost as sick as she is thinking that my daughter wants to marry a Gath."

"What can I do to help?"

"I believe you know the answer to this."

"If magic could alter the girl's heart, I'd be sorely tempted. But you know your daughter better than I do, so I don't need to tell you that her heart is not in an alterable state." He rubbed his beard in contemplation. "Truth be told, the time to act was when she brought the boy here. I should have quarantined the lad to keep her away."

"Bah. You make it sound as though he's human."

Hilkiah ignored her reply. "But now, they have experienced much together. Like it or not, they've become a couple. The bond established while they were in Gath is, I'm afraid, made of an epoxy that will endure in such a way that if you attempt to dissolve it, you will lose her."

"I know that much," Miriam sighed. "I was her age, too, once."

"We can't attribute this strictly to the typhoons of the teenage heart."

She nodded at this. "She's a smart girl, Hilkiah. She's never fallen for one of our boys. Why is that? And why . . . *him*?"

"The purity behind the mystery of love is an absolute I'll never trifle with."

"So you approve of this error. Oh, dear Hilkiah, what am I doing? My daughter suffers, and I'm assaulting her choices. What kind of mother does that?"

"One who cares. And to answer your question," Hilkiah waited a beat, "it's complicated. I've spent considerable time with the lad. I've seen his heart. And I approve of his heart. I vouch for the boy in the most absolute terms. Like everyone here in Moria, I have no love lost for the Gath. Aurilena's life will become more challenging than it would have been if she had found herself a nice boy from Moria. That is my only concern, and I have no illusions about that. But as for the boy himself? If he survives, he'll grow to be an impressive young man. And he'll be one of ours. I'll see to it."

There was little more to say. Miriam knew that Hilkiah's arguments regarding Aurilena's emotions were cogent enough. She also knew she could simply call on the Legions and ask that they forbid the marriage and try to force Aurilena to stay away from the Gath, but she knew Aurilena would easily circumvent the order. These kinds of actions were classic blunders by parents trying to control their children's destinies. One thing she had always been determined to do was to allow her children to set out on their own journeys. This was a particularly difficult journey to observe, but Miriam thought, her desire to alter the path was her problem, not her daughter's.

"I guess the best way for me to deal with this is to try to make her comfortable," she said. She set to that task after giving Hilkiah a warm embrace goodbye.

They lodged Aurilena in a room on the fourth floor of the Hall of Legions. Miriam called it a healing room, and she invited several healers from around MagicLand. She wasn't surprised when a few, somewhat impolitely, declined the invitation. Others were more eager. Aurilena had always been well-liked, and part of what people liked about her was the perception that she liked taking risks. Marrying a Gath, of course, according to a saying spreading through Moria, was more reckless than risk.

3

"Father," Aurilena greeted Hiram as he walked in after a long day away from their home.

"Hello, my sweet." He kissed her forehead and went into the kitchen. There were apple biscuits on the counter, and he took one.

Aurilena padded in behind him, wearing a bathrobe and big feathered slippers. Her hair was still wet after a long bath, and she felt refreshed enough to make a demand. "Father. I saw this hat while looking at books in the library. It's the perfect riding hat. Have you seen such a thing?" She had learned how to project images of things she'd seen, and she did so now, which forced Hiram to view a canvas hat rimmed with fur and a pointed top rounded off by a small ball of fur.

Hiram nodded. "Ah, yes. An ancient look from the Mongolian steppes. But how did you find this in the library?"

"I just kind of ran into it looking at other stuff. Can you get one?"

"A hat like that?"

She nodded.

"Why on earth do you want such a thing?"

"Don't you think it would make me look regal?"

"Since when did you care about regality?" her father replied.

"Since I saw this hat," she laughed. "Please, Daddy. I love it."

Even though it was one of the few times she had asked for anything, he tried to explain to her that he was too tired to go on a mission like this for a hat, but the truth was that the death of his son had worn him down and dispirited him. At one time, he would have enjoyed the unique challenge of searching for such an antiquity. He no longer hungered to acquire anything, be it a slab of marble or a hat. Aurilena was discouraged, but she put on a brave front as she walked away.

Hiram only wished he felt worse than he did about his unwillingness to find Aurilena the item she craved. But he didn't feel much of anything these days. He felt no joy at a feast or at one of Hilkiah's prayer circles, nor any regret at the increasingly frequent conflicts with his wife. He felt no anger toward his wife, either. He simply felt nothing. He was slowly being molded into a different soul, one made of the coldest of stone from the kind of impossible grief that can only be acquired when a parent loses a child.

Aurilena mentioned the hat several more times over the next year but eventually gave up when it was clear Hiram never seemed to be in an acquiring mood. The distance from his family began to define him, slowly stripping away the productive details that had once formed the ballast of a more honored reputation. He loved his daughter still, this he knew. He hoped that he still loved his wife, as well. But it was as if he faced an emotional blockade, a force that couldn't be reasoned with that shifted hope away from every one of his living moments. There was no way of turning back from this, he felt, unless someone could somehow use magic to bring back his child.

4

Hiram's heart was heavy with guilt. He had heard about Aurilena's sickness through an Empath in a pub. His growing distance from the family since Seth's death, and from Miriam especially, on some levels often seemed like a necessary respite. But it was accompanied by a persistently deep depression, the cause of which couldn't only be attributed to the grief of his lost son. Some of it was the grief over what he was now losing. After grumbling to himself that an Empath had no business being in a pub, he gathered up his mental strength to visit Aurilena at her bedside.

He stood for a moment outside her doorway, wondering what to say. He knew that even when he was at home, he wasn't. He knew that she knew that, too. He thought of all the times he'd had to stand with Hilkiah and others to defend Moria and felt that summoning the courage for this visit was far more difficult than any of those moments.

He decided to cheat. Maybe he had lost all true courage when he lost his son, he thought. It had certainly seemed that way to him on more than one occasion. He thought about the riding hat, which he hadn't provided Aurilena during her moments of grief after the death of her brother. He thought about her persistent requests and his silly denials. A strong wind from the steppes of Mongolia whistled through the hallway, blowing his hair back and drying his lips.

He staggered to the floor from the force of the blast as he fell to one knee, then reached to the floor with one hand while his heart, larger and happier, pounded inside his chest.

"You didn't have to do that," she said weakly as he entered her room with a large shepherd's hat. "Your being here is enough."

"I haven't been here at all," he replied with a gentle smile. He placed the hat on her stomach. She slowly caressed the horsetail at the end of the hat and smiled faintly. "I think about him every day, too, Dad." She took his hand as a tear fell off the corner of her eye. "It's better to cry than to run," she said, and he broke down into tears.

5

One of the healers Miriam had recruited to the cause of Aurilena's improvement was a youngling named Amanda, one of Hilkiah's favorite young protégés and one of those rare magicians who had many talents despite her youth, a trait she shared with Aurilena.

She immediately began looking after Aurilena like a parent, night after night, watching her deteriorating body writhe and wondering, not unsympathetically, why she wouldn't die.

Sometimes, she would tell people later, she had hoped that Aurilena would die because watching her suffer was an excruciating experience. It wasn't a true wish, just the kind of random dagger of illogic that can strike when someone wants to escape hardship.

Thankfully, days passed, and Aurilena wouldn't die. Her body weakened, but she somehow held on, and each passing hour filled Amanda with inspiration as she watched her new friend toss and turn during terrifying battles against her ailment. As Aurilena hung on, Amanda, thinking back to her first encounters with magic, grew closer to her, a nursing cheerleader rooting against dispiriting odds.

6

"Your aunt has some serious issues," said Beth to Amanda, who was sticking pins into a doll's head with some fury, pretending it was the magician.

Amanda was not quite nine, but she was already able to display a vast array of magical skills. "Why do you say that?" she asked, focusing intently on the doll's head, her tongue poking out of the upper corner of her mouth in concentration.

"Because look, that's why."

Her aunt, who was Amanda's adoptive mother, was just outside the door of Amanda's house, on her knees, planting flowers again. "That's like the twentieth time she's replanted that flower bed this week," said Amanda.

"See? What's that all about?" wondered Beth out loud. Beth was a little round girl who hadn't lost any of her baby fat. She had short hair and bright, pale skin that looked unhealthy in sunlight. Beth watched Amanda studiously trying to kill her victim. "Who is that?" she asked.

Amanda's long sandy-blonde hair kept trying to drape over the doll, and she'd impatiently push it away. "It's the magician," she said.

"Aren't you a magician?"

"I mean, it's a mean magician. He took my auntie's mom away a long time ago and killed my whole family even before that. That's why I'm here."

"Oh," said Beth. "Are you trying to kill him then?"

"Uh-huh."

"Where is he?"

"Come on!" Amanda jumped up and tugged on Beth's hand.

But as they went outside, her aunt stopped them by saying, "Look, honey, it worked. It finally worked."

Her mom had been planting rocks in the soil for weeks. Finally, what she had hoped for blossomed out of the soil and brought a tear to her eye and a smile to her face. She grabbed Amanda's head and kissed her forehead, her disheveled curly hair rubbing Amanda's forehead. "Ice plants. Aren't they beautiful?"

1

The days wore on without much change in Aurilena's condition. "You're so sweet for watching her with such attention." Belex was bending over and looking into the concerned eyes of the youngling they called Amanda. He had been told she had many gifts and that having her here could only help. "We're trying as many avenues as possible for her recovery," Hilkiah had said.

Belex watched as tears of sweat cascaded down Aurilena's skin from the curves of her hairline. Miriam, who was keeping a constant vigil on her daughter, sat on a chair on the other side of the bed from Amanda.

Belex knew Aurilena had a fever and feared she wouldn't survive, and he felt oppressed with guilt. *I did this to her* was an unbearable new anchor of thought in his daily living.

Aurilena's body seemed to be in a perpetual state of angry vibration. When he tried to cup her head in his hands, her head shook them off violently while it shuddered up and down against the pillow, throwing sweat against everything that surrounded her. Her pelvis jumped up, her body thrashed about, and her arms whipped up and down.

Miriam, seething at the Gath and unable to witness the charade any longer, removed herself from the room.

Aurilena clutched the sheets and looked at him desperately, wishing that she hadn't discovered him the way she did in the land of the buffalo. In the small instances of what was left of her consciousness, she allowed herself trickles of what may have been. Maybe if she had been an actor in one of his cinescapes or a young producer in his world. Or an old one. Maybe a director . . . or a friend of one. So many people she could have been in his world, and she was none of these. Instead, she was fading away from him, becoming a stranger to him again, and she was unable to even say goodbye through the strands of her remaining thoughts.

Belex wanted only that his eyes could say at least one last thing to her, to let her somehow know he understood that he was aware he had erred in his judgment of her and MagicLand. He had even grown fond of the city's dirt and grime. He wanted to tell her how much he longed to stay here and how strongly he knew the people here would rightly refuse that wish.

He had never considered death before, although he always had a sense that he was afraid of it. But not now. Having met her was solace enough to know that he, too, could enter this next phase. It hadn't been perfect, and he had never really spoken to her how he really felt, but it didn't matter. The opportunity of having experienced the young sorceress pursed the smallest smile upon his lips as he watched her through what he was sure was the end.

He grasped her hand and looked up at the ceiling to bring forth the light he knew should save her, but instead, her body grew wilder in its sweat and restlessness. *Where is the magic in this place now?* He wanted to believe in it. How did these people first tap into it, as ancients, before they evolved into the spirit race? Because that was what he needed to do. He needed to harken to those olden days when the first magicians learned how to summon magic.

Her eyes no longer looked at him but at the ceiling. Her wild eyes seemed desperate to escape her shaking body, and her body seemed relentless in its fury. His own fury was now almost the same as her body's, and in this instant, he screamed against everything he knew and ran out of the room, collapsed onto the floor of the hallway, and sobbed.

Miriam, in that very same hallway on the other side, was also sitting. She looked up through her despondent, wet eyes and began to feel a tenuous hint of empathy for the Gath boy who had fallen so in love with her daughter. One part of her mentally kicked herself in the head as she slowly rose, sorrowfully ambled over to him, and sat down beside him. She took his hand and smiled weakly at him. "We can do better, young Gath. Right now, the only one with her is a youngling she barely knows." She stood up, still holding onto his hand. "Come, let's forget our differences for this moment." She said this to herself more so than him. "And find the magic to save our beloved Lena."

Belex nodded and stood up, afraid to let go of Miriam's hand and this new bond. They walked into the room together, hand in hand, and walked to the side of the bed opposite Amanda, who looked up at them and smiled.

8

Belex could hear Sherealla laughing in the back of his head. Belex, annoyed as always with her, wondered how anyone could laugh in a time like this.

"Hey," she said. He wanted to slap her, even though she was buried deep in the neural network of the hive mind. "They did it. They found the cure."

"The collective?" he asked disbelievingly.

"Yes, of course the collective. You won't believe what they say it is."

"Try me," he said flatly, still annoyed.

"You have to pray."

I think I just did, he said to himself. He felt like he had just asked somebody, he didn't know who or what, for the bond with Miriam to expand into an even more sacred moment.

He still found room in his heart to be aggravated at Sherealla for residing in what amounted to her own strata within his being. "Do you have any idea how sick she is?" he asked her. "This is no time for levity." He also thought he had shut her out. He guessed that he couldn't easily tell, since he was still unable to make any permanent, reliable connection with stoven.net.

"Of course, I realize. And I'm telling you, that's what they're saying."

"And coming from stoven.net, I can see why they may think it's funny, but if they saw her now, they wouldn't."

"They know. Of course, they know," she said resolutely.

"And that's what they came up with? Asking us to pray? What do they know of prayer? You know how it is there, Sherealla. Everything is fun and games to three-quarters of them."

"Oh," Aurilena's weakened voice ruptured his thoughts.

Miriam had heard that sound before, but not in that way. It wasn't a groan or yelp. Somehow, she knew it was a voice that had seen death.

She released Belex's hand and took both of Aurilena's hands in hers.

"It's so loud," Aurilena wheezed from what must have been her lungs, so hoarse and quiet was her voice.

Miriam tightened her grip too hard, she knew in excitement, and instinctively looked for red rings around Aurilena's wrists.

"What?" begged Miriam as she released the wrists gently back into the world.

"My head," Aurilena whispered through dry, chapped lips.

Miriam shook her head. "Wait," she said. "Don't say anything more." Her heart pounded. "Can I get you some water?"

Aurilena lifted her wrist, but Miriam didn't see or feel it.

"I'll go get some help."

Aurilena snapped Miriam's arm like a striking snake.

"Don't go," Aurilena hissed quickly. Then, more subdued, she said, "I'll die if you leave."

"Okay," said Miriam, wanting to scream at the top of her lungs but whispering to Aurilena like only a mother can when distress corrodes faith.

"It's like a siren in my head," said Aurilena.

"Here, take my hand," said her mother. She could see Aurilena's grimacing face contort, and Miriam understood there was little comfort she could provide.

Aurilena tried to look around but couldn't find her caretaker or her caretaker's hand.

"Where?" Aurilena gasped. "Where is it?"

Miriam locked her fingers with Aurilena's. "I'm right here."

Miriam wondered if every dying person heard sirens in their head.

Meanwhile, Amanda took a doll out of her small duffel bag as she sat next to Aurilena. "I don't know why I didn't think of it before. I guess because I think it's bad to use. But I got a new trick I want to try, okay? It's not black magic like I've used before."

"Before?" asked Miriam.

"Yeah, he was a bad man though, and I was only nine." She was still only eleven now but didn't feel young at all. She suddenly felt as if her dead mother was here to fix things.

"Okay, sweetie, whatever you want to try," Miriam encouraged, faintly smiling at the sweet child.

Amanda took out some flowers from her bag, sat the doll into a sitting position, and put the flowers on its head. She closed her eyes and said, "I pray to Yehoshua . . . that he helps my friend Aurilena. I hope you love her as much as I do and that you want her to get well."

9

"They are serious, Belex," Sherealla was saying to him during a conversation that happened in an instant of time, so swiftly passing that it was almost a separate existence from the other proceedings in the room. "Pray, just like they say. Belex, the conversation within the collective is all about the belief in the magic of MagicLand—it's almost like they believe in it even more than the people in MagicLand do. They saw what magic can do during the wars. They're sold, you know? They're believers. And something about that little girl magician inspired them to a solution."

"The little girl? Amanda?"

"Yes. They've been watching her when I'm in the room with you. She's the darling of the collective now. And they saw how Miriam came to you in the hallway." He considered all this revelation to stoven.net a danger, and he said so, but Sherealla ignored him. "And they think, if you get in there and put your hand on Aurilena's head and hold Miriam's hand and just ask Yehoshua to bring everyone who loves Aurilena to the room, that he will. They say that the lifeforce and love of all those people will help her."

"And what do you think?"

"It doesn't matter what I think. It's what you think that matters."

He glanced at Miriam bending over next to him trying to comfort Aurilena as he said, "What have I got to lose, I guess."

He tried to tune her out, but he heard Sherealla's voice saying, "Oh, and Belex? One more thing. You must actually believe it. You have to believe that Yehoshua will help Aurilena."

10

When Amanda finished straightening out the doll's crown of flowers, Miriam looked around, and there suddenly appeared to be thousands of ghostly people in the room. She noticed that someone was holding her other hand. It was Belex.

Belex looked solemnly at the youngling and instructed her to come to his side of the bed. When she did so, he placed his other hand on Aurilena's forehead. "I don't know who you are, Yehoshua, but I can feel your presence here in this room," he said soulfully, and he could. Amanda leaned into him and took his elbow. "I ask you to bring the dance of life back into my beloved." He closed his eyes and went into a trance. Miriam was bewildered at this turn of events, and Aurilena's eyes closed as if she had dozed off. She knew Belex was not of magic, and when she looked at his other hand, her bewilderment turned into mistrust, then fear. The fear that she had been right all along about the intruder from Gath.

His other hand had let go of Miriam's and metamorphosed into a machine with long, needle-like fingers. One of them was withdrawing from Aurilena's neck. Miriam cursed silently for not having seen it sooner and wanted to grab his wrist, but it was too late. Whatever Belex had been doing was done.

She couldn't know that Belex knew the nanobots also needed to be touched by this spiritual moment and that he sent some of his medibots into Aurilena's body to mingle with the bots sent by Maoch—to essentially order them to divert all their resources into healing her, which they did instantly.

What struck Belex, however, was that the idea wasn't his. It came from someplace else. A part of him, perhaps a part of his mind—*no*, he thought, a part of someone else's mind. Something or someone had told him to do this, and that same someone told the nanobots what they must do and transformed them from machines into a kind of spiritual fertilizer.

Belex looked around and turned his palms outward to face the ceiling. He smiled warmly at the young girl, then at Miriam. "You all have *really* allowed me into your homes. And now," he placed one of his palms onto Aurilena's forehead, "I believe she is cured."

Aurilena sat up in the bed. The hat her father gave her had fallen to the side and instead of reaching for it, she said to Belex, "Give me that hat!" And she smiled. When Belex obeyed and retrieved the hat, she happily put it on. "How did this happen? I feel—"

"They did this," said Belex. He looked at the people in the room.

"Not just them," said an ethereal visual representation of Sherealla, who had stepped out from the ghostly figures.

"You did this?" Aurilena asked, looking at the incorporeal manifestation. Then turning her attention to Belex, she said, "And you?"

"And the collective," added Sherealla. "We are all the collective, now."

Belex bent toward the youngling again. "And you. Especially you, young lady, where would we be without you?"

People later said that in that moment, Amanda the youngling strapped the largest grin onto her face ever worn by any soul in Moria.

Amanda, beaming, was still wondering about the ghosts. As a youngling, many things about magic puzzled her, even her own magic. Hilkiah walked out of the crowd of apparitions, pulled up a small chair that had been next to Aurilena's bed, and sat in front of Amanda. Even sitting in the chair, he towered over her. It helped that one of Hilkiah's magical abilities was that he could almost read the minds of children, so strong was his ability to read sentiment.

"These are not parlor tricks, youngling, and these are not ghosts. Those who love Aurilena are here, but truth be told," and he chuckled loudly, "this room is simply too small to hold us all." Amanda looked at the wispy crowd, each person stacked as if in bleachers—but in such a way that each shared space with others. It was a big pile of upright, translucent, happy people.

"You see?" Hilkiah said to Amanda. "We come out as needed." Miriam leaned into Aurilena and sobbed, embracing her tightly as each of their faces plunged into the other. Miriam brushed Aurilena's silky black hair with one hand and then stood up to face Belex.

"I can't promise I'll ever get used to this," she said to him, grasping his shoulders gently, "to you. But I'll try. You deserve that much. And so, I make this vow: No matter what terrible things I say to you in resentment toward your people, know that I will always love you for helping to save my daughter."

Belex bowed his head a little. It was all he could do because he believed Aurilena never would have suffered were it not for him in the first place.

CHAPTER XIII

1

Hilkiah called for a celebration in the Legions' Auditorium.

"Now we can get you married!" he proclaimed. His goal was to lure as many Morians as possible to the event, so the following day, he employed a specialist to see to it that invitations reached everyone. The celebration would be a complete transition into womanhood for Aurilena, who would also be turning eighteen soon. Hilkiah thought it made perfect sense to celebrate both occasions at one time.

2

Sarah of the Enclave's name came from her ability to immediately alter surroundings and thus make it her "enclave." She had grown into middle age often wondering about the practical use of such a skill. She usually only used it as a joke.

As she was sweeping the front of her small home along the southern slopes of Moria, she saw that her straw welcome mat was changing color and texture. It became smooth and glossy white, almost like the marble in the Hall of Legions. She had to think for a moment to make sure she hadn't done something to trigger such a thing but decided with certainty that she had not. She watched curiously as a handwritten note seemed to appear on what used to be her mat:

You are cordially invited to the gala event of the year.
Our lovely Aurilena is turning 18 and getting married!
(to you know who)
Please join us at the Legions' Auditorium as we celebrate!

The animated writing then provided the date and time, and the white mat unfurled itself from the straw mat (which had been underneath all along, apparently) and slid itself inside Sarah's home.

3

Shage had heard about the possibility of one of the witches at the top of the hill getting married to someone from Gath and assumed it was a prank, but it made him realize that if something like that happened, those who lived a charmed life in the central city might decide to end the war, which might or might not change things for people like him. After all, Shage had little opportunity to get excited about anything the outside world slung this way. Shage was a stone thrower who sometimes used his ability to help construction crews build large buildings, but he rarely used his skill. The end of the wars would mean he'd never get a chance to lob stones at Gath, something he often wished he could do.

He was still young, and he wondered if there was other magic he could learn, but the truth was, he had little incentive.

When he was younger, sometimes for kicks, he would hurl a small stone at a friend or acquaintance, but that was an unsatisfying way to entertain himself. As he grew older, it no longer seemed funny. As a result, he felt stuck with this useless skill.

People often called him Shage the Stone Thrower anyway, which was funny since, to him, it was a name that ought to be associated with large, athletic, burly men. Shage was overwhelmingly thin. His skinny arms were as thick at the bicep as they were at his skinny wrists.

He typically didn't think about this kind of stuff much these days, but today, something was happening that returned him to these thoughts. He was outside picking green beans from his vegetable garden when a rock fell on the ground just to his right. From somewhere. Then another and another. He looked up at the sky but saw no hints as to their source. He wondered if old Saul next door was playing tricks on him, but he knew Saul didn't have powers like this. Saul was more of a card shark.

The rocks continued to fall out of the sky until they built a frame. Then, inside that frame, a volley of pebbles fell and seemed to be spelling out words. They poured out of the sky quickly, and the words were completed seemingly in an instant:

You are cordially invited to the gala event of the year.
Our lovely Aurilena is turning 18 and getting married!
(to you know who)
Please join us at the Legions Auditorium as we celebrate!

"Not my kind of witches, they aren't," he said, and he furiously kicked at the new formation, sending the rocks and stones scattering.

4

Those in Moria who didn't know Aurilena was marrying the Reckless from Gath soon did. Aurilena had stored up a significant amount of goodwill over the years, which her illness strengthened. This was a good thing because the reaction in Moria to her marriage to a Gath had generally not been favorable, even met with hostility among some.

Hilkiah fretted over this and wondered how to win over hearts and minds. Even Aurilena's mother continued to grumble about the marriage whenever she had a chance, despite her witnessing Belex's true self up close. Her father seemed hostile, too, but, as was usual with him, he was also adrift, although not as severely as before Aurilena's illness.

Hilkiah thought a grand party celebrating Aurilena's birthday, along with her wedding, would unite the town, but factions seemed to be forming, which was a nightmare scenario in the middle of a conflict with people as formidable as the Gath.

When he consulted with the Legions on whether the wedding should proceed, the Legions were universal in their encouragement. This surprised Hilkiah. "You have not read the sentiments of the people?" he challenged them.

The Legions spoke as one. "The only guide for countering such sentiment is love." He nodded at that.

"Very well, then. We shall have a wedding for the ages."

The Legions nodded, and the forum was over.

5

Sherealla wanted to upload a recording of the wedding to stoven.net so that all of Gath could see the ceremony. This was, after all, the culmination of their history's greatest romantic cinescape. But Sherealla was also motivated by the strategic value of such a recording: it would seal the hearts and minds of Gath in favor of Belex and his bride forever. The only way to get a recording into stoven.net was for Belex to record it while he was participating in the ceremony. A view of the wedding ceremony from the groom's eyes, Sherealla thought, would tender a remarkable volley of conversation within the collective.

"Belex will release the recording when he and Lena visit Gath," declared Hilkiah. "Keeping the recording of the event just out of their reach, I believe, guarantees their cooperation when he arrives. Once they are married, everything from that point becomes anti-climactic."

"The Gath may simply turn their attention elsewhere if we release it before our arrival," agreed Belex. "And then our arrival will be a non-event."

Marriages in Gath were quite rare and only done for amusement because the fertility-related basis for marriage had disappeared nearly two thousand years ago. But there was still interest in the romantic notions underlying ancient marriage rites, and although it had previously not been at the forefront of anybody's thought process, that changed the instant Aurilena asked Belex to marry him.

Belex's comment annoyed Sherealla. Not because she thought Belex was wrong but because of the reminder that she didn't know her own people. She had been sent to MagicLand as a child, and now, as an inhabitant of stoven.net, was without a true home, mingling with a million strange voices with no frame of reference.

6

On the day of the wedding, the Legions Auditorium was so full that Aurilena wondered how everyone could fit. She was in a waiting room, of sorts, with a full mirror on one wall and another wider mirror in front of a long table and cushioned seat at another wall. The other two walls were draped in ornately woven woolen tapestries. Long strips of decorated satin hung from the high ceiling.

Her dress was a gift from her circle of immediate friends, most of whom she had been ignoring during recent weeks as she found herself consumed with crisis and Belex. She was grateful for their patience and equally grateful for the beauty of the dress they had made for her.

Her off-shoulder sleeveless gown was made of dark green satin and a rippled court train. Her hair was set with a waterfall braid that wrapped around the back of her head but was largely hidden by an extravagant headdress consisting of a red fur-brimmed hat wrapped by a gold band with inlaid topaz. Attached to the band on each side of her head were diamond-shaped silver medallions adorned at their ends with several hanging strands of pearls.

Her ears held earrings made of smaller matching sets of pearls, and her neck was surrounded by a black ring that fit over her head as if someone had thrown a flattened tire over her shoulders and tilted it upward just enough to display its inlay of rare gemstones acquired from around the world. All this attention and glamor made her terribly uncomfortable, but the crowd and the man she was marrying dislodged those feelings quickly. She only wished her friend of the last seven years could be at the ceremony. She wondered what, if anything, Sherealla could witness through Belex.

The man she was marrying, she thought. She considered this as the musicians warmed up in the auditorium, and the crowd settled in while she waited for Judith and Miriam in the little dressing room. Just yesterday, it seemed, she had been a child, running up and down the hills of Moria and, as she grew, riding her horses to places away from Moria where she probably should not have been. *Anything,* she thought, *to avoid growing up.* And now, here she was, in a formal catacomb of childhood and a maturation dictated more by circumstances, like Belex's arrival and the endless series of crises that followed, than by biology.

She felt a combination of joy and dread. Whenever she was near Belex, she felt intoxicated with love. She could not have imagined herself getting married a year ago. There were no suitable candidates, for one thing, but it was also the furthest thing from her mind. It had also been the furthest thing from her mind after she met Belex until that sudden moment in Gath where the spirit of joy embraced her heart and nudged her toward this new kind of life with another person.

Her friend, Abilene, and Judith were her primary caretakers on this day of nerves. "I'm more nervous than the day I met Hilkiah," she said to Abilene.

"You were such a rebel soul," said Abilene, "that I doubt you were nervous at all when you met Hilkiah."

Abilene's comment reminded Aurilena that Abilene had not always been an Acquirer.

7

"Isn't this the most amazing fabric you've ever seen?" Abilene was unrolling a bolt of a silk and cotton blend of dark blue fabric.

"You're so obsessed," said Aurilena, shaking her head.

"Yeah?" Abilene replied, rubbing the fabric with her palm to flatten it on the table in front of her. "Someday, you'll love my obsession. Someday, I'm gonna make you a fancy wedding dress."

Aurilena scoffed and asked, "Where did you even get that?"

"Joan," was all Abilene said, her eyes focused on her treasure.

"She's an Acquirer? I had no idea."

"She doesn't brag about it. It was quite by accident."

"Isn't it always?"

"Anyways, she says that there are ancient bolts of fabric all over the world that haven't been eaten away by time."

"Or in the case of silk, moths."

"Yeah, that too. I dunno anything about it. She's teaching me how to acquire but I'm slow, I think," she giggled. "All I know is I want to make a dress!"

"Some people don't need magic. For people like you, it's all in your hands," said Aurilena, smiling at her friend.

"I know! And someday, I'll be able to find my own fabric and make whatever I want!"

8

"Where did you find all these tapestries?" she asked Abilene because she was the only Acquirer Aurilena knew who could possibly find such exotic fabric in such a short time. "And this dress!" she exclaimed. "How could you know it was exactly what I'd want?" She tried to think about her empathic and clairvoyant friends but couldn't think of any with such skills.

"Silly girl," Abilene said. "Your sister knew exactly what you'd want. So that was easy. And you know me and dresses. Your dad found all these tapestries and jewels for your headdress. On the other side of the world, Judith says. I'll take a bow for the awesome headdress, but it's your dad that found the amazing stones for it."

My father, she thought, with a tear welling up in her eye. She wasn't sure if the tear was about the efforts of her father or the effort Abilene had put into the headdress.

Aurilena was looking in the mirror when Judith and Miriam walked in. Judith nudged her mother and said, "Oh . . . look, Mom, Lena's engaging in her favorite pastime." The three women cackled, and Judith and Miriam embraced Aurilena warmly.

"Are you ready, little sister?" Aurilena could hear a milling crowd die down as the gentle sound of a piano added its musical fragrance to the adjacent room.

She nodded nervously.

Miriam hooked her arm into Aurilena's elbow.

9

Belex was in a prayer room with Hilkiah, a long hallway away from Aurilena. The room, as most interiors in MagicLand, he thought, was austere. There were a couple of black leather couches that he assumed had been foraged from distant places and times by Acquirers, a small mirror hanging on the light blue wall— blue sandstone, Hilkiah had said—a couple of tall wooden chairs, each with backs high enough to hold all of Hilkiah's height, and a small oriental rug in the middle of the breccia marble floor.

All of this would have seemed laughable to Belex just a few months ago. He would have considered the ceremony contrived and gratuitous. He guessed, if he was being honest with himself, that it still did seem so, but he felt this without the rancor he would have felt before.

"Most men think that way about these ceremonies," said Hilkiah, pouring them both a small glass of fruit juice. "This is palm juice from the southern reaches," he said, handing Belex a glass.

Taking it, Belex said, "Is mind reading another one of your talents?"

"More like sentiment reading, young friend. Sentiment sniffing might better describe it. Like a dog sniffs that out a variety of odors and can respond to each, I do the same with sentiments. Alas, there are no mind readers here in MagicLand. I would know it if there were," he chuckled. One eye glinted at Belex as if sharing a secret. "It is tradition for the groom to drink a glass of palm juice with the giver just before the wedding."

"The giver?"

"That's me." Hilkiah lifted his glass higher. "And this is the palm juice. And you, my young Gath friend, are the groom. Drink."

Belex drank it all in one gulp.

"Outstanding," said Hilkiah, who did the same. "And now, I shall give you to the bride."

"I'm not sure the word "give" is an appropriate word," Belex said with a guilty smile. "My presence here has exacted a heavy toll."

"Nonsense," said Hilkiah. "I shudder to think what would have been the results had they sent someone else. A Gath of no character, for example."

"That's probably the strangest compliment I've ever had, but I'll take it on this day."

Hilkiah bowed and led Belex to the ceremony.

10

The full auditorium held 20,000 people. The large stage in the middle was accessed by small sets of stairs on each side. In the middle of the stage was a large, inked circle etched into the wood floor. Two long aisles approaching the stage from opposite directions cut through the seated crowd. The musicians had transitioned from piano to strings and were now giving way to the crowd, which had begun singing in adagio, almost like a twenty-thousand-person a cappella slowed down for a long romantic interlude.

When the couple appeared along their respective aisles, the crowd's only reaction was the crescendo of their shared song. Belex thought it was the most beautiful thing he had ever heard. It was more magnificent than anything he had heard through stoven.net, which, even though most of its musical efforts were a farrago shaped by the collective's maze of discordant creative minds, managed to offer the occasional masterpiece. But nothing like this. This sound shot into his spine and reverberated throughout his body.

Aurilena was mesmerized by the sound of the audience, and the tighter grip she felt on her arm testified to her mother's response, as well. They strode forth, a mother leading her wayward child into the arms of the enemy, it seemed to many, but it was a song worth finishing because there were forces far stronger than those who seemed insistent on this destiny.

11

A long-robed man and woman stood waiting for the couple in the middle of the circle on the stage. Hilkiah and Miriam brought Belex and Aurilena together onto the stage. The couple clasped hands and walked the short distance to the priest and priestess as Hilkiah and Miriam returned down their respective aisles amidst the continued singing.

Aurilena tilted her head and noticed her father nodding at her in the front row. Just then, a Turillion scarf appeared around his neck underneath the wide grin on his face. When Belex recognized the scarf from his early wanderings, his heart filled with joy.

The couple faced the priest and priestess, Belex in front of the man and Aurilena in front of the woman. Belex smiled at the man, Aaron, who had originally been introduced to Belex in a prisoner intake role. Aaron nodded politely. He wore an elegant robe of green and blue, with an intricate insignia, shaped as a letter Belex didn't recognize, overlaid over a large circle with a cross in the middle. The robe's wide sleeves were trimmed with a gold band.

The priestess's robe was identical. When they had rehearsed a day ago, the role of the priestess had been played by one of Aurilena's friends, so this was the first time Belex had seen her. She was an older woman. Belex couldn't guess her age, and since he was now more fascinated than horrified by old age, he wanted to take a DNA sample from her to determine her precise age.

His fascination took him into the process of examining the lines and grooves on her face. She had crow's feet around the corners of her eyes, and her cheeks were grooved with thin lines that acted as thoroughfares for a network of thinner, smaller routes that spread across her face. Her lips ended at upturned corners, each splashing into a handsome dimple.

Belex began to understand something that had eluded him his entire life— simply because he had not been exposed to age. There was illustrious beauty in the wisdom reflected in a face such as hers, whose name he had learned yesterday—

Ha-Kodesh—because it was said, she could talk directly to the spirit of the Great Shepherd, something not even Hilkiah had done. He had learned she was rarely seen in MagicLand, or, as he now referred to this land, Moria.

Her presiding over his wedding was either a great honor, he thought, or he was in a lot of trouble. He glanced over at his betrothed, stunned by her almost perplexing beauty, and decided whatever trouble he might be in would be worth enduring.

Ha-Kodesh took Aurilena's hands and began to recite a canto from a long poem written by one of Aurilena's friends. When she was finished, she said to Aurilena, "Are you prepared to journey with this man to the ends of the earth and for eternity?"

"I am," said Aurilena quite solemnly.

"Are there any obstacles that can prevent you from fulfilling your destiny with Belex Deralk-Almd?"

"No," she said.

Aaron then asked the same questions of Belex, who answered the same. He was then directed to face Aurilena. "You, Belex Deralk-Almd and Aurilena Kingston, are now the bride and groom of God and Heaven for eternity," the priest and priestess said together. Belex got down on one knee and Aurilena extended her hand to him, which he took in both of his.

"Thank you for the honor of being my bride," he recited with truth in his voice. This was a traditional Morian wedding with an untraditional groom, but he was playing the part perfectly, thought Aurilena adoringly. *And it's the happiest day of my life.* They walked off down one aisle together, as the congregation burst into more festive song.

12

The wedding was a greater success than Aurilena's highest expectations. Even Orpah, who had once bitterly opposed Belex's very presence in Moria, participated by providing a grand wedding feast after the ceremony.

The feast, naturally, was held in the Hall of Feasts and its many ancillary dining rooms. Hilkiah had some concerns over safety, but he acquiesced to Aurilena's demands that the round, wooden wedding table be centered in the middle of the wide hall. He had heard murmurings of treachery, but with Orpah's support, he decided that such murmurs were not worth heeding and probably the result of the usual jealousies that large weddings occasionally aroused.

Hilkiah had even invited Orpah to the wedding table, and although she refused, she made herself visible enough to suggest that she had given her blessing to the event. She made sure that everyone knew she was the master of the feast, which featured lamb and mutton from distant lands, wild game fowl from the middle forests, citrus from the southern reaches, and drink from everywhere. The many people who had been convinced by Orpah that this was a heinous affair were likely now confused into a state that gave way to nothing more harmful than a few questioning looks.

Hilkiah gave the first speech, a grand one, Aurilena thought, one of praise for Belex and his usual accolades toward her. Then, he called on Miriam to speak, which wasn't part of the plan, and Aurilena gulped. Her mother loved her unconditionally, though, didn't she? She knew it was so, but her confidence gave way to a shaky hand as she picked up her glass to drink a sip of sparkling wine. She very much wanted to drink it all down quickly and have much more, but after a sip, she listened instead.

"This," Miriam began sternly. "is a most unusual affair." She shook her head. "Is there one soul here who does not know what I think of the Gath? Of course not. What a question. And yet here I am, honoring the wedding of my own daughter to a Gath. Has this ever happened in Moria? Such a thing."

Aurilena downed her drink and hurriedly signaled for more.

"We here in Moria are called to a greater calling than perpetual warfare, I think. This event, this ceremony that only a few days ago I considered a ghastly turn of events that challenged my patience in ways I could never have conceived, was handed to me with great resistance on my part.

"One could say that a daughter such as mine could have any man here in Moria that she pleases, and one would be correct in saying so. And what does my darling daughter do?" Miriam raised her voice in bitter denunciation as she scanned the crowd, avoiding eye contact with Aurilena. "She cavorts with the enemy!" Aurilena downed her drink then demanded more.

Miriam's voice then fell to a quieter, softer tone. "But none of this was her intent . . . any more than mine. And it wasn't his intent, either. These two young people met as enemies. Do you know the first thing he did when he met my daughter? He tried to kick her!" She laughed, and the discomfort that had filled the room gave way to a few islands of laughter.

"No. He had no intent to wed my daughter when they met. She certainly had no intent to wed him. So, how did this come about, then? This unlikely pairing?

"Well, I believe it was truly born of the spirit world we so cherish. Their shared experiences, their shared horror of the ancient people who preceded us, people who are in the ancestral lines of both Gath and Morian, this helped bring them together. That, and their own shared fanciful notions of love and whatever else strikes the fancy of two smitten young people.

"When one examines the steps that brought these two together, one can only conclude that this was a union truly brought together by heaven. Who am I, a simple healer, to resist what Yehoshua himself has ordained? You see, my friends, this is much bigger than we are. This signals to me that a much grander scheme is afoot. Perhaps even an end to the war that strikes us down with inhuman regularity.

"I therefore, renounce my denunciations of this man who has married my lovely daughter, and I proclaim that he is no longer Gath. He is no longer our enemy. He is Morian. His journey is now our journey, and our journeys are now his. He has united with my daughter in a union blessed not just by the more cynical among us," and she looked over to Orpah as she said this, "but by the Great Spirit who governs our every action."

She lifted a glass into the air, "A drink to them, a drink to this union, and a drink for a new and enduring age of peace in our land. And if there is more war before the peace," she said, looking at Belex, "know that we have a new ally who can lead us to victory. A drink, then, to all of you who have come here to honor my wonderful daughter, and a drink to you, my beloved, who, in honor of your eighteenth birthday, we shall hereafter refer to as Magdalena of Moria. And you, Belex Deralk-Almd, are no longer of Gath. You are Boanerges, Sons of Thunder, Son of Moria."

Chapter XIV

1

The next day, Aurilena and Belex were taken back to reality. They knew Maoch was not sitting idly while they were getting married. They feared an imminent attack, despite the lack of any direct evidence. Sherealla had not heard any chatter in military channels, but Belex felt she was probably compromised and no longer able to access such information.

Everyone seemed happy. Children were playing in the streets outside. The replica of the ancient streetcar was running along the tracks. People were haggling over goods in market stalls in the city's plazas.

The tension fueled by Aurilena's sickness gave way to a happier interlude buoyed by the relief of her recovery, her wedding, her birthday, and Miriam's rousing speech.

"She's always been such a popular girl," Judith said to her mother at a restaurant along the Malecón. Her mother was treating her to lunch. "She'll be okay." The day was sunny, hotter than usual. The sky was a crystal-clear blue. "Not a cloud up there today," she noted. "Such a rare sight." Fog usually rolled in by this hour of the day.

As she said that, a long, wide, waving strip of black specks appeared as if breaking through the blue expanse from a hidden tunnel in the sky. The specks swirled around like the tail of a supersonic kite and dove toward the ground at the other end of the city.

"Oh, no," said Miriam.

"Gath?" asked Judith, knowing the answer.

"Uh-huh."

"What do we do?"

"How fast can you ride to the hall?" asked Miriam, referring to the Hall of Legions.

"Fast."

"Tell Hilkiah we have visitors."

But they were more than visitors. Judith could already see debris getting sucked up along the path of the nanobots. She cursed and ran off but then halted in mid-step. "Mom, come with me."

"I'll just slow you down. And we should just transport ourselves."

"We don't know where everyone is. Come!" Judith ordered, and Miriam jumped up and followed her daughter out to Judith's horse.

2

Aurilena and Belex were eating a late lunch at a small eating establishment on a hill between the Hall of Legions and Aurilena's home. The street sloped at such a degree one had to hold onto a rail on the way into the diner to avoid feeling concerned about tumbling down the street.

While they were eating, they noticed small streams of people running frantically down the hill. They looked at each other before dropping their forks on their plates and scampering outside. They looked toward the top of the hill but couldn't see anything that would be causing the flight. But Aurilena recognized the look of fear she saw now on the faces of the people running past her. One person stopped after recognizing her. "It's the Gath," he said, and he scampered away.

"They couldn't just give us this one day," Aurilena said bitterly.

Aurilena grabbed Belex by the arm and didn't bother saying anything when she transported them both to the Hall of Legions, where she knew Hilkiah would be if he was aware of the attack.

They arrived instantly. Hilkiah was at a doorway at the end of the hall, frantically urging people toward various directions. When Aurilena and Belex ran to him, he calmly said, "There are several Metamorphics already attending to this, but I'm afraid they've had no luck this time. The Gath are quick to adapt to our defenses."

"This is Maoch's doing," said Belex. "Sherealla has confirmed it. There is no activity in stoven.net regarding this attack. The average Gath has no idea that it's happening."

"We could alert them, alert the collective?" suggested Aurilena.

"We could, but I'm afraid the destruction will be complete before they have time to react." Belex shook his head. "They might not even react. They'd blather about what a terrible shame it is and resume their forays into their various gaming strata tomorrow."

"We have to find a way to stop them here, then. Now." As Hilkiah said this, they could hear the destruction getting closer. They didn't have to see it to understand what was happening. Swarms of nanobots were ripping buildings and people to shreds, pulling long fluid clouds of debris and flesh into the sky as an unnecessary show of force.

Judith appeared on horseback with Miriam sitting behind her. They dismounted and ran to Hilkiah, Aurilena, and Belex.

They all sprinted through a vestibule to the door at its far end and peered outside, which provided an overlook from the hill on which the tower of the Hall of Legions was perched. Every building in their view looked like a participant in a violently choreographed dance of flames, with showers of sparkling cinders kicked and scattered about by the ignited feet of fiery dancers, fueled by crumbling walls and roofs and beams born of the northern forests.

Teams of firefighting wizards, acquiring and applying copious quantities of water, struggled to keep the entire city from burning down as the fires rapidly spread.

"It's all happening too quickly," said Hilkiah despairingly. "We can't get a handle on it. Inside, all of you. Come now."

"And do what?" asked Aurilena, her chin quivering, not in fear for herself but for the place she loved so desperately.

"Pray."

3

Shage was the type of fellow who wanted to protect everything and felt like he could protect nothing. He wanted to cover up his tomatoes, beans, and peas to make sure they didn't meet the fate of the rest of Moria. Everywhere he looked, he saw flames or bodies flying up into the sky, sucked up by the black streams of nanobots that were terrorizing the city.

His heart felt like it was ripping open as he watched the sky of death, wondering how it could all end like this in defiance of so many talented magicians. People like Aurilena, whose wedding he had reluctantly attended and who had warmed his heart with kind words. People like Hilkiah, the great priest. And Aurilena's mother, the great healer.

He began to feel sick to his stomach as he fell to his knees. He tried to avoid looking at the catastrophe above. "Oh, Yehoshua," he said while on his knees, unable to do anything else, "Hilkiah, our great high priest, tells us to pray to you, and I want to, but I don't know how. All I know is that I feel helpless and wish I could help. So much death. So much suffering. What can I do? If only I could move those little black sand pebbles in the sky, I would. If only, if only . . ." He sobbed as he covered his face with his hands. "If only you'd let me, I'd hurl them into the surrounding waters where they'd turn into steam that rises to your honor, and we'd be safe from this Gath horror." His heart was heavy, and he had that awful feeling when sadness devastates us to the point that our head has too much weight to carry. He kept his eyes covered as they filled with more tears because he knew this was the end—the Gath had finally won.

4

Hilkiah, despondent, terrified, and nearly broken, had been given no time to think about how Maoch had found a way to attack the city. He had no time for even a short moment to pray. The noises of carnage continued, but suddenly, something seemed different. When he looked up, he saw no thick streams of nanobots in the sky. Fearing another onslaught, he ran to the far corner of the vestibule where Belex and Aurilena were sheltering. He could see Aurilena praying with her eyes closed as Belex held her. "Aurilena, do you sense your horse?"

She nodded silently; she, too, feeling the heaviness of pure despair.

"And White Star? Belex's horse?"

She nodded again. "Both alive for now, I guess," she whispered, knowing they, like everything else in Moria, would soon be gone.

"Ride to your home. Take Belex."

She was too frightened for her people to even consider that possibility and shook her head as she trembled.

"Do it. I believe they've stopped. But our window is short. You can confirm they've stopped by riding to the top of the hill. To your parents' house. And scan the skies."

She looked up at him and said, "It would be safer to just transport myself there."

"Do whichever you prefer. You can do this, right?" Hilkiah took her hand, and she nodded.

She got up and pulled Belex up with her. She decided to go by horseback so she could survey the wreckage. They found the two horses, agitated but okay, still tied to their posts outside. They mounted and galloped up the hill against the background glow of a flaming city to her parents' empty home. She opened the front door, and they raced to the deck outside.

"Look," she said, pointing to the water. The nanobots were pouring into the water from the sky as if attacking it. The water where they entered roiled and coiled and turned into a raging whirlpool as the black streams poured in. Steam rose from the water as if a hot pan had received a sudden shock of cold water.

"What are they doing?" asked Aurilena.

"I don't know," Belex answered. "It's as if they are committing suicide."

As soon as one stream of nanobots finished pouring into the bay, another behind it did the same. There were dozens of streams queued up behind one another, harmlessly swirling and swarming in the sky above. One after another dove into the sea and the wild waters of their target area, but nothing came out of the bay.

"I don't understand."

"Neither do I," said Belex. "It's as if they think their mission is complete."

"Why would Maoch stop at . . ." but she couldn't finish.

"Almost destroying us?" finished Belex.

"Yeah."

"He wouldn't. Something else is happening." He kept silent as he watched. Then he softly grabbed Aurilena's shoulder. "Magic?"

She shuddered in an involuntary reaction to the trauma and the sudden possibility that Belex raised. "Maybe. But who?"

5

Shage's agony was subsiding but only because all the activity around him seemed to be subsiding. It took him some time to notice the calming environment. He had been wallowing in the brokenness of the moment and had lost all sense of the world around him. He slowly got to his feet and looked around. There was still much consternation and strife among his neighbors, but something else had introduced itself to the proceedings. A strange quiet in the air made him look up. He saw nothing except four turkey vultures circling a few hundred feet away within an arc seemingly painted on the sky by the burning city. He grimly realized they would not go hungry.

He brushed himself off and walked to old Saul's home. Nobody was outside, so he knocked hard on the door. "Saul! You okay?" He knocked to more silence before walking to a window and peering in. It was dark. "Saul?"

"I'm back here, behind the house," yelled Saul.

Shage hurried to the back and saw Saul looking east. He pointed up. "They went that way, and that way, and that way," he said, pointing east, north, and west. "But not that way," and he pointed south. "Don't make no sense. Why not go back to Gath? I can't tell from here, but it's like the little devils all picked their own spot of water and just kind of dive-bombed in. I saw one group go up, way up high, like so," and he motioned an area high above, "then they swooped down and went over there, toward the eastern bay, and dove straight down. And now I don't see 'em. Any of them. Anywhere."

6

There are many stories and legends of heroes that have been told throughout history, great tales of courage that inspire us to persevere through the darkest of times. But for every great hero story, there is a heroic story more like that of Shage the Stone Thrower, a modest man with humble ambition, who only wanted to see the end of his people's suffering but had no idea how to stop it.

But stop it, he did. His story was never told in Moria because not even he knew the narrative. He was too caught up in the moment during his lamentations to Yehoshua to realize that he had referred to the swarms of nanobots as pebbles, and thus, they became stones, which he then, unaware, threw into the surrounding waters.

Sometimes, Shage would ponder the sudden change of events while his mind would drift into his last thoughts before what he had been sure at the time was his certain death. He'd think about that little prayer he made, hopeful, for no discernable reason, and how it may have made a small difference.

He continued living what he considered to be a small life, never knowing that he was bigger than all Moria.

7

Aurilena and Belex, too numbed by the stress of the events to feel hopeful, rode down to tell Hilkiah the news. They wondered if his pleas to Yehoshua worked in the end after all.

"Something else, something else," said Hilkiah when they reached him and asked. "I'm afraid I don't know what, but something else sent those devil stones into the seas that surround us."

"How can you know that?" asked Aurilena. "It had to be the Great Shepherd answering us. It had to be that."

"Perhaps in some way. And you're sure they are gone?"

"They are in the water. But you can be sure," warned Belex, "that the next batch Maoch sends will not be destroyed by something as simple as water."

"Indeed. And that means I'm afraid your journey to Gath must begin posthaste, before Maoch finds a way to win the hearts and minds of his people."

"I'm not sure he can ever do that," said Belex. "Look. I know what everyone here thinks of my people. But we were used—all of us. It wasn't just me. We are decent folk. Just like you. Maoch manipulated us. All this destruction and mayhem, that's on him. If he's going to win, he'll have to take the next phase of the battle to his own people."

"Are you certain you can live with the consequences of helping him do that? If you leave this alone, he will probably leave them alone."

"Hilkiah, I want to set my people free. I can live with that."

8

The next morning, Aurilena and Belex set out to rig their horses up for the journey to Gath. A part of Aurilena had wanted to try transporting directly to Gath, but the risk was too great. She didn't have enough confidence in her skill to get them to a safe place within what still needed to be considered a hostile city.

They went outside the Hall of Legions to untie their horses and take them to Judith, who could help prepare proper packs for the journey. As they were untying the horses, a few people, looking dirty, mangled, and tired, began to berate them.

"You did this," one woman said. "You and your stupid Gath boyfriend and your repulsive marriage to that beast." She stalked toward them, pointing at Belex, followed by three or four, then five, then six people behind her. "You drew attention to us. If not for you, they'd never have found us. Never have killed my son."

"Or mine," said a woman behind her.

"Or my daughter," said a man with the group, which seemed to grow with each word.

Aurilena, startled and heartbroken by their words, released the lead to Remembrance that she had been holding and stood to face them. Her horse neighed and stamped its feet, so she held one palm up to Remembrance behind her while still facing the angry gathering, and the horse calmed down.

"I lost my brother to the Gath," said Aurilena defiantly, "and now this Gath, who is no Reckless, has come to redeem his people and end this war, which is not of his doing. It's not of his peoples' doing. Any of you who have heard of the being who appeared at the Hall of Legions knows that the Gath are prisoners to an entity named Maoch, who has been directing the Gath policy of relentless extermination."

"It's all a trick," said one of the men. "You!" he pointed to Aurilena, "are a traitor. There's only one right punishment for the likes of you." He moved forward, which prompted the rest of them to do the same.

The angry group lurched ahead as if pushed forward from behind by an unseen force. And what surprised Belex, as he saw the group encroach upon their space, was the calm that allowed him time to study every angry line on each face, every arched brow, and every bulging vein within the storm of their fury. He realized at that moment that it wasn't the people in the crowd who were his enemy. He examined the crowd as he approached it. He was now ahead of Aurilena, facing the group alone.

"I am Boanerges, Sons of Thunder, Son of Moria," he said to them. "I am here to avenge the deaths of your loved ones." He walked up to one of the men with his hands clasped together and knelt on one knee before the man. "In the name of Yehoshua, I say to the hatred that surrounds us, be gone!" He smiled gently at those in the fringes of the crowd still approaching, and they stopped upon those words.

One of the men looked at the others and then at Aurilena. Then, the woman who had led the charge did the same, as the tension ran out of her face, and her eyes loosened away from their gash of fury. They all stopped when she did. Their hands fell to their sides when she spoke. "I don't know why you are here, Gath. But know this. We will be watching you. The Great Palisade of Moria will be watching you." She turned to walk away, and the rest of them, grumbling, followed suit.

9

They brought their horses to Judith. Hilkiah and Miriam were waiting for them. Miriam had prepared a noon meal for everyone, and they all sat down to eat outside. Belex opened the conversation with, "It feels like a last supper of sorts."

"You will be back with my daughter," Miriam said sternly.

Aurilena took her mom's hand. "We'll be back," she promised.

"If they're not," Hilkiah started as he swept his hand around Judith's land. It was impossible to underappreciate the beauty of their surroundings, the forested cliffs with their thick, red trees that reached hundreds of feet into the sky and dusted the surrounding air with the scent of pine. "All of this disappears, I'm afraid."

"No pressure," mumbled Belex, extracting a few grapes from their nest in a nearby bowl.

"Did you know," said Judith, looking up at one of the soaring trees, "that the bark of these trees—just the bark—can be a foot thick?" She measured the air with her hands. That brought forth the silence of the woods, which wasn't silent at all but for the forest sounds of whistling blue jays and surrounding songs of woodland birds. One hawk's screech bounced around the canopy.

They all finished eating in this form of arboreal quiet, and finally, after Aurilena pushed away her cup of tea, Belex stood and played the old song he had played for her not so long ago.

But he managed to change one word, and Judith smiled broadly when she heard it, the voice of the singer perfectly replicated, as if the injected word was part of the original song . . . when he asks if Empire trees, rather than lilac, are in the heart of town.

Belex paused the song for a beat to let Judith enjoy the moment, then continued. Aurilena came up to Belex, and he twirled her around in a dance as the song neared its end.

Aurilena giggled and asked, "Is that the only song you know?"

"I have a few million more we can listen to on the way," said Belex. He stopped dancing and brushed her hair back. "Are you sure about this?" said Belex.

She nodded eagerly. She was ready.

"So, you're okay," he said.

"Right as rain."

About the Author

Charles Bastille self-published his first series of books in sixth grade, when he folded up stacks of notebook paper and wrote and illustrated hand-sized comic books called *The Adventures of Dr. Maums* and distributed them to his classmates. He has been writing fiction ever since.

Charles has had several books on web software development published by Sybex, IDG, and Wiley. He retired from the software development business to concentrate on fiction writing. *MagicLand* is his debut novel.

He currently lives in Atlanta, Georgia.

You can find him at www.charles-bastille.com.

A free ebook edition
is available with the
purchase of this book.

To claim your free ebook edition:

Visit MorganJamesBOGO.com
Sign your name CLEARLY in the space
Complete the form and submit a photo of
the entire copyright page
You or your friend can download the ebook
to your preferred device

Morgan James BOGO™

A **FREE** ebook edition is available for you
or a friend with the purchase of this print book.

CLEARLY SIGN YOUR NAME ABOVE

Instructions to claim your free ebook edition:
1. Visit MorganJamesBOGO.com
2. Sign your name CLEARLY in the space above
3. Complete the form and submit a photo
   of this entire page
4. You or your friend can download the ebook
   to your preferred device

Print & Digital Together Forever.

Snap a photo   Free ebook   Read anywhere

CPSIA information can be obtained
at www.ICGtesting.com
Printed in the USA
LVHW041944051121
702546LV00005B/160